Set in eighteenth century Dorset
novels follow the life and times o
who, in 1750, is wrongly convictec
America. This is just the beginnin¡
tale of his adventures introduced
Exile, and continued in his second, ...
stone carving and this eventually wins him a fifty-acre headright and the
chance of a contented farmstead life with his new wife, Rose. But it is
not long before he feels compelled to return to England to clear his
name, soon pitching himself against the violent men who set him up and
who want to see him dead. His quest for justice and revenge exposes him
to dangerous repercussions that he could never have foreseen; he faces
action in the Atlantic, in the Chesapeake, and in the forests of frontier
territory.

In *The Road to Fort Duquesne*, it is 1758, when Jack finally honours a
commitment to serve in a southern Maryland militia, raised to do battle
with the French in what will become known as the French and Indian
war. The militia has orders to rendezvous with Brigadier General Forbes'
armies as a military road is cut through the mountainous Pennsylvanian
wilderness to recapture Fort Duquesne on the forks of the Ohio. This
key objective is one of three identified by William Pitt, British Secretary
of State, in a campaign aimed at defeating the French in north eastern
America. But this is not the only challenge that Jack Easton will face
during a critical year that will see British and provincial forces victorious
in the middle colonies. Although he believes he has settled the score with
his old enemies, Pettigrew and Hayward, both captured while attempting
to escape to New France on a hijacked tobacco ship, he will not be
satisfied until they are tried and punished for their crimes. Wounded in
pursuit of Judd, the third member of the malicious triumvirate that has
tormented him, Jack recovers to learn that Judd's body has mysteriously
disappeared. And the road that Jack must now follow to fulfil what he
believes to be his duty is not the only journey he will have to make.

The Road to Fort Duquesne

RON BURROWS

Published 2012 by arima publishing

www.arimapublishing.com

ISBN 978 1 84549 538 1
© Ron Burrows 2012

Printed and bound in the United Kingdom

Typeset in Garamond 11/14

Swirl is an imprint of arima publishing.

arima publishing
ASK House, Northgate Avenue
Bury St Edmunds, Suffolk IP32 6BB
t: (+44) 01284 700321

www.arimapublishing.com

For my family & friends

CONTENTS

British North America

Part of

1758

Miles 0   50   100

Approximate scale

Ohio River

Fort Duquesne

ALLEGHENY MOUNTAINS

Youghiogheny

Ford

Loyal Hannon

Pennsylvania

Virginia

Braddock's Road (Southern Route)

Fort Cumberland

Fort Bedford

Fort Loudoun

Forbes' Road (Northern Route)

APPALACHIAN

Potomac River

MOUNTAINS

Frederick

Potomac River

Patuxent River

Georgetown

Charlestown

Maryland

New Hope

Baltimore

Annapolis

Chesapeake Bay

Cape Charles

Princess Anne

Philadelphia

New York

ATLANTIC OCEAN

Chapter One

Having grounded the hijacked tobacco ship, Miranda, on the Chesapeake mud banks, Judd has slipped over the side with a stolen fortune. But he is spotted by Jack Easton as he makes his escape towards the shore, and hotly pursued. Meanwhile, Miranda's sister ship, Rebecca, another former sixth-rate, has arrived from Annapolis, coming to her aid...

Judd snatched a frantic glance over his shoulder as he scrambled up the empty beach. Behind him at the water's edge, the smoke from his pistols had already drifted clear, and he saw at once that at least one of his two shots had met its mark. The leading oarsman in the pursuing long boat lay collapsed over his oar, the bloody evidence of his wound already spreading across his shoulder.

Miranda's crew had chased him and his stolen craft relentlessly across the open waters of the Sound, but now they fell about the boat in utter disarray, piling forward to the aid of their wounded comrade. Only minutes before, Judd had cursed his luck as *Rebecca's* cannon shot had brought down his sail and forced him to his oars, his bid for freedom quickly becoming a gruelling sculling race against the six angry oarsmen who closed upon him with every powerful stroke. He had beaten them to the shore, but only by a few boat's lengths. If he had simply fled in panic then, he would have made an easy target for their muskets, but he had resisted the urge to run; he had stood his ground and waited for the range to close before firing.

Now it seemed that his gamble had paid off. The longboat was slewing helmless across the surf, its oars abandoned and askew, its crew scrambling to regain control. Escape might be possible after all and he congratulated himself for achieving his objective. His careful shots had bought him time; he had waited for Captain Goddard and his men to come uncomfortably close before letting off his precious rounds. He had staked everything on that last ditch stand for, had he missed, he would have been a sitting duck. The chaos at the water's edge had justified his resolve.

He pressed onwards up the beach with new vigour, running for his life on yielding shingle that ground noisily beneath his feet. But he had not gone more than twenty strides before his legs began to weaken, his thighs to protest as the loose footing drained him of his strength. Yet he could not rest - every faltering stride was a step closer to the safety of the dunes. Even without a rearward glance, he knew his pursuers would soon be taking up the chase again. Rage would spur them on; their determination to get even, to recapture the stolen fortune in the saddlebags across his shoulder, surely the more intense now that he had drawn first blood. He felt the hairs on the back of his neck bristle at the imagined muskets already taking aim; at any moment he might feel the impact that would bring him down.

Ahead, the sanctuary of the dunes beckoned; they represented cover in which he could reload and fire again. He must reach them! Only a score more strides! But there was soft sand beneath his feet now - shifting sand into which each exhausting step sank so deep that forward momentum began to stall. He scrambled desperately, his legs on fire, his sinews stiffening as if nearly spent. He felt his face contorting into the grimace of a silent scream; the pain was so intense, yet he drove himself onwards to the very limit of endurance. Only a dozen paces to go! Surely he must make it now? His hungry gasps for air roared inside his ears and scorched his throat; his heart pounded as if at any moment it might explode.

When the musket ball hit him, it knocked him clean off his feet. It was not the sharp stab of pain that he might have expected, but more like a blow from a heavy boot to his right shoulder, and so fierce that it knocked the wind from his lungs and sent him flying headlong. He heard himself grunt. Then time itself seemed suddenly to slow, the instants lengthening as if each quantum moment had become stretched to full width, wherein each detail of the sand below was registered, yet with curious detachment. He noted, even before his shallow flight path had reached its apogee, that all sound had gone; it was as if he had been struck deaf. His breathing had stilled; the pounding of his heartbeat had ceased. Nor did he hear the loud report from the distant musket that had sent its speeding ball upon its way. He seemed for a moment to hover in mid-flight, to be defying gravity, to float in mid air as the beach inched past below. Then he saw the rock sticking up in front, and in that instant reckoned his head's unlucky trajectory towards it. Slow in its approach at first, as if making up its mind where to strike, the rock then seemed to

2

accelerate. Instinctively, he twisted in mid-air so that the impact might fall upon some less vital body part, but he saw at once that his attempt would fail. And abandoning himself to his fate, he let himself be taken.

The rock propelled itself towards his head like a missile aimed with particular and personal malice. At the moment of collision, there rang out a resounding bang deep within his skull that sent shock waves throughout his crumpling frame. He became aware of the taste of blood in his mouth as sand ground into his teeth; and then there came a flash of bright, white light. Surprisingly, he felt no pain. And then darkness enveloped him.

It seemed only an instant later that consciousness returned. It was like waking from a nightmare in which he fell from a great height, coming awake with a jolt at the very moment of impact. He lay quite still for a long time, lapsing into and out of consciousness, his mind a jumble of dark and turgid images spiralling before his mind's eye. He wondered if he were descending into the pit of hell.

Judd must then have fallen back into a longer period of unconsciousness for he came awake again with the same jolt as before, only this time he was aware, even through closed eyes, that gentle light and warmth played upon his cheek. If death had taken him, he thought dreamily, it was not unpleasant. Time then drifted for a while as sensations of the flesh returned - until he came eventually to the certainty that he had not taken leave of life after all. It was a pleasing realisation.

And then the troubling images returned, more coherently than before: his frantic scramble up the beach, the impact of the musket ball, his headlong flight and collision with the rock. These thoughts moved through his head like a procession that seemed to turn upon itself and repeat; and it was only after several passes that the picture of his angry pursuers took its place in the parade. It was that image that brought him at last fully to his senses, and he made at once to rise. But his body seemed made of stone and, unwilling yet to test its function lest he should find himself broken, he opened an eye. An empty scene formed in his narrow view, an oblique view across dimpled sand towards the low, tufted dunes that he had tried desperately to reach. The sound of distant surf entered his ears from somewhere as yet invisible, and thoughts began to come like pages turning in a breeze, each a fragment of broken memory.

He wondered why he still lay upon the beach unmolested; he wondered where his pursuers were now? Perhaps, he thought more urgently, he had only lain there for a short time? Perhaps the boatmen were even now thundering up the sand towards him, bent upon tearing him limb from limb?

Pulse and mind now began to race as the adrenaline of flight took hold to impel him into action; there might yet be time to flee before they pinned him to the ground! He jerked his head up to look about, but his right eye was gummed up and he could not see clearly from the other. Instinctively, he brought an exploring hand to his head. There was a sudden sharp stab of pain from his temple as his fingers found the wound - a flap of buckled, gritty skin that was clammy and cold to his touch. He winced as he probed around it. Hair on the right side of his scalp was hard and matted. He examined his fingertips for blood; the bleeding seemed to have stopped, but a membrane of dried blood had sealed up his right eye. He prised it open clumsily, the salty sand stinging as he rubbed it clear. Bleary sight returned. He found his lower lip swollen; his mouth was full of grit and blood - he spat it all out. He forced himself to his knees, his head thumping as if with repeated hammer blows, the effort of his movement making him feel nauseous and dizzy.

Judd began to wonder if he had the strength to run for it after all, but fear is a powerful motive force and it got him to his feet and signalled his unwilling legs once more into action. Yet for all his fright, he seemed unable accelerate, and soon he realised that he would never be able to outrun a determined pursuit. Terrified, he glanced over his shoulder, expecting grasping hands already to be reaching out to grab him.

The empty view astonished him - the beach was deserted! Where were his pursuers now, he wondered, hardly believing his eyes? It was as if they had vanished into thin air. He stopped in his tracks and swung his gaze around. The two sister ships, *Miranda* and *Rebecca*, lay peacefully to anchor some distance out, their sails furled to their yards. The two merchantmen had swung on their anchors but otherwise they were exactly where he had last seen them as he had sailed towards the beach. The muddy waters of the lower Chesapeake stretched out beyond, calm and empty but for a single sail on the distant horizon. The damaged skiff in which he had made his escape lay abandoned much as he had left her, her shattered gaff and sail still lying in a tangled heap across the thwart. Her tiny jib flapped lazily in the on-shore breeze as if beckoning for company. But something about the sight struck him as odd and it took a few heartbeats to appreciate what it was. The little boat lay well above the gently lapping surf, left high and dry on the beach - and yet the tide had still been rising when he had made his escape. He was quite certain of this because he had left *Miranda's* foredeck crew kedging the vessel off the mud on the tidal flood. His face puckered in consternation. He could make no sense of this. And then before he could apply reason to the conundrum, he realised that something else was missing from the scene. The sleek two-masted schooner in which Jack Easton and Captain Goddard had intercepted him was nowhere to be seen. He clammed his eyelids shut to squeeze out the residue of gritty debris that still blurred his sight. When he opened them again, he half expected to see some clue that he had missed before. He swung his gaze again, puzzled to the point of incredulity. But no, he had not been mistaken; the schooner had indeed disappeared – he wondered if she might be the distant sail making off in some haste? And though he hardly believed what his eyes told him, he was most certainly alone, alone on this isolated beach on the tip of this desolate peninsula at the bottom of the Chesapeake. It seemed for some unknown reason, that he had been let go.

He stood bewildered for a while, trying to piece together the train of events that had led him to be here. He remembered the schooner blocking the *Miranda's* path and forcing him aground as he had tried to steer a way through the shoals into the Atlantic - realising too late that the schooner had been the Trojan horse that hid Jack Easton and his friends, all set upon recapturing the hijacked vessel. He remembered finding Pettigrew and Hayward trussed up in the aft cabin where he had abandoned them to their fate, taking the saddlebags full of money for himself. He remembered making his escape in Easton's own skiff, and the feeling of elation at getting away unseen - until the *Rebecca's* longboats had been launched to round up Pettigrew's fleeing band of pirates, thus drawing attention to his escape. And finally he remembered being chased towards the shore, and running his skiff onto the beach with his pursuers hot on his heels.

But where, he wondered, were his pursuers now? It was mystifying. His head continued to throb and his right shoulder seemed suddenly very tender. He cast his eyes about. A few paces away, he saw the blood-smeared rock into which he had been thrown so violently and went back to examine it. Blood had stained the nearby sand, and on inspection, he noticed that his jacket shoulder was stained too. But when he examined the material more closely, he found no penetration. The musket ball had certainly hit him very hard, but for some reason it had not even pierced the cloth. It was only as he mused on this that he realised that the light had changed; dusk was by now fast approaching. He frowned in thought for a moment, reckoning by this observation the number of hours that must have passed since his fall. And then he realised that his saddlebags had also vanished – and with them, the small fortune stolen from the tobacco agent's safe in Charlestown! He swung his gaze about vainly searching for the bags, but quickly guessed what must have become of them - and his pistols too. Judd's befuddled mind had worked slowly, but now he realised at once what must have occurred: he had been left upon the beach as a corpse. His pursuers must have thought him dead; they had recovered their precious saddlebags and simply left him for the gulls to feed upon.

But he knew that it was really he who had won the day. He had cheated them again, just as he had cheated them before. They might have got their money back, but the victory was really his. And the best thing about it was that they would not know it! While he might have lost his fortune, he still had his life and his freedom. With that thought, a smirk spread across his bloody, swollen lips as he contemplated the sweet revenge that might now reach out from his supposed grave. Quietly he resolved that he would rise from the dead and strike again at those who had persecuted him.

Perhaps if he had known that the oarsman struck by his careful shot had been none other than Jack Easton himself, the man who Judd held responsible for all his recent troubles, he might have felt his honour sated. But in his warped mind, the very thought that Easton had deprived him of his hard-won prize was poison in his veins.

Captain Goddard stood impatiently at the *Miranda's* quarterdeck rail squinting into the gathering darkness, watching the lanterns of his boatmen criss-crossing the distant beach. Now that Pettigrew and Hayward and the other prisoners had been transferred to the *Rebecca* to be taken to Annapolis, his ship was once more his own. At last he could concentrate on getting his ship ready for her return to the Potomac at first light the following day. Before he departed to his cabin, however, he wanted the satisfaction of seeing Judd's body brought aboard so that it could be displayed in a manner that would demonstrate just punishment for his crimes. Goddard would not believe himself to be a cruel or vindictive man, but Judd had driven him beyond the limits of civilised condemnation. Judd's attempts to blackmail him and threaten his family, his thieving and conniving as boatswain, and now his audacious attempt to hijack his first command, had put the scoundrel beyond mercy. The

6

captain felt an irresistible craving to inflict mutilation on the face of the man who had caused so much misery – not only the misery felt by himself, but also by his good friend, Jack Easton, who by Judd's hand had already lost a son and may yet lose his life. With Jack thus coming into his thoughts, Goddard offered up a silent prayer:

'Pray God that *Warrior* will deliver him back to New Hope and into the hands of a competent surgeon in time to save him!'

It made him angry to think of his friend's peril. And for this and all of Judd's crimes, Goddard would have the man's body swung from the bowsprit for the gulls to peck his eyes out, and then cast the remains to the hungry fish of the Chesapeake! But as he watched the continuing meanderings on the distant beach, he began to fear that he had left it too late to send his men ashore. With the distractions of ferrying his prisoners to the *Rebecca*, he had lost track of time. And in the darkness, his men were clearly having difficulty finding the corpse, or else they would not be taking so long.

Eventually the lanterns converged into a single point of light, which after several minutes of uncertainty became recognisable as the bow light of the returning boat. The light made steady progress towards him, and soon he could make out the vessel's shape from the foamy splashes thrown up by its oars. The captain watched hopefully as the craft drew nearer, eventually seeing towed behind it as expected, the damaged skiff used by Judd for his escape, its severed gaff and bundled sails collected in a pile and strapped across the thwarts. The tandem vessels bumped alongside in an untidy fashion, entering the pool of light thrown down by the ship's lanterns.

Goddard leant over his rail to scan both boats intently.

'Where's the body?' He snapped. 'In the skiff?'

'Couldn't find it, sir,' came a hesitant reply from below. 'We looked where you told us, sir - and right across the beach.'

The man's tone became defensive as he continued. 'But in the darkness we just couldn't see it, sir,' he said lamely. 'I thought it best to bring the men back rather than waste more time blindly stumbling about! We'll go back at dawn, sir. We'll have no trouble finding him then – if the wolves haven't got to him first!'

There was no doubt in Philip Goddard's mind that Judd had been shot dead; he had seen the prostrate form lying on the beach from the longboat as he attended to his wounded friend. Major Lawrence had confirmed it and he would know; he was the one who had brought Judd down with a single shot and then led his scouts up the beach to retrieve the saddlebags. Judging by his description of Judd's body on his return, the shot must have been instantly fatal – a conclusion that had been no surprise to Goddard at the time; the major was reputedly an expert shot and this had surely been the proof of it! However, since getting Jack back to the ship urgently for medical attention had then been the priority, the recovery of Judd's corpse had had to wait.

By now, however, Goddard had expected to have the corpse back on board. That his boatmen had failed to find it irritated him intensely; sending them back to the beach at dawn would inevitably delay the ship's departure. And now the suggestion that predators might be on the prowl had made him think that he may yet be deprived of his trophy. His lips tightened in vexation:

'Then make sure you're ashore at first light,' he snapped. ' - and get the body back before we're ready to weigh or you'll be rowing it all the way to Charlestown!'

Goddard threw a sarcastic snarl at the dejected boat crew and retreated crossly to the stern rail where his first officer stood supervising his watch in securing the ship for a night at anchor.

'When the ship is secure, number one,' he said, 'have a boat made ready to take me across to the *Rebecca*. I shall not have another chance to speak to her captain, for he will certainly be away before us tomorrow morning while we await our boat's return from the beach! I want to be sure that he properly understands the charges to be brought against the prisoners when he arrives in Annapolis.' His voice descended to a growl. 'Pettigrew and Hayward must feel the noose around their necks for the murder of my watch-officers that night!'

The first officer nodded soberly. 'Aye, sir! But I fear that we ourselves may be called as witnesses if it goes to trial. We cannot leave it to an intermediary if we want to secure a conviction; and the men will want to see their shipmates avenged.'

'Then they'll have to send a chaise across to collect us in Charlestown, won't they,' Goddard replied shortly. 'We have a cargo to clear!'

Aboard the *Rebecca*, Pettigrew and Hayward remained curiously composed as they began their first night locked up in the dim lantern-light of the ship's brig. The *Rebecca's* heritage as a former Royal Navy ship-of-the-line had bestowed no favours for the likes of them. The tiny space allocated for their incarceration was part of the old gunpowder magazine buried in the ship's orlop to protect its contents from enemy fire. While the rest of the criminal cohort had been locked up in the airy forepeak with at least a little space to stretch their legs, the two leaders had barely enough room to stand in an airless cubicle with only a guttering candle to light it. Indeed, since both men were relatively tall, neither could get to his feet without adopting a pronounced stoop under the low deck beams.

It had been the warning from Captain Goddard earlier that evening of the particular dangerousness of these two hijackers that had persuaded the *Rebecca's* captain to separate them from the rest, lest they rally the others to some mischief. Indeed, the captain had detailed a burly crewman to be their gaoler and keep them under constant guard. Had Jack Easton been present at the time the warning had been given, he would no doubt have added the additional cautionary note that Pettigrew and Hayward were skilled in all the guiles of deception. But still fighting for his life aboard the *Warrior* speeding back to New Hope at that very moment, Jack was in no position to communicate his counsel.

The two prisoners had been somewhat contemplative ever since being bundled through the low hatch into the tiny space. Both squatted on their haunches in the flickering candlelight gazing morosely at the opposite bulkhead from which two buckets hung on hooks: one, water for refreshment, the other, their lavatory. Although dishevelled by their rough treatment at the hands of Sir Michael's militia scouts after the recapture of the *Miranda*, the two prisoners had borne the discomfort with brooding stoicism. Inwardly they blamed themselves for the loss of their prize. But neither would admit openly that it had been their inattention on the quarterdeck that had allowed the scouts to get aboard while Judd and his foredeck crew had been kedging the grounded vessel into deeper water.

'You should not have put so much faith in Judd,' said Hayward at last, clearly needing an outlet for his frustration. 'His grasp of chart work was tenuous to say the least. I watched him closely - the man was incompetent,' he sneered. 'How you could ever have thought him capable of navigating us all the way to the St Lawrence, defies me. You were taken in, Pettigrew; you chose the wrong man!'

This was Hayward the former card-sharp and trickster speaking, the man who had never done or said anything without first calculating the likely benefit to himself, the smooth talker who could charm an old widow out of her life savings and be proud of it.

'Yes, well we both know that now, don't we,' replied Pettigrew, irritably. 'As was patently demonstrated by his running us aground!'

With this, he gave his companion a haughty glance, looking down the length of his aquiline nose. 'And I don't remember you offering your services or doing anything to help!' He raised his eyebrows as if waiting for a protest, but when Hayward merely sneered again, he continued unperturbed. 'Post-mortems are a little futile in our current position, I'd say, but it was not as if we were able to take our pick of master mariners when it came to recruitment, was it? At least Judd won't be around to complicate things for us any more, will he? The man apparently got what he had coming to him, the double-crossing swine!'

Hayward grunted an endorsement. 'And good riddance too! I'd have put a bullet in him if they hadn't!'

The pair fell into a sullen silence for a while which, due to the enclosing heavy timbers, was as soundless as the inside of a tomb. The candle continued to gutter, throwing long, dancing shadows from the hanging pails, while the absence of any apparent movement told the pair that the ship was not yet underway. Pettigrew surmised that it was already to late for her captain to start back up the Chesapeake. As a former ship owner he knew how to read a chart, and from his recollection of those aboard the *Miranda*, he estimated that Annapolis was at least a full day's sail away, and more likely two. This then was how much time he would have to think about their eventual escape. Despite the setback, he had not abandoned thoughts of reaching the sanctuary of French territory. Even if his plan to sail into the St Lawrence had been a little too ambitious, there was bound to be another way.

'Rather than lament our misfortune, however,' he said at last, 'I would suggest that we have more pressing matters to consider.'

Hayward flicked up an ironic eyebrow. 'Such as how we get out of the little pickle you seem to have got us into?' he offered sarcastically.

'Quite!' came Pettigrew's laconic reply; the former master smuggler would not be ruffled by a silly comment from his idle companion. 'If I had had more of a contribution from you, Hayward, perhaps we might already be well on our way to safety instead of sitting here in this god-forsaken hole!'

Hayward frowned but remained silent.

'From now on we have to work better together,' continued Pettigrew, perhaps realising now more than ever that he would need a man familiar with the territory if he were to accomplish the new plan that was beginning to form in his mind. 'I'm sure that it has occurred to you that we are both likely to face the gallows if we are brought before a judge and jury. As well as for the hijack, we're both likely to be charged for the murder of the *Miranda's* two watch officers whose throats were cut when we took her. And I'll also be blamed for the two hostages killed when my knuckle-headed friends and I escaped from our transportation ship when we first arrived in this damned colony. I'm afraid that it will be your unlucky lot to be joined with me when we stand alongside each other in the dock!' Pettigrew said this with a supercilious smile, almost as if he enjoyed he prospect of taking his companion down with him.

'Hmmm!' muttered Hayward, flashing Pettigrew a surly look, 'I can't say that my record was entirely unblemished before anyway. My face is too well known in the colony. Once I fall into the hands of the authorities, there will be a reckoning of my long and, dare I say, illustrious past. I'm afraid that you are right, Pettigrew. We sink or swim together!'

'Then I'm glad we agree, Hayward,' returned Pettigrew after a long pause. 'For, as you might expect, I already have a fall-back plan in mind.'

It was as well that the dim light masked the sly look on his face as he threw another glance in Hayward's direction.

'So I would suggest that we should prepare ourselves to escape when our chance comes - and we must make sure that it does!'

Chapter Two

The first rays from the rising sun shot across the distant dunes to find *Miranda* and *Rebecca* still lying to their anchors in the navigable channel running northwards from Cape Charles. The two handsome square-riggers, suddenly resplendent in the sun's golden light, lay separated by a cable's length with bowsprits set across the Chesapeake like thoroughbreds nosing a starting line. Both ships' decks and yards already swarmed with hands already at their stations, with an urgent cacophony of shouted orders and ships' machinery echoing between the two hulls as if competing for attention. The breeze that had arisen with the dawn had raced across fifteen miles of open water from Virginia to ruffle the canvases already hoisted on their forestays but not yet sheeted in. Astern, lay the low sandy island that Jack Easton had used as a transit, piloting *Warrior* for her ambush the previous day. And in the starboard quarter, the shoreline of the eastern peninsula, broken by marshy creeks and headlands, stretched northwards into the haze until lost from sight.

Captain Goddard had been on *Miranda's* quarterdeck since the early light had woken him, his telescope trained upon the distant beach. Behind his glass, his brow was furrowed in concentration. With his magnified sweep, he had followed his shore party's renewed search as they had quartered the entire length and breadth of the sandy shoreline to which he had directed them. He had watched closely as they had disappeared into the dunes behind, hoping to see them soon returning with Judd's corpse. Yet as far as he could make out his men were returning empty handed. He swept his view up and down the coast to other sandy stretches nearby, beginning to fear that he may have sent his men to the wrong part of this long and empty shoreline. Due to the shoaling mud banks, he had been forced to anchor his ship nearly two miles out to ensure a safe depth under her hull. At such a distance, his glass was simply not up to investigating every little shadow and indentation ashore. Any one of these could have been a prostrate form - indeed his heart had missed a beat on several occasions as his eye had stumbled upon some dark feature that could have been the dead Judd. That his ship had swung on her anchor with the tide turning overnight had confused things further, so that he was no longer certain of his earlier identification of Judd's location. Moreover, the only other witness to Judd's shooting had gone off with Jack aboard the schooner, so there could be no corroboration of the precise geography. And the recovery of Jack's skiff the previous night had now removed the only landmark to go by. Thus, ever the optimist, the young captain would not accept the boatmen's empty-handed return as proof of anything sinister or untoward.

Furthermore, he was reluctant even to consider the possibility that Judd had not been killed. The idea, therefore, that the former boatswain might suddenly have become mobile and walked away was simply inconceivable. Even if the musket ball had not killed Judd outright, Goddard was convinced that he would anyway have perished in the cold of the night or from loss of blood. It had been a grievous wound after all, or so Major Lawrence had reported.

And yet, the alternatives did not seem credible either. That Judd might have been dragged away or buried by some inhabitant in the darkness seemed ridiculous – the peninsula appeared so sparsely populated that he could not imagine such an event. So too, the notion that wolves had carried the body away, although he admitted to himself that this possibility was marginally more likely. None of these thoughts, however, could deflect him from the growing (and more palatable) conviction that his search party had gone to the wrong part of the beach! Or else that they were stupid or completely blind! And while their ineptitude would deny him his opportunity to display Judd's corpse as a trophy, he began reluctantly to accept that this had been the case. Some mental conjecture continued in Goddard's mind, nevertheless, even as his hapless oarsmen came alongside and reported their inconsequential search - until his first officer distracted him by calling out:

'*Rebecca's* weighing, sir!'

Captain Goddard turned to watch *Miranda's* sister ship swinging her fine prow sedately across the wind under a backed foretopmast sail. He watched the manoeuvre with a critical eye – the *Rebecca's* captain was as newly promoted as himself and no doubt coveted the same ambitions to progress. Amongst such a professional cadre, one was wise to mark a potential rival's performance in order to gauge the competition! And Goddard had to admit that it was a well-executed drill. With the wind put abaft the beam by the manoeuvre, the *Rebecca's* topmen, already poised along the yards awaiting instructions from below, were called to let go the main, the fore-top and the topgallant sails, which tumbled down in a great cascade almost simultaneously. Even from the deck of the *Miranda*, the thunderous flapping of the mighty canvases could be heard as they were sheeted in and braced into propulsive form. And in less than a minute, the *Rebecca's* masts were leaning before the wind in harness of the straining sails, a healthy wake soon swirling at her stern.

'We'll not be long behind her, number one,' Goddard replied, snapping his telescope shut. 'Our boat's alongside – empty-handed I'm afraid - but we can't waste any more time on another search! Hoist the boat aboard as quickly as you can and prepare the ship to weigh; we'll race *Rebecca* to the mouth of the Potomac before we have to leave her!' And under his breath, he added: '- and the gulls will have to see to Judd's remains wherever they are!'

Only a few minutes later, with *Miranda* picking up speed in *Rebecca's* wake, the boatmen attended the captain on the quarterdeck formally to confirm what he already knew. It was just as he dismissed the men to their posts that the first officer called out from the helm:

'Can't get full throw on the wheel, sir! Feels like it's jamming at about half its travel. Must have been damaged when she went aground, sir.'

And with that, any last concerns regarding Judd's disappearance were thrust aside.

Goddard strode immediately to the wheel to try it for himself.

'Number One! Get the carpenter below to investigate,' he said quickly; and to the helmsman he added: 'Hold her as steady as you can for the time being; let me know if she falls off the wind.'

The damage report was not long in coming:

'Chippy says the tiller's been fractured, sir. Looks like they ran her into the mud rudder first. He'll need to cut out the split timber and bolt some new in place. The starboard steering pulley's been pulled askew too, and the cable's jamming on it. It's that that's causing the restriction in the wheel's throw, he says. He's also saying that he'll need some heavy equipment and a forge to fix it, sir.' The first officer looked glum.

'Confound it man!' retorted Goddard sharply. 'Should have checked it out before, Number One!'

The captain flashed an accusing glance at his junior, but he knew that he was ultimately at fault. It was Judd's mysterious disappearance that had distracted him, but that was no excuse. The ship should have been given a proper checking over after her recapture and it was his responsibility to ensure that it had been done! He sucked his teeth.

'Would it get us to Annapolis?' he snapped.

'Wouldn't trust it, sir, even in this wind,' replied the first officer, throwing a concerned glance at the closeness of the land and shoals to starboard. 'It could seize up at any time, and we'd certainly not be able to heave to or bring her about! We're on a lee shore, sir...'

The captain nodded and came to a quick decision.

'Signal to *Rebecca*: "we require your assistance"!' he said. 'Call her attention to our flags with a cannon if you have to. We'll get her to take us in tow. Should be an interesting exercise!' he muttered these last words under his breath, then added more buoyantly: 'I suppose it's as well to discover the damage with our guardian angel still near at hand, number one! This'll be the second time in twenty-four hours that she has come to our assistance!'

The original plan had been for the *Miranda* to return to the port of entry at Charlestown (where she had been loaded), so that Thomas Harding, the port's shipping agent, could clear his cargo of tobacco for export through customs. However, in consequence of the rudder damage she would now be towed to Annapolis, since it was only there that the ship's owners had facilities for repair. In a fair wind, either vessel under full sail could have made the journey up the Chesapeake in one or two days at most, but with the *Rebecca* towing her disabled sibling all the way, it would take a full four days. Moreover, because it was thought best to lock *Miranda's* rudder central (to avoid it becoming stuck deflected thus making the combination impossible to steer), she could raise only limited sail to assist progress. More might have brought both vessels into danger. It was therefore not until the close of the fourth day that the vessels were secured in tandem on the busy Annapolis waterfront. On top of all the difficulties en route, an inconvenient wind blew up on entering the harbour and this had required some deft seamanship to bring both vessels alongside in any semblance of order. It had been an exercise requiring a great deal of bellowing from the two quarterdecks and the motive power of all the ships' boats.

The *Rebecca's* crew were thus exhausted and hungry at the end of all their efforts, and not as alert as they should have been when the prisoners were brought on deck. Moreover, the *Rebecca's* officers (unlike Captain Goddard and his first officer who remained aboard the *Miranda* to instruct the repair party the moment it arrived) were not so keenly aware of the ruthlessness and guile of Pettigrew and his men. Perhaps too much had been assumed about the prisoners' continuing docility after their demoralised surrender at the retaking of the *Miranda*. Perhaps it was thought that four days in confinement would render them weak and more submissive yet. However, even without the benefit of hindsight, it was surely courting disaster to bring upwards of twenty criminals on deck at the same time, especially since all faced the hangman's noose for piracy, and therefore nothing to lose. Furthermore, while the seamen had endured four long days of hard labour managing an unwieldy waterborne combination, the prisoners were fully rested and had had ample time to prepare. Certainly, they were tethered at the wrists as they were brought on deck to be handed over to the city constabulary, already waiting on the quayside with muskets on their shoulders. And no doubt any reasonable observer would have considered the crew's weapons sufficient to arrest any misbehaviour. But the determination of the criminal cohort to seize the first (and perhaps most obvious) opportunity to make their move was grossly underestimated. Indeed, it was the sheer crowdedness of the deck and the patent dangers of crossfire that both facilitated the attempt and frustrated an effective response.

It was when the prisoner cohort was brought to the head of the Rebecca's gangway, prior to being led down to the waiting constables, that trouble started. The twenty or so men previously locked in the forepeak had been marshalled out in two lines and led across the main deck where they were brought together in a single group (presumably to await the arrival of Pettigrew and Hayward being brought up from the brig). It must have been at this time, when the guards' view into the now quite large assembly of prisoners became obscured, that the restraints of some must have been severed. (It was suggested in the subsequent enquiry that nails or scraps of metal from the forepeak must have been sharpened into blades during the four days of the journey.) Until this point the cohort had been impeccably behaved - an obvious ploy considering what was about to happen - and this had lulled their guards into complacency.

Soon, Pettigrew and Hayward were brought out of the forward hatch accompanied by a burly gaoler and two armed seamen. The two captives, their wrists shackled with manacles and chain, appeared pale and weak on their legs, both affecting to need some support from their guards. Hayward, in particular made a great play of this as the pair were led across the main deck towards the waiting assembly. And he had not gone far before he stumbled, pulling his helpful supporter off balance and causing them both to fall to the deck with some theatricality. This drew the attention of all on deck and proved to be just enough of a distraction to allow the now unrestrained prisoners in the main group, about eight to ten in all, to disarm a few adjacent guards and turn them into human shields and hostages.

With captured pistols now in their hands, this break-away cohort formed themselves into a protective circle at the head of the gangway into which the main body of guards seemed reluctant to fire, no doubt afraid of wounding their comrades. For several long seconds there was a sort of standoff. Hemmed in at the top of the gangway by the *Rebecca's* seamen and at the bottom by the sheriff's constables, their muskets now aimed threateningly into the melee, there appeared to be no escape. At the same time, both sides seemed to understand the nature of the predicament in which they found themselves. There was quite a lot of jostling for position amongst the two groups, and a noisy exchange of taunting soon broke out, with much provocative gesturing. But no one seemed willing to open fire. It must have been obvious that a blood bath would have followed if someone had.

Meanwhile, the remaining prisoners, those who had not already slipped their bonds, had become cut off from their comrades in the commotion by an intervening wall of guards, and they now milled about in an agitated fashion causing yet further distraction. The situation was rapidly becoming quite angry. The *Rebecca's* captain and first officer, alerted by the sounds of disorder on the main deck, made to return from their dinner table below, but found themselves trapped in the companionway by the press of men outside. Hayward in the meantime was still lying on the deck where he had fallen, apparently unconscious; and Pettigrew, feigning unsteadiness, now rested on the arm of the burly gaoler, by then abandoned by his erstwhile comrades, both of whom having been drawn into the scuffle across the deck. Clearly they had thought their two charges too frail to cause trouble, but this, of course, was exactly what Pettigrew had intended. The burly gaoler was thus taken entirely by surprise when his prisoner took hold of the arm used as support and twisted it into an arm lock. The seaman resisted, of course, but not quickly enough to release himself from Pettigrew's grip before Hayward, springing up from the deck with breathtaking agility, grabbed the gaoler's pistol. And before the man could cry out, a swift blow to the back of his head with the weapon's butt silenced him. It took only a few seconds more for Pettigrew and Hayward to unfasten their restraints with the key from the gaoler's belt.

With the others' attention still fixed upon the continuing confrontation at the gangway head, none of this was noticed - until several of those seamen at the rear of the jostling group were quietly overcome. And by the time the rest realised the danger that had crept upon them from behind, it was too late. Pettigrew and Hayward had armed themselves with two pistols each and posed a clear and pressing threat. With the *Rebecca's* deck crew now effectively encircled, a degree of confusion reigned, and it was at this point that the remaining prisoners, those until now who had remained tethered and apparently compliant, now asserted themselves, taking the guards by surprise with the violence of their uprising. Amongst these were the two knuckle-headed thugs, formerly Pettigrew's accomplices in his earlier escape from the transport ship. They knew the form, and now, using their tethers as nooses and snares, they employed their brutish strength to deadly effect, rallying their comrades into unrestrained action. It is surprising that only a few of the guarding seamen opened fire – wounding several prisoners and fellow guards as a result - but the scrum was so confined that it was not easy for them to be careful with their aim. The sheer weight and recklessness of the attack overwhelmed them before they could really get organised. Moreover, Pettigrew, Hayward, and their by now fully armed collaborators systematically disabled the seamen at the periphery.

The speed with which the *Rebecca's* deck had been transformed from orderliness to violent mayhem had caught the sheriff's men off guard too, for they had watched from the quayside bemused, with no one thinking to give the order to take cover. When the first shots rang out, therefore, there was an abrupt awakening and somewhat of a panic as the line of special constables (conscripted for this special duty) scattered to the four corners of the quay with surprising alacrity. The sheriff's belated orders were lost in the general din of the retreat, and Pettigrew was quick to take advantage of the disarray, ordering his men down the gangway to snap at the fast disappearing heels as if in pursuit. The rout was thus completed. And unfortunately for the officers, the great majority of the escapees now making for the lantern-lit lanes and alleyways of Maryland's colonial capital were faceless petty criminals who would be the devil to identify.

Only Pettigrew and Hayward stood any chance of recognition by lawmen in the colony. Pettigrew was already the subject of a wanted poster that had been widely circulated (made from a print of Jack Easton's charcoal sketch a month or so before); while Hayward's face would be well known in Charles County, especially by those who had had the misfortune to fall victim to his deceptions in the ordinaries and gambling houses of the district.

From the quarterdeck of the *Miranda*, Captain Goddard had watched mortified as the incendiary mixture on the deck of his sister ship had exploded out of control. The disorder had developed so quickly that he had had no time to react, and he had watched dismayed and angry as the prisoners had fled across the quay. Behind them, on the main deck of the *Rebecca*, were left a pitiful array of defeated, dazed, and injured seamen being brought to order by a bewildered captain and first officer. Their hangdog glances, thrown across the decks of the two adjacent vessels towards the captain of the *Miranda*, said it all. The *Rebecca's* officers had failed in their duty, and both quite clearly knew it. The sheriff and his men, no longer visible along the whole length of the waterfront, were by now assumed to have taken up the chase, but it would be some time before they returned.

Chapter Three

'Jack!' shouted Rose Easton crossly from the door of the bedroom, to which she had just returned carrying a breakfast tray. She had found her husband on the edge of the bed as if about to get up and that simply would not do, for in her opinion he was not ready. Nevertheless, she could not help being amused at the sight of him in his nightshirt and his nightcap, dangling his bare legs to the floor, his toes feeling for his moccasins, just out of reach. There was a sort of comical pathos about him that she found endearing. In full health, he had been a picture of fitness and strength, a handsome man, she had always thought; but now he looked pale and somehow fragile after his ordeal - as if he'd had the stuffing knocked clean out of him by his injury. At his groomed best, his long dark hair would have been combed back smoothly over his head into a neat ponytail tied with a ribbon, but now it hung dull and tousled around his ears and neck. His face, though fuller and with more colour now as he continued his recovery, still showed a painful legacy. She knew how close she had come to losing him, and she thanked the Lord for the wind that had delivered him on the schooner so quickly into the surgeon's hands. Jack would certainly have perished without it. But while his current weakness evoked feelings of maternal care and nurture deep within, there was a little bit of her that resented his plucky bravado, for she suspected that he itched to be off on his adventures again just when she had really had enough of his absences. There was a brooding obstinacy about him too that Rose had come to know too well, and she feared it and disliked it.

'Now Jack, you get back into bed this instant! You know what the doctor said.' Rose spoke in a matronly tone. 'You know that you're not supposed to get up before he says you're ready!' The breakfast tray clattered as she strode breezily across the room where she took up a position to block her husband's intended ascent. Dressed in her blouse and long skirt, and with her hair drawn up into a tight bun, she exuded command.

'Oh Rose, have pity on a poor soldier!' Jack grinned, trying some humour. 'I have just got to get up; I cannot stand this confinement any longer!'

But he saw at once that he had lost the battle and rolled himself submissively back onto his pillow with a sigh. He saw the little, impatient shake of his wife's head as she put her tray onto the dresser, and he smiled mischievously behind her back - he knew that he would win in the end.

'I am so bored with this,' he said petulantly when she returned to his bedside. But he got no sympathy as she pulled over the blankets that he had cast aside in his failed bid for freedom. 'And anyway, my shoulder is feeling much better now, and I'm sure that it would be good for me to be up and about rather than stuck in here!' Jack protested. He had been an invalid too long. 'Besides, I have to get myself fit and ready to go north. I cannot let Sir Michael and Major Lawrence and the scouts get too far ahead of me or I shall never catch them up.' He moved his bandaged shoulder tentatively as if testing it, his face creasing in pain as he stretched the damaged sinews to their maximum extent. His secret exercise regime of recent days was paying off, he thought; despite the discomfort, full movement of his damaged joint was now just about attainable - if still somewhat uncomfortable. He forced a grin as if to say: 'It's almost normal, see!'

'Oh Jack!' Rose sighed wearily as she brought back his breakfast tray. She was about to continue with her entreaty but she put the tray down on his lap rather too firmly, causing some of the contents of a steaming mug to spill over. Despite her obvious impatience with her husband, she did not seem able to stop herself fussing about the little mess that had been spilled upon the tray. She stooped over it, sighing impatiently to herself, and used a corner of her apron to dab it dry. But the job was not half finished before she straightened and gave Jack a piercing glance.

'Look Jack,' she said, giving her supposed invalid a withering look. 'Don't you think that you have done enough for Sir Michael now? He has his money back; and we have ours. You don't owe him anything any more. Anyway he has quite enough men in his militia not to miss you in his ranks!'

But she saw that he was about to protest and stiffened visibly. She had heard her husband's arguments before and held up her hand to prevent him from rehearsing them again.

'No, I don't want to have another argument!' she said firmly. 'Someone has to protect you from yourself!'

And with this, she strode to the window and snatched back the curtains - an act done as much in exasperation as to let in the morning light. She stood there for a moment gazing at the slow-moving river below, her arms folded resolutely over her apron bib, her lips tightly clamped. The tranquil summer morning outside did not reflect her mood.

'You cannot go! I will not let you!' she said at last, as if that were the end of the matter.

Rose had nursed Jack unstintingly through the weeks of his convalescence, and knew him well enough to realise that he she could not keep him cooped up in this bedroom for much longer. It was true that the gunshot wound was healing very well under the care of Sir Michael de Burgh's physician. Indeed, Jack's strength had recovered surprisingly quickly, aided no doubt by the good food sent up from Lady de Burgh's kitchen. But, perhaps a little deviously, she harboured the notion that the longer she kept him confined, the more likely it was that he would give up the idea of following Sir Michael to the battlefront - the further away the militia was, the more difficult it would be for Jack to catch it up!

Sir Michael and Lady de Burgh had been so generous with their help since Judd's malicious hands had set their cabin aflame, and she knew that she must be grateful for their kindness. Without their help in the aftermath of that dreadful fire, life would have been difficult to say the least. The rooms that had been made available in the plantation owner's house at New Hope - this comfortable bedroom and the small snug adjacent to it - had been her home for nearly two months now, ever since Judd's spiteful act. Rose could not deny that Lady Caroline's support had helped Jack's recovery too. But until their home was eventually rebuilt, she and her husband would remain dependent on their hosts for almost every detail of their living; and the strains of this rather too-close relationship were beginning to tell. Moreover, well-meaning as it was, their charity would place them more and more in Sir Michael's debt, a debt that she feared would put Jack under yet more obligation.

The rebuilding of their cabin, furthermore, had not yet even started, and if Jack should go off again, as he seemed quite determined to do, it could be a year before she would have her own home - an interminable time to be languishing at New Hope as a reluctant and lonely guest. And while Ned and Matthew would undoubtedly do their best to help with reconstruction, they would also have to work the farmstead and so would constantly be diverted – moreover, sixty-year-old Sebi was no longer up to heavy work since his fight with Judd and his injuries in the fire. With all these thoughts in her mind, she was becoming increasingly bitter at

Jack's apparent eagerness to rejoin Sir Michael's militia, by now well on its way north.

She deserved more consideration from her husband, she thought, especially after all they had been through. She had not objected when Jack had first joined the regiment because his enlistment had been a condition of their tenancy. But things had developed worryingly, and had become much more dangerous too - ending up with his near-fatal wounding. That Jack had been instrumental not only in recovering the tobacco consortium's money but also its entire year's produce aboard the recaptured *Miranda*, must surely have fulfilled any debt of honour owed to his former master! And what vexed her more was that her plea to Sir Michael to reward her husband's bravery by relieving him of his undertaking to serve had been ignored. On this matter, she had quite expected her host graciously to consent - Jack was a farmer and a stonemason after all and not a soldier - but Sir Michael had been ambiguous and evasive with his reply, and had soon after left New Hope to rejoin his company without mentioning it again. Despite Sir Michael's help and kindliness in other respects, Rose now found herself offended by his indifference to her plea.

But Jack was his own worst enemy; he seemed somehow driven by ambition now. That he was recovering so quickly seemed miraculous, but his run of luck was unlikely to last. 'No,' she thought, suddenly feeling very angry, 'Jack has done his bit, and Sir Michael can do without him very well!' Jack may well have shown himself to be a fighter, but he was not a military man! And now that Judd and the two others who had tormented him had finally been dealt with (or so everyone at New Hope still thought), he had achieved everything that he had set out to do.

More importantly, Rose felt that it was now time for Jack to focus on rebuilding their home so that it would be ready for their new baby (which she was now certain she carried, for her period was overdue). She would tell her husband this wonderful news today, she had already decided – later, when the time was right - and she was sure that this would change his mind about going off on another of his reckless endeavours! After the torment of losing her first as a result of Judd's assault, and indeed after suffering *all* the discomforts that she had been forced to endure since her expulsion from England all those years ago, he surely owed her that!

'I respect your sense of duty, Jack,' she said at last, still gazing through the window. 'And I did not try to stop you going when you set off with

Sir Michael last month. But this last adventure of yours - recapturing Judd and Captain Goddard's ship, and nearly getting yourself killed in the process - has changed things. I told Sir Michael, that you had done enough, Jack, and that he should not expect more…'

'You spoke to Sir Michael, Rose?' retorted Jack shortly. He was clearly put out by his wife's admission and frowned angrily. 'You should not have done that without speaking to me first! I would not want to cross him; his goodwill is important to us and we owe him so much…'

'You owe him nothing, Jack - not any more!' Rose turned back sharply to face her husband, her features strained. 'You recovered his fortune and he should be more than satisfied with that! Besides, you had already cleared your name when you returned from Portland - you were already a free man! In the sight of the law you had been wrongly convicted and wrongly transported to Maryland; when Sir Michael came aboard the *Rotterdam* looking for convicts to indenture, neither of us should have been for sale!' She had raised her voice progressively as she had spoken and was near to shouting now. 'Jack, in law, you have no obligation to him at all!'

Jack sighed wearily. 'Rose, we have discussed this before and I don't want to go over it again,' he said. 'The fact is that we are here in Maryland – wrongly or not - and it's given us the opportunity to make more of our lives than we could ever have dreamed of in Portland. And Sir Michael has been very generous to us, first in releasing me from my indentures, then in giving us our fifty-acre farmstead, and now in accommodating us since Judd burned down our home. I don't want to let him down; he could be very important to us in the future.'

But Rose was not to be deflected. 'I grant you that he and his wife have been kind, Jack – especially since the fire,' she said, making her tone conciliatory. 'But you should never have been a convict in the first place, and you have repaid Sir Michael with all your stonework many times with the profit he has made from it! When he offered you the tenancy, his motive was to keep you here and make yet more from the quotas that he imposed upon you. He has given you nothing that you have not earned, Jack – nothing that would not ultimately benefit him more! And I do not understand this compulsion you feel to follow him to fight the French!' Rose was beginning to sound really angry now. 'His little regiment will do no more than get in the way with so many British and colonial regulars already moving west. Besides, I half suspect that he and some of his plantation-owner friends have less noble motives in mind!'

'Like what?' answered Jack defensively, as if he did not already know what his wife's answer would be.

'Like the acquisition of more land, for instance! At the expense of the native people living there already,' she said, throwing him a fierce glare. 'And at the expense of the French who have just as much right to be there as we have on this side of the Appalachians. I talked to people on the plantation while you were away; this whole thing is a squabble over land, Jack, don't you see? There is nothing noble about it! For all their brutality, the French and Indian attacks on British settlements would never have taken place had our colonists not encroached upon their trade and our settlers moved so far west! We would be living in peaceable co-existence otherwise!'

Jack could not meet her angry eyes. 'We both know that there is more to it than that,' he said evenly. He had heard her thoughts on this subject before, but she seemed to be becoming more and more entrenched in her attitude, and her arguments more cogent. In his heart of hearts, he shared some of his wife's misgivings about the war, but he dare not voice them now. He feared that if he conceded even a single point to her, it could fast become a rout, the proud bastion of his contentions crumbling completely under the siege of her logic; it would leave him looking feeble should he follow Sir Michael as he intended. He was committed to the militia now and he would lose face if he did not at least make the effort to rejoin it. Moreover, if he were not seen to have played an honourable part in the campaign, there could be uncomfortable business and social consequences for him in Maryland when the company returned. He began to marshal a rebuttal, but Rose changed tack:

'Lady Caroline is of the same mind, you know;' she said abruptly. 'The two of us talked about you and Sir Michael quite a lot while you were ill. In fact, she confided in me that she tried to talk her husband out of going too – obviously to no avail! It seems that he is as obstinate as you, Jack!'

With this, Rose seemed suddenly to run out of words. She sighed heavily and shook her head.

'Anyway, if you are so important to him,' she said more calmly, 'why could he not wait for you to recover before he set off? Does he expect you to find your way through those mountains and forests alone?'

Jack was tiring of his wife's onslaught and his voice began to sound a little patronising.

'He was simply anxious be on his way, Rose - he didn't want to leave Sanderson in charge too long. The man's apparently considered a bit of a buffoon, and Sir Michael just doesn't trust him. So once he and Major Lawrence knew I'd be all right, they pressed on to Georgetown to save time – given a fair wind up the Potomac, they'd only have been a few days behind the regiment when they got there. They said they'd send someone back to wait for me in Charlestown.'

Rose looked put out by this. 'I see! It seems you've already made up your mind,' she said coolly. 'You didn't think to include me in this conversation, I suppose?'

Jack shifted uncomfortably on his pillow. 'I can't let them down, Rose,' he admitted, his tone becoming at once defensive. He could see by his wife's expression that she was furious.

'Look,' he said, deciding to be plain, 'fighting this war is a patriotic responsibility, Rose, and I can hardly remain at home while others in the county take up arms in our defence. I would be failing in my duty to them as well as Sir Michael if I did not go.'

Jack's statement was boldly asserted but it sounded hollow in his ears.

To Rose, Jack's sudden declaration of patriotism sounded pompous; if he thought that evoking patriotism would win him the moral high-ground, he was badly mistaken.

'Duty?' she snapped. 'Do not talk to me about duty, Jack! I stayed with you when I could have gone back to Portland when my four years were up. And then, after we both nearly broke our backs building up a farmstead and a home from the tangled wilderness we were given, you just upped and left me pregnant while you went off looking for Smyke! Even when Judd followed you back and destroyed the cabin out of pure nastiness, I did not blame you for it.' Rose was angry now. 'And in spite of that, I still supported you when you went off again with Sir Michael soon after, leaving me to sort out the mess! And have I not tended to your wound and cared for you? You know I care deeply for you, Jack, but do not lecture me on duty! It is not duty that drives you, and you know it! You are putting pride and comradeship before your duty to me; it is as simple as that!'

Rose bit her lip as if to stem her outburst, and she glared crossly at her husband through reddened eyes already welling with tears. Jack was quite taken aback by the vehemence of his wife's attack and his mind was thrown into a whirl of indecision while he wondered how he might defuse the tension. Unfortunately, he wondered just a little too long. Abruptly, she turned back to the window and stood motionless for a while with her arms folded defiantly across her chest as if expecting a conciliatory response. But Jack was still at a loss for words. He found himself unable to argue further. He knew his wife's analysis had more than a grain of truth in it, although he could never admit as much. His instinct was to go to her, to wrap his arms around her and console her, but something held him back. What could he say that *would* console her, he wondered. That he would not go? That he would come back quickly? That he would not get hurt again? He knew that he could promise none of these. He sank back on to his pillow and allowed the silence to endure. Later he would realise that this had been a bad mistake, that his silence had stiffened his wife's resentment and made this growing rift more difficult to heal.

When Jack spoke again he spoke softly yet his tone sounded oddly resolute. 'Could you try to see it my way, Rose?' It sounded like an instruction rather than a question. 'We stand to lose so much if I do not follow Sir Michael. I am a free man now and will soon have earned our fifty-acre freehold from him. And with all my work these past years, I have won some respect for us in our community. If now I should be seen as a coward by not joining in the fight when so many of my peers and betters have done so, we would find ourselves outcasts again – like when we arrived and I was thought to be a criminal.' He shook his head and shrugged his shoulders. 'All that I risked by going back to Portland to clear my name, all that I fought for in my search for justice would be lost! We would be reduced to peasantry again, Rose.' He sighed helplessly. 'Try to understand,' he pleaded almost in desperation, 'if I felt that I had a choice...'

With these last words, uttered in a tone of finality, Jack thought that he had said enough.

Rose had listened mutely, but as Jack fell silent she stiffened then turned away abruptly to hide her tears. She fumbled for the handkerchief in her apron pocket, brought it out and wiped the tears away, dabbing her eyes quickly, almost angrily, as if cross with her womanly weakness. With a sniff, she pulled herself up and turned back to face her husband; her eyes were red-rimmed but now curiously steady, and the strong tone of her voice took Jack aback.

'You *do* have a choice, Jack, and you must make it carefully,' she said firmly. 'But hear me: I will not be left alone again to wait for you to return on a stretcher – or worse, for you not to return at all! Our farmstead was a joint endeavour, but I begin to see that your priorities have become entirely your own and do not seem to take account of my feelings at all. I will not accept the role of the dutiful and neglected wife that I appear to have become with all these adventures of yours! Even now,' she said incredulously, 'even now you cannot wait to be off again, can you?' And seeing no denial, she shook her head in disbelief. 'Well,' she said, taking a breath as if steeling herself to say something important, 'I am with child again, Jack; I have become sure of it these past few days.'

Jack's eyes widened in a look of pure delight at this news, but this brief pleasure was squeezed from his happy soul by his wife's continuing onslaught.

'It is a pity that I have to tell you like this, Jack, but there it is! And I do not intend to endure another pregnancy without you around. After all the pain that we have suffered, I will not bring another baby into this world without its whole family around it!' Rose bit her lip as if trying desperately to keep control of her emotions. 'If this does not change your mind, Jack, then I shall...I shall return to have our child in Portland, where he will at least receive the love and protection of his grandparents until you are ready to give yours.'

This hot tirade had issued from her lips as if swept before the flood of her sentiment. She might have employed her threat more appropriately after other womanly devices had failed to get her way, perhaps as a last-ditch salvo in a losing war of words. But she had made it her opening shot! And the moment her ultimatum had spilled out, she realised that they had taken her much further than she had intended. For a moment, she was as shocked as Jack appeared to be, and she stood staring at his stultified reaction just as he stared back. Her first instinct was to retract what she had said and plead that it had slipped out in haste or heat. How could she hurt him so with such a barbed attack, she asked herself? Surely she would never leave New Hope after all that they had both endured? Even if a woman disagreed with her husband, this was no reason to abandon him - and a wife should surely yield to her husband's wishes in return for the security that he provided? But as she considered the matter further, her feelings began to harden; she was determined to make of her life what she wanted, and she wondered if she might very well have meant what she said after all!

Jack's face had become flushed during Rose's heated monologue but now it seemed to drain of colour. For a moment he was speechless, his mouth held slightly open as if poised to form words that he could not find. He tried to swallow but his mouth was dry. Again, he did not quite know how best to respond. His first instinct was to try to pacify her; his second was to take up the argument again, expressing it more persuasively this time, thus talking her around. But as he dithered, wondering what to say next, he saw that her face had set. Her eyes had become cool and appraising, as if she had expected but failed to receive a gesture of conciliation or compromise on his part. Yet he knew that he could not make that gesture. She had thrown down a gauntlet that he could not pick up. For an instant he resented her challenge to his authority - a man should be the master in his own home after all! And then he thought: 'It is a ploy; she cannot mean it. She will come to see that I am right.'

It was at this point that a gentle tap at the door broke the uncomfortable silence that had descended on the room. In their different ways, both Jack and Rose felt grateful for the diversion, each hoping that the interruption might offer some way back, some way to bridge the abyss that now seemed to separate them. They noticed at once that the door had been left ajar after Rose's earlier entry with her breakfast tray. The uneasy look that passed between the pair acknowledged the possibility that their heated words had been overheard. But when the face of Lady Caroline appeared around the edge of the door, her expression was so innocent and pleasant that it gave no clue. Either the lady had heard absolutely nothing of the angry intercourse or, as Jack suspected, she was careful about what she chose to reveal.

'Ah,' she uttered in a voice that had no side to it, 'you *are* in after all! It was so quiet that I though Jack must be sleeping.' It was a clever deception.

Rose tidied her face with her handkerchief with such quick gestures that she hoped they passed unnoticed. She forced a smile.

'Oh, do come in Lady Caroline,' she said, brushing down her apron.

Lady de Burgh entered breezily, proceeding directly to the foot of Jack's bed with an air that suggested urgent business.

'You are looking better today, Jack,' she said in a matter-of-fact tone. 'Isn't it time for you to be up! It isn't healthy to stay in bed too long, you know!'

Rose flushed to have been contradicted, especially by another woman, and she flashed her husband one of those tight little smiles that was designed to show vexation when in the company of another. She picked up Jack's untouched breakfast tray and made to take it away.

'Jack seems to have no appetite this morning, Lady Caroline,' she said stiffly. 'It has gone quite cold.' She was probably referring to his scrambled eggs, but she might equally have been speaking of the atmosphere.

Their visitor smiled innocently.

'A messenger arrived this morning, Jack,' she said carefully, ' – sent back from Sir Michael. It seems that my husband and Major Lawrence called in at Charlestown to see Mr Harding on their way up river to Georgetown. Apparently there have been some worrying developments that he wants you to be aware of immediately, and he would therefore like you to visit Mr Harding as soon as you are able. The messenger would give me no further details on the nature of the matter, other than to say that one of Major Lawrence's scouts would be sent back to meet you there as agreed. It seems that it is important, Jack. The messenger would like to know the date of your expected arrival at Charlestown so that he can report it back – he is still waiting outside for your reply.'

Rose had continued towards the door carrying the tray as her former mistress had relayed Sir Michael's request, but now she paused and turned back. Jack caught her expectant glance. He saw the glimmer of hope in her eyes – and he realised that she must be longing for him to say that he would or could not go. With this, his heart sank; suddenly he had been backed into a corner - the need to declare his intentions had been thrust upon him. He had hoped that he would yet have time to bring Rose round to his way of thinking, if not to endorse his decision to rejoin the regiment then at least to understand it. But now he was being put on the spot for an answer. He hesitated, flicking his glances between the two women as the seconds ticked by. They both seemed to be watching him expectantly. He shifted uncomfortably in his bed; he wanted desperately to please his wife, to enjoy again that ease and mutual trust that had existed between them before this issue had arisen.

But Sir Michael's message had been both demanding and unsettling at the same time – something must have gone wrong for him to have sent it. Surely Rose would understand that he could not give in to her wishes now he thought, feeling some relief. Sir Michael's instruction had lifted the burden of the decision from his shoulders; it had conveniently absolved him from responsibility; it was the justification he needed for doing what he anyway felt inclined to do. He pretended not to notice that Rose still lingered at the door awaiting his response. Instead, assuming a defiant and manly bravado that seemed fitting in front of the wife of his militia colonel, he set his jaw into a sort of stoic pose.

'Then I must be up and get these legs to work again,' he said firmly, and he swung them out of the bed with an agility that surprised both ladies in the room. 'And Lady Caroline, perhaps you'd kindly send the message back that I'll be in Charlestown before the week is out!'

And thus it was that for the first time in their married lives, Jack and Rose found themselves on different paths, their minds set proudly one against the other.

Chapter Four

Nicolas Pettigrew never disclosed his first name because he hated the sound of it. Its ring evoked unsettling feelings from the past. It was what his father used to call him - more often than not in a mildly deprecating tone, even from his deathbed. Pettigrew rarely looked back on those years now, but when he did, his memory conjured a picture of a young man greatly misunderstood. He saw himself different from the crowd, someone gifted with faculties and insights superior to his peers. And being so precocious, he had grown to despise his father for being the gritty, plain-speaking, self-made man he was. Pettigrew junior looked down on Pettigrew senior for being bluff and uncultured, for not having the refined qualities that he himself had acquired at the best of boarding schools. Moreover, in comparison with the families of his young friends, amongst whom he was a frequent weekend houseguest, his own embarrassed him for their lack of social grace. In this self-image that he constructed, he allowed no acknowledgement that it had been the profits from his father's modest shipping company that had funded the privileges he enjoyed. And as an only child, he did not see that his father's constant critique might be meant helpfully as an antidote to his mother's indulgences, or an attempt to correct his languid ways. Young Pettigrew did not mourn his father's death when it came, nor did he much comfort his grieving mother whom he soon neglected. Instead, he dedicated himself at once to exploiting his shipping inheritance to the full. In a self-obsessed crusade to build personal wealth and power, he soon came to view other men as merely vassals, whose shoulders were the steps on which he climbed, whose souls he could pervert where and when it suited his cause. By his middle-thirties, he had achieved a position in polite society that looked unassailable. A magistrate, wealthy businessman and landowner, with fingers in many pies, he used his guile and influence to make his shipping company the most profitable on the south coast. That his burgeoning wealth was acquired largely through evading tax on his imports did not trouble him, for he had no social conscience to be pricked. Indeed, secretly he regarded his ability to cheat His Majesty's Revenue, to lie convincingly, and to manipulate others for his own gain as special gifts to cherish and hone.

Pettigrew's smuggling empire and his power and influence had, however, come abruptly to an end after falling, along with Smyke, his customs-officer protégée, into the trap that Jack Easton had set in Weymouth when he returned to clear his name. Ironically, like Jack before him, Pettigrew too had been transported to Maryland, convicted and disgraced. But ever with an eye open for opportunity, he had escaped to mastermind the ill-fated hijack of the *Miranda*, an ambitious scheme designed handsomely to restore his lost fortunes. Yet despite its failure and his recapture, Pettigrew remained curiously buoyant even now. Such was his enduring belief in his own supremacy that the set-back was seen merely as an early round lost in some long game that would ultimately be won.

This was the game that was still in play seven days after his audacious escape from the *Rebecca* on the Annapolis quayside, a game that would take a long time yet to play out.

'No, my dear Hayward,' asserted Pettigrew over his wavering companion, 'we must stick to our plan, 'We have to continue west, and that is that!'

Pettigrew was surprisingly composed for someone unused to the physical deprivations suffered since the pair's escape. The unrelenting effort required to travel through largely untrodden terrain may have worn his frame but not his spirit, despite the rigours of sleeping rough and meagre sustenance. The two men now rested on a mossy knoll in sunlight dappled by a high canopy of birch leaves that fluttered in a breeze that did not stir the damp air below. They soothed their bared and aching feet in the clear water of a sparkling stream that descended a shallow gully into the nearby river. The rippling cadences of tumbling water filled their ears. Pettigrew allowed a moment for the strength of his assertion to sink in. Hayward was the sort of man who sought an easy path in life, he thought, the sort of man who exploited opportunities to the full but did not make them. He was a chancer who could too easily become disaffected in their joint venture. He needed constant coaxing if he was to be of any use.

'You know that neither of us will be safe if we remain in British territory,' Pettigrew continued. 'By now, news of our escape will have spread to Pennsylvania and Virginia. If we want any peace in our lives, we have to reach French territory and do a deal with them. I know the French; they'll be interested in what we can tell them of the British mobilisation, especially if we make it our business to find out more as we travel. If we play our cards right, we could earn ourselves some favours.'

Hayward lay flat on his back, his arms cradling his head as the sun's warm rays played upon his face. He smirked derisively.

'They would have been better disposed to favour us had we delivered the *Miranda* and its cargo into the St Lawrence as we had planned! And we would have avoided this goddamned footslog too!'

'Well, we have Judd to thank for that as we both know!' Pettigrew said lightly. 'We must play the hand we have, I'm afraid, and not the one we might have wished for. And so far, I think we've managed to play our hand rather well, don't you? We are still free men after all, and now we are on our way to safety! Anyway,' he added with a lift of an eyebrow, 'I have not heard you coming up with a better idea!'

Hayward scowled. He felt cornered by his companion's logic, but he had to admit that Pettigrew's plan made some sense. With the furore that would have been stirred up by the hijack and the subsequent mass escape, there did not seem to be much of an alternative. There was certainly no safe future now for either of them in the British colonies, even if he doubted that his companion fully appreciated the challenges of the journey he proposed. He wondered if Pettigrew truly understood the sheer scale of this vast country. The mountainous, forested terrain through which they would have to pass to reach New France would be physically exhausting as well as dangerous. They would have to be constantly wary of being identified, yet finding food and shelter would inevitably bring them into contact with people along the way, and every exchange would increase the danger. Moreover, neither would describe themselves as hardy, yet they would have to cover over two hundred miles on foot. Such a daunting undertaking made Hayward feel apprehensive, yet it seemed that making some sort of deal with the French was the only certain way to gain a fresh start.

It was not only the dangers of the journey that troubled Hayward, however. He also disliked the prospect of placing himself entirely in Pettigrew's hands when it came to negotiating with the French, especially since he did not have the language. The prize that Pettigrew promised was alluring, but it would make Hayward dependent on someone he could not trust – and his companion had already shown himself to be ruthless when it came to allegiances that were no longer useful. On the other hand, he knew that they would have a much better chance of surviving the journey and gaining a good outcome by working together;

he certainly could not imagine doing it alone. And so, with some misgivings, Hayward found himself going along with Pettigrew's plan, even though he knew that he would never be able to let down his guard.

'Well, if we are really going to be able to set up afresh,' he said, choosing his words carefully, 'with the land and status in New France that you seem sure will be ours, then I suppose that that might make all this purgatory worthwhile.' In saying this, he swept a dismal gaze around the surrounding wooded wilderness. 'But I warn you, Pettigrew, do not try to get the better of me for I would prove a determined enemy if crossed.' It was an empty threat, but making it made him feel a little better about putting his companion effectively in charge.

Pettigrew's look of hurt surprise was intended to disarm. It hid his real feelings, which were more calculating. As fugitives, both had benefited from each other's company in staying alive and out of trouble. The partnership between them had provided mutual support and motivation through the trials of living rough since their escape. There was still a great distance to travel before they would be beyond the reach of British colonial law, and cooperation could mean the difference between escape and capture (or even life and death!). A colonial born and bred, Hayward was better acquainted with the territory than he; and despite the man's urbane persona, he was a known street fighter with practical skills and resourcefulness better suited to survival. Pettigrew, on the other hand, recognised that there was nothing in his own background that prepared him for the kind of challenge he now faced - in short, he needed Hayward more than the other way round. Yet Hayward must always believe the contrary if he were to remain the loyal servant that Pettigrew would require.

Thrust into an alien world, Pettigrew had had to employ deceit and guile in the place of the wealth and influence stripped from him in by an English court. Had he not been able to turn others to his will with such artifices as he now constructed to draw Hayward into his cause, he would certainly not have survived. He had learned that men like Hayward had within them a spark of greed that could readily be fanned into a compliant flame. It required merely a confident manner cultivated to mislead, or the lure of some imagined reward to ignite the latent avarice that would fuel a willingness to be led (and led astray!). Pettigrew often congratulated himself on his ability to do this; and he knew that while he dangled the illusion of a new life, land, and riches before Hayward's imagination, he could count on his compliance too. But he also knew that once they were safely on French soil, Hayward would quickly become a complication that he could do without.

'My dear chap,' he said, placing his hand upon Hayward's shoulder in a companionable manner, 'I have often dealt with the French and have always found them more than willing to repay favours. If we can offer something in return, I am sure that we shall receive all that we both aspire to. The French territories extend from Canada, right down the Mississippi to the borders of New Spain. With all that land available, I am quite sure that we shall be able to negotiate some for ourselves – why, we might even gain the grant of a proprietorship for the founding of a new colony!'

Pettigrew cast a glance to judge his companion's reaction to this grandiose notion and was satisfied to see a glint of self-interest flare in the man's eyes. He decided thus to continue on the theme.

'Although my assets in England were confiscated when I was convicted, I still have property and station in France that give me credentials and standing. And an undertaking on our part to tame and populate land in the name of France and produce tax revenue for the French treasury, I'm sure would be attractive – especially since they seem to have difficulties in attracting settlers themselves. Why, you might even find yourself its first Deputy Governor indeed!' (He laughed - and Hayward guardedly laughed with him.) 'We have come so far together, Hayward;' Pettigrew continued smoothly. 'Let us learn to be more trustful of each other and work in partnership towards this end. It is the only sure way that we can avoid being permanently on the run - or else strung up as menaces to polite society!'

And so it was that Hayward's loyalty was cheaply bought.

After their bold escape from the Annapolis waterfront, Pettigrew and Hayward had made no attempt to join up with the band of ruffians that had scattered to the four corners of the quay. Indeed, the pair had seized the opportunity to strike out on their own. At that moment of escape, Pettigrew had been quick to recognise the possibility and threat of recriminations. Although it was Judd's poor navigation that had run the *Miranda* aground in the Chesapeake, as leader for the group, he would be blamed for their capture. Before being recruited in the Brandywine hotel, those vagabonds might merely have faced a night or two in the stocks for their petty misdemeanours, but being hunted for a capital offence would put them in fear of their lives, and they would bear a grudge for the unwelcome notoriety. Pettigrew and Hayward had therefore waited for their criminal comrades to vanish into the dark streets and alleyways of Annapolis before setting off unseen in the opposite direction. It had amused the pair on reflection later, that having been inept as sailors, the blackguards had finally served some useful purpose by drawing away the sheriff's constables while they had made their own discreet escape.

Lying low for a few days to confound any cordon thrown up around the capital, the two men had eventually struck southwards to the shoreline of a wooded creek, which they then followed, believing it to be the quickest way into open country. But soon they found a major river estuary (the South River) blocking their path. And for the best part of the following week, they had trodden a tortuous and meandering route along the river's craggy shoreline, forced to circumnavigate its many tributaries, often having to come dangerously close to the town's perimeter in finding places to cross. They dared not risk being seen so near to habitation with word of their escape certain to have been quickly spread. Two wandering strangers were bound to attract attention, especially with Jack Easton's confounded 'wanted' poster spread about the county - there had been a price upon Pettigrew's head even before his latest infamy. Consequently, the pair travelled mainly in the twilight hours of early morning and late evening, sleeping and resting by night or day. Thankfully, the weather had remained dry, and the summer temperatures had made sleeping out a tolerable discomfort. This was just as well, for they had been forced back upon themselves so frequently that even after a full week, they were still only fifteen miles as the crow flies from the harbour!

In the following weeks, however, they would find themselves able to make better progress westwards, less hindered by the meanderings of the waterway they eventually left behind. They soon found themselves moving more easily along tracks and paths that wound through a partly cultivated landscape that undulated gently, where huge tracts of woodland provided ample cover. There were more opportunities too for petty thieving from isolated farmsteads and fresh water aplenty in the many woodland streams. But foraging for food occupied more and more time as each day passed. They had started their journey with a small stock of foodstuffs and a few other useful items, such as the invaluable tinderbox (with flint and steel) and a couple of decent knives stolen from a back street store in Annapolis. But when that little stock of nutrition had eventually run out, survival demanded more inventiveness. Hayward with the luck of a beginner once managed to snare a rabbit, which was spit roasted on an open fire and devoured voraciously. But more often it was other, less palatable woodland creatures that formed the protein of a sparse diet, supplemented by any other pickings that they could lay their hands upon.

By the end of the second week at large, however, being by then at what they considered a safe distance from the capital, both had become less nervous about being seen. Coming in due course upon a small settlement, therefore, it was decided that Hayward would venture in. He was later to reappear with a smug and mysterious smile upon his face for, not only had he a quantity of dried meat, bread, cheese and apples stuffed into the capacious pockets of a stolen overcoat, but he also carried a leather purse bulging with coin.

Pettigrew, still apprehensive of being recognised from Easton's 'wanted' poster, had remained outside the settlement. But unshaven, unkempt, and somewhat gaunter than he had been, he looked a very different man from that depicted in Jack's sketch. The benefit of this natural disguise eventually dawning upon him as he waited for Hayward to return, he risked a brief exchange with a mounted traveller who happened by. And seeing that he had not been recognised, he was emboldened to engage with the man at greater length, quizzing him on possible routes west. From this fortuitous conversation, he learned of the progress of the military road being cut by Brigadier General Forbes to move his troops from Philadelphia to the Ohio valley. Pettigrew had heard talk of this new thoroughfare before during his earlier time at large, but only now did he realise its significance as a possible escape route.

Thus fortified with Hayward's booty and given useful directions by the mounted traveller, the pair made their way into the Patuxent River valley, and followed the river constantly as it diminished towards its head. The watercourse led them steadily north-westwards in the direction of Frederick, a town identified by their helpful guide as a suitable place for replenishment. It was another tortuous trek along winding, undulating paths, which would take a further arduous week to negotiate. But at last they caught their first sight of the town, visible in the far distance across a swathe of cultivated fields and open grazing land, all carved from the surrounding woods. Weary from the day's walking, they selected the first likely looking building in which they might find safe refuge overnight - an isolated barn on the outskirts of the town.

'Ah! At last a decent bed,' cried Hayward gratefully, on pulling open the rickety door to see quantities of dry straw and hay piled up against the old building's far wall. And without another word, both men slipped inside, closing the door behind them, and threw themselves into the soft embrace, each letting out a long sigh of sheer exhaustion.

Some little time passed before either man stirred, both eventually waking from their naps. Hayward was first, raising himself abruptly from the straw as if in some alarm, but after swinging a worried gaze about the otherwise empty barn, he seemed to relax. Rummaging in his pocket, he pulled out a small package.

'Here,' he said, offering his still sleep-befuddled companion a piece of something taken from the wrapping.

'What on earth is this?' said Pettigrew taking it and raising it to his nose. 'A bit past its best, I'd say,' he said wincing, but popped it into his mouth nevertheless. 'Ugh! Tastes of something I'd prefer not to imagine!' He screwed his eyes up tightly as he chewed and swallowed it, then looked back at Hayward as if expecting an explanation.

'The last of the cheese!' said Hayward.

His thievery and basic woodman's skills en route had provided sustenance for the pair to endure the journey so far, but their diet had only been barely adequate. 'And it'll get more difficult to steal food after Frederick,' he said, falling into a glum mood. 'The population will thin out, so we can't depend on it any more. And if we have to depend entirely on what I can catch, I'm afraid we're going to go hungry!'

Pettigrew nodded. 'Then we'll have to stock up well before we set out, won't we?' he said in a tone that seemed to make light of Hayward's concerns.

Hayward was by now used to Pettigrew's languorous optimism, but still found himself riled by it, especially since it seemed that he was the one who had to do most of the providing!

'And it gets hilly after Frederick, Pettigrew!' he added, wanting to inject some realism. He was tired and fed up, and Pettigrew's naivety was infuriating. Of all his companion's traits, it was his manner that he disliked most, the way he seemed to take everything for granted. Hayward was apprehensive about the serious challenges that the pair would soon face and he needed his companion to take his share of the burden and become more engaged.

'We'll see the mountains rising in front of us soon,' he said, continuing the gloomy theme. 'And once we've reached them, the going will get a lot tougher. We've got a good hundred-and-fifty miles of forest in front of us – maybe more.'

'Oh, you're such a pessimist, Hayward!' replied Pettigrew coolly, 'Brigadier Forbes new road will practically lead us where we want to go, saving us the trouble of finding a route ourselves! What more do you want? I'd say that we have to use it, wouldn't you? It would be ridiculous not to.' He flashed Hayward an enquiring glance as if challenging him to contradict; but when Hayward remained silent, Pettigrew continued:

'And to intercept it, it seems all we have to do is follow the road going northwards out of Frederick - up a river valley apparently. That traveller fellow reckoned we'd reach the junction in a few days. And I'm quite sure from what he told me that the going won't be half as difficult as that dreadful river path,' he said blithely, as if the route onwards was the New York to Annapolis turnpike.

Hayward was irritated by Pettigrew's blind faith in the traveller's advice but he did not show it. As usual, his companion's logic made sense, and that made the man even more irritating; but Pettigrew had patently given no thought at all to the hazards of penetrating a potentially hostile wilderness.

Hayward's nod was ambiguous. 'Well, as long as we're properly equipped,' he said grudgingly. 'Finding the road is probably the least of our problems, but at least if we stick to it, we shouldn't get lost! And I guess it might be easier to find food and shelter too - an army marches on its stomach, as they say!'

'Good, then we're agreed! And no one's going to be interested in the likes of us, so why worry? Once we're on it we'll be in the clear!' Pettigrew paused, shot a triumphant look at his companion, then added lightly: 'You know, if we can keep up our current pace, we'll be enjoying French hospitality within the month!'

Hayward threw Pettigrew a sideways glance while suppressing a facetious laugh. Somehow, he knew that their journey would be far more difficult than the fellow imagined. Hayward's knowledge of the territory beyond Frederick was only second hand, picked up from fur traders or returning settlers, but they had painted a daunting picture of rugged terrain and dense forest, populated with wolves, bears, and poisonous snakes. Worse, the further west one travelled, the more likely it was that hostile Indians would be encountered too - like those who had recently brutally raided several of the exposed settlements in Pennsylvania and New York.

'Yes, but as I said, it's still a long way on foot, and we'll need to equip ourselves properly for the journey,' said Hayward, trying to salvage his authority. 'If we could get hold of a couple of horses, I'd be more confident of making it.' He took the stolen purse from his pocket and emptied its contents into his hand. 'We'll need a lot more than this though!' he muttered as he sorted the coinage with his finger.

Pettigrew flicked a desultory glance at the collection, raised his eyebrows and nodded gravely. 'I'm sure we'll think of something,' he said with an ambiguous smile. 'Nothing too clever this time, though. The last thing we want is to attract attention to ourselves!'

The pair sat in sullen silence for a while, consuming the last item in Hayward's cache – some kind of sausage, which appeared to be composed of little pieces of meat and fat compressed within a dark substance that looked like dried blood. It had fallen to pieces on being pulled out of its muslin pouch, and the two men now picked at it with their fingers. It was one of the things that Haywood had found in the outhouse of an isolated homestead, but it had been languishing at the bottom of his coat pocket for quite a long time – probably because it had looked so unappealing. It had a rank smell too, which was a bit off-putting, but the pair were so hungry that they would eat practically anything that they could sink their teeth into. It had been chance findings such as this that had kept the pair alive, despite the intestinal irregularities that had been a frequent preoccupation for both. The sausage soon disappeared.

'So, Hayward,' Pettigrew said at last, wiping his hands clean with some straw, 'if we want a few little comforts for our journey ahead, we had better put your gambling skills to the test, hadn't we?. A little bit of your slight-of-hand amongst these country yokels should win us enough to buy what we need, don't you think?'

Hayward jutted his jaw, throwing his companion a resigned glance. As usual, Pettigrew underestimated the risks involved!

'But can I rely upon you, Mr Pettigrew, to do exactly what I tell you?' he wondered to himself.

Chapter Five

Jack was disappointed (though in his heart, perhaps not entirely surprised) that Rose did not come down to the quay to wave him off. His damaged skiff still aboard the *Miranda* in Annapolis, he had requisitioned one of Sir Michael's little fleet and set out from the creek without the comfort of her usual farewell. Even as he and Ned headed out of the river and into the Potomac, he looked for her on the beach, hoping that he might see her standing there, waving as she had the last time he had sailed away. He must have cast a dozen hopeful glances astern, searching for her lonely figure at the water's edge, before finally giving up. The borrowed skiff was friskier than his own and it bore him away quickly on the breeze like a filly given her head, her sail and rigging eagerly tugging the little vessel through the slight chop. And soon, even if Rose had belatedly appeared, Jack would hardly have seen her across the opening distance, for all his hopeful searching. Feeling let down, he fell into a dark mood, handing the tiller to Ned to steer the little craft while he brooded in silence, sitting hunch-backed on the forward thwart. The summer day was bright and warm, the wind favourable for a speedy track up river, yet even the prospect of a good sail did not cheer him. His thoughts drifted back to his departure from the house. The leave-taking had been a somewhat strained affair, and as he reflected upon it now, a gloomy temper came over him.

Gazing glumly at the passing waves, Jack wondered at his wife's intransigence. Why could she not understand? At least her threat of going back to Portland for her confinement had not been repeated during the days of hurried preparations. And she had seemed attentive in ensuring that he went off well prepared. But now that he reflected upon her attitude towards him, he saw that the coolness in her manner went beyond the stoic resignation at his leaving that he had come to expect. Moreover, when he and Ned had set off for the quay with Sebi in the wagon, she had gone inside before he was out of sight so that he had not got her customary wave of farewell. That fond gesture had become a comforting ritual, and that she had denied it had upset him. He tried to persuade himself that his disquiet was unfounded, but he could not quite shake off the thought that trouble loomed. And now it was too late to put it right!

'She'll come round, Jack,' said Ned, noticing his friend's glances at the fast receding beach.

'I hope you're right, Ned.' Jack replied glumly. 'She doesn't seem to realise that everything I do is ultimately with her best interests in mind. I've tried to explain, but I...' His voice trailed off as he shook his head with a sigh of exasperation.

'Jack, I think she...' Ned started to say.

But Jack had not finished. His tone turned earnest, as if he felt a need to justify himself and his actions.

'If people didn't do what they thought had to be done just because it was difficult or uncomfortable, Ned,' Jack blurted, finding it difficult to find the right words, 'if...if no one ever rallied to the call of duty, then where would we be? I mean, nothing noble or lasting would ever get done if all we ever did was live from day to day in contented domesticity, would it!' He shook his head again, this time more in frustration. 'Sometimes I wonder about women, you know – I mean, what drives them. They crave security and a comfortable home, but they don't seem to appreciate that a man might have to take some risks and make sacrifices to achieve all that!'

Ned threw his friend a puzzled glance but said nothing for a time. Meanwhile the passing water played a rippling tune on the bow as the skiff ploughed on, her sail pulling boisterously in a playful south-westerly wind. Instead, with his big hands firmly on the tiller to hold her steady, he set a thoughtful gaze upon the horizon. At present, his westerly course would clip the southern tip of St George's Island a mile or so ahead. Rounding it, he would then turn the boat northwest to follow the coast up river. These were familiar waters. The Virginian shore, some five miles further on across the wide Potomac, was a shimmering mirage - a fine brush stroke in purple, drawn with an unsteady hand across the thin watery yellow line of its sandy shores. It seemed to hover like a magic carpet above a sea of dazzling reflections laid down by the bright sunshine. The illusion made the distant beaches appear much closer than they really were. For a while Ned fell into a whimsical muse as he cast his gaze about. Unusually, this normally busy waterway seemed devoid of other craft. To the southeast, the expanse stretched into the distance to the empty horizon of the Chesapeake. From the boat's low elevation, the nearer shores of Maryland revealed no signs of habitation amongst the tall, dark trees marshalled along the waterline like an impenetrable stockade. He might have been the helmsman of the Ark or the Dove arriving to found the new colony a hundred years or so before. He imagined himself as one of the first settlers gazing upon a virgin landfall.

But these shores were so well known to him now, after seven years at New Hope, that a sort of proprietary pride had begun to swell his heart. For him, this land represented his rebirth, and he was grateful for the succour that it had provided. And how lucky he had been, he reflected, to team up with Jack Easton on the transportation ship; he doubted that he would have fared so well otherwise. Ned Holder was as unassuming a soul as could be found outside childhood. But while he was certainly without guile or ambition, he was anything but simple. And in his reasoning, everything that he had achieved in recent years he owed to Jack - his long decline halted, reversed indeed, by this happy association. A decline that had started with eviction from the common land on which his family had scraped a meagre living, his poor parents driven into penury and early graves thereby, and he to the squalor of the English gutters; a descent that had continued with his conviction, and imprisonment to the purgatory of transportation and virtual slavery. That indignity had been the lowest point of his existence as he reckoned it; but in retrospect he now saw it as the turning point that marked his new beginning. Without it, he would not have found Jack. And without Jack, he could never have become a freeman, with a stake in his own land and with a respected place amongst the community at New Hope. Modest though it was, his life was far richer now than he could ever have imagined before; and it had been Jack that had led him along this path of reconstruction, this road to reclaim his self-respect.

Jack, sitting hunched upon the forward thwart, was evidently lost in thought and staring with such sullen concentration at the horizon ahead. Ned gazed at his friend's back and wondered about him; he seemed somehow to have drifted from the path that they had set out upon together so successfully - the stone carving workshop and then the building up of their farm. Ever since Judd's disastrous visitation, Jack's soul seemed to have become possessed by a strange obsession. Why was he so driven, Ned pondered? Jack's quest for revenge on Smyke was worthy enough, but the exacting of it had brought consequences that must have caused him to question it if not regret it? Ned had been somewhat ambivalent when Rose had sought his support to stop Jack going off on that first, fateful occasion. Now he wondered if he might have been a better friend if he had taken her side, for Jack's retribution had indirectly brought Judd amongst them, and his malice had played out with terrible consequences. Then came Pettigrew, another unfortunate legacy of Jack's action in Weymouth; Pettigrew, who had torn through the colony leaving a trail of dead in his wake. Once again, Jack had thrown himself into the chase to track these two criminals down – nearly getting himself killed in the process! And now this curious haste to catch up with Sir Michael and his regiment and go to war? It was as if some dark medicine had got into Jack's veins and displaced all reason.

Ned had come to know his impetuous friend by now. Jack had been headstrong even at that very first encounter aboard the *Rotterdam*, but now he seemed to be turning his back on everything that he had once held dear. He wondered what counsel he should offer his friend, but in his heart he feared that he had already missed his chance to help.

When at last Ned brought himself to speak, his words were tentative:

'She went through quite a hard time when you went off to Portland, Jack,' he offered, as if he had become the lady's champion. 'Six long months, it was…over a hard winter too. An' she took quite a lot on herself with you not there; more'n you'd expect for a woman.' (With this, his broad face revealed more than a hint of admiration.) 'We never got no news of you either, an' none of us was really certain that you'd even make it back. Why, you might have been lost at sea, let alone arrested in England and hanged as a returning transportee!'

'I did write, Ned,' Jack protested quickly, 'but Captain Goddard wasn't able to find anyone he could trust to bring the letter back!'

Ned threw Jack a kindly look that was fashioned to show understanding. 'She knows that *now*, Jack,' he said, 'but as the months went by without word from you, she got herself more and more worked up about it. I guess that she began to harden herself up in case you never *did* return. And no sooner than you came back, there was talk of your going off again pretty much straight away with the militia - so that put paid to any thought of things returning to the way they were before! She'd hardly a day to come to terms with that before that bastard Judd appeared and…and…'

'I know, Ned; she had a tough time of it - the cabin burning down, our baby…' Jack exhaled a long and thoughtful breath. 'She's shown real strength getting through all that, and I love her and admire her all the more for it,' he added softly.

'An' you showed her that by going off with Sir Michael so soon after...? Ned's tone was gently accusing.

'That was my contract with him, Ned, and I think she understood that!' Jack objected crossly. 'Do I need to remind you that this was the contract that gave us all our farmstead and the living that she and I, *and you*, now enjoy!' he said pointedly.

'Yes Jack, and I think that she was almost reconciled to your goin' off with Sir Michael for that reason. But when you were brought back on the schooner with a wound that almost killed you, I think things changed for her...I think that she thought that was enough.'

'Yes, I know,' Jack returned impatiently, 'she told me as much in no uncertain terms - but it didn't change my contract and my obligations did it Ned?' he snapped.

'But you *have* been very quick to leave again, Jack...' Ned left the accusation hanging in the air. 'Your injury is not a month old an' you're on your way again – as if nothin' matters more in the world than to be with your militia friends and join in their adventures!'

Jack frowned and went silent for a while. 'It is a duty, Ned!' he replied quietly. 'Surely you can see that we must fight to defend ourselves from the French. Why should I be excused from that duty just because of some little flesh wound?'

'Well, you know that that's not the way Rose sees it...'

'Well then she's not being fair to me! I've tried to reason with her, Ned...tried to explain why I have to go. It is important for both our futures, and in the end she will come to know that - when we start to prosper ...because of my loyalty to the cause, and the recognition of my contribution! This is my chance to make something of myself, Ned – to rise above the ordinary, to be recognised as something more than a mere artisan chipping stone and tending the fields!'

Ned raised his eyebrows at this. 'There was a time when these things would have been enough, Jack,' he said evenly. It was a mild rebuke but it was kindly spoken, and the two men exchanged glances that signalled and acknowledged Jack's admission to the truth of Ned's assertion.

Jack gave out a heavy sigh and nodded a reluctant assent. 'All right Ned, I admit that adventure fires me too – life would now seem a bit dull without it as a matter of fact. Man to man, Ned; you must surely understand that, even if Rose would not!'

Ned's face crinkled into an expression that somehow managed to combine disapproval with manly fellow feeling.

'Thought as much!' he said. 'It's got into your blood, hasn't it? A heady combination, I would say, Jack – a sense of duty and adventure at the same time – kind of lends a sort of legitimacy to doing what you want, doesn't it? But take this advice from a friend - you can't have your cake and eat it. While you pursue your duty - or thirst for adventure, or great ambitions, or whatever you want to call it - you might well leave the ones you love behind. You might then find yourself on your own with only the memories of your brave deeds to console you! I can't say it plainer than that, Jack. I was goin' to say that you will have to decide what's important to you, but clearly you already have!' With this, Ned shrugged helplessly as if to say: 'I've said my piece and will say no more.'

The cross frown that had creased Jack's forehead during Ned's attempt at wise counsel took some seconds to unravel.

"You are a good friend, Ned,' he said at last. 'You'll have to do your best to pacify her for me until I get back. Perhaps if you tell her how a man feels amongst other men about playing his proper part and doing what he thinks is the right and honourable thing, she'll understand?' Jack flashed his friend a hopeful glance. 'Besides, now that Judd is dead and Pettigrew and Hayward are safely behind bars, there is only my service to the militia to put behind me, and that can't go on for long. The men only signed up for three months, so we'll all be home for Christmas with a bit of luck. And once we've rebuilt the farmstead, Ned, things will very quickly return to normal, you'll see.'

Ned gave his friend an indulgent smile and nodded thoughtfully. He would do his best to mollify Rose until Jack returned; but it was difficult to imagine that it would be easy to change the heart of a lady almost as obstinate as her husband!

Chapter Six

The town of Frederick had been the seat of Frederick County, Maryland, for barely a decade, but it had already acquired several buildings of note including the brick-built county courthouse and several other municipal edifices that marked its newly elevated status. Being also a convenient stopping point for traffic on the major thoroughfare between Pennsylvania and Virginia, and also on the migration route to the colony's western frontier lands, it had become a busy conurbation by the standards of the day, with a tidy grid of streets and a central square on which a number of hotels, boarding houses and residences had been erected. It was also the main commercial centre of the county and a general meeting place for the county's dispersed population, which had grown in earnest in the last quarter century since the Maryland General Assembly first offered inducements for migration. Since then a sizeable number of German immigrants had arrived by way of Pennsylvania along with English and Scots from Virginia and southern Maryland. It was thus a cosmopolitan settlement, a melting pot of peoples of different languages, accents and religious interpretations, all brought together in a sort of guarded interdependency where differences were relegated to the mutual cause of stability and prosperity. The town also served as the site of the periodic county market when farmers, traders, and anyone with anything to sell or barter would bring in their livestock and produce in the hope of a good exchange.

The day of Pettigrew and Hayward's arrival in the town was just such a day, and the square had a positively carnival atmosphere about it, with all manner of noisy trading activity taking place. If earlier the pair had looked like emaciated vagrants, the result of living rough and lying low for weeks, they looked the better for a meal, a bath, a shave and a haircut - and new boots and riding clothes. Pettigrew, still cautious of Jack Easton's 'wanted' poster being on display, had instructed the barber to fashion his beard into a neat goatee so as to modify his features, and he had bought himself a wide-brimmed hat as further concealment. Hayward, having no such fears in Frederick despite his notoriety elsewhere, had reclaimed the clean-shaven, honest businessman's appearance that had been an essential persona for the successful charlatan that he was. Both men thus waded confidently into the crowd milling about with excited interest amongst the livestock pens and produce stalls, and made their way towards the most prominent of the hotels on the square.

The Town Hotel was always well patronised on market days, but being relatively early in the afternoon there were still a few tables still unoccupied as the pair entered the saloon. Even though not full to capacity, the room nevertheless resounded with exuberantly chattering men who, judging by their clothing and conversations, were farmers or traders. And most seemed in high spirits. Hayward surveyed the scene carefully through the haze of tobacco smoke that floated in the air like a thin blue veil. Adjacent to where he and Pettigrew now stood, there was a long bar attended by a waiter wearing a leather apron who from time to time moved between the tables conveying drinks. In all, there were about twenty tables in the saloon, most occupied by ordinary customers like themselves. But near the bar Hayward located what he sought, the *Stammtisch*, a German word for the table set aside for favoured regulars, and regarded as a sacrosanct domain. A glance at the half-dozen or so individuals seated there told him what he wanted to know. Then, selecting a vacant table on the opposite side of the room, he led the way towards it, pursued soon after by the attentive waiter carrying a pitcher of frothy ale. Seating themselves at the table, Hayward made a play of paying from a bulging purse, which, depleted by the morning's indulgencies, had been supplemented with folded sheets of paper to make it look fuller than it was. Assuming an immodest air, Hayward explained the thick wad as the upshot of a lucrative trading day – it was a little bit of pantomime, but it soon produced the desired result.

Not long afterwards, a slick-haired individual, dressed down to his waistcoat, was seen to rise from the *Stammtisch* and begin to move about the room. Above the background din his voice could not be heard, but it was clear that he was canvassing interest in a game of cards for he carried a pack of playing cards with him, which he held up as a sort of advertising placard to attract interest. Hayward's practised eye saw at once that the man's circulation was not random, but directed instead at those he might have identified as having money in their pockets. Hayward watched the man carefully, pleased that his work was being done for him in setting up a table at which the stakes were likely to be high – exactly what he needed for a quick and substantial win. He was not surprised when he and Pettigrew were eventually approached, and, after an initial show of cautious reticence, he allowed himself and his companion to be persuaded to join in. The table to which the entourage was led was rather larger than the others and situated in an alcove off the main saloon. Seated there already was an older man with a shock of greying hair who had three card decks of different colours laid out before him. Hayward caught Pettigrew's eye – things were going exactly as they had predicted.

The group took their seats, Hayward occupying the chair with its back to the main saloon; Pettigrew, the chair directly opposite as had been agreed.

'Just a friendly to pass the time, gentlemen,' the grey-haired dealer said with a pleasant smile as he shuffled the first of his decks. 'In town for market day?' His manner was no doubt designed to be disarming.

Pettigrew replied from under the broad brim of his hat:

'Yes, and a successful one, too!' he said, patting his jacket pocket smugly.

The waist-coated gambler rubbed his hands in a show of amateurish enthusiasm.

'Well then, what will it be?' he asked brightly. 'How about five-card stud? Penny a card?'

And so it was agreed.

The host and his grey-haired companion were convivial, the house treating the players to a round of drinks even before play commenced. The first few hands then proceeded with small coins and notes moving from one side of the table to the other to be scooped up with some theatricality and good humour. Hayward's winnings were modest but steady, and soon he had enough to bring his strategy into play. Another round of drinks was ordered by the winner of a larger sum, and then another soon after, and before long the whole table was in a happy and garrulous state. That is to say, all except the apparently despondent Hayward who, having artfully raised the stakes a little recklessly during the most recent round, had lost a visible portion of his precious pile. Contriving to look flustered, he then bid rashly and lost a few times more, until he felt he had convinced the other players of his ineptitude. Thus when a good hand eventually came his way, his artless manner drew them in. But this time, he raised the stake repeatedly until the larger part of his remaining cash was committed, causing a few wry glances to be exchanged around the table. Pettigrew had dropped out early, making a play of shaking his head and throwing in his hand; another player folded not long after, declaring the stake too high to call. But the remainder, including the waist-coated host, called Hayward's bluff, each covering the stake with notes and coinage from their own piles. The pot by this time amounted to a useful sum, but it was not ostentatiously large. So that, when Hayward revealed a winning hand and scooped the heap of cash towards him, it was taken in good humour and written off to luck. Luck it might have been, but Hayward's pile had now grown considerably - and it was proudly heaped up on the table in front of him for all to see.

It was during all this that Pettigrew, appearing to have run short both of money and of luck, excused himself with a little harrumph of exasperation. The other players watched him leave with disdain upon their faces, but they paid him no attention when he returned ten minutes later to join the small group of spectators gathered at the alcove opening. By and by, new players took the places vacated by those retiring, and under that distraction, Pettigrew manoeuvred until he was directly behind Hayward's chair. The game went on, each round being dealt from a different pack from the three in circulation, the house seen overall to be paying out more than it was winning. Eventually, the dealer good-naturedly suggested raising the stakes.

'Come on boys! Give this poor ol' house a chance to take back some of your winnings!' he said, with some evident chagrin.

Hayward's features may have displayed disquiet at this suggestion, but inwardly he rejoiced - it was exactly what he would have proposed if he had been wearing the waistcoat. With a shrug and a tight smile, he nodded his assent, thinking wryly as he did so that if a few would lose their shirts that night, his would not be amongst them.

The dealer now dealt with enthusiasm, and it was as the cards fell onto the table that Hayward felt Pettigrew's light but distinctive touch upon his shoulder - three taps from a finger of the hand resting with such apparent innocence on the back of Hayward's chair. Pettigrew had used the distraction of an earlier changeover to slip a card into Hayward's jacket pocket, and with this pre-arranged code he had signalled that it was the ace of hearts – a suitable card secreted from one of his own hands before he had quit the game. In planning the ploy, the pair thought it unlikely that the absence of just one card would be noticed with several packs being brought regularly into play, as was the norm. Thus Pettigrew had needed only to wait until the particular pack was dealt before he gave the signal - and by giving it, he had told his companion with which coloured pack to make his play.

It was not many rounds later that Hayward was dealt a hand in which substituting the extra ace for a lesser card would make a winning combination. The exchange was accomplished under cover of a convenient distraction with practised sleight of hand (although, as it would turn out, not quite practised enough). At first, Hayward let the stakes be raised by his companions, simply matching their bets to stay in the game - his fellow gamblers it seemed were either supremely confident of a win or else attempting to bluff it out. Hayward was quietly content to let the bidding run its course without interfering, for he soon constructed a hand that he thought would beat them all. The pot thus increased steadily until, inevitably, the resolve of some of the players began to waver as the stakes increased, attrition eventually taking its toll. It was, therefore, not long before only three players were left in the game: the slick-haired host in the waistcoat, Hayward himself, and a rather cocky newcomer dressed in the smart uniform of a militia lieutenant-colonel. If there had been any light-heartedness around the table before, this now evaporated as concentration became intense. The atmosphere in the alcove was electric with expectation, and necks craned amongst a growing circle of spectators, who soon fell into a sort of reverential hush.

Hayward was initially in the satisfactory position of simply matching escalating stakes in what seemed quickly to become a battle of wills between the other two. In other circumstances, Hayward might have left them to their suicidal romp and quit the game, but armed as he was with his reinforced hand, he quietly bode his time. The little frenzy of bidding did not last for long, however. Sweating profusely and quite alarmingly red in the face, the military newcomer pompously called the other's bluff, matching the recent raise with what appeared to be the last of his pile. With this, there came the briefest hint of triumph in his waist-coated opponent's face that Hayward savoured, for he was certain that that triumph would soon be his own. He let the moment linger until all eyes had turned upon him, clearly in the expectation that he would do the same. Unhurriedly, he took a look at his cards then raised his gaze upon his host. This time his eyes showed none of the earlier artful uncertainty - instead it was the steady and confident gaze of a master of the game. He imagined the dreadful cold fingers of doubt that must now be taking hold of his opponent's heart; he could almost sense the man's confidence draining away. Hayward knew this feeling well – the awful dawning realisation that perhaps too much had been assumed - and he revelled in the defeat that his skilful trickery was certain to inflict. It did not disquiet him that his opponent's face remained passive and unrevealing, or that the man's eyes fixed on Hayward's were unflinching. No, Hayward was not to be deceived; he was convinced that he saw dread in the very steadiness of his opponent's gaze; he was certain that the man simply feared to look away.

And so Hayward did not fold. Instead, in a quiet and measured voice, he raised the stake again. There were a few gasps of astonishment from the crowd as he moved his entire mound onto the table. The militia officer's brittle nerves now shattered abruptly - this was apparently the final straw - and he threw down his cards in disgust quite as if they had turned to filth in his hands and he could not be rid of them quickly enough. Visibly deflated, he sat back in his chair, uttered a barely audible groan, and shook his head despairingly at the ceiling. The hovering crowd seemed to hold a collective breath as seconds ticked by slowly. The waist-coated gambler took his time to respond, his face meanwhile impassive, his body almost statuesque. For a moment, Hayward wondered if his opponent would also capitulate, but guessed not. His instinct proved sound, for a moment later the gambler put his cards face down on the table before him, counted out the required amount from his own diminished pile, and pushed it out.

'Call,' he said quietly.

Hayward regarded himself too much of a professional to let his triumph show, but he threw his cards - three aces and two tens - upon the table with more than a little flourish, and then sat back looking rather pleased with himself. There were a few muted murmurs of approval amongst the crowd at the revelation, but curious eyes quickly settled back upon the house gambler's cards, still lying face-down on the table and mostly hidden by the man's resting hand. For several seconds, the suspense was maintained during which time both players seemed frozen in their poses, still eye to eye. Some in the crowd evidently began to assume that the player's hesitation signalled defeat, for knowing glances were exchanged between a few. Indeed, Hayward became so certain of his win that he started forward in anticipation of scooping up the pile. But it was not to be so. The host's hand was lifted from the table with a single finger raised above it as if to call attention to itself, a gesture seemingly independent of the player's form, which otherwise remained strangely unmoving. Hayward flashed his opponent an inquisitive and, at once, anxious glance. The host returned it enigmatically as, slowly and deliberately, he turned over his cards one by one. Hayward watched

fixed as the lucky sequence in spades was revealed. He sensed
Pettigrew shifting his weight uneasily behind his chair, and both must
have known, even before the face of the fourth card had been displayed,
that the game had been lost. Under the excited uproar that then erupted
from the crowd, Hayward rocked back in his seat in disbelief. Even
above the din, he heard Pettigrew's single but forceful expletive as the
shock of his defeat turned quickly into rage. The chances of his
constructed hand being beaten were so slim that he was sure that he had
been tricked. He shot an accusing glance first at his opponent and then
to the dealer in turn, but found himself already under their mocking gaze.
And on the dealer's lips he saw the barest smirk as the grey-haired man
picked up the remnant of his deck and flicked it with his thumb as if
counting the cards within. With the man's knowing look, Hayward
realised that his sleight of hand had been discovered after all, and that he,
the master trickster, had been out-tricked.

It soon became apparent from a disturbance in the crowd behind him
that the hotel's musclemen had been called to the table, and before he
could react, Hayward found himself pulled to his feet. Forceful hands
were then felt to delve roughly into his jacket pockets until, with a
triumphant hoot, someone shouted: 'Here it is!' And his ears were
assaulted by an affronted jeer from those who now jostled him on all
sides. The restraining arms then forced him to turn about, and there
before him now stood a hatless and fuming Pettigrew similarly restrained.
And, held up like a trophy by the burly lieutenant colonel was a single
card – the two of diamonds that Hayward had discarded from his hand in
favour of Pettigrew's ace. Despite their carefully planned deception, the
pair had been well and truly undone! And in the frontier town of
Frederick, justice was swift and rough. Within the hour, both fugitives
found themselves thrown headlong into the dusty street and hounded out
of town.

So much for their grand scheme of setting off quietly from Frederick
properly equipped! And bruised and limping from the summary hiding
received, they were already two miles out of town before they paused for
breath.

Chapter Seven

Jack and Ned's journey up the Potomac to Charlestown was uneventful (unlike the pair's last trip together when they were nearly run down by the *Rebecca* charging up the river under full sail), and the two men arrived at the town's quay during the following afternoon. The weather meanwhile had turned unusually inclement for a summer day, and it was dressed in oilskins, hurrying against the sheeting rain that Jack and Ned burst into the shipping office in search of the tobacco agent, Thomas Harding. The pair proceeded at once to divest themselves of their bulky outer garments with some good-humoured banter, depositing in the process a pool of water that spread half way across the floor - much to the obvious annoyance of the clerks behind the counter. It was the commotion caused by this untidy arrival that brought Harding rushing from his office at the rear. His face, at first puckered in vexation, turned immediately into a broad grin of delight on recognising his visitors.

'Jack!' he exclaimed. 'Good that you have come! And so quickly too!' he said, offering his hand to both men in turn. 'And so heartening to see you back on your feet!' he added warmly, giving his young friend a good looking over. 'You're looking fit!'

'And feeling it too, thank goodness!' said Jack, rotating his shoulder as if to demonstrate it. 'Anyway, Thomas, what's all this about?' asked Jack at once, getting straight to the point of his visit. 'Sir Michael's messenger said that there had been some worrying developments...'

'Yes, well,' said Harding looking awkward, his face soon turning grave, 'you had better come into my office, Jack. I'm afraid that events have taken an unfortunate turn for the worse.' And with this he turned on his heel and led the way into the gloomy depths of his back office, made gloomier yet by the forbidding skies visible through the high and narrow window.

Harding's working space was dominated by a large oak pedestal desk and accompanying library chair upholstered in green leather, but there was enough space left over for two side chairs opposite, to which with a careless flick of Harding's hand the visitors were directed. The two men settled themselves expectantly while Harding took his seat. Behind the agent's chair, a gilt-framed oil canvas of a Tobacco River scene hung upon the bare plank wall, and nearby, a notice board had pinned upon it several printed bills, including a copy of Jack's 'wanted' poster from which Pettigrew's features stared out blankly.   The hated face caught Jack's eye immediately and it shocked him; it seemed almost as if the man were present in the room. The image had been endowed with a strangely mocking expression that Jack had not noticed before – and he would reflect soon enough that somehow this impression had been a warning. He tore his eyes away, not wanting to be reminded of the figure that had been the root of his troubles. In the far corner of the room loomed a disproportionately large cast-iron strong box that looked as if it would have taken one of Jack's Portland stone derricks to lift into place.

Harding noticed Jack's eyes surveying the new safe.

'Ah yes,' he said, 'if that monstrosity had been in place when Judd broke in, we might all have been spared! As you see,' he continued, sweeping a hand towards the window, now heavily barred and reinforced, 'I have taken other precautions too. And so now I can assure you, Jack, that your money is absolutely safe inside – along with Sir Michael's consortium deposits, which you and your militia scouts thankfully recaptured!'

With this, Harding's demeanour changed abruptly to one of distinct discomfort, and when he spoke again he seemed to be choosing his words most carefully.

He cleared his throat uneasily.

'Ah, it is about that that matter that I need first to relate some rather disquieting intelligence received from Captain Goddard. He remains even now in Annapolis, the *Miranda* having apparently been towed there from the Cape - where you last saw him I think - with rudder damage from her grounding.'

Jack looked surprised at this, for he had expected the *Miranda* already to have sailed for England by now, but he did not interject.

'The first news to relate, Jack' Harding went on, shifting in his seat, '- and you had better prepare yourself for this - is that when he sent his shore party to retrieve Judd's body from the beach where he was brought down by Major Lawrence's excellent shot, it was not found - despite apparently protracted searches soon after your departure aboard the schooner and again the following morning.'

Jack's forehead creased into a frown and his lips began to form a question, but Harding held up his hand.

'Before you jump to conclusions, Jack,' the agent said quickly, 'Captain Goddard regarded it as entirely possible that locals had removed the body or even buried it – evidently he did not have the time to enquire or search further.' Here Harding paused thoughtfully. 'I suppose that is indeed a possibility,' he said plainly, his quick glances giving away his doubts. 'Another possibility might be that the body was dragged away by wolves, although I think that unlikely too, as evidence would have been found I'm sure!'

Jack's expression had gone from disbelief to derision

'Yes, and such evidence would have been so plain to see,' he said dismissively, 'that I think we can discount that idea completely. And I would not be confident either that the kind people of the eastern shores would have disposed of the body for us as their good deed for the day!' He paused briefly, his forehead furrowing. 'But even if Judd had merely been wounded by the major's shot rather than killed outright, he surely could not have got far? If he managed to crawl away from the beach and hide himself somewhere behind the dunes, he could not possibly have survived for long. He must have lost a lot of blood, and it would have been a pretty desolate place for him to last overnight.'

'I hope you're right, Jack,' said Harding, sitting back in his chair. 'But I'm afraid that there is more to tell you – something I spotted only recently – pointed out by Sir Michael, in fact.'

Without another word and looking rather sombre, Harding rose from his seat and went to the safe, unlocking it using two large keys pulled from separate pockets of his long coat. He took hold of the brass handle with both hands and pulled the door ajar, his arms and shoulders clearly under strain from the door's huge cast iron mass.

'Judd wouldn't have been able to break into this little beauty,' he grunted as he swung open the door to its full extent. Then, reaching his head, arms and shoulders well inside the container's cavernous depths, he emerged some moments later with a pair of saddlebags in his hands. Jack and Ned recognised them at once; and it was quite clear from the way Harding handled them that they were empty of the quantity of notes that they had once contained. Harding secured the strongbox door, pocketed the keys, and threw the bags upon the desk.

'Now listen Jack, neither Sir Michael nor I consider this certain, so don't be too hasty in your judgement!'

Harding looked Jack directly in the eyes with an expression that gave away his own feelings on the matter, and then rearranged the bags so that the wide leather strap and metal buckle connecting the two pouches were uppermost. The buckle was particularly noteworthy. It looked as if it might have been of military origin by its large size and its solid and hefty casting, embossed with what looked like a crest of some sort in the centre of its bridge.

'Come closer and take a look,' Harding said, offering it up.

Jack was first to step forward and examine the buckle, turning it over in his hands. He passed it to Ned who did the same. The right-hand side of the buckle's broad bridge had been badly disfigured by a circular indentation about an inch across its diameter and about half that in depth.

Jack caught the meaningful glance that passed between the two other men.

'What have I missed?' he asked, puzzled.

Ned was little hesitant in his reply.

'You wouldn't have seen Judd escapin' up the beach would you, Jack? In fact, you probably don't remember anything after you got hit, do you?'

Jack shook his head. 'Not a lot,' he said.

'Well, although Captain Goddard and me was proppin' you up in the boat at the time,' Ned went on, 'we got a good view of Judd makin' a run for it up the beach as the major and his boys leapt over the side and levelled their muskets. The major was the only one who needed to fire! He brought him down first go! We saw Judd sent flying. Sir Michael was still on the tiller and he got a clear view too.'

'Yes?' uttered Jack, still not making the connection. 'So?'

Ned hesitated again. 'Judd was carryin' these saddlebags over his shoulder, Jack,' he replied finally, throwing his friend an awkward glance.

He did not need to say more.

Jack now understood exactly what the two men were suggesting and didn't like it one bit. He picked up the buckle and examined it again; the ball fired from Major Lawrence's musket could well have caused the indentation; but he still resisted the idea as the only possible conclusion – if it were true that the buckle had stopped the bullet, it would have unthinkable implications.

'But Ned!' Jack objected. 'Judd was found dead on the beach when they reached him! With a bloody head wound! Everyone was so convinced. You all told me he was dead!' he persisted, not wanting to believe what his logic was already asserting.

'We were in a rush, Jack!' protested Ned, quickly. His look was suddenly sheepish; he was clearly anxious to explain, 'We had to get you back to the ship for some medical attention! You were in such bad shape that you were everyone's priority – mine included! When the scouts saw Judd's head wound they thought that the Major's shot had hit home. It was a reasonable assumption at the time – the major apparently rarely misses!' Ned spread his hands apologetically. 'But now seeing this…!' He gestured at the buckle and shook his head. 'Seeing this,' he repeated in a meeker tone, 'well, perhaps I'm not so sure.'

There was a long period of silence during which all three men seemed to be staring at the buckle almost as if in a hypnotic trance. Eventually Ned continued.

'Maybe the buckle was damaged before?' he offered hopefully, but his tone was not very convincing.

'And maybe Judd tripped and fell and cut his head!' countered Jack in a sarcastic tone. 'Maybe he was only stunned?'

'But the major's shot definitely brought him down, Jack – I *saw* him sent flyin' with my own eyes. He was definitely hit! It wasn't just a trip! And when the scouts reached him, he looked stone dead and they were sure he was - there was apparently a hell of a lot of blood all over his face! And as we were hollerin' at them by then to get back to the boat quickly so that we could get you to the ship fast, they just grabbed the saddlebags and his pistols and ran back down the beach as quick as they could… There was no real doubt in anyone's mind - even Sir Michael and Captain Goddard were convinced!' he protested.

'Well, my guess is that this gives the lie to that!' said Jack, holding up the buckle angrily. 'No wonder he wasn't there when Goddard's landing party went back!'

He threw the disfigured fastener down in disgust and turned to the window where he stood in silence for a while, his breath steaming the cold glass. Low dark clouds could be seen hurtling past overhead; rain pelted against the window pain like gravel hurled from some lofty shovel. A gloomy mood descended upon the room while Harding and Ned exchanged doleful glances. Harding cleared his throat.

'Sir Michael did think that it might be prudent to assume the worst,' he agreed quietly, 'and I have already taken the precaution of sending word of our fears to the sheriff in Annapolis - with my strong recommendation that he alert his colleagues on the peninsula. No doubt they will already be on the lookout in case Judd shows up.'

Jack turned from the window and raised his eyebrows.

'Oh good!' His voice was heavy with irony. 'So we can all sleep soundly in our beds tonight!'

Harding sagged. 'Yes, I know Jack,' he said lamely. 'It wasn't the news you wanted to hear, was it? Not after all you've been through.' Conceding this, he might have dropped his eyes to avoid Jack's angry glare, but instead he held Jack's gaze steadfastly, as if coolly analysing his friend's frame of mind.

Jack knew Harding well enough to guess that the grave look on his face signalled that there was something more to come. Jack's puzzled frown must have given this away for Harding nodded with a wry look.

'Yes Jack, there's more bad news, I'm afraid,' Harding confirmed in a low voice, signalling the two men to resume their seats, while seating himself at the same time.

Jack glared crossly as he backed into his chair. 'It can't get much worse than Judd being on the loose!' he said angrily.

The tobacco agent shifted his glances uncomfortably between the two men now sitting expectantly before him.

'I received this note a few days ago from Captain Goddard in Annapolis,' he said, taking a piece of paper from his waistcoat pocket. 'It seems that Pettigrew and Haywood ...' he started to say.

'No, don't tell me...' Jack interjected. 'They've escaped too!'

Harding did not answer at first but simply raised an eyebrow making an expression that was as incredulous as Jack's.

'I'm afraid so.'

He shrugged feebly.

'Apparently the whole damn lot of them made a break for it when they were being assembled on deck for transfer ashore. It seems the *Rebecca's* crew were overwhelmed. Goddard watched it all from the *Miranda* apparently – too far away to be able to do anything about it unfortunately. He is, needless to say, furious with *Rebecca's* captain for his incompetence! And happily he reports that most of the prisoners were recaptured within the city limits that night – mostly found in the taverns drinking themselves silly by the sound of it! But as far as the two men you will be most interested in – Messrs Pettigrew and Hayward...' Harding sighed heavily, 'well, the sheriff and his men are still looking for them.'

'This is too much!' gasped Jack, exasperated, throwing himself back in his chair.

Harding and Ned looked ill at ease, unsure of what to say next.

The agent tried to be consoling: 'They'll catch them, Jack…your poster with Pettigrew's likeness is still scattered around the colony…' he said, flicking an acknowledging glance at Jack's 'wanted' poster pinned upon his notice board.

With a heavy, exasperated sigh, Jack rose, crossed the room to the notice board, and carefully removed the poster.

'I may need this,' he said, folding it and slipping it into his jacket pocket. 'Pettigrew by himself in a strange land might not get very far, Thomas,' he said firmly, 'but with Hayward as his guide, the pair will be more difficult to find. You'll remember how slippery Hayward is. He made enough of a nuisance of himself here in Charlestown without ever getting caught!' (Harding skewed his lips at Jack's retort, reluctantly acknowledging the truth of it.) 'Anyway, how much of this does Sir Michael know?'

'He was here when Captain Goddard's note arrived,' Harding replied simply. 'That's one of the reasons he's sending a one of his scouts back to accompany you…'

'Hah!' Jack spat. 'To make sure that I don't go rushing off again, trying to track them down, I'll bet!'

Harding sighed wearily. 'More to lead the way I think, Jack,' he said quietly, rubbing his eyes with the palms of his hands. 'Sir Michael and his militia will be well ahead by now and you'll need help to find them.' He shook his head as if to signal a change of tack. 'But look, Jack,' he reasoned, 'even if Pettigrew and Hayward *do* get away,' '– and that's by no means a foregone conclusion – they'll hardly come back in this direction, will they? Not with the sheriff and his men scouring the county for them! And that goes for Judd too.' He paused to let the validity of his words sink in, while the rain still drummed against the window. 'Just assuming that Judd still lives…' he held up his hand to silence Jack's impending interruption. 'Just assuming Judd still lives,' he repeated patiently, 'he's got one hell of a way to go northwards even to get off the peninsula; and like the other two, he's hardly likely to hang around anywhere he's going to be recognised, is he? My guess is that he'll just disappear – and we'll never see *any* of them again.'

'That's not the point, Thomas, and you know it!' Jack snapped. 'I thought I had settled the score with them, and now I find that all three of them are on the loose again! And likely to be up to no good too - with who knows what scheming intentions in mind! What do you expect me to do - forget that they exist?'

Harding shrank in his chair at Jack's attack; but Ned broke in, speaking in his usual measured tones:

'We had words about this, Jack, remember?' he said calmly. 'Give it up, man. You've got enough on your plate without worryin' about those three wasters. You've got other priorities now with Rose expectin'. Get this militia thing put behind you, like you said, then get yourself back to New Hope and be done with your gallivantin'! You can't hold yourself responsible for *all* the world's evil. Good must eventually prevail if God's in his heaven!'

Jack bowed his head and clasped his hands tightly. It may have looked a bit like a posture of prayer but it was far from it. 'God may need a bit of help with this one, Ned.' He said quietly.

Chapter Eight

The greater part of Maryland, that is to say most of the colony's territory lying to the east of the meridian through Frederick, perhaps more so than any of the other twelve colonies of British North America, is characterised by so many tidal estuaries, rivers and creeks, that on maps of the colony there seems almost as much enclosed water as land. To the south and west, the Potomac marks its border with Virginia; to the east lies Delaware and the Atlantic coast; and penetrating its tidewater heart, as if the colony is being torn apart by its upward thrust, the Chesapeake and its tributaries reach into the very soul of the land. Maryland's eastern counties, thus almost completely severed from the western shores by this watery thoroughfare, are connected only by a narrow isthmus at the very top of the Bay, so that any traveller by land would have to go almost as far north as Pennsylvania to find a way across (by way of the Susquehanna River ferry).

It was on these eastern shores of the Chesapeake that Judd had made his astonishing escape, saved from almost certain death on the beach at Cape Charles by a mere brass buckle. And since that time, after the remarkably good fortune that had confounded Captain Goddard and the members of the *Miranda's* search party, he had set himself the task of moving northwards with as much haste as his legs would bear. His course was set because at first he thought it likely that Goddard's crew would pursue him along the shore by boat and cut off his escape, then later because there seemed no other choice. He had thus struck inland and found a straight route up the middle of the peninsula which, more by luck than judgement, had also saved him from a tortuous winding and boggy trek along a coastline riven with creeks and marshes.

Limping slightly on blistered feet, his shoulder still bruised and sore from the impact (though not the penetration) of the musket ball, Judd had nevertheless made steady progress in the days since his escape. The head wound, washed and cleaned in the saline waters of a creek, had become a blackened scab on his right temple, but since the blemish was partly covered by his hair, it would not now draw too much attention. Even after a long week of days and nights on foot, he could barely believe that he was still free when by all rights he should at least be hotly pursued, if not imprisoned or dead.

The settler population hereabouts appeared thinly spread and confined mainly to the navigable creeks that opened into the Chesapeake. Almost every tributary he encountered was cluttered with little boats and surrounded by a patchwork of small, cultivated fields. Most of these, Judd noticed, were planted with wheat or flax and not the tobacco that had seemed more common on the other side of the Bay. He had tried to keep out of the way of people for the first few days - until hunger had forced him to take chances when opportunities arose to steal from fields, or orchards, or isolated farms. But he had always given a wide berth to the larger settlements so as not to leave a trail, still fearing that he might be followed. The terrain was almost entirely flat and the going thus relatively easy, except when occasionally he encountered marshy ground or dense thicket, which sometimes forced him to detour or even double back.

Eventually he found what appeared to be a wide track going in his intended direction, noticing as he walked on the sandy ground, the imprints of iron-rimmed wheels and horses' hooves. One stretch, heavily trammelled by scores of smaller hoof prints, was clearly in frequent use as a drove between fenced-in fields that lay to one side or other of the track. Some of these were lined with new green shoots but others had evidently been cleared for grazing, for the ground in those was stumpy and untilled. He saw no animals at all, but spotted smoke rising here and there above the surrounding woodland, probably from isolated farmsteads hidden amongst the trees - but he never ventured close enough to find out. There were a few rudimentary shelters along the route too – refuges for animals or herdsmen, he surmised. They served him well as protection from the frequent squally showers that hounded him for days at a time, under a leaden overcast that seemed to stretch into infinity in all directions. The taste of salt in the damp air told him that the Chesapeake was never far away.

All this evidence of human presence kept Judd continuously on his guard, but as the days went by he got used to it and soon began to think that he could risk encounter should an appropriate opportunity occur. Indeed, he began to crave the decent meal and comfortable bed that such an opportunity might win. However, not wanting the sight of him - a lone, ill-equipped, foot-weary traveller - to frighten people off or raise suspicions, he anticipated the need for a plausible reason for being on the peninsula in the state he was. His devious mind constructed one quickly and he was soon ready to try it out, but his road would remain empty for some days yet, and so no immediate opportunity arose. The track continued thus northwards, taking an easy winding route, skirting the frequent watery obstructions that seemed a characteristic of the area. Sometimes he found himself in dark woodland, under tall pines, cedar, and holly, and sometimes amongst broad, open swathes of tall marsh grasses extending on either side as far as his low view could encompass.

Eventually his hoped-for encounter arrived - although it was not in the manner that he had imagined. He had only just set off one morning (having rested overnight in one of the rough shelters already mentioned) when the chance meeting occurred. A fresh wind blew in from the west (as it had most mornings) straight off the Chesapeake, of which he had been able to catch a glimpse or two on his left hand side through scattered clumps of vegetation. The breeze carried the scent of tidal mud and bent the tops of nearby birch trees, rustling the silver leaves in their swaying branches. The airy hiss ebbed and flowed like the distant waves of the Bay so that he was deaf to the soft clip-clop of horse hooves approaching from behind. A sudden snort from the sharply reigned-in beast so close at hand made Judd's heart leap into his throat. He turned in alarm, ready to flee or fight, expecting to be set upon. But he was faced not with a posse of Goddard's pursuing seamen that he, in that frightened instant, conjured in his mind, but with a lone horseman in a grubby leather tricorn who looked down upon him suspiciously from his saddle.

'You lost?' the man enquired in a rough voice.

Judd must have looked a ragamuffin, dressed in a crumpled seaman's jacket and baggy breaches, dirtied at both knees, and the horseman's expression showed that he was wary.

Judd felt his heartbeat racing. 'Fisherman from St Mary's across the Bay!' he offered by way of explanation, still slightly breathless from the unpleasant surprise. 'Went aground - down near the Cape. Couldn't get off that damned mud! Boat broached and flooded.' He contrived this latter detail with a look of dejection.

The horseman gave Judd a withering look. 'You're not the first,' he drawled. Then, after a moment's thought he added, suspiciously: 'You've travelled a fair distance from the Cape, friend; where're you making for?'

'Other side of the Bay – back to St Mary's eventually!' answered Judd, trying to sound resigned to a long walk - and he put on a little show of exhaustion by pulling off his neckerchief and mopping his brow.

'Hah!' The rider jerked his head in amusement. 'Well, it's a long way on foot!' he scoffed from his lofty seat, his eyes giving Judd a careful going over, his manner and tone remaining distrustful.

At this point, Judd noticed the musket slung across the man's shoulder and a brace of wildfowl hanging limply from his saddle post. Further glances at the rider's apparel revealed a powder horn and a water flask hanging from straps across his chest, and a bulging leather pouch on a belt around his waist (Judd guessed the latter contained lead shot and wadding for the musket). With this inspection, he was careful not to let his eyes to linger, for fear of giving himself away.

'You've had a good day, by the look of it,' he said innocently, flicking a glance at the rider's catch – a couple of long-necked geese with black heads and opaque white eyes

Judd calmly weighed up his chances of pulling the man to the ground – the rider was no bigger than he and could thus probably be overpowered, especially if taken by surprise. But it would also be too easy for him to spur his horse out of harm's way in any move that Judd made to unseat him. Worse, if the alarm were raised it would inevitably mean pursuit by lawmen who by now must have been alerted. Judd decided thus to play for time.

'Anywhere on this coast where I might find a boat to get me back across the Bay – to save me the walk?' he asked, his voice the tiniest bit flaky, as someone dog-tired might sound after several nights without sleep (which was not far from the truth). 'And an inn would be welcome too!' he added with a weary and disarming smile.

The rider lifted the flap of his saddlebag, rummaged inside, and pulled out a small fabric-covered bundle.

'Here!' he said, throwing it down.

Judd caught it, and unfolded the fabric to discover a bread bap wrapped up inside. Judd sniffed it tentatively; it appeared to have a filling of goose fat or dripping.

'Grateful,' Judd said, taking his first hungry bite.

'Your best bet is to press on to Princess Anne,' the huntsman continued as he stroked his stubbly chin thoughtfully. 'You couldn't do better than that – it's the busiest little trading town you'll find on this part of the peninsula - pretty little place; it's not on the shore, but there's a navigable river from the Bay right up to the town quay.'

'Grateful, sir,' said Judd again, his mouth bulging at the cheek. 'Far from here?' He crammed the last remnant of his fatty bread into his mouth while he chewed greedily, open lipped, the macerated contents of his mouth churning sickeningly behind his yellowing teeth.

'A day on foot from here, I'd say,' replied the hunter helpfully. 'Keep going north along this track for about five miles until you reach a river (he pointed) – that's the Pocomoke. If you're lucky, the ferryman will already be on your side where he has his cottage; but if not you'll have to shout for him – and he usually takes his time!'

The rider shifted in his saddle and swept an airy gaze around the horizon. 'It's just possible you'll see a boat alongside the grain wharf opposite that might be heading across the Bay, but there's not a lot else there. So if you want an inn and some comforts, keep going! Then after crossing the river, you'll come to a fork about a mile or so further on - go left there and it'll take you direct to Princess Anne – about ten miles, I'd say. You'll stand a better chance of finding yourself a boat there – there're usually quite a few vessels of one sort or another moored along the river. And there's a decent ordinary in Princess Anne too, and a hotel right on the wharf that'll give you a clean bed for the night.'

With this, the horseman gathered up his reigns as if making to spur his horse on. 'Well, sir, if you'll excuse me,' he said breezily. 'I must bid you farewell and be on my way. I have a distance yet to travel before I see my bed tonight!'

'Grateful again, sir!' said Judd, wiping his mouth with the back of his sleeve, and, seeming to give way, he took a few steps backwards to allow the rider room to pass.

But as he did so he contrived to lose his footing on some loose stones at the edge of the track where the ground fell away rather abruptly; and he stumbled and fell headlong into the long grass, letting out a grunt of pain as if he had been winded or hurt by the fall. This was, in fact, quite convincingly done. Of course, he had not been hurt at all - it had been a hastily constructed deception - but it was all the more realistic for its spontaneity. Nevertheless, Judd had to wait a little time for the act to bring its intended effect. And while he lay waiting face down in the long grass, he squirmed a little and moaned from time to time. And when the rider seemed at first reluctant to dismount, Judd squirmed and moaned a little more, before falling still as if he had lost consciousness. Some seconds then passed in silent indecision until the horse's hooves were heard at last to stir. The equine tread came closer, clattering on the loose stone as the animal descended off the track and into the long grass. Judd remained perfectly still as he sensed the beast's hooves being brought to a halt very close to his head.

'You all right, fellah?' he heard the rider call from his mount.

A draught of warm, fetid breath suddenly assailed Judd's senses as the horse's soft nostrils sniffed around his ear. His heart leapt at the shock of the unexpected blast, and he was only just able to resist the impulse to yank his head away, managing to remain completely motionless even as the animal's olfactory investigation ran its course. Eventually the beast seemed to tire of Judd's prostrate form and turn its interest instead to nearby grass, which was torn up and masticated very close to Judd's right ear, a sensation almost impossible to bear. And it seemed a long time before the horseman's boots were heard to land heavily upon the ground and come towards him. But then Judd felt hands grip his shoulders and begin to turn him onto his back - the moment he had waited for so patiently.

By using the turning motion as cover for his action, he brought his arm over rapidly as it became free. The heavy stone clenched within his fist made his limb a sort of trebuchet that arced into his helper's skull with substantial force. Judd saw the startled look in the man's eyes an instant before the stone hit home with a heavy and sickening thud. And he watched consciousness drain away as the man slumped onto the ground beside him, the man's mount interrupting its grazing only briefly to cast Judd a doleful glance.

***

Jack's departure from their lodgings at the de Burgh residence at New Hope had not brought tears to Rose's cheeks as it had done before. This time, his going produced more a feeling of resentment in her heart than sorrow. She had bid Jack farewell coolly and had made a point of going inside even while he remained in sight as the wagon trundled down the track towards the quay with Ned and Sebi seated at his side. And hidden from him behind the windowpane, she had seen him look back for her as the wagon approached the bend that would take him from her view. Even at that distance, she could see Jack's face plainly turned towards her, searching. And once he had started looked back, she never saw him turn his gaze away, even to the moment when he disappeared from sight. Instinctively, her hand had come up to wave, but she had checked it as it reached her lips, where her fingers lingered, hesitating, uncertain. Then she realised that he would anyway not be able to see her behind the glazing.

Part of her had wanted desperately to give in, to rush outside before he disappeared completely from her sight, and by her wave let him know that she loved him still – that despite all her vain arguments against his going, she at least admired him for his spirit. But the stronger part of her took hold at once and stayed her at the window. She had known perfectly well that it would hurt him not to see her waving, but she felt no guilt.

And then he was gone, and with that she felt her resolve become suddenly stronger; her little demonstration of defiance seemed to have filled her with a sense that she could describe only as liberating, even triumphant. And in the minutes that came afterwards, as she reflected upon the manner of their parting, when remorse might have stolen into her strong heart, she found her feelings just the same. Indeed, she felt stronger; and she gazed down the now empty track with a defiant look upon her face. Jack had to know how strongly she felt about this, she thought crossly. If there had been any notion remaining in his obstinate head that he was going off to fight a noble war on her behalf, then her coolness should have disabused him! She would show him no approval, no indication of her support! It was a boys' game that he was going off to play – and one that had no room in it for her! And that he could leave her to another lonely pregnancy, especially after all the misfortune that had beset them, beggared belief! (How could he be so cruel and unthinking!)

Sebi came back to the de Burgh house some hours later in the day after delivering Jack and Ned to the quay, and helping the pair prepare for their departure in the skiff. For Rose, Sebi's visit was not anticipated; he did not have any business at the house and thus would have been expected to have gone directly to his cabin on the farmstead where undoubtedly Matthew and his kitchen garden would be waiting. It was curious, therefore, that despite this, Rose had found herself glancing down the track frequently throughout the afternoon. It is difficult to be certain what was in her mind with this preoccupation, but perhaps hope lingered there that Sebi might bring some parting message of contrition from her husband, or perhaps even that Jack himself might return (though if she hoped the latter, it might make one wonder if her earlier resolve was already beginning to waver). Whatever was in her mind, it took some hours of waiting in vain in this strangely anxious state, glancing through the windows at each fretful passing, before her pacing had ceased. If it had been these slender hopes of reconciliation that had fuelled her disquiet, perhaps she had at last given them up? Or perhaps she had come to terms with the bleak fact that neither of her fancies had come to pass?

The clatter of hooves and wagon wheels on the gravel drive beneath her window woke her from a doze. She woke gradually as the gritty sounds permeated her consciousness, and for a moment she remained drowsily in her chair, staring through the window at the passing clouds, wondering what had disturbed her. Then came the distinctively uneven crunch of Sebi's lame tread on the loose stones of the drive, and the tentative knock at the front door a few moments later. In a flash, she knew that Sebi had come after all, and the thought sent a tingle of excitement through her. She leapt from her chair and, without so much as a glance in the mirror, she rushed down the stairs two at a time with her long skirts gathered up around her. Sebi stood at the threshold with his cap gripped in his hands as if he were wringing it dry from a soaking. But the dour expression on his crinkled, black face deflated her hopes immediately.

'Sebi!' She forced a smile while distractedly tucking a loosened strand of hair behind her ear (she was still breathless from her downstairs gallop). 'You're back!' she said lightly, not wanting to give her feelings away.

'Yeah, Miss Rose, I came to say that they're on their way!' Sebi replied laconically, looking a little sheepish.

Rose knew instantly from Sebi's evident discomfort that Jack must have confided some sentiment or disappointment concerning her. Sebastian was a tall stick of a man, but his long years as one of Sir Michael's plantation slaves had given him a pronounced stoop that brought his head down to the same level as hers. He had become the wise counsel, the grey-haired father figure of the Easton farmstead since Jack had taken him in. But now he seemed stuck for words and unable to meet her enquiring gaze.

'Well, thank you for telling me, Sebi...' Rose said hesitatingly. 'Did they get away all right? Oh, do come in and tell me?'

Rose thought she had better draw him out a little for it was obvious that he had something more to say.

'Erm, why thank you, Miss Rose, but no - I'd better get back to see what that young kerl Matthew is up to...probably asleep on the hay by now!' He spoke in the lilting cadences of African plantation English. 'Yeah, they got away all right. I kept the skiff in sight for a bit, followin' down the shore path to the bluff, and I watched 'em until they set headin' in the estuary for St George's. T'was a good wind, and they'll make good speed for Charlestown for sure,' he said emphatically.

Sebi saw Rose's tight smile and thrust his hands into his pockets, shifting uncomfortably where he stood as if steeling himself to speak plainly.

'To tell the truth, Miss Rose,' he blurted, 'Jack seemed a bit down in the mouth before he left.' He flicked up a kindly glance, and smiled crookedly. 'Sum'n not right between you two?' he asked, not seeming to expect an answer.

Rose glanced evasively at her feet.

'Anyhow, he tol' me to give you a message,' Sebi continued unabashed, 'an he was most partic'lar that I should give you his exact words.'

Rose felt her heart give a little leap. 'Yes?' she answered quickly, finding herself suddenly impatient with her old friend's slow drawl.

Sebi wondered aloud: 'Now what exactly *did* he say? Ah yes...he said to tell you that whatever you might think, he goes knowin' in his heart that he has to go. He said...erm, that he found it hard to explain to you, but that it was important and necessary for him to take part. Yes... them's the words he used...*important* and *necessary*! ...and that you should trust his judgement - and that he would be thinking of you constantly, Miss Rose.'

It had been imprudent of Jack to have such a message relayed, for the tone with which it was conveyed was all important to its spirit, which was inadvertently misrepresented by their mutual friend. Where Jack had meant it warmly, hoping even now for her understanding and support, it had come out in a rather pedantic, even hectoring way, that seemed to Rose to be admonishing her for her own recalcitrance.

So much for contrition or change of heart, she thought bitterly!

'What *is* it about men?' She complained bitterly to Lady de Burgh on taking tea together in her parlour the following afternoon. 'Action,

71

action, action! They cannot seem to sit and think. They must rush off and *do* something!'

'My dear,' smiled Lady Caroline indulgently at her lodger, 'they are all the same. They are like little boys. When God got round to making them, He seems to have skimped on patience and subtlety. Men are far too quick to puff themselves up at times when caution and reflection might achieve a better outcome.' She laughed, and then smiled conspiratorially. 'However, as they are occasionally useful to have around,' she said with a wry glance, 'I suppose we have to indulge them from time to time. And I have to admit that sometimes a display of manly chest-thumping sends out the required message - especially when it is other men who threaten us.'

'Hmmm!' retorted Rose, 'Then you ascribe to us the role of holding the reins - of knowing when to spur them on and when to hold them back, Lady Caroline! But I am not at all sure that individually we have the power to do so, especially when they are all fired-up by stirring rhetoric. And I have certainly failed to temper Jack's recklessness...'

'Perhaps so, perhaps not, Rose,' counselled the older woman, holding a finger to her smiling lips. 'Such messages take time to sink into men's minds!'

'Well, Jack's mind seems firmly closed to *my* reason!' Rose's tone had now become quite sulky. 'After all the misfortune that has beset us, he still races off to enjoy his manly camaraderie while I am left behind carrying his child - and I must also bear the responsibility for the rebuilding of our home alone.'

'You must not worry about the rebuilding of your cabin, Rose,' Lady Caroline said pleasantly. 'Now that Sir Michael and his regiment have departed, I can spare some labour from the fields to assist you.'

Rose's sullen mood seemed to lift a little at this kindly offer, but her brow remained creased in a frown. 'I am grateful, Lady Caroline; help would certainly be much appreciated - but Jack should be here to play his part nevertheless!' she said petulantly.

Lady Caroline threw an amused glance at her companion. 'Why, I do believe that you envy his adventures, Rose!' she laughed.

It had been on this last taunt from Lady Caroline that Rose had pondered on over the coming days, and she found her feelings towards her absent husband becoming more contrary. There were times when she fell upon her borrowed bed at night still resentful, angry, and tearful that she had been abandoned yet again. And there were other times, especially when she visited Sebi and Matthew at the farmstead to discuss plans for the rebuilding of her cabin, when she began to feel a little remorseful of her coolness towards her husband at their parting. And her feelings continued to alternate in this fashion until the evening that Ned, returning late from his trip with Jack to Charlestown, arrived at the house panting after running up from the quay.

Ned had some alarming news to convey, and in his rush to tell Rose all that Harding had revealed in his office, he blurted it all out, hardly pausing for breath. She listened dumbfounded as the details of Pettigrew and Hayward's escape were retold; but it was Ned's embarrassment about Judd's likely survival that had her more concerned. Ned's obvious unease rekindled in her mind the still vivid images of Judd's murderous attack upon her home. Perhaps she had blanked them out before; perhaps with the report of his death, she had put that nightmare behind her. But the thought now of Judd still alive and at large brought all these thoughts rushing back, and they triggered a most ignoble and revengeful alchemy in her veins. The surge of anger and recrimination took her completely by surprise; she wanted Judd destroyed, torn limb from limb, utterly extinguished! She had not thought herself capable of such base desires. But as she struggled to calm herself, vindictiveness gave way to apprehension. What evil schemes might now be brewing in Judd's twisted mind, she wondered. He surely must also bear a grudge? It was her husband after all who had brought him to justice for his embezzlement aboard the *Rebecca* - losing the boatswain his employment and reducing him to the status of a vagabond. It was Jack, too, who had pursued him across the Chesapeake to recapture the stolen fortune and make him the fugitive that he evidently had now become. Why, she herself might be a target too, for she had wounded him badly on the face with her kitchen knife in defending herself from his attack!

Suddenly, she felt very frightened. 'He will come here, Ned, I know it!' she said quietly.

Ned looked perplexed. 'Look Rose, the county sheriffs all the way down the eastern peninsula will be on the lookout for him by now' he pleaded, trying very hard to reassure her. 'It won't be so easy for him to escape this time.'

'Does Jack believe that?' she challenged.

Ned took a breath as if to speak but instead sighed and shrugged his shoulders.

'No, I didn't think he would!' said Rose triumphantly.

Rose would not be consoled. This was not the first time that Judd and Pettigrew had outwitted their captors. And with such evidence of incompetence, how could she ever trust the forces of law and order? Moreover, she sensed that beneath his brave words, Ned was just as apprehensive as she for she could see it in his eyes – those dear, doleful, guileless eyes that were incapable of concealment. And as she studied him in his discomfiture, her pious words with Lady Caroline came back into her mind to taunt her. Her easy condemnation of the male propensity for action rather than caution rang suddenly trite. There *was* a time for action and it was *now*!

'I must go to Jack, Ned!' she said firmly. 'We have made ourselves Judd's targets, and I will not wait here idly like some tethered bait for him to make another strike! I have seen the malice in his eyes, Ned. He has been here before and I know he will come again!'

And inwardly Rose also knew that Jack *must* be her protector. Together, prepared, they could defend themselves; alone, here at New Hope, she would be too easy a target for Judd's bent mind, obsessed with retribution. Moreover, her very presence might endanger others on the estate, just as it had already endangered Sebi and Matthew when Judd had set the cabin aflame. No, she *must* be with her husband now. For all his faults, Jack had been designed for such occasions: he had demonstrated the courage to act upon his convictions, and had risked all to see them through. Evil *must* be fought and wrongs redressed! She had challenged Jack's claim of duty to Sir Michael's militia in protecting the colony, but now faced with a threat nearer to home, she began to understand what drove him. And she found herself grudgingly admiring of his doggedness. His were the very qualities that were necessary for right to prevail, to protect the meek and liberal-minded from themselves.

'Is Jack still likely to be in Charlestown, Ned?' she asked quickly, even as Ned started to protest.

'Yes, it is quite likely, Rose;' he surrendered uncertainly. 'When I left him last night, he was still awaitin' one of Sir Michael's scouts bein' sent back to accompany him.'

'Then I want you to take me to him! And as speedily as you can!' Rose was quite insistent.

Ned looked dismayed.

'Look, Rose, even if Judd manages to slip the net,' he protested, 'the basta'...' (he checked his language) '...the man's not likely to risk coming back down here.'

'Then you don't know Judd like I do!'

'Rose...' Ned seemed about to continue his protest, but he stopped mid-breath and let out a weary sigh of capitulation instead. 'Then if it's a speedy journey you want,' he said wryly, 'we had better go in the wagon. I came down river runnin' before a good north westerly all the way, an' I'm damned if I'm goin' to tack against it all the way back!'

'Then get the wagon ready, Ned! And be back for me first thing tomorrow morning,' she said turning on her heel. 'And be sure to explain things to Sebi before you leave!' she called over her shoulder as she went in. 'Tell him what has happened and warn him to be prepared in case Judd turns up! And tell him to get started with the work that we discussed - he'll know what I mean! Tell him that Lady de Burgh has offered help from the hands on the plantation. All he needs to do is organise it with the overseer!'

Chapter Nine

Wearing the grubby tricorn hat and hunting garb that had been stripped from the hunter's lifeless body, Judd rode northwards following the directions he had received. Across his back he carried the hunter's musket, around his belt the dead man's powder flask, shot pouch, and bag of flints and wadding. Without doubt, he looked every inch the part. A mariner rather than a horseman, however, Judd had not dared to urge his stolen mount forward at more than a steady walking pace for fear of falling off. The beast anyway did not seem much inclined to move faster, being lazy and long in the tooth. Nevertheless, Judd's progress up the peninsula, while far from swift, was now considerably faster and less wearisome than it had been on foot. Skirting several small plantations encountered along his route, he came thus upon the river that had been mentioned.

At the point he met the reedy riverbank, the Pocomoke was wide, slow moving, and evidently navigable for medium-sized vessels. Indeed, a channel had been marked along the waterway by a ragged avenue of withies. The river wound its way out of sight to the east through yellowing reed beds, rimmed in the distance by dark woodland on a horizon that was so uniformly flat that it might have been drawn with a straight edge. In the other direction, on the opposite bank, Judd saw the wharf and the adjacent grain store about which the hunter had spoken, but both wharf and store seemed deserted with no vessels lying alongside. Judd's hopes of a ready passage across the Chesapeake from here were thus quickly dashed. But further downriver, he spotted the thatched roof of a small dwelling sticking up above the reeds like a hayrick, and guessed by the smoke curling from its crooked chimney that the ferryman was already on the near side of the river. He was right in his assumption, and fetched scurrying from his cottage by Judd's impatient shout, the ferryman did not take long to have his boat ready to push off (in fact, it departed as soon as Judd had coaxed his reluctant horse aboard).

Princess Anne was a settlement of some sixty edifices, mainly clapboard with shingled roofs but a few were built in brick and tile. The larger part of the accommodation in the town was residential and trade – the housing and premises of administrators and local tradesmen who

76

served the wider settler and farming communities in the southern part of Maryland's eastern shores. Being the county seat for Somerset County, created only fifteen years before by the Maryland Assembly, it also boasted the county's municipal offices, a courthouse, the sheriff's office, and a gaol. A busy and thriving market town, the main street was a cluster of the usual commercial enterprises and facilities necessary to support its wider service area. And located at the first point on the River Manokin that could easily be crossed (originally a wading place but now a bridge), it was connected to the Chesapeake by water navigable by shallow-draft boats. Thus, not only did the town straddle one of the principal north-south thoroughfares on the peninsula, it was also an important trading port.

Judd made himself as inconspicuous as possible on arriving in the town, keeping to the side streets as he sought out the quay. He suspected that word of his escape was likely to have reached all the county towns on the eastern shores by now, and even in his new disguise, he dare not risk too much exposure. His intention thus was to get out of town and off the peninsula as soon as he could find a vessel to convey him. The focus of his revengeful obsession, meanwhile, had firmly settled upon the Easton farmstead at New Hope, which he knew lay little more than forty miles across the Bay. If he could find a passage to take him there quickly, he thought, he could leave all these potentially suspicious eyes behind and put himself where he would be least expected.

The quay was a noisy and bustling place, and the multitude of men working on the several craft moored alongside seemed far too intent upon their business to notice Judd's arrival. Feeling thus secure, he watched the activity from his saddle for a time, gauging his chances of a speedy embarkation. Directly across the harbour, the arms of two derricks swung nets bulging with sacks of grain into the holds of a large and beamy vessel. While in the harbour basin to his right, a three-masted barque was being warped about by a dozen stevedores to bring her bowsprit to point back towards the Bay, from where she had evidently recently arrived. And a glance to the left from his elevated seat revealed several other craft arriving or departing along the river, with some more distant masts visible beyond the low trees of the first bend. A sudden burst of activity around one of the moored vessels nearby then drew Judd's attention. By the sight of her battered woodwork, she was a hard-worked lugger with two tall masts carrying a full set of sails, already hanging on their spars. Her rig was a cross between square and fore-and-aft, which would endow her with some of the advantages of both; and by the cluster of busy men about her on the quayside, she looked about to depart. Without dallying further, Judd spurred his horse down the path and rode right up to the vessel, even as her warps were being singled-up to slip, and engaged the skipper forthrightly at once. The craft was bound for Norfolk, Virginia, at the southern end of the Chesapeake; the vessel was apparently one of many similar that paid back the cost of their construction by transporting dry goods around the shallow harbours of this inland sea. The captain was a rotund and amenable fellow and, in exchange for the brace of black-headed geese that he spotted dangling from Judd's saddle post, he agreed to deliver Judd and his steed to Point Lookout on the Potomac River mouth. He got himself a bargain, for in the southerly wind prevailing, the straight tack across the bay hardly counted as a detour, for the vessel would be tacking back and forth to windward all the way down to Norfolk!

'Why, my crew and I would take you all the way to Annapolis for a decent roast duck dinner, wouldn't we boys!' he bellowed to his two crewmen standing patiently fore and aft, waiting for the instruction to let go. (It was a dinner that Judd would not share, although he would smell the enticing aroma of cooked meat coming from the galley oven before he stepped ashore on the other side of the Chesapeake.)

Thus it was with such expeditious transportation, that Judd was already far away from Princess Anne before the huntsman's body was discovered (as had been intended) - lying at the roadside, dressed from head to toe in Judd's travel-worn clothes.

By dusk, Judd and his horse had been disembarked. In the dwindling daylight, he did not turn back to watch the lugger sail away from the wood-stilt quay upon which he had been landed, but made his way immediately along the shallow beach for the cover of trees. His point of disembarkation lay a mile or so to the northwest of Point Lookout, the slender gravel spit that marked the southern extremity of St Mary's County and the northern arm of the Potomac estuary. Behind him, the wide, slow-moving river merged quietly with the Chesapeake, bringing to an end its former identity and its long, winding, and sometimes turbulent journey through the Appalachians and across the piedmont. Had Judd paused for thought and considered the confluence for a moment, he might have seen it as a poignant metaphor for his own dramatic change of situation. This very morning, he had been a fugitive with an unknown, somewhat daunting journey ahead of him. Now, at the close of that same day, he had cast off his old identity and become a hunter and a traveller, endowed with the wherewithal and means of transportation to propel him wherever his sullen mood took him. Moreover, with this fortuitous landing, he now found himself little more than ten miles from New Hope. All this good fortune had helped to crystallise his thoughts. It seemed as if some guiding hand were leading him; for even without seeking them, these opportunities had been laid in his path as if he had been meant to pick them up. Indeed, he felt as if mysterious forces were drawing him back inexorably to Jack Easton, as if some strange magic were at play. Only briefly did it cross his mind that he might also be being drawn into danger, for his new persona gave him a most powerful sense of invulnerability. He decided thus to let fate take him, to let one step follow the next, and to see where chance might lead him.

On reaching the sanctuary of the trees, Judd dismounted and set about organising himself for the night. And taking his first inventory of the contents of the hunter's saddlebags, he found, amongst other useful items, two rolls of oiled sailcloth. Unfurling these on the ground, he found one to be roughly twelve feet square, the other a rectangle about half the size; and noticing the lines attached to the larger of the two, it was clear that it was intended for use as a shelter, while the smaller would serve as a ground sheet. He soon made himself a tent of sorts, using the boughs of adjacent trees for support and rocks for restraint, and the night was thus passed protected from the cool breezes off the river. But it was a fitful sleep. Judd was troubled in his dreams by the uncertainties ahead and so eventually he gave up his quest for slumber, deciding instead to decamp and make his way towards New Hope with just the moon's grey light to guide him. And with this early start, fate had dealt him another helpful hand.

Rose Easton too had risen early at New Hope (although not as early as Judd, who was by now already closing in).

'Are you sure you know what you are doing, Rose?' exclaimed Lady de Burgh, rudely brought from her bed by her lodger's early knock at her door, and thus still in her nightgown, the curls of her hair still tied up in little pieces of white linen. 'If Judd does come back, you'll be at greater risk in the open on the road than here where I can task some of the men to protect you.'

'I'll not be put under siege, ma'am,' replied Rose calmly. (She already wore her cloak, and the travelling bag at her side signalled her quiet determination to proceed with her plan.) 'I am truly grateful for your consideration, but I do not want to cower as a prisoner in my home, worrying that he stalks outside and afraid of every shadow or rustle in the undergrowth; and I especially do not want others to be put in danger on my behalf.' Her dark eyes flashed.

'But Jack will have left Charlestown by now, Rose.' Lady de Burgh persisted. He must already be on his way north, surely?' Lady de Burgh tied together the cords of her nightgown as she spoke.

'Ned says that he is still there, Lady Caroline - that he awaits the return of one of the scouts who is being sent back by Sir Michael to guide him. If I go now, I am hopeful of seeing him before he leaves.'

'But even if he *is* still there when you arrive, what can you do?'

Rose shrugged helplessly and sighed. 'I'm not sure, ma'am. Nothing by myself, I admit.' She frowned, concealing in her heart a slender hope that, in the change of circumstances, her husband might think again about rejoining the militia, and choose to remain with her instead. 'But at least if I am there with him, he will not be concerned for me,' she continued evasively. 'While Judd is known to be at large, I am sure that Jack will not want to think of me here alone.'

Lady de Burgh looked sceptical. 'This news seems to have thrown you into some confusion, my dear. This threat of Judd's returning may be more imagined than real! Surely he will have other things on his mind to occupy him rather than risk dallying on some spiteful errand? He has done you enough harm already! And Jack must go north eventually, you know - leaving you alone in a strange town. Surely that would put you in an even worse position? Won't you reconsider?'

Rose bit her lip. Lady de Burgh had certainly seen the weakness in her argument, and she now began to wonder if anything she had said made any sense at all. But deep down, she also knew that there was something else that drove her, and for honesty's sake she had to admit it. She sighed resignedly.

'Ma'am, I admit that I have also begun to feel some remorse that I sent Jack off too coolly...' (her tone became regretful here) '...and I now realise that I was thinking only of myself. I need to put things straight with him - it is important to me that he knows that he has my love and support. Whatever he chooses to do, wherever he goes, I do not want him to be uncertain of that - even if I have yet to decide what to do if he stays away too long.'

Hearing Rose's admission, Lady de Burgh smiled knowingly.

'You know, sometimes I think that you and your husband are like two peas in the same pod!' She laughed, putting her hand gently on Rose's arm. 'You are just as impulsive as you accuse him of being!'

'Well then,' Rose replied with a light smile, 'perhaps he feels the same as I do, and my seeing him will do us both some good? And if I am too late, I am sure to receive Mr Harding's hospitality in Charlestown, so you need not be concerned for my safety.'

'Ah yes, of course,' Lady de Burgh said thoughtfully, 'the good Mr Harding will help you.' And she smiled indulgently as Rose took her hands in hers.

'Then farewell, m'lady,' said Rose warmly. 'Ned is calling for me soon with his wagon and I shall wait for him outside on the veranda. You have been so free with your generosity since we lost our cabin to the fire – our rooms here, your constant attendance while Jack was ill; why, even these very clothes!' With this she spread her cloak to reveal her dress – a riding habit handed down from her ladyship's wardrobe. She smiled demurely at Lady de Burgh's look of approval and returned a little mock curtsey. 'We are so grateful for your hospitality,' Rose continued, 'and I especially for your friendship. I pray that both the war and this Judd business will soon be over so that Jack and I can return to the settled lives on our farmstead that we once enjoyed.'

And with a further squeeze of the lady's hand, Rose turned and vanished down the stairs - leaving Lady de Burgh standing on the landing with a bewildered wrinkle on her forehead. She heard the front door slam.

'Grace!' the lady called sharply to her house servant who, even at this early hour, was already busying herself in the scullery below. And she waited at the banister until the young girl appeared at the foot of the stairs looking rather flustered, with her hands blackened with soot. 'Have word sent to the foreman, Grace,' Lady de Burgh called down without waiting for the girl to complete her bob. 'I wish to see him this morning as soon as I have had my breakfast!'

Hidden in the leafy shadows of the woods surrounding the Easton farmstead, Judd watched the driver mount his wagon and depart. He did not recognise the heavy-set man sitting hunched upon the driver's seat in his long coat. Perhaps if he had studied the man's profile a little longer, he might have remembered Ned as one of the leading oarsmen in the boat that had pursued him from the *Miranda* (indeed, the one who had briefly been his target as the boat had closed upon the beach - until his aim had settled unwittingly on Jack Easton's back instead.) But Judd had recognised Matthew sure enough, and the lanky, grey-haired, black man too, who he had watched earlier hitching the horse to the wagon and who now waved the wagon off. Matthew had been ship's boy aboard *Rebecca* when Judd had been its deceitful boatswain; the black was the old slave who stubbornly defended the Easton woman when Judd had first come looking for the money. So Judd could certainly not afford to be seen by either, or else his game would be up, his subterfuge immediately undone.

Holding his horse still for a time, Judd waited for the pair to go back inside and the wagon to disappear from sight; meanwhile the grinding of its wheels upon the gravel slowly receded. The air of this new dawn was already full of joyful birdsong, but Judd's heart was still as black as night. His waiting gaze was drawn eventually to the blackened heap of cinders that had once been the Easton's cabin. A single charred timber lay propped upon the heap, pointing in his direction like an accusing finger; it glistened with dew in the yellow rays of sunrise that now blazed a path between the trees. The ashes were long cold now, but his nostrils caught the reek of charred wood, the acrid smell a lingering legacy of his arson, inflicted to spite the man he had made his enemy. A smirk of satisfaction twisted his lips as he imagined Jack Easton's likely distress on losing his home; it was no less than he deserved, Judd thought grimly – and there would be more to come, for he was not finished with Easton yet.

When all, at last, had fallen still around the farmstead, Judd decided to follow the wagon, obeying an instinct that he did not question. And so, pulling firmly upon the reins, he turned his mount about and heeled the creature's flanks to start back along the wooded path of his earlier approach. He soon emerged into a cultivated clearing, bathed in the bright new sunlight of the emerging day, and saw at once, off to his left in the distance, a prominent and well-proportioned house. Taking this to be the wagon's destination, Judd headed towards it along the field's edge. It was soon evident that his route must have cut a corner, for when he converged upon the track taken by the wagon, he found himself only a hundred or so yards behind. He followed it as it approached the house, only just in time pulling into the greenery of a copse, for no sooner had he taken cover, than a woman was seen to step out of the front door.

The house was a post and clapboard construction, painted white, with three small gables set into its shingled roof. It was not a building of any architectural note, but its height and the massive brick chimneys at each end of the house lent it a more imposing appearance than its construction might otherwise suggest. It sat above a bend in the river facing roughly southeast, its front aspect now emblazoned in the early morning sunshine. A wooded, sandy spit extended in an arc beyond the house like a protecting arm, shielding it from the winds off the Potomac, which shimmered brightly through gaps in the trees. The site seemed well chosen. A covered veranda ran the length of the house, with a shallow flight of steps and railings at its mid-point making an entrance to the front door.

It was in front of these steps that Judd soon saw the wagon brought to a halt, its driver dismounting immediately to engage in conversation with the woman who evidently expected him, for she carried a travelling bag and cloak. Judd's eyes appraised her womanly curves – she had a tall and slender figure. Her raven hair was pulled back quite severely into a long, loose ponytail that rested over her right shoulder; and on her head she wore a tricorn with green-braided edges. Judd thought at first that she must be the lady of the house, for she had a commanding air about her. Dressed in a fine, dark-green riding habit, she held herself uprightly and confidently, with a poise that he found striking. It was only as Judd examined her more closely that it dawned upon him that the female was none other than the Easton woman. And as he recalled his last violent encounter with her and her kitchen knife, he found his hand straying to his cheek, fingering the weal that still scarred it. And in that moment, the lustful thoughts he had just begun to harbour turned into something far more sinister as he pondered the sweet fruits of his intended revenge.

Judd watched the pair now with heightened interest as they climbed into the driving seat and set the wagon once more into motion. He should have anticipated that the vehicle would turn about and retrace its route, for there was no other way out from the house. But he had been so taken with the woman that he had not thought of it before. And so he was nearly caught out as the wagon suddenly turned towards him, and forced to pull back sharply into the copse. For a few racing heartbeats he thought he must have been seen, for both faces seemed to be looking in his direction as they approached. But the wagon came upon a fork in the track before reaching the copse and turned northwards, away from where he hid. Judd let out a sigh of relief as he watched it move out of sight. And he knew he could afford to wait before he made his move; the Easton woman's travelling bag had given him the clue – he was now quite confident that the wagon would lead him to her husband – the very man he sought.

In the stillness of the early morning, the grating of the vehicle's wheels upon the track ahead carried far upon the air, and this was all Judd needed to remain at a safe distance. The thoroughfare wound gently north westward through dense copses of trees, with outcrops of bushy vegetation encroaching upon it here and there from one side or the other. There was rarely a time, therefore, when more than a few hundred yards could be seen ahead before a bend took away the view. Judd rounded each twist and turn gingerly so as to remain unseen by any rearward glance, but the distant grating sound drew him on unerringly like a homing beacon for his ears. The morning continued thus, the air remaining so still that the telling resonance hardly ever failed him - except that occasionally, the sound was broken by abrupt, mysterious periods of silence. He quickly learned to be wary of these, finding the sporadic stopping and starting suspicious of a trap. Perhaps the vehicle might be being stopped to listen, he wondered, as if its driver might suspect his presence and be waiting for the telltale sound of pursuing hooves. But nothing came of these silences. Judd listened very carefully, and every time the wagon was heard to halt, he brought his steed up sharply too, holding himself quite still - until the distant grating of the wheels continued. The day wore on in this manner, hour by hour, with the wagon making steady progress northwest despite occasional interruptions. And by and by, as daylight began to fade to dusk, Judd found himself on the approaches to a small town, later remembered as Chaptico, at the head of the Wicomico River, another of the many navigable tributaries of the lower Potomac.

The settlement of Chaptico was distinguished by its brick-built church, which was constructed to a Christopher Wren design (like many in England and its colonies), and around which the town had expanded to become a modest terminal for trading. Catching an early sight of the church elevations above the trees ahead, Judd realised that this was not the first time he had seen it. Indeed, he had passed through Chaptico some months before (going in the opposite direction), following Jack Easton and the scent of his money to New Hope. And so here he was again, still on that same weary trail, he thought, suddenly impatient to have his satisfaction and be done with it. But he knew that he must be patient; just as he knew that his tenacity would eventually be repaid.

Judd rounded the last bend and came into the main street of the town, his horse still walking at its habitual pace. And he spied ahead, still at some distance, opposite the church that stood so prominently at the crossroads, the horse and wagon left tied up in front of the hotel. By now, Judd was confident that the driver and his companion must be making for Charlestown, for there were no other likely destinations along the road. Besides, Judd also knew that Jack Easton had connections there, in particular with the port's shipping agent, Harding. Indeed, it had been in Charlestown that Judd had had his first encounter with the pair in the hold of the *Rebecca*. (Judd remembered that occasion well and often cursed his luck. If the bales that he'd set tumbling down upon their heads had done the work intended, his embezzlement might never have been detected!) Deciding thus that Charlestown must be the goal, he concluded that there was no longer any need to dawdle tiresomely behind. And with the woman and her driver presumed to be arranging accommodation for the night, Judd decided to keep on going for a while. He would pitch his cover further along the road at a place of his own choosing, and await the wagon's passing in the morning.

Ned had led Rose into the lobby of the Chaptico Hotel carrying her travelling bag. She had followed him in reluctantly and now hovered in the hallway while Ned waited at the desk. Worried that she might miss her husband in Charlestown, she was anxious not to waste time. Having set her mind on seeing him, it had become a vital necessity to do so, as if by missing him she would bring about some bad fortune sent by angry gods. She thus fretted more and more as the minutes passed, reckoning each minute as somehow crucial, seeing in her mind's eye Jack departing those same lost minutes before she reached the quay. She had tried in vain to press Ned to travel through the night but he was adamant that they break their journey at this halfway point for rest. And so she had conceded for his sake. But now she found herself regretting her acquiescence, pacing to and fro as she glanced through the window at the fading light outside.

It was during one of these glances outside that she saw a lone horseman coming down the main street in the direction of the hotel - by his dress, a hunting man, she thought. For no obvious reason, the image of Judd suddenly flashed through her mind as she scrutinised the approaching figure, a strange sense of foreboding coming over her at once. Ever since she had left New Hope the thought of Judd had dogged her, and she wondered now if she would ever shake him entirely from her mind. During the journey indeed, she had found herself frequently glancing over her shoulder, or searching the shadows between the trees as they passed by. She had thought more than once that she had detected sounds of distant hooves behind. And Ned had grown quite impatient with her obsession - especially on those occasions when she had snatched the reins from his hands and pulled the wagon to a sudden halt. Ears pricked, she had waited then with bated breath for her suspicions to be confirmed; but only the faint echoes of their own passage came back from the trees to taunt her. She had eventually persuaded herself that she was being silly, that it would be too much of a coincidence for Judd to turn up right here and now. But the fear of his doing just that was not far beneath the surface of her composure.

As she watched the rider pass abreast the hotel, he seemed to turn a glance in her direction, and for a moment she found herself looking at him square in the face. His features were hidden in the shadow of his hat and so no immediate sense of recognition struck her. Nor did she believe that he could see her behind the glazing due to the relative darkness inside. But something in the manner of his glance made her pull back and look away. Was that glance directed, she wondered? Was he looking for her through the panes? But she chastised herself at once for her foolishness. Of course not, she thought! And impatiently she thrust her fears aside and returned to window. But when she looked out, tentatively at first and then more boldly, the rider was already almost out of sight. It was indeed a silly notion to think that Judd might be so near, she reasoned, becoming cross with herself for such timid anxieties; the man she watched go on his way was probably a local huntsman returning home at close of day.

Behind her, at the far end of the lobby, Ned still waited for someone to answer his knock on the counter. The clerk eventually arrived in the hallway, but catching sight of the caller clutching a travelling bag, he at once threw his hands in the air. The man shook his head vigorously.

'No more!' he groaned, as if buckling under some invisible load, and was quick to explain that because of the arrival of a vessel at the quay that afternoon, the hotel had been filled to capacity. There were simply no more rooms available, he insisted.

By this time, having heard the clerk's apologies, Rose had left the window and was already at Ned's side, pulling at his sleeve as her companion allowed this disappointing news to sink in.

'Some refreshment then?' Rose shot at the clerk, in hope, seeing the lack of room as just the excuse she needed to get back underway. 'And an hour's rest in your lounge, sir! You'll see, Ned! With some food inside us and little nap we'll be as right as rain!' she said, becoming suddenly more buoyant. 'And then we'll get ourselves back on the road. Why, the moon will light our way; and you can nap in the back while I drive!' she added, with a winning smile.

Her mind was evidently made up. She had already forgotten her anxieties at the passing of the rider.

Ned rolled his eyes. 'Our poor mare will last no longer today, Rose, even if we might,' he sighed, shaking his head dolefully. 'And if there are no rooms, then we'll just have to join her in the stable! There's bound to be some dry straw to make ourselves a bed.' His manner was stoic, but it might have been possible to detect a hint of triumph in his voice, as if his concern for equine welfare had won him a good night's sleep.

'But you'll have a livery, sir, surely?' Rose addressed this to the clerk. She was determined now to get her way.

The clerk nodded.

'Then we can exchange horses, Ned!' said Rose, 'and pick up ours on the way back!'

Ned's shrug and wrinkled smile was a clear sign of imminent defeat, but hope had not been completely extinguished in his breast. Perhaps the inn would *have* no fresh horses, perhaps he might get his good night's sleep after all? He threw an expectant glance at the clerk as if willing the man to reply unhelpfully, hoping for any obstruction that would deflect his companion's persistence. But unfortunately for Ned, the clerk's reply was anything but unhelpful.

'Liveryman's still out back, ma'am; he'll sort you out,' he said, his tone quite matter of fact; 'we're a coaching inn - we always have a few horses ready for harness. And you'll get some refreshment in the saloon.' And with this he hurried off with an impatient air.

It thus appeared that Fate had played another hand, this time in Ned and Rose's favour: the pair would dine and rest awhile, and then continue on their way to Charlestown by moonlight with a fresh horse harnessed to their wagon. And they would drive through the night to reach their destination. Moreover, when eventually the metallic grating of wagon wheels echoed again in the still night air, it went completely unheard by Judd, who by that time had settled down comfortably for the night under his cover, and had fallen fast asleep.

Chapter Ten

Having taken turns on the reins during the cold and moonlit night, Rose was back in the driving seat (and Ned back under blankets in the rear) as the wagon trundled into Charlestown's approaches the following morning. She managed a bright smile and cheerful wave at children lining the fence of the little school hall as they passed by, just as its mistress rang her bell. It was this shrill ringing that brought Ned abruptly from his slumber, and the wagon had not gone ten yards before his tousled, sleep-befuddled head popped up above the blankets like a puppet pulled up sharply by its strings. One of the children caught sight of the bleary-eyed emergence and pointed it out to the others even as they obeyed their teacher's call, and before long the entire playground was a riot of shrieking youngsters, splitting their sides with laughter. Ned got an admonishing glare from the teacher who brandished her bell as if it were a weapon. The children's excited screeching could still be heard long after the school disappeared from view.

'You should've woken me earlier, Rose,' complained Ned, somewhat taken aback by his rude awakening. 'Are we there?'

But they could not have been anywhere else, for all roads in this part of Charles County led to Charlestown, the County seat, whose position at the head of the Tobacco River made it also a busy port. Ahead, the steeple of the familiar white-painted church stood up above the roofline like an aiming mark for the town centre. Ned climbed up and joined Rose on the driving seat as the wagon rattled steadily towards it. They passed a tobacco-curing barn, its double-doors agape, from which aromatic vapours of the drying weed issued out a heady draught. Next, they passed the long, open-sided workshop of a rope-maker's shed extending to the river behind, on whose banks the fresh-cut timbers of a new hull stuck up like a carcass of sun-bleached bones. In Ned's fuzzy head, the syncopating beat of the shipwrights' distant hammering tapped out the complicated rhythm of a well-known tune. He found himself nodding to it in quiet amusement while his back warmed in the morning sun, shining down from a near-cloudless sky.

The town was waking up to a fine new day, and townsfolk were setting out in fresh new clothes, looking bright and ready to take it on.

The wagon trundled on, soon passing a line of cottages, all of similar clapboard construction but painted in different hues so as to make a colourful picture. It seemed the neighbourhood habit to hang out bedding to air, for all the cottagers had done so. Dazzling in the sunshine, the array of linen might have been the bunting of a welcome for the new arrivals. But no smiles or waves came the way of Ned and Rose; so undone and dishevelled were the pair after their rough night on the road that they must have looked like peasant folk on an outing.

Nearing the town centre, they then came upon all manner of stores and service providers - doors already opened, boardwalks swept and stacked with articles for sale - all evidently ready for the new day's trade. Coming from the rural backwater of New Hope, the activity of such a relative metropolis was simply breathtaking; and for Rose especially, who unlike Ned had never been in the town before, it was a veritable wonder.

Eventually, they reached the square, which Ned knew well from his short stay in Charlestown the previous year (when he accompanied Jack on the first stage of his journey to Portland). On one side of the square stood the church, its east front now emblazoned in full sunshine, the chime of its little bell ringing out its early matins call. On the other, stood the familiar Centennial Hotel, where Ned and Jack had been accommodated at the town's expense (after assisting in the capture of Hayward's ruffians). And ahead, dominating the square was the imposing brick-built courthouse that served also as a municipal hall and meeting place. It was behind this judicial edifice, situated on the town quay, that the office of Mr Thomas Harding Esquire was located. And it was in this direction that the wagon was now steered, for the shipping agent would be the pair's first port of call.

The shipping office was a single-story timber building abutting the northern end of the courthouse. It was set back from the quay by some thirty yards, across a gravelled hard standing that served as a loading area for the shallow-draft craft able to come this far up the river. (Ocean-going vessels would be loaded and unloaded at quays and landings downstream in deeper water, and at Neal's landing, the naval port of entry.) The gravelled area was cluttered with neat stacks of boxes and casks, but a path wide enough for a wagon to pass had been kept clear. Having now taken over the reins, Ned negotiated the vehicle along this path towards the office steps, where Mr Harding could be seen with a small group of men. The agent, standing elevated on the boardwalk with his audience on the ground below him, seemed to be issuing forth a briefing of some sort; the men appeared to be listening attentively. From their rough clothing and demeanour, it seemed that these burly individuals might be stevedores receiving their instructions for the day.

Rose knew Harding only as a softly spoken, gentle man who had been friendly towards her at New Hope while Jack had been away. But now, in his professional capacity, he seemed brusque and commanding. Dressed down to his shirtsleeves and breeches, wigless with his silver hair cut short, he appeared the master of his waterfront domain. Rose caught his friendly glance as Ned reined the wagon to a halt some yards behind the gathering, but both remained seated until the men dispersed.

'Rose, my dear!' Harding called across their retreating heads, his face beaming with delight. 'You know, I half expected you to arrive today! And you, Ned! Welcome back to Charlestown!'

Harding descended from the veranda, strode the short distance to the wagon, and was at its side in time to assist Rose alighting. Ned meanwhile had jumped down from his seat, tied the reins to the hitching rail, and come round to join them. The two men shook hands, but it was Rose who could not wait to speak.

'We have travelled through the night to get here as quickly as we could, Thomas,' said Rose anxiously. 'Are we too late? Has Jack departed already?'

Harding laughed. 'No, to both enquiries, Rose; you have arrived in time – although only just! Sergeant Schluntz arrived yesterday - you may remember him as one of Sir Michael's scouts – the tall German fellow? One of those who helped bring Jack up from the schooner…?'

Rose shook her head – she had been far too preoccupied with Jack's unconscious state at that time and could not recall the scout.

Harding continued, nevertheless, 'Ned may have told you that Sir Michael was sending someone back to lead Jack to rejoin the regiment,' he said, waiting for Rose's nod. 'Well, Sergeant Schluntz is to be Jack's shepherd. Having said that…' He cast a quick glance around the quay. '…I have not seen either of them today, but I do know that they were intending to spend some time this morning buying additional supplies to transport forward to the militia - but I am sure they will be back soon. I hear from my clerk that they have booked themselves on the two-o'-clock packet boat to Georgetown. They're apparently taking a wagon and some horses on board, so they'll need to deliver them for loading by mid-day.'

Rose looked relieved and perplexed both at the same time.

'I am so glad to have caught him, Thomas;' she said, 'although it is a pity that we shall have so little time together – that is…' She hesitated. 'That is if he *must* depart this afternoon! Perhaps I can persuade him to delay his departure?'

Harding looked uncomfortable. 'I doubt that he can delay, Rose, I'm sorry. There is only one packet boat a week to Georgetown, so they'll have to be on it, I'm afraid. The regiment has sent back for some urgent supplies, you see, items that Sir Michael seems to have omitted from his inventory, and Jack and Sergeant Schluntz must be the delivery boys.' Harding laughed lightly, rolling his eyes. 'The good Sir Michael never was a man for detail, you know, and having lost Jack as his adjutant, he was bound to forget something! It also seems that his militiamen are a ravenous lot and costing much more than he expected - and so that the men don't go hungry, he's also requested that Jack takes back some money from the estate's deposit!'

However, it was as if none of Harding's words had had any impact on Rose at all, for she continued almost where she had left off, clearly still thinking that Jack might have the opportunity to stay on.

'You see, Thomas, this news of Judd's escape has really worried me,' she said. 'I just need to spend some time with Jack before he leaves…to talk with him about it…I am so frightened that Judd will return to New Hope…'

Harding held up his hands and smiled indulgently. 'Let us not discuss the matter of Judd until Jack arrives, Rose,' he said, with a mysterious glint in his eye, 'as of this morning, there is a good deal more to say on this, but if you can please be patient, it would be better if we waited for him!'

Harding took Rose on his arm and led her up the steps into the front lobby of the building, Ned following in their wake, where the visitors were invited to take a seat. The lobby enjoyed pleasing views of the river, and cool air wafted in pleasantly through its open double-doors.

'Now,' Harding said brightly, rubbing his hands with unexpected fervour, 'after your long night, I expect that you and Ned would like some refreshment?' (Both Rose and Ned nodded gratefully.) 'Then let me organise that straight away!'

The agent turned and stepped over to the long counter opposite where he spoke briefly to a clerk seated at his desk. The clerk nodded, rose from his chair, and hurried out as Harding returned to his guests.

'However, I *can* tell you,' Harding continued, barely containing his suppressed excitement, 'that I received some most encouraging news from Annapolis late last night. And when you hear it, Rose, I think your mind will be eased considerably.' He beamed meaningfully. 'But first, if you will follow me, we shall go at once to the hotel where you can refresh yourselves and enjoy the breakfast which my clerk should by now have ordered for you.'

It was a little later that morning, while descending the steps of the Centennial Hotel veranda, hanging onto Thomas Harding's arm, that Rose recognised the figure of her husband driving a loaded wagon across the square. Beside him on the driving seat sat the shaven-headed militia scout, Schluntz, who she now recognised as one of the stretcher party who had carried the wounded Jack back from the quay at New Hope. Neither of the two men seemed aware of her presence and Rose could not resist calling out:
'Jack! Jack!' She shouted loudly, waving an arm wildly in the air.
Not only did this catch Jack's attention at once, but it also turned the heads of others in the square. And several pairs of amused eyes watched as Rose skipped down the steps and ran towards her husband who, at the same time, leaped from the wagon and ran towards her. They met in the middle of the square, and threw themselves into an embrace that seemed so fierce that both might have been returning from the jaws of death rather than a few days apart.
'Rose!' Jack grinned from ear to ear. 'I'm so pleased that you've come! I had this terrible feeling that I'd lost you somehow - what with my pig-headedness and going off again, I mean.' He looked contrite. 'It's just the way I am, and you've every reason to hate me for it. But I do love you, you know, and there'll come a time soon when it'll all be over...' Jack was not sure what else to say so he embraced his wife again and kissed her again tenderly.
'I love you too, Jack,' she said, eventually pulling herself away from his amorous grip. She meant it too, and Jack saw that she did, but her manner became teasing at once. 'And it's not just your single-minded obstinacy that makes me love you, my darling,' she said with a cheeky smile. 'It's your self-centred, headstrong, impetuous...' she shook her head madly as she searched for adjectives, 'thick headed, insensitive and, and ...' and not able to think of any more, she burst out laughing. 'And I

suppose I shall have to put up with it!' she grinned. 'But not for long, Jack! Do you hear me?'

Jack nodded and laughed with her, but then became more serious.

'I expect you've heard about Judd?' he asked, and seeing that she had, added: 'I thought the news might bring you here. Although I don't know what on earth we can do about it. Let's hope they'll find him.'

And he took her hands in his and held them as if all the troubles in the world could not diminish the pleasure of her arrival.

Meanwhile, Schluntz had brought up the wagon and was climbing from his seat just as Ned and Harding arrived from the other side of the square. The latter could not help overhearing Jack's last words.

'Well, I have some good news for both of you on that score!' he announced enthusiastically, and he waited until he had the attention of everyone in the little group before continuing.

'I received news this morning by messenger from Annapolis that Judd's body has been found!'

Harding was so thrilled to be the conveyor of such good news that he could hardly contain himself.

'Yes, it's true!' He laughed delightedly at his audience's stunned surprise. 'It's official! The sheriff received the news from his opposite number in Princess Anne – somewhere way down south on the eastern shore, apparently,' he added, noticing some puzzled frowns. 'It seems that someone found Judd's body lying at the roadside a few miles south of there on the route up from the Cape – just where he was expected to be found, in fact. The sheriff in Princess Anne evidently was in no doubt – the description that Captain Goddard had sent over matched exactly, right down to the head wound and the clothes he wore. It seems that the bla'guard eventually succumbed to his wounds – loss of blood or infection, I should think!'

Jack, Rose, Ned and Schluntz had all listened intently as Harding had given his report, and now Rose and Jack exchanged glances that were both incredulous and delighted at the same time.

'The major, he never misses,' chipped in Schluntz, nodding, his Hanoverian accent still strong. 'His shot eventually did its work - just as I knew it would!' he added, triumphantly slapping his thigh.

Jack flashed another happy glance at his wife, let out a little chuckle of delight, and took her in his arms again.

'Thomas, that is good news indeed!' he enthused as he released her. 'Justice at last!'

And the little group fell into a sort of mutual congratulation of hand shaking and hugs - much to the bemusement of those in the square who still watched.

Rose joined in the celebration of Judd's reported demise with just as much gusto as the others at first, but it was not long before a seed of doubt took root in her mind. She so desperately wanted to believe what she had heard that she tried to put aside her misgivings, but she soon found her faith in Harding's second-hand report beginning to waver, and a sudden wave of pessimism checked her buoyant mood. She could not put her finger on what troubled her and thus could not voice it at the time, but later, as she wandered the town's emporia and Jack and his companion finished off their calls to various provisions stores, her reservations began to multiply.

It was around noon that she returned to the hotel, in a strangely melancholy mood. By then, the loaded wagon with its team and two spare horses had been delivered to the landing where the packet boat had berthed. Jack and Sergeant Schluntz had waited there until their convoy had been loaded and secured before returning to join the others for a farewell luncheon in the saloon. But the imminence of Jack's departure made it an uneasy affair – with Ned's brave attempts to keep it bright and cheery doomed to fail. It was Harding eventually, perhaps noticing the awkward glances passing between Jack and his wife, who seemed to know what was required. Rising, he suggested lightly that Schluntz and Ned join him in his office to count out the cash manifest requested by Sir Michael, and all three soon took their leave.

'Walk?' Jack suggested, finding himself at last able to speak freely with his wife. Rose nodded her assent. And taking her hand, Jack led her out of the hotel and down to the quay to a bench under an old oak tree overlooking the river. But it was not Jack's parting words that Rose needed to hear, nor were her parting sentiments uppermost in her mind. She needed first to voice the doubts that troubled her.

'You know, Jack, this news of Judd's death seems almost too good to be true,' she suggested tentatively as they seated themselves in the shade of the oak's spreading branches. Not wanting to deflate Jack's buoyant mood just when parting was upon them, she was reluctant to articulate her misgivings too directly. She meant her approach instead to be more circumspect, to probe gently, to establish if Jack remained as confident of

Judd's demise as he had been earlier. Perhaps if he were, she thought, it would be reassuring and help to ease her qualms.

But Jack was not slow in picking up his wife's ambivalent mood. He knew that Ned's earlier report of Judd's likely escape would have frightened her when he delivered it at New Hope. That she had come to Charlestown so soon afterwards was testament to that. And after such a fright, the sudden reversal in fortunes brought about by Harding's news that day sounded, indeed, too good to be true. It would take her time to adjust to, and he must try to help her do this, for he could not bear to depart on his journey knowing that she still worried. But how to reassure her? His instinct was to try to coax her into thinking along similar lines to his own, but first he had something to get off his chest.

'Look, Rose, I want to say straight away that I would not have been so quick to leave New Hope last week had I not then been sure in my own mind that Judd was dead.' he began. 'So when a couple of days ago we were given reason to suspect that he might have survived, my first thought was that I should return to you immediately. But then I thought: well, if he *had* lived, and *if* he still bore a grudge, it would be *me* that he would come looking for, not *you*. And in that case, returning to New Hope would have been exactly the wrong thing for me to do – after all, I led him there once before with disastrous consequences and I would not want to draw him back!'

With this, Jack paused, hoping for some indication of understanding from his wife. Her head was bowed in thought, but he caught her quick glance, and from this it seemed that she had accepted what he had said.

And so he went on.

'Even thinking this, I still wanted to believe that Judd was dead – everyone had been so certain that he had been left dead on the beach that I found it hard to credit that they could *all* have been so wrong. And even if he had survived, and had somehow dragged himself away to where Goddard couldn't find him, I reasoned that either he would perish from his head wound or else try to get away from Maryland altogether. I mean,' he protested, holding up his hands helplessly, 'I mean, if he had lived, he would not have been so stupid as to show his face in these parts again - not with the hue and cry out, surely? And so, persuading myself that there was no danger to you either way, I decided you were better left out of it – and I would have gone north with Sergeant Schluntz this afternoon without any concerns for your safety.' He glanced at his wife again, meeting her eyes with his. 'This morning's news proves me right, doesn't it?' He waited for her slight nod her agreement. 'So now neither of us needs to worry any more, do we?' Rose's hands were clasped in her lap, and he patted them reassuringly.

Jack had used the opportunity to rationalise his own thoughts without realising that his tortuous reasoning betrayed his own niggling uncertainties. Perhaps Rose had picked this up, for she did not yet seem willing completely to put her doubts aside.

'But maybe I should still be concerned for *you*, Jack?' she answered pointedly. 'Judd has tricked us before.'

'The man's dead, Rose - all the evidence points to that!' Jack retorted boldly. 'The location, the clothes, the head wound, surely that's enough?' He was beginning to find Rose's unwillingness to give in to reason irritating. If he had been absolutely certain in his own mind, he might not have felt that his back was against the wall.

'Anyway,' he added smoothly, 'Judd would hardly be likely to follow me into a war zone, would he? And especially not with Sergeant Schluntz and the militia to protect me!'

Rose fell quiet at that. 'Hmmm, perhaps you have a point there,' she said thoughtfully, prepared finally to acquiesce, at least for the sake of a happy parting.

Jack turned to her and took her hands again.

'Promise me you'll not worry any longer, Rose,' he pleaded, confident at last that he had satisfied her.

She smiled, leant towards him and kissed him on the cheek. Then hand in hand the pair returned to the shipping office where the others would be waiting.

A curious omission in Jack's treatise was the matter of the shot-damaged buckle. And if he had revealed this detail to his wife, it might have turned her residual misgivings into something far more tangible.

Chapter Eleven

Amongst those who had been in the square at the time of Rose and Jack's joyous reunion was the very man at the centre of the news that Harding conveyed. Judd's attention had been drawn to that reunion by Rose's first shout from the steps of the hotel. Otherwise he might not have noticed the pair at all as he plodded through the bustling centre astride his slow-footed mare. He then observed the meeting that followed with sly interest from his saddle. Had he been closer he might have overheard the report of his own demise and been cheered by the success of his deception. But he dare not press his luck, and remaining at a safe distance, disguised as a common hunting man, he entered a side street unrecognised.

Later, from the path on the opposite side of the river, Judd watched Jack and his shaven-headed companion deliver the wagon and the horses to Neal's Landing. And he had watched them return to the hotel on foot. Then in the early afternoon, he observed the Easton couple stroll along the quayside, hand in hand, and spied their little tête-à-tête under the oak tree, and their intimate embraces. And then later still, he followed the whole group discretely as they drove to the landing in Harding's four-wheel chaise to see Jack and the tall scout embark and sail away. It had been a touching farewell.

And so Judd had found the man he had been looking for, but then had just as quickly lost him. However, with such an encouraging start, Judd's resolution in his new quest would not so easily be shaken. It would take no more than an inspection of the shipping notices posted at the quayside to establish that Georgetown was Jack's destination. And Georgetown, as Judd would quickly calculate, was only two days away on horseback. Moreover, he now had double cause to continue his pursuit, for he had spotted the familiar saddlebags slung over Jack's shoulder as he went aboard the packet. And while Judd could not possibly have been certain what the bags contained, his instinct told him that the prize so recently lost was once again within his grasp. Of course, we know that Judd's instinct was sound, but perhaps he was becoming just a little bit too sure of himself, too confident of his disguise and the cadaverous deception that he had played. So confident indeed that, from under the lean-to roof of a tobacco-curing shed, he was still watching the boat departing when Harding's chaise retraced its route back towards the town. And although he quickly backed into the shadows as the chaise passed by, his presence was noticed.

Seated in the rear of the returning vehicle, Rose had registered the mounted figure within a casual sweep of her gaze. His presence would not have lodged in her unconscious mind at all had she not seen him once before from the window of the Chaptico hotel. Her eyes merely took in the image of the hatted rider sitting in the shadows and moved on. The sinister presence had been so briefly seen indeed, that her conscious mind was not prompted to react. But it did not take long thereafter for a quite inexplicable gloominess to come upon her. Her doubts about Judd's death had been temporarily displaced by the melancholy of Jack's farewell, but now they returned like phantoms to haunt her. She soon allowed them voice.

'This report of Judd's death, Thomas,' she called forward to Harding, sitting in the driving seat with Sergeant Schluntz at his side, 'are you quite sure that it is true? Judd seems to have the nine lives of a cat! First, Captain Goddard and Jack were so confident in Cowes that he had been put away for good, and yet he turns up on my doorstep! Then everyone was so sure that he had been shot on the beach, and yet he escaped. Now, on the basis of a third-hand report from across the Bay, everyone seems convinced again that he is dead. He has outwitted us before, Thomas - perhaps this is another of his deceptions?'

She saw Harding and Sergeant Schluntz exchange glances, but got no reply to her question. Irritated by the silence, she pressed her point:

'When Ned told me that his body had disappeared from the beach, Thomas, I knew at once that he'd escaped, and was afraid that he would try to take his revenge on Jack. And I have to say that I am finding it difficult to put this thought entirely from my mind despite this morning's news. It is silly of me, I'm sure, but I have the strangest feeling that he is watching us even now. I suppose I have been so frightened by the thought of him returning that I am seeing him everywhere...'

Harding threw her a reassuring glance over his shoulder. 'I am *quite* sure, Rose,' he said emphatically, 'that you do not need to worry anymore. All the evidence fits so well. And anyway, who else could it have been with that description!'

Ned, sitting beside her, nodded sagely. 'We've seen the last of him, Rose,' he said, patting her hand comfortingly, 'you can be sure of it.'

Rose put on a little smile as if persuaded, returning Ned's reassuring gesture with a gentle squeeze of his arm. It may well have appeared to her companions that her concerns had been assuaged, for she resumed her casual gazing of the pretty river scenes passing by. But she soon found herself feeling strangely irritated by her companions' apparent complacency. These men are too easily convinced, she thought crossly. But then she began to question herself, began to wonder if it were she who was being unduly pessimistic in the light of so much evidence contrary to her feelings. And so for a time she forced the matter from her mind. It would not be until the following evening, back at New Hope, that Rose's doubts would return.

Rather than going straight to her rooms on returning to the estate, Rose decided instead to accompany Ned to the farmstead to share in telling the good news of Judd's death to Sebi and Matthew. The pair were extremely glad to hear of it for both had suffered under Judd's malicious hands on that fateful day when he had set the Easton cabin aflame. Indeed, in trying to defend Rose, Sebi had been knocked unconscious and left to die inside the burning building as Judd had made a run for it; and Matthew and Rose could so easily have perished in rescuing the old man from the fire. And so it was with an air of quiet triumph that the group celebrated Judd's demise over supper that evening, the company regaled again by Ned's embellished story of the schooner chase across the Chesapeake. Rose laughed as much as the others at first (the cider was an especially heady brew), but she soon found her mood changing as her mind began again to sift through her doubts.

It was when Matthew was relating his part in Sebi's rescue – in particular, the bit when he saw Judd rushing from the cabin with a hand clutched to his bleeding cheek, the wound inflicted by Rose's kitchen knife – that she realised what had been troubling her. From being somewhat relaxed in her chair in a moment of quiet thought, she suddenly sat forward and brightened.

'That's it!' she exclaimed, causing the others at once to cease their happy bantering and turn their eyes upon her in puzzlement. 'No one mentioned the scar, Ned!' she said levelly, in the silence that endured.

The eyes of her companions remained expectantly upon her, while the gap between Ned's heavy eyebrows narrowed.

'No mention was made of the scar on Judd's cheek,' Rose repeated, more confidently this time, now that she had their attention.

It took some seconds before anyone else spoke – indeed it seemed as if no one moved in that short time. And meanwhile, the three male members of the group stared at Rose blankly, frowns eventually coming to all their faces as her words sunk in, the slow reckoning behind their eyes almost audible. Ned was the first to speak, but he seemed at first unwilling to accept the implications of what Rose seemed to be suggesting.

'It is such a detail, Rose,' he snorted, while shifting uncomfortably in his chair. 'Mr Harding said that the body had a head wound, perhaps the blood masked the scar in some way.' He shook his head in denial. 'Or as likely, the detail was left out from the report 'cause...' he hesitated, apparently searching for some other reason, '...'cause there was enough other evidence to prove that the body *was* Judd's?'

Sebi and Matthew exchanged glances. From their expressions, neither seemed confident enough to voice an opinion either way. Sebi's brow creased.

'Ned's right, Miss Rose,' he said, speaking in the usual cadences of his African roots. 'That scar might very well have been obscured or maybe jus' forgotten when the message was relayed. That other evidence seemed pretty strong to me – his clothes an' all. Anyways, I don' see what we can do about it now – he's either dead or he ain't. Less'n he turns up again, I guess we'll never really know.'

Matthew pouted. 'I'd have liked to have seen the body,' he complained, pulling his lips into a tight little smile, 'just to have been sure that it was he! Judd would have done us all in that day if he'd had the chance - begging your pardon, Miss Rose, for I know your loss was the hardest to bear.'

It may have been that the memory of the little coffin, carried to its grave on Jack's shoulder, came into the mind of everyone at the table at that moment, for all four seemed to drop their eyes into their laps.

Matthew threw Rose an abashed glance before he continued. 'When Judd was bosun on the *Rebecca*, most of us hated him for the way he and his cronies pushed us around – while they lined their pockets with their thievery,' he sneered. 'I'd have liked to have seen his dead face, Miss Rose – just to be sure that that nasty smirk of his had been wiped off it for good!'

Rose was shocked by the boy's crude vehemence, but when she examined her own feelings, she found them much the same. 'Well, why should we just sit here and brood on it?' she asked at last. 'I think we should settle this once and for all. Ned -you and I will sail across to Princess Anne tomorrow and talk to the sheriff ourselves!'

Ned looked pained. 'But...' he started to protest, but then evidently thought better of it.

The shortest sea route from New Hope creek to Princess Anne measures about forty-five miles in all. Once out of the St Mary's river, the route first heads south-easterly down the lower Potomac to Point Lookout before taking up an easterly course across a thirty mile width of open Chesapeake. About two-thirds of the way across, passing South Marsh Island to larboard, the direct route then turns east-by-northeast to enter Manokin bay. Maintaining that same course, following a line straight up the centre of this broad, fissured estuary, the river entrance is reached ten miles further on. And even from there, a vessel still has five miles or so of winding river to negotiate until arriving in the basin of the town's quay. It is not a journey to undertake lightly in a small boat.

Ned had often sailed from New Hope creek on fishing outings, but he had never navigated into the Chesapeake; indeed, he had never sailed beyond sight of his familiar Potomac shoreline. Crossing the Bay's entire width, therefore, was an intimidating prospect, especially with the added burden of responsibility for Rose's safety and comfort, a burden that he bore with due gravity. At this latitude, moreover, the Chesapeake would appear like open sea with no visible far side. It was a sea that Ned and Rose would have to cross in a little, vulnerable sailing boat – an open boat that might easily be swamped should a wind come up. His heart was thus in his throat as he put Point Lookout astern and headed out into the featureless, grey haze the following morning with only a compass to guide him. Ned's hand-drawn chart (copied from a St Mary oysterman's) showed that the eastern shores of the Chesapeake must eventually appear, but it was an act of faith on his part nevertheless, for he had his doubts about his draughtsmanship. And it was not long before the haze closed in behind them, making it feel somehow as if there could be no turning back. For hours thereafter the pair sailed on as if in an amorphous dome, enveloped by a gloomy miasma, with nothing to fix their eyes upon save for the wind-whipped waves. The little skiff was soon leaning before a brisk little breeze that came up from the south-east. And with her sails sheeted-in so tightly that they shivered at their leeches, the boat plunged headlong into a shortening sea. Stinging salty spray thrown up by her prow with every lunge was taken by the freshening wind and whipped back to hit Ned full in the face, but he set his jaw to it and gripped the tiller with his great big hands, and held her solidly on her course. Rose meanwhile mostly stayed wrapped up in her cape in the shelter of the cuddy looking glum; perhaps she wondered what on earth she had got herself and faithful friend into, but she bore the discomfort without a murmur. And from time to time, in little flurries of exertion, she might set herself to bailing out the bilges, or else delve into her picnic basket to find some offering to keep Ned's spirits up. It was this recurring routine that lent a structure to each hour and helped the time and distance to pass. But it was a sort of mutual, grim doggedness that kept them both going. Brave ventures into the unknown are often acts of sheer endurance just like this; and having set themselves to it, neither Ned nor Rose would be beaten by the challenge.

The brisk but favourable wind held throughout the morning as the gloom slowly melted, the grey dome turning a hazy blue as the overcast thinned into a flimsy blanket of mottled cloud. And, as if sign-posting the way, a sudden shaft of sunlight penetrated the dissipating shroud and lit up the searched-for landmark two points off the larboard bow. There illuminated in the yellow light was the low, sandy extremity of South Marsh Island, like a sliver of gold shining on a grey sea. Ned had swept his gaze in vain for it over the past anxious hour, first doubting his chart, then his compass, then recalculating his estimate of course and speed; but now here it was! It was such a stroke of good fortune to have his navigation confirmed, for it was the vital turning point for Manokin bay. It crossed his mind that the timely shaft of light was heaven-sent, and just in case it had been, he turned his gaze skyward and thanked the Lord for it. It might have been God's reward for his steadfastness, he mused, smiling to himself.

With the change of heading to east-by-northeast and the main sheet eased for a broader reach into the wide, and as yet invisible mouth of the Manokin estuary, the skiff now sailed more comfortably on an even keel. The sun soon began to warm and dry the pair too, and with less than ten miles to the river entrance, they knew that they had put the worst of the journey behind them. It was a little over an hour later that land at last became visible under a thinning haze, and only minutes later, a bright, sunlit bay opened up before them. It was as if a veil had been drawn back and colour had been returned to sight, as if the sun had finally prevailed against the lingering airborne moisture with a mighty solar blast. In the clear air, Ned now found his little craft equidistant between two long, wooded promontories that made the estuary a rough funnel, the headlands reaching out on both sides in an embrace that seemed to draw the skiff in. But as if that guidance were not enough, there now appeared several other sunlit sails ahead, all heading in the same direction. These would be Ned's pilots to the Manokin river mouth.

The pair reached the quayside at Princess Anne as the summer twilight turned from crimson to purple in the western sky. The wind had died at sunset, and thus becalmed, Ned had dropped the sails and taken to the oars; and with Rose on the tiller, he had rowed the last few miles to reach the town. When they arrived in the deep pool that formed the harbour, theirs was the only movement on the water as they glided silently to the quay. There followed that moment of complete tranquillity that often accompanies the end of a long voyage, when all movement ceases and peace falls like a curtain. As the pair sat for a moment's quiet reflection on a voyage accomplished, the silence was broken only by the watery slip-slop-slapping on the hulls of other boats moored up nearby – caused by the spreading ripples of the pair's arrival across the glassy surface.

By the time the skiff had been properly secured for the night, Rose thought it too late to start seeking out the sheriff and Ned was quick to agree, declaring himself to be in urgent need of food, drink, and a comfortable bed! A helpful seaman smoking his pipe on the afterdeck of the adjacent vessel, overhearing the conversation, recommended the pair to a guesthouse on the southern outskirts of the town where, in short order, these three requirements were tested - and not found wanting. And so it was not until the following morning that Rose and Ned were striding down Bridge Street looking for the sheriff's office just as doors and windows were being opened to let in the new day.

They found the sheriff already at his desk in an office between the county court building on one side and the gaol on the other. The officer got to his feet as Rose led the way in and greeted them cordially, beckoning with a sweep of his hand, for the pair to take the two seats opposite.

'Early birds!' he exclaimed as he sat himself down, reaching at once for the mug of steaming liquid before him. A platter with the residue of his breakfast lay at his elbow.

'To catch the worm, sheriff!' Rose replied flippantly, not knowing how close she was coming to the truth of the matter. She settled into her chair, unable to stop herself arranging the folds of her skirts to hide the marks and creases from the day before. When she looked up, she found his eyes upon her. He had been waiting expectantly.

'Well ma'am, what can I do for you?' he asked.

Rose took a liking to the man for his courtesy, but knew somehow from his taciturn demeanour that she would have her work cut out to get her way. He was a tall man - in his late thirties, Rose guessed - with an intelligent, clean-shaven face, flushed at the cheeks. He wore a hunting jacket, unbuttoned so as to show his shirt, and riding breeches and dusty boots, as if he had just returned from an early ride. Rose made her introductions and explained the reason for her visit.

The sheriff was interested in the affair, telling her that he had been the author of the report sent over to Annapolis (and thence on to Charlestown) of Judd's body being found.

'He met the description exactly;' assured the sheriff confidently, '- brought in by a Worcester county deputy - on his way here when he discovered the body – a few miles south of the River Pocomoke on the north road coming up from the Cape. He'd been dead for a day or two, I'd say, and as soon as I saw him, I had no doubt in my mind that it was the man we sought.'

Rose got straight to the point. 'Was there a scar on his cheek, sheriff?' she returned lightly.

'The man's forehead was covered in congealed blood, Mrs Easton,' the officer retorted, instantly going on the defensive; 'and his clothes matched the description exactly!'

'But did you see the scar?' Rose persisted.

The sheriff sat back in his seat and gave Rose a hard look. He had probably set out to be helpful, Rose thought, but there were clearly limits as to how far he might be pressed.

'I do not remember a facial scar being part of the description sent over from my opposite number in Annapolis,' he said tautly. 'And therefore I cannot say that I looked specifically for such a feature. However, with all the grime and blood on the dead man's face, it may well have been there, but hidden.' He shrugged dismissively.

Rose thought for a moment. Something that the sheriff had said puzzled her.

'This head wound, sheriff: how old was it, do you think? From what you describe it was a fairly new wound, and yet he is supposed to have received it some weeks ago when escaping from the *Miranda*. It would have been quite well healed by now, surely?'

This observation took the officer a little by surprise, and he reacted in the manner typical of someone defending a position too quickly taken. There was a slight pause before he spoke.

'The wound looked more recent, I admit,' he said slowly. 'But it is also likely that it had been reopened - perhaps by his fall?' He paused in thought, before continuing more confidently, as if convinced by his own reasoning. 'Yes, perhaps in his weakened state, he blundered into something, or perhaps stumbled and fell and hit his head?'

Rose pursed her lips, wondering whether to press her point. She needed the lawman's cooperation; the last thing she wanted to do was antagonise him with hostile interrogation.

'It is too late to see the body, I suppose?' she asked tentatively, already anticipating the answer. 'To my great cost, I have encountered Judd before and could thus identify him with one glance.'

The sheriff looked shocked and shook his head adamantly. 'He's six feet under, Mrs Easton!' he said, raising his hands in protest. 'And wrapped in sacking rather than in a coffin, the worms will have got to him by now! Anyway, I'll not have him exhumed on a mere whim. As far as I'm concerned, it was Judd that we buried, and that must be the end of the matter!'

Rose tried one last time.

'I accept what you say, sheriff - it is *quite* possible that the scar was hidden and that the head wound had been reopened,' she conceded. 'But Judd has deceived us all before, and I have a horrible feeling that he may have deceived us again. The only way to be sure would be to open up the grave…'

The sheriff held up his hands again and smiled indulgently. 'Mrs Easton, I have to suggest that you are being irrational now. You appear to accept my arguments and yet you persist with this unreasonable demand! It is at least half a day's work to dig up the grave – and we do have other calls upon our time, you know! Anyway, who else could it have been *but* Judd?'

And with that, the officer picked up some papers and shuffled them in a rather peremptory manner. 'Now, you really must excuse me,' he said, shortly, 'I have work to attend to.' He laid the papers down upon his desk, bent over them, and began to study them intensely.

Rose hesitated for a moment, wondering if there was anything left to say, anything that might change the sheriff's mind. But soon she became aware of Ned's nearing presence, then felt his hand upon her shoulder. 'No! I'm not finished yet,' she thought at first, flashing her companion an angry glance and shrugging her shoulder free of his grip. But then something made her doubt herself again. 'Perhaps,' she began to think, 'the sheriff has a point? Who else, indeed, could it have been?' The evidence was almost overpowering. 'Perhaps I *am* being irrational?'

'Well, I'm grateful for your time, sheriff,' she said meekly, rising to excuse herself and her companion to take their leave. The sheriff mumbled a sort of acknowledgement as the pair departed, but he did not look up from his desk.

It was about the middle of the morning when the pair found themselves back out on the street, by now busy with pedestrians and horse-drawn traffic hurrying this way and that. Ned and Rose, standing together on the boardwalk, swinging their gazes about, looked like two lost souls in a strange land wondering what next to do. An awkward silence had developed between them since leaving the sheriff with their tails between their legs, with neither seeming to know quite what to say.

Ned imagined that Rose's thoughtful introspection signalled an admission of defeat, or else that she had been persuaded against her earlier conviction by the sheriff's argument (with which he himself had secretly sided). He wondered what he could say that might console her, for he admired her pluck in seeing her conviction through and did not want her to feel too badly let down. Nothing came into his mind, save that perhaps the matter that had dragged them all the way across the Chesapeake could now at last be put to rest - like Judd himself who, Ned was convinced, was dead and buried like the sheriff said. And with the day still relatively young, Ned's thoughts turned to the return journey to New Hope, which he now felt sure would be Rose's next wish. But suddenly he felt anxious at the prospect.

'We can't go back today, Rose,' he said plainly, in order to pre-empt the suggestion that he anticipated. 'It's already much too late to get all the way back in daylight, and this wind looks a bit strong for a long flog in open water,' he said, flicking a nervous glance into the shivering trees. 'Anyways,' he insisted, 'I want to find myself a better chart before we set off, just in case the mist rolls in again.' (Ned would not admit that he had been frightened by the poor visibility of their crossing, and the inadequacy of his hand-drawn chart.)

But Rose did not object. Instead, she nodded absently. She was not ready to go back anyway. Her unsatisfactory meeting with the sheriff still rankled, and she needed time to think. Perhaps some new argument would yet occur to her, she thought, or some new insight would come to mind with which she might persuade the officer to take her intuition seriously.

With Ned setting off happily in pursuit of an improved chart, Rose found herself alone. But rather than find some quiet place to sit and ponder while waiting for his return, she decided instead to browse the local stores - it was not often, after all, that she got the opportunity. Thus it was, having taken a fancy to a bolt of pretty cloth displayed in the window of a haberdashery and fabric store, that she found herself drawn inside. She browsed awhile, bemused and enchanted by the variety of fabrics on display. The touch and smell of woven cotton entranced her, and the vivid colours too - what pure delight! These very sensations transported her to her mother's shop in Fortune's Well on Portland where she and her sister, Elizabeth, God rest her soul, once worked as seamstresses. Every corner of the cluttered store, the trays of thimbles and needles, the racks garlanded with a hundred reels of coloured thread, the dusty floor littered with strands of cotton and fragments of cloth, a mannequin swathed in rich velvet; all of these things brought back such bitter-sweet memories that her heart was full and torn at the same time. A great melancholy came over her as her eyes drank in this little cameo of a former life left long behind on the other side of the Atlantic. And soon she found herself dreaming of her sunny Isle. The sad countenances of her parents drifted before her mind's eye, just as she had last seen them on Weymouth quay – distraught and tearful - as she had been led aboard the *Rotterdam* as a prisoner in such ignominy. She wondered wistfully if she would ever return; and then asked herself why ever should she not contemplate it? There was indeed nothing now to stop her. Perhaps one day, she resolved; perhaps one day when all these troubles are behind us, and when Jack and I have time to think at last about our future; perhaps one day we shall!

It was while lost in this reverie that Rose's eyes fell upon a newssheet lying upon the counter. A customer in another corner of the store was occupying the proprietor at that moment, and so Rose picked up the newssheet and ran her eyes across it. It had been an idle impulse to do so, but she would come to wonder later if some guiding hand had been at work, for her attention was drawn immediately to an inconspicuous headline half way down the page. It read: *"Worcester Hunter Missing."* Something made her read on:

"Questions were expressed last night about the whereabouts of duck hunter, Edward Fitzpatrick of Worcester Count, Maryland. When Fitzpatrick, an indentured servant on the Stockbridge Estate, failed to return when expected from a recent hunting trip, his Master, plantation owner Henry Arundel Esq. contacted the Worcester Journal for help in trying to track him down. 'I have allowed Fitzpatrick a leave of absence each year when he can be spared from his duties, so that he can go duck hunting,' said Mr Arundel. 'He's generally away for a few weeks at a time, so I was not overly concerned when he did not return as expected last week. But now I am beginning to think that he may have taken advantage of my generosity and absconded.' The Journal's Missing Slaves and Servants reporter, Mr Sean O'Dowda, would like to hear from anyone who might have seen Fitzpatrick, last known to have been hunting in the marshlands south of the Pocomoke estuary. For Fitzpatrick's description and other notices of runaways, plus rewards for missing slaves etc., see below."

With the newssheet rolled up tightly in her hand, Rose ran from the store without a word, leaving the storekeeper looking puzzled at her fast retreating back.

'That's who it is!' she said triumphantly, slapping the sheet down on the sheriff's desk.

The sheriff picked it up and scanned it, but then looked blank.

'The last thing you asked me this morning,' continued Rose stridently, 'was who else could it be? You can call it feminine intuition, sheriff, but I've a notion that this is the man you buried – not Judd. I challenge you to prove me wrong!' And with this, she managed a little smile that would soften the most resolute of masculine objections.

Chapter Twelve

It would be early evening before the evidence confirming Rose's assertion would be revealed at the bottom of an unmarked grave just outside the town limits. The sheriff had not been far wrong with his estimate of how long the exhumation would take. It was midday even before the gravedigger had even been tracked down (to a quayside tavern where he was already well ensconced); and it was well after that before he had been persuaded to put down his tankard and go to work on his day off. And he had gone about it with the sort of petulant self-importance that one might expect more of a civil servant than the horny-handed navvy that he was, despite the promise of one-and-a-half times his normal rate. The sheriff, Rose, and Ned had waited patiently in the shade of a nearby tree, trying to ignore the digger's bad-tempered muttering as he had descended from their sight behind the growing pile of sandy soil thrown up by his spade. Eventually his flushed face reappeared above the earthy mound, and with a grunt and the curl of a bony finger, he beckoned the group to come closer. With handkerchiefs clasped to their noses, the threesome thus approached and peered down into the grave to see the sackcloth-covered corpse lying prone below, the gravedigger standing astride the shrouded form awaiting instructions. At the sheriff's nod, the man took out his knife and with unexpected delicacy cut three neat slits in the material to form a loose flap around the corpse's head. The spectators bent closer, seemingly transfixed by the procedure, as the mud-caked sacking was peeled back to reveal the grey and blackened lineaments of a human face. That it was human was undeniable, but the weight of earth that had pressed upon the decomposing flesh since its interment had flattened it grotesquely, so that it would have been difficult to identify even if the features had been those of a familiar countenance.

Rose gasped in revulsion at the grisly scene and could not prevent herself from turning away in disgust.

Ned felt his stomach churn at the sight, but steeled himself to examine the face more closely. It was truly unrecognisable. But even if this were Judd, Ned would not have known it, for he had only ever seen him from a distance (lying prostrate on the beach while Ned remained in the longboat nursing the wounded Jack). After a while, he too drew back, and, wrapping his arm around Rose's shoulders, gently coaxed her forward so that the dead face once more came into view.

'Well, is it Judd?' he asked gently.

The sheriff seemed just as anxious as Ned to hear Rose's reply, for his eyes were fixed upon her expectantly.

Rose glanced into the grave again then shook her head uncertainly.

'I cannot be sure,' she admitted. 'The face is so horribly distorted, and so caked in mud and blood.'

She took a breath, brought her handkerchief to her nose, and braved a closer look while the two men stepped back to give her room. Eventually, she turned to face them.

'It is quite impossible to tell,' she said, 'Can it be cleaned up, sheriff? I'll need to see if there is a scar upon his cheek to be sure either way.'

The sheriff now stepped forward and peered down into the grave.

Still standing astride the corpse with knife in hand, the digger glared impatiently upwards, looking for all the world as if he had been caught in the act of some murderous deed.

'Get some water and wash the man's face,' the sheriff ordered sharply. 'We need to see his cheeks.'

The gravedigger cursed under his breath as he clambered from the grave, returning a minute or so later with a pail of water. He descended again, clumsily missing his footing on an earthen step that he had carved for himself, and rode the ensuing landslide down into the pit, landing on his knees on the corpse's chest. Miraculously, the water did not spill. Then, muttering further obscenities, the digger dipped a piece of sacking into the pail and commenced to rub the face clean, doing this so gingerly that he might have feared waking the dead. And with his action the pasty flesh was caused to move as if some life force were indeed returning, the digger's troubled muttering meanwhile adding voice to this impression. To Rose, who watched intently as the grime and blood came off, the corpse might well have been uttering some last message from the grave. But she needed no unearthly voice to reach her conclusion; as soon as the digger leant back from his gruesome endeavour to reveal his handiwork, it was at once clear that the man in the grave was not Judd.

'It is as I suspected, sheriff,' she said evenly. 'This man has no scar upon his cheek; he is not Judd.'

Rose had wanted to be proved wrong. She had wanted to see Judd's face revealed at the bottom of the pit so that she could at last put her fears to rest. But with this contrary evidence now laid bare before her, her suspicion that Judd remained alive at once hardened into firm belief. Judd had tricked them all again! In her former state of uncertainty, she had allowed her secret hope of being wrong to obscure an unpalatable possibility and the reckoning of its consequences. With this graveside revelation, however, that hope was stripped away to leave naked fear exposed in its place; the door in her mind that had, until that moment kept the phantoms of her nightmares at bay had been torn open and the spectres of her worst fears, released from their restraint. These were now given free reign to taunt her. The dusty rider on the street at Chaptico, the shadowy figure hidden in the lean-to on the river path at Charlestown - these images flashed into her mind's eye, and in that instant, the connection between those observations and her underlying sense of foreboding was made. She recalled too, those moments along the road to Charlestown when she had felt evil lurking somewhere near at hand, making her skin creep. All these demons now joined in an unholy union to form a new and terrifying reality.

'Judd is alive, Ned; I know it!' she said at last, her heart pounding.

Ned sighed heavily. 'That this is not Judd does not prove that he still lives, Rose,' he cautioned calmly.

'I saw him, Ned!' Rose countered - and she related her observations of the mysterious rider at Chaptico and at Charlestown. And she also reminded him that she had forced him to stop the wagon several times on their way to Chaptico thinking that she had heard the sound of following hooves.

'I thought it all a silly obsession then, Ned;' she said, 'but now that we know that this poor man is not Judd, it all adds up. Don't you see? It *was* Judd that I saw! And he was on the road to Charlestown behind us - he followed us from New Hope!' she asserted. 'Of that I am now quite certain. And he must have seen me with Jack and watched him depart on the packet boat!'

Ned looked grave. It did not take him long to set his lingering doubts aside, and he decided at once to back his companion's intuition. 'Then we must warn him, Rose,' he said solemnly. 'And let's hope that we're in time; if Judd saw those saddlebags on Jack's shoulder, he'll have good reason to be bold!'

Rose turned to the sheriff who had clearly been listening attentively to the conversation.

'Well, are you convinced now, sheriff?' she asked.

The sheriff clamped his jaw. He was evidently not quite ready to answer Rose's question either way. Instead, throwing her a hounded glance, he stepped forward to the graveside and barked a further instruction. 'Let's see his clothes!' he called sharply. 'Pull back the sacking, man' he shouted irritably when the digger did not instantly respond. And again, all three bent down and peered into the pit as more of the sacking was removed.

'I'm satisfied now, Mrs Easton,' the sheriff said at last, stepping back from the graveside. 'There is no scar.' He shook his head grimly. 'We'll get Arundel over here from Worcester to identify him properly in due course, but I'd say this is likely to be his missing servant. There are not many hunters who'd be wearing a reefer jacket, and I'll wager your man Judd's dressed as a hunting man – just like you said, ma'am.'

'Then may we ask for your help? Firstly, can you send word of this discovery to your colleagues in Annapolis and Charlestown? Ned and I will set off at first light tomorrow for New Hope and then onwards to Charlestown. If the sheriff there is forewarned by your report that Judd is still at large, he is likely to be ready to help us when we arrive.'

'This is sheriffs' work, Mrs Easton,' returned the sheriff stiffly. 'And if Judd has added this poor fellow's murder to his list of crimes, his capture is as of much interest to me as my colleagues across the water! I will send word to Annapolis as you suggest, but since the quickest way to Charlestown is by boat, I shall accompany you tomorrow – and I shall requisition a vessel more suitable for the journey than that little tub of yours!'

A glance at Ned's face as the sheriff made his proposal might have revealed relief that the navigational burden of the return journey had been lifted from his shoulders. But the sheriff misinterpreted his expression as one of concern for what might become of his boat.

'No need to worry on that score, Mr Holder; once I've organised a suitable craft for us, I'll have yours put on board - we'll take her with us to Charlestown.'

Ned nodded his agreement readily as the lawman continued.

'There are a few things that I shall have to organise before we leave,' he said grimly, flicking a glance into the grave. 'And after this man has been formally identified, he will need a proper burial in consecrated ground!'

The gravedigger's groan echoed in the pit.

One of the first responsibilities of the administration of a newly designated county seat is to create road connections with those of adjacent counties. Thus a network of roads was growing within Maryland that was passable to wheeled vehicles and on which goods could be carried in the furtherance of trade. One such road had already been constructed between Georgetown and Frederick, and it was along this thoroughfare that Jack and Sergeant Schluntz had driven their wagon following disembarkation from the packet boat. The distance between these two county towns measured some forty miles, and being maintained assiduously on both sides of the county boundary so as to avoid unfavourable comparison, the road's graded surface permitted a good average speed. It was thus still the afternoon of the day following their departure from Charlestown, that the pair entered the courtyard of Frederick's Town Hotel. The small enclosure resounded with the clatter of hooves and the scrape of metal rims on cobblestones as Schluntz brought the wagon to a halt before the hitching rail. A familiar white charger stood there already, its saddle still in place; and from the sweat on the animal's coat, it appeared as if it had been ridden hard.

'Looks like Colonel Sanderson's here already,' said Schluntz as he descended from the driving seat. 'Sir Michael said to expect him.' He gave out a disapproving grunt and raised his eyebrows contemptuously. 'My favourite officer - I'd follow him anywhere!'

'Out of curiosity?' Jack laughed - and Schluntz laughed with him.

Jack remembered Sir Michael's second-in-command from his encounter in the briefing tent at New Hope - and he reckoned it his good fortune not to have had to deal with him since! Jack had taken a dislike to the pompous lieutenant colonel from the very outset. Like Sir Michael, Sanderson was the owner of a large tobacco estate in St Mary's County but he wore the distinction haughtily, affecting a disdain for anyone he considered below his station.

'The man's a pretentious fool,' said Jack, remembering the colonel's ostentatious arrival at the New Hope quay, leading the column of militia from the high saddle of a conspicuous white mare. 'Still, we'll need someone to draw the fire when we come face to face with the enemy!' he added with a smirk.

The pair collected their personal things from the back of the wagon and started up the steps, Jack carrying the cash-laden saddlebags over his shoulder. But just at that moment, Colonel Sanderson came out of the hotel.

'Lieutenant! Sergeant!' came the colonel's sharp call. And he strode along the boardwalk towards them, coming to an expectant halt some two yards or so short. Jack and Sergeant Schluntz stopped in their tracks, their hands encumbered with belongings, and nodded a simple greeting.

'A salute is customary I believe,' said Sanderson shortly, and he waited while the arriving pair put down their bags, came to attention, and saluted (which they managed without a hint of satire). Indeed, the salute was exceedingly smart, and must have pleased the colonel because he returned it with similar precision.

'Stand easy,' he ordered self-importantly. 'You've brought the money, I hope, lieutenant?' (Jack nodded and patted the saddlebags on his shoulder.) 'Good, then I'll take it if you please,' the colonel said, holding out his hand. (Jack handed the heavy bags over.) 'I'll be the custodian from now on,' the colonel added, managing to infer somehow by his tone that Jack, as a mere subaltern, was somehow less trustworthy than a half-colonel.

Jack's face gave nothing of his feelings away as he watched his superior lift each flap in turn and carefully probe inside as if checking the contents. And as those few moments passed, Jack had an opportunity to study his superior officer more closely than he had had before. The colonel was perhaps a little shorter than himself, his figure certainly a little fuller; and while Jack and Schluntz's uniforms were already the worse for wear, the colonel's appeared to be freshly cleaned and pressed, for there was not a mark upon his jacket nor a button out of place. The colonel's smoothed-back hair was already flecked with grey despite his young face, which, unlike Jack's, was not grimy with the dust of the road. Jack realised that the colonel must have washed and changed the moment he arrived, since his horse had not yet been attended to. He wondered at the man's priorities.

Sanderson finished his delving, buckled down the flaps, and looked up to find his subordinates still standing stiffly before him. 'I shall be accompanying you onwards from here,' he said brusquely. 'Have the wagon prepared for an early departure tomorrow morning. I want to leave at dawn, so make sure that you're not late!'

'Yes, sir,' said Jack.

'Yes, sir,' echoed Sergeant Schluntz (both managing not to let their irritation show).

'And I'll meet you tonight in the saloon after you've eaten,' the colonel went on, pointedly not inviting the pair to join him at his table for supper, 'I'll brief you then on where we're heading for.'

'Yes, Sir,' acknowledged Jack and Sergeant Schluntz together.

The colonel turned and began to walk away but stopped in his tracks after a few paces, performing a neat little pirouette to face the way he had come. His two subordinates by this time had bent down to pick up their bags, but now they straightened as if expecting something more to be said. They should have realised what was required from the senior officer's expectant manner, but it took a moment or two for the penny to drop. With a quick exchange of glances, they came smartly to attention (if perhaps with slightly excessive zeal) and saluted.

'Thank you, gentlemen,' the colonel said in a satisfied tone as he languidly returned the salute, 'then I'll bid you a good afternoon.' And turning on his heel he made again to go, voicing casually over his shoulder as he departed: 'And see to my horse, would you?'

The two men raised their eyebrows as much in amusement as affront.

'He doesn't change!' said Schluntz, shaking his head wearily.

The three men met as arranged later that evening in the saloon, Jack and Sergeant Schluntz having finished their meal by the time Sanderson arrived at their table.

'I took my meal in my room; I haven't kept you waiting too long, I hope,' he said, his voice pleasantly mellow, as if a glass or two of some alcoholic beverage had already passed his lips.

Jack caught Schluntz's eye with a conspiratorial wink as he poured the half-colonel a large measure of ale from the pitcher on the table. Perhaps with the help of the fermented brew, they might make this haughty officer a tolerable travelling companion after all!

The room resounded with loud and boisterous chatter; drinking men crowded the dozen other tables in the room. A haze of tobacco smoke floated in the air as shafts of amber sunlight streamed in from the setting evening sun, throwing the room into stark contrasts of light and shade. In a shadowy alcove off the main saloon, a game of cards was in progress. The few spectators who had gathered behind the table stood observing it. Evidently the game had reached a crucial stage, for an expectant hush had descended. A waist-coated player with slicked-down hair seemed to be the centre of their attention; by the size of the pile of cash on the table before him, he would go home a happy man tonight – unlike the others, whose grim looks and small piles told a different story. A grey-haired dealer meanwhile looked on expressionlessly while shuffling his pack.

Sanderson took a mouthful of ale from his tankard, helped himself to a further full measure, and took another long draught. 'Right,' he said, getting down to business straight away. 'Let me bring you up to date.'

Against the noise in the room, Jack and Sergeant Schluntz had to lean forward to hear the colonel's words, which were delivered in the laconic manner of a military briefing.

'Our militia passed through Frederick about a week ago,' Sanderson reported. 'I travelled with them as far as Fort Loudoun, about three days north of here, before being sent back to meet up with you two.' He drew a map with his finger in the thin film of dust and nicotine tar deposited on the table. 'We're here,' he said. 'And Fort Loudoun's here - the first of the frontier posts on Brigadier Forbes' new military road.' He threw a sideways glance before adding: 'The garrison there apparently got massacred by Cherokee a year or so back, by the way, but it's pretty calm now, so nothing to worry about. Anyway, from there, the road goes north a stretch (he continued tracing the route in the dust), before turning westwards for Fort Bedford.'

Jack and Schluntz examined the smudgy drawing on the table closely while Sanderson downed another mouthful from his tankard. After topping it up again from the pitcher, he went on:

'We're told that the road will reach the Ohio Valley by winter, where Forbes' is having an assembly post built from which to re-take Fort Duquesne when everything's ready. (Again he used his finger to trace the general geography and the route of the road through it) 'He's got several thousand British and provincial troops already on the way, and when you see it, you'll find it quite a sight! You'll see some Indians with them too.' He leant back in his chair, ruminating like some student of military philosophy, a look of admiration coming into his eyes. 'You know, it's an amazing feat to cut through such a vast stretch of mountainous wilderness. And not only that; every three or four days along the new road, there's a new fort – that's one thing the British seem to have learned from Braddock's experience – to secure the logistic tail!'

'Impressive,' said Jack – and he meant it. The more he learned about Forbes' attention to logistics, the more confident he became that Sir Michael de Burgh's militia would be well deployed and led. Jack's earlier apprehension at being drawn into an amateur brigade of southern landowners supported by reluctant conscripts was diminishing – now he was beginning to feel more optimistic about the whole affair. He might even admit to a growing sense of pride at being part of something really big. If this mobilisation were indeed to be successful in driving back the French and creating a lasting settlement with the Native American population, then he could be truly proud of his part in it (and Rose would be too, he thought!).

'Then our militia has already joined with Forbes?' posed Jack.

'*Brigadier* Forbes to you lieutenant,' Sanderson corrected. 'Anyway, I'm told that he directs the operation from his sick bed,' replied Sanderson, 'He seems to suffer from some mysterious ailment – he will apparently come forward when the road is completed. Our troop has joined up with a British regiment of fusiliers from the south of England who marched ahead from Philadelphia. We're under their overall command from now on.'

Jack was intrigued. 'This English regiment, sir, it's not the South Coast Fusiliers, by any chance is it?' he asked, remembering his journey with them on his last Atlantic crossing.

'Why yes, as a matter of fact,' replied Sanderson, apparently surprised that his lieutenant should be so well informed.

'Hah! I sailed from England with a large contingent of them – under a Major William Green,' retorted Jack, delighted by the coincidence. 'Perhaps you came across him?'

'Indeed I did,' said Sanderson. 'He's one of the battalion commanders. Not as full of himself as some of the British officers I have known, either! You'll get to meet him soon enough, for tomorrow we set out on the road to catch them up.'

Schluntz cleared his throat. 'Probably not as speedily as you would like, Colonel,' he interjected. 'With our loaded wagon, we'll not be able to travel much faster than they can on foot! They'll have reached Fort Bedford by the time we join them.'

Sanderson seemed somewhat irritated by Schluntz's interruption.

'The plan, sergeant,' he continued rather too pedantically (for the alcohol was having its effect), 'is for them to await us there – providing that we're not too far behind, that is. They'll assemble at Fort Bedford for training and victualling before moving on to this new fortification I mentioned at Loyal Hannon for the winter - that's about fifty miles short of Fort Duquesne and well into the territory where we might expect an unfriendly reaction from the French. So for our own safety, we have to join them before they leave Fort Bedford!'

The conversation was at this point interrupted by a loud uproar from the spectators in the alcove, and all three men turned to look. Evidently, someone had done well at the card table; and from the satisfied look on the face of the slick-haired player in the waistcoat, it was he who had taken the pot. Sanderson threw a rueful glance at his two companions.

'I learned a hard lesson at that table last week,' he grumbled, taking another draught from his tankard. 'We had two travellers at the table. It turned out that one of them was passing cards to the other, but before their sleight of hand was discovered, I had already lost rather heavily and had left the game. They were found out in the end, but it was too late for me! That fellow in the waistcoat there,' he said, flicking his glance towards the gaming table, 'is the hotel professional; it seems that he was on to them from the start, playing them at their own game. He took everything they had!'

Sanderson seemed to be enjoying the recollection of the summary justice meted out to the cheating duo. 'We had great pleasure in throwing the pair of them out of town too - a card-sharp and his distinctly English upper-class accomplice – both educated too, but rather too clever for their own good!'

Jack sat up at this.

'Colonel,' he interrupted, 'Sir Michael must have told you about the escape of the *Miranda's* hijackers in Annapolis? I wonder...'

Sanderson frowned and shook his head.

'I know of the *Miranda's* recapture,' he offered, cutting Jack short. 'Indeed, the whole regiment knows of it! Sir Michael regaled us with his story of it almost as soon as he had rejoined us. And a dramatic and entertaining tale he made of it too - no doubt embellishing his own part in the affair! But he didn't mention any escape.' Sanderson still looked puzzled.

Jack summarised the report of the escape relayed by Harding in Charlestown.

'It seems that most of the hijackers were recaptured pretty soon after,' Jack concluded, 'but two of them, Pettigrew and Hayward in particular - the two ringleaders - are still on the loose as far as we know. Your mention of an Englishman and a card-sharp made me wonder...'

'Surely you can't believe that they would have travelled this far west?' replied Sanderson, incredulously.

'It's possible, Colonel,' replied Jack. 'They'll not be safe in British territory. Perhaps they're attempting to reach New France? It may well be that that was their objective all along with the hijack of the *Miranda* – perhaps they were making for the St Lawrence?'

Sanderson still looked doubtful. 'You know these men?' he asked.

'Yes, I do: both of them in fact, to my great misfortune! And I know Pettigrew has connections with the French too – that's indirectly how I came into contact with him in the first place. He ran a French contraband operation on the Dorset coast in league with a Weymouth customs officer who killed his own captain just to stop him interfering. And I was made the scapegoat for it. It's why I was transported to Maryland all those years ago!'

It was now Sanderson's turn to frown.

'These men - what did they look like?'

Jack described them as best he could, then remembered the 'wanted' poster that he had taken from Harding's wall. He removed it from his pocket and unfolded it upon the table.

'This is my sketch of him,' he said. 'I made this after his first escape. I got my revenge in getting him convicted in England, but it rather backfired when he was transported here himself. It's a complicated story – I'll tell you sometime. He may have changed his appearance since then though; he's a slippery customer.'

Sanderson scrutinised the picture – a print of Jack's original charcoal drawing – but he looked doubtful.

'Hmmm; not sure,' he said. 'The man had a goatee and wore a broad-brimmed hat which mostly hid his face – until it got knocked off in the scuffle! I only saw the back of him after that - as we chased the pair of them up the street and out of town!'

Sanderson sat back awhile reflecting for a moment, holding the drawing before him and studying it closely.

'I'd have a score to settle too if I ever caught up with him,' he muttered almost to himself.

Eventually, he put the poster down and shook his head uncertainly.

'Best man to ask is the dealer over there - or the chap in the waistcoat. They will have got a really close look at him.'

And picking up the poster again, the colonel raised himself from the table and crossed the room to the alcove, where several despondent players of the recent game were just dispersing. Through the haze, Jack saw Sanderson catch the attention of the two professionals and engage them, showing them the poster. Some serious discussion then ensued before all three faces were seen to glance in Jack's direction, directed by the colonel's pointing finger. Soon, the threesome in procession picked their way towards him through the maze of tables that cluttered the saloon.

It was the waist-coated man who spoke first.

'This could be one of the men we ran out of town,' he said, speaking as if unsure. 'But like your friend said, he wore a hat.'

Jack glanced across at the adjacent table, noticing a clay pipe that had been abandoned there. He rose, stepped across and picked it up, making some apology to the table's occupants before returning to his seat. His new companions had watched him, puzzled; but they began to understand what Jack had in mind as he dipped his little finger into the blackened bowl and proceeded to amend the drawing with a delicate touch.

'A goatee, you say, Colonel? And a broad-brimmed hat?'

He dabbed his sooty finger here and there, then drew in some bolder lines.

His audience looked on closely as he worked; and eventually there were some mutters of approval.

'Like that?' said Jack, tentatively.

'That's the man,' said the waistcoat at last. 'He's a bit thinner than the picture shows, but I'm pretty certain that he's your man.'

The grey-haired dealer nodded his head sagely in agreement.

'Gentlemen, we're grateful,' said Jack. 'I believe that that is as close as we're going to get to an identification.'

The card players soon departed leaving Jack and his two companions to consider the consequences of the unexpected turn of events. Sanderson posed the first and obvious question:

'But why Frederick?' he asked. 'Where on earth can they be heading from here?'

'If Pettigrew will cross into French territory, as you say, Jack,' offered the German Schluntz in his slightly imperfect English, 'then he will use the military road – just as we do. The two of them would not find it easy on another way through that wilderness.'

Sergeant Schluntz knew Pettigrew and Hayward well enough to appreciate the kind of characters they would be dealing with. The sergeant was one of Major Lawrence's militia scouts aboard the schooner with Jack, Sir Michael and Captain Goddard in the race to intercept the hijacked *Miranda*; he was also a member of the boarding party who deceived Pettigrew and Hayward to get aboard the grounded vessel in the

Chesapeake; and it was Schluntz personally who had overpowered Pettigrew on the quarterdeck and tied him up below.

'I know these lands very good,' he continued. 'From Annapolis, their best route to reach the military road is to follow the Patuxent river valley at first. That would bring them to within ten to fifteen miles of here. Frederick would be an obvious place to come. And from here, if they are sensible, they will use the same road north as we must now.'

Jack let out a long and thoughtful breath. 'Then there is every reason to make haste!' he said. 'We must catch them before they can make contact with the French and barter for their freedom.'

Chapter Thirteen

The road leading northwards from Frederick is little more than a rutted track that winds its way through sharply undulating and forested terrain, following the course of an old Indian and fur traders' path. Pettigrew and Hayward had been on it since their inglorious episode at the gaming table in the Town Hotel - and their subsequent summary expulsion. And without the provisions, without the weapons or equipment, without the horses that Hayward's gambling had been intended to finance, the pair was soon in a parlous state. Continuing their earlier pattern of petty thieving from the few farmsteads and small settlements encountered along the way, they had kept themselves alive. But sleepless nights – dark nights on damp, cold ground, tormented by the incessant whining of flying insects and the hungry echoes of creatures on the prowl - had extracted a heavy toll. Though they were as yet far from finished, their gaunt faces and intense glares revealed a growing desperation in a long and inevitably losing battle to survive, unaided and unprepared. Until now they had moved furtively, dodging into the surrounding undergrowth at any sound of others on the road; but the sheer effort of remaining out of sight had drained them further. And now they cared less and less about being seen – indeed they almost courted it, for in their harried frames of mind, even capture began to offer a prospect of relief.

It was in this reckless and distracted state, in the twilight of the seventh day, that Pettigrew and Hayward came upon a farmstead in a clearing beside the road ahead. Slipping quietly into the shadows of surrounding trees, they observed the settlement for a while, noting the layout: a single cabin, a barn, and several outbuildings placed around a yard - with a paddock nearby in which two mares grazed and a dozen chickens roamed freely on the grass. The two men's hungry eyes saw at once an opportunity to improve a sorry lot. And where once fear of discovery might have made them wary of entering such an open site, desperation now drove them to be bolder – though not yet so bold as to risk a daylight approach. They decided to await the fall of darkness before making a closer reconnaissance, and hid amongst the undergrowth, setting themselves to watch as the light faded.

Soon, they saw a tall, young-looking, dark-haired man come out of the barn swinging a halter in his hand. A small boy, probably aged four or five and similarly dark-haired, skipped along behind. They were clearly father and son, for the boy caught up quickly and grabbed the man's hand, and together they continued into the paddock. Faint sounds of childish laughter drifted on the air as the two approached the first of the two mares. The father threw the halter over the animal's head and secured it. The horse did not resist. Pettigrew and Hayward watched all this with interest; transport was high on the list of their requirements now and these mares seemed to fit the bill exactly. And so they continued to watch closely as the man and boy led the beast into the barn. Some minutes later, the pair came out again and returned to the paddock. This time it was the latter who carried the halter; or to be more accurate, dragged it along the ground - for which it appeared he was quickly admonished, for under his father's critical eye, he stooped and gathered up the leather straps in a bundle, which he held to his chest. The bundle tidied eventually to the father's satisfaction, the pair continued into the paddock in close procession, attaching the apparatus to the remaining mare, which was then led in to join its companion. Being abandoned in the paddock, the chickens seemed suddenly to take fright as if some invisible predator stalked the gathering gloom, for they scampered after the procession as if of one startled mind, and followed it into the barn. After a while, the man and boy came out again, pushing the tall doors closed behind them, and walked hand-in-hand towards the cabin. And as the pair approached, a young woman in long skirts and apron appeared in the doorway and greeted them, before all three disappeared inside.

Against the darkening background of the forest that stretched beyond unendingly, the cabin windows glowed with welcoming lantern light. It looked a haven of warmth and safety to the two cold and hungry observers waiting uncomfortably outside. Through the windows, movement could be seen inside until the curtains were drawn. And in the still air of descending night, luminescent smoke was soon rising from the chimney. The evening wore on thus, until eventually the cabin lights were extinguished; and by and by the homestead and its surrounds fell quiet, with only the tumbling water of a nearby stream and the occasional hoot of a distant owl to disturb the silence that descended. A further quiet hour was allowed to pass while Pettigrew and Hayward dozed - until a three-quarter moon ascended the star-studded sky.

The two men then rose from their cover, skirted the paddock, and quitly moved towards the barn. Opening the tall doors fully to admit the moonlight, they slipped silently inside. The earthen floor was littered with straw, and one wall of the barn was heaped untidily with straw bundles on which the chickens were now roosting. Some of the silly creatures were already craning their necks in alarm at the untimely intrusion. The soft chorus of their anxious clucking soon filled the air as Pettigrew and Hayward penetrated their sanctuary. The horses had been placed in individual stalls at the far end of the dim and cavernous space – but they too were soon reacting to the strangers in their domain. Their wide-open eyes had become dark, glistening pools in which the low moon was reflected. As the men came closer, their hooves began to shift restlessly and stir the straw.

Hayward noticed some saddles and harnesses hanging on pegs nearby and beckoned Pettigrew over to help collect them. But as they entered the stalls carrying the saddlery, the horses shied back, rearing up their big heads as if challenging the trespassers to stay away. Stiff and cold from so much waiting, the two men were in no mood to be put off; putting down the saddles, they pressed determinedly into the stalls carrying only the halters, which each then attempted to throw on, thinking that if the horses could be led out of their confinement it would be easier to saddle up. But each time the men raised the leather tackle, reaching up on tiptoe to put it over the animals' ears, the beasts recoiled and bucked their heads. The wooden slats that hemmed in the protesting creatures soon became sounding boards for their hooves. The two men made several more clumsy attempts to put the halters in place, but it seemed a hopeless task – the moonlight and the intruders seemed had spooked the horses into a rebellious frame of mind. Eventually, Hayward gestured Pettigrew to retreat to give the beasts some time to calm down, whispering that a gentler approach might be more successful. They were waiting thus, with the halters still dangling in their hands, when an angry shout startled them almost out of their wits.

'Who's there!' a male voice resounded from somewhere still out of sight. 'Come out, damn you! I have a musket and I'll shoot if I have to!' The voice grew nearer.

Pettigrew and Hayward froze - their pale, moonlit faces turned towards each other in alarm. Then, at Hayward's signal and with breathing stilled, they moved apart, treading silently in opposite directions to find cover. Hayward had already concealed himself when a tall man's dark form appeared in the open doorway, silhouetted against a lunar backdrop. He carried a musket in one hand and a lantern in the other, but its light was enfeebled by the strong moonlight behind him. Pettigrew, rather slower than Hayward to react, was still tiptoeing across the barn and was thus seen immediately. The man put down his lantern, raised his musket and cocked it.

'One more step, and I fire!' he called. 'Put your hands up where I can see them!'

The voice trembled a little but the man's aim did not waver. Pettigrew was caught in the full glare of the moon's rays and there was no escape. Obediently he dropped the halter and raised his hands.

'Don't shoot!' Pettigrew called out, genuinely frightened that the man's nervous finger might inadvertently squeeze the trigger. 'Don't shoot,' he called again. 'I'll cause no trouble.'

'We shoot horse thieves around here!' the voice growled. 'Who the devil are you?'

Pettigrew remained mute. Some instinct suggested that it would be wise to play dumb and look scared out of his wits - which he managed to do quite convincingly (it was not difficult, for his heart was palpitating wildly).

The man now took a few tentative steps into the barn, glancing nervously from left to right.

'Are you alone?' he called gruffly. And throwing a few more quick glances into the shadows, he came a few steps closer.

'Who are you,' he repeated, now close enough to poke his long barrel into Pettigrew's chest.

'I am a poor traveller, sir,' whined Pettigrew, thinking quickly on his feet. 'I was only looking for somewhere to rest the night...'

'You liar!' returned the voice sharply. 'You had the halter in your hands, you blackguard; you were going to steal one of my mares!' And with each alternate word, the man prodded his weapon firmly into Pettigrew's chest, causing his victim to back away with each painful thrust.

Despite his discomfort, Pettigrew knew that he must play for time and cause enough of a distraction to give Hayward the opportunity to come to his rescue.

'Down on your knees!' called the man gruffly.

Seeing Pettigrew complying with his instructions, he backed towards the door and shouted over his shoulder:

'Martha!' he called out sharply.

A woman's voice was heard to answer from somewhere near at hand, and seconds later she trod cautiously into view, wearing a nightdress so thin that against the bright backlight, the form of her naked body could be made out beneath.

'Fetch the other musket quickly, Martha, and come right back!' said the husband triumphantly. 'We got ourselves a horse thief!'

And with that, the woman disappeared from sight.

It was only then that Hayward emerged from his hiding place and began to creep across the floor behind the armed man's back - with a wooden handle of some sort held threateningly in his hands. Pettigrew saw the stealthy movement at once and knew to keep his interlocutor engaged. He began to let his arms drop.

'Keep you hands up!' shouted the man.

Pettigrew raised them again with an obvious effort.

'I can't keep them up much longer, sir,' he replied honestly. 'I'll cause you no trouble; I'll pay for a horse if you have one to sell - and be on my way.'

It was a deception, but the words had covered his companion's quiet steps across the littered straw.

'I don't do deals with thieves. Best place for men like you is behind bars,' the man growled, 'and that's just where you're headed!'

These were the last words that he would utter for a while, for as he spoke, Hayward moved closer yet. A moment later, he sprang forward, and with a sweep of his arm, he brought the handle down so heavily on the man's head that he sank to the ground without so much as a gasp.

By the time the woman returned, Hayward had retreated back into the shadows so as to ambush her from behind. Pettigrew meanwhile had set himself up as bait in the trap to draw the woman's attention, her unconscious husband lying inert at his feet. The ploy had worked before, but this time both Pettigrew and Hayward were taken by surprise by the speed and aggression of the woman's reaction.

'You murderer!' she screamed. And without a moment's hesitation, she raised her weapon and pulled the trigger. The ensuing flash of powder and the resounding explosion that followed half a second later were both blinding and deafening in the hollow void of the barn. And the shot that issued from the barrel would certainly have been fatal for Pettigrew had not Hayward's hasty lunge spoiled the shooter's aim. In his quick dash, however, Hayward tripped awkwardly on some hidden object buried in the straw and was sent flying headlong into a pile of fencing stakes, which fell about him with a resounding clatter. The roosting chickens had already taken fright at the commotion and by this time were scuttling about the floor clucking and squawking in mindless panic - until eventually they made a bolt for the door and disappeared into the yard. The woman meanwhile had recovered from the glancing blow that had toppled her to her knees, but she now found herself looking up the barrel of her husband's musket - held in Pettigrew's hands. Yet even this did not restrain her. Enraged and screaming like some cornered beast of the forest, she sprang up and ran at the startled Pettigrew with her arms outstretched, her fingers set like claws intent upon his throat. Her hands found their target and her nails sank deeply into the flesh of his neck. Pettigrew was caught off guard, and his weapon was knocked from his hands in the woman's mad and unexpected rush. The force of her charge overwhelmed him, knocking him to the ground as he tore frantically at the vice-like grip around his windpipe. He struggled and writhed under the ferocious onslaught, but he was too weak to dislodge her. Her grip had hold so tightly that sight and consciousness soon started to slip away.

Hayward meanwhile struggled to disentangle himself from the heap of fencing posts that had fallen about him in such confusion; and when at last he got to his feet, his companion had gone quite limp under the woman's stranglehold. Within a few quick steps, however, he had picked up the handle again and had rendered the woman unconscious with one sharp blow to the back of her head. The woman's iron grip at once released, and Pettigrew recovered his senses to feel the weight of her limp body slumped across him - it took the efforts of both men to roll her off.

It was at this point that the couple's young son appeared in the open doorway carrying a pistol that was so long compared to his height that it reached his ankles. Still wearing his nightshirt, he peered into the barn with wide and frightened eyes. As can be imagined, a ghastly scene confronted his gaze, a scene made nightmarish by the cold, unearthly light. Immediately before him, his father lay sprawled upon the ground, inert, his long limbs bent at odd angles. Further inside, grunting obscenities, two shadowy figures manhandled the unconscious form of his mother, tossing her aside as if they were ogres of the night and she no more than a rag doll. Neither of the intruders appeared to have noticed the boy watching, speechless and open-mouthed, from the doorway. The men got to their feet, panting and flushed; one of them distractedly dabbed at his bloody neck with a handkerchief, the other offhandedly dusted down his coat as if the still figures lying in the straw were mere carrion. The scene was the very stuff of childhood terror, but the boy remained calm - and schooled by his father to take action against the foes that might threaten this frontier family, he knew what he must do. The heavy pistol wavered in his two hands as he brought it up to aim.

'Put your hands up!' the boy shouted, adopting his most manly bravado. (It was the script of one of his father's bedtime tales.) 'Or I'll shoot!'

The two men raised their hands at once, but Hayward was quick to spot that the firing arm of the boy's weapon had not been cocked. At that same instant, the boy realised it too and made a frantic attempt to correct his error. But the firing spring was strong and his little hands fumbled with the mechanism. And so, before he had managed to pull the arm back into its firing position, he was seized, disarmed, and thrown roughly to the ground.

'Enough of this!' said Hayward testily, while stuffing the captured pistol into his belt. And he grabbed Pettigrew by the arm and propelled him towards the stalls (thus distracting him from fussing over his bleeding neck). 'Let's get the bloody horses and get out of here before we have any more trouble!'

Behind them, the boy got to his feet, ran to his mother's side where he fell onto his knees beside her, his hands instantly upon her shoulders gently, rocking her as he sobbed 'Mommy, Mommy' in such a forlorn tone that it would have moved the hearts of most men. But neither of the two intruders was moved at all by the boy's plaintive sobbing. Indeed, neither really noticed it; and in their haste to bridle up the horses, nor did they notice that the woman soon began to stir.

The woman opened her eyes to find herself gazing into the tearful face of her distraught son. She moved a finger to her lips to silence him as she cast a glance about the barn. Seeing the two intruders preoccupied in the stalls, she quietly got to her feet and gestured the boy to go to his father's side. Her head throbbed painfully, but she ignored it as her eyes searched for the weapon that she had knocked from the intruder's hands in her mad and reckless charge. The musket lay amongst the straw a few paces off. She moved over to retrieve it, thinking that she would turn it on the two men there and then and regain control. But when she examined the flintlock, she found that the powder had spilled out of the firing pan. The weapon would need re-priming before it would fire; she would have to retreat. With a glance over her shoulder, she saw that the thieves were still struggling to get the halters on her two mares, both being typically uncooperative. She had often cursed them for their waywardness, but now she blessed them for it. It would give her time to regroup and rearm; and if she and her family could get back to the cabin quickly, she thought, these thugs would have a nasty surprise waiting for them when they came out of the barn!

Under cover of the intruders' noisy activity, she crept across the barn to join her husband and son - the former still unconscious, the latter now kneeling at his side. There was a little blood on her husband's forehead where he had been hit, but it did not seem serious and his breathing was regular and even. She shook him gently, and eventually he came to. She pressed her fingers to his lips to stifle his attempts to speak, but seeming immediately to become aware of his family's peril, he struggled to raise himself at once. He managed to get to his knees but his efforts left him gasping. The woman glanced anxiously towards the stalls; the dissenting horses were still making a fine commotion, kicking and shying and snorting all manner of protest; the rumpus would provide good cover for their escape. She took hold of her husband's arm, gesturing the boy to take the other, and, acting both as prop and crutch, they helped the dazed man to his feet and from the barn unseen.

When eventually Pettigrew and Hayward had harnessed the mares and led them from the stalls, they saw at once the family gone. The musket too had disappeared, leaving only the man's lantern burning in the doorway as evidence of the earlier confrontation.

Immediately on their guard, both men used their steeds as shields as they stepped tentatively into the open, half expecting a shot to ring out straight away. Moonlight bathed the yard, throwing long, stark shadows that both pairs of wary eyes at once probed closely, nervous of the dangers that might lurk within. But nothing stirred; the coast seemed clear. The cabin door was closed; several of its curtained windows were now dimly lit by lantern light - the family had evidently retreated inside. Pettigrew threw a confident glance in Hayward's direction as if to signal danger past, and led his horse forward towards a hitching rail barely ten paces in front. Hayward seemed less sure. He held back until his companion had been exposed long enough to have drawn a reaction from the cabin, which appeared eerily still in the cold, pale light. Only the gentle gurgling of the nearby stream broke the expectant silence that seemed to have descended. Eventually Hayward followed Pettigrew to the rail and tied up his mount. Then, glancing about themselves nervously, both men returned to the barn, half stooping, half running with a curious loping gait, to collect the saddlery. They came out some minutes later with their arms full.

It was Hayward who first noticed that the cabin lights had been extinguished and that the cabin door was now ajar, but by then both men were fully exposed in the open space of the yard. Hayward stopped in his tracks and called an urgent warning to Pettigrew, a step or two in front. But before either could retreat, a shot rang out and Pettigrew was knocked sheer off his feet, landing heavily on his back with the saddlery falling to the ground around him. Fortunately for him, the bullet had struck the saddle that he carried rather than his chest (at which it had been aimed), but the force of the projectile had transferred its momentum to both. It took him a second or two to realize that he was unhurt.

Meanwhile, Hayward had thrown himself to the ground, erecting his saddle as a shield before him, and had pulled the pistol from his belt ready to return fire. A further report resounded from the cabin. This time, it was Hayward who felt the hammer blow of the bullet's impact upon his protective leather shield. The shooting had been accurate, but now was the time to make a run for cover, he thought quickly, while the hidden marksman (or woman) reloaded. He shouted forward to Pettigrew to follow, and both leapt up simultaneously and raced for the barn, finding cover inside just as a third report rang out, sending a shard of timber from the doorpost flying into the air. The sheer speed of their reckless flight had carried them as far as the stalls before they realised that a careless foot had kicked over the abandoned lantern in the doorway. The ominous crackle in the dry straw behind them was unmistakable and it drew their immediate attention. Looking back in alarm, they saw fire spreading across the straw-littered floor so rapidly that the doorway was already an impenetrable wall of flames. Hayward saw at once that there would be no stopping the blaze now. The straw was tinder dry, and before a minute was out, a growing swathe of the floor was well alight, forcing the men further and further back into the recesses at the rear of the stalls. The fire moved so quickly that at first it almost stultified the frightened pair into inaction. There seemed hardly enough time to think. But suddenly the drive to escape was both instinctive and imperative.

'The back door!' shouted Hayward, choking in the smoke. 'Over there!'

Alarm turned to outright fear as the pile of stacked straw bundles caught light, quickly turning into a thundering inferno, the flames lashing the timbers and roaring greedily upwards in a gathering tempest of the fire's own making. The blaze was becoming a voracious beast, devouring everything it touched. A muffled detonation somewhere within the pyre sent a plume of sparks shooting upwards into the loft where further bales of hay could now be seen illuminated in the flickering glare. Within a second, they too were alight, and within ten, unfettered tongues of orange flames darted and dived like hungry fry amongst the clouds of billowing black smoke that would soon engulf the building.

The men ran from the flaming edifice into the cool night air behind. It was a blessed relief to breathe it. But Hayward realised at once that now was not the time for grateful reflections on salvation; if the pair were to make good their original intentions to re-supply and re-equip, they must take advantage of the distraction and press home an attack. Pettigrew seemed thunderstruck, gazing almost in awe at the growing conflagration as he panted for breath, but Hayward's shout for him to follow was the rallying call. The two men now circled into the shadows at the rear of the cabin where they found the open window of a bedroom and climbed inside. Crossing the room on tiptoe, they cracked the door open and peered into the living space beyond. The large room was unlit by any artificial means, but pulsating shafts of fiery light, radiating through the windows from the blaze across the yard, pierced the darkness. The shadows in the room were thus thrown into stark contrast and it was at first difficult to see where the family had placed themselves. But gradually, as eyesight adjusted, the profiles of the farmer and his wife were seen crouching beneath the open panes - dark, hunched shapes edged in flickering gold by the fiery glow. Both adults peered into the yard outside, their muskets resting on the sills but not aimed in any particular direction. The boy knelt dutifully between the pair with a powder flask and bandolier of shot across his shoulder; his gaze too had been drawn outside. All three seemed at that moment transfixed by the horrific conflagration that confronted them. Even at this distance, the roar and crackle of the fire had by now become thunderous. But even ascending the din, the man's shout was heard clearly:

'The horses, Martha! They're too close to the fire! I'll have to bring them back!' And with that, he put down his weapon, sprang up, and rushed out of the front door.

Seeing him go, the two intruders cracked open the bedroom door a little further to catch sight of the farmer through the windows opposite, first racing across the yard and then leading his frightened mares back towards the cabin. His wife and son seemed frozen in their earlier positions at the window, their attention completely taken by the man's dangerous endeavours, as first he led the horses to safety and then went back to retrieve the saddlery. The woman must have thought that he two intruders had either fled or been burned alive for she had raised no objection to his going. It had obviously not occurred to her that she might already have been encircled and be in imminent danger from behind, for when Hayward strode across the room and thrust his pistol into the small of the woman's back, she was entirely taken by surprise. His hand muffled her scream, just as Pettigrew swept up the boy and clasped a hand over his mouth too. Both captives struggled for a while but both were swiftly and brutally subdued.

When the man re-entered the room some minutes later, he was confronted by a scene that was as terrifying as it was unexpected. His wife and son knelt side-by-side in their linen nightclothes as if forced into some act of penance, tethered to a structural post, their wrists tied behind their backs, their mouths agape, gagged with a strip of cloth. In the devilish light from the blaze, they might have been sacrificial offerings prepared for hell's inferno. And standing over them like manifestations of Satan's henchmen, the two shadowy intruders held a pistol and a musket to their bowed heads.

'Now, you do exactly as I say,' growled one in a low and threatening voice, 'and there'll be no further harm done tonight.'

The farmer held up his palms and took a step back. 'Alright, alright!' he pleaded urgently. 'Take whatever you want! Just leave them be!'

At this, the other came towards him quickly and without warning struck out with the butt of his pistol. Then everything went dark.

Less than half an hour later, Pettigrew and Hayward had saddled the waiting horses and were on their way. Having ransacked the cabin, taking anything that might be useful and carried conveniently on horseback, they had simply departed the fiery scene, leaving the family to their fate. They had got what they had wanted from their raid – horses, weapons, clothes, supplies – and that was all that mattered. Neither seemed to have given a second thought to the likely outcome of abandoning the settler family, secured or unconscious inside the cabin, with the flames of the blazing barn so dangerously close by.

When the two men reached the road, the pair paused to look back and saw the shingles on the barn roof already well alight. They sat in their saddles and watched the fire rage from this safe distance - it was a spectacle sure enough. The cabin, a low, dark silhouette against the background of the rampant blaze, was very clearly in great peril, but it was as yet untouched by the flames. It would still have been perfectly possible to pull out the family and lead them to safety, but neither observer seemed taken by that noble notion. The barn was soon an inferno of such intense brightness that it lit up the whole clearing, almost as if bathed in daylight. Sparks, flaming shingles and other glowing debris were soon being propelled high into the air like the efflux of an eruption - the roar of it, quite deafening. Even now, the cabin had not caught alight despite the rain of flaming fragments that showered down upon it in profusion; even now, a rescue might have been achieved. But still, neither of the two men calmly watching were moved to act, nor even shift in the saddle, yet the potential for tragedy must surely have been recognised by both. If there had been an ounce of compassion in their hearts, surely one or both would have realised that this was their last chance to redeem themselves. Yet they let that moment pass with such cold indifference that any normal person watching would have found beyond comprehension; and if guilt or remorse troubled the two men, it did not show in their faces as the cabin roof first smoked, then smouldered and then ignited in a flash, like tinder from a spark. Unmoved, Pettigrew and Hayward watched the flames take hold of the low building and then spread rapidly to engulf it.

'No witnesses then!' said Pettigrew coolly, as he yanked the reins to turn his horse upon its way, leaving the conflagration to run its fateful course. And with just a few rearward glances over his shoulder, Hayward followed without a word.

Chapter Fourteen

Had the winds been less favourable for the packet boat on which Jack and his companion had sailed from Charlestown, Judd might have beaten them to Georgetown, as he had hoped. But as it was, he missed their disembarkation on the town's bustling quayside by a good day and a half. He had not been blessed with particularly good fortune either, as far as navigation was concerned. A distance of only some thirty miles as the crow flies, his route to Georgetown had not been at all easy to follow, due mainly to a paucity of signage and his misreading of the lay of the land. His sense of direction confused in the dense woodland of the Potomac hinterland, he had been forced to retrace his tracks on more than one occasion. Moreover, an infuriating deviation of at least ten miles had become necessary to find a way to across the Anacostia River, just when the tall masts in Georgetown's harbour had come into view across the river's wide and muddy estuary. All this meandering was made doubly frustrating by the reluctance of Judd's stolen mount to move at more than a slow walk.

Despite Judd's belated arrival, however, it was not difficult for him to discover the pair's intended route. Talk of war with the French was rife in the waterfront tavern in which he sought solace and refreshment, and the progress of Sir Michael's militia through the town was much discussed. So too, was the later arrival of two of Sir Michael's scouts, who had arrived by packet boat and had soon followed on the heels the militia in their loaded wagon. Judd was thus on the trail early the morning following - as if nothing other than his pursuit was of the slightest consequence.

Jack Easton, Colonel Sanderson, and Sergeant Schluntz meanwhile were now well on the way northwards from Frederick, making for the military road as they had planned. The frosty relationship that had existed between the Lieutenant Colonel and his two subordinates had melted just a little since the revelations in the Town Hotel regarding Pettigrew and Hayward. But despite this, Sanderson still chose to ride ahead of the wagon rather than with it. And determined now to catch up with the two fugitives, whom they all guessed would be on the same route only a day or two ahead, the threesome had elected to ride from dawn to dusk, thereby increasing the daily distance travelled. It was thus early in the second day out of Fredrick, travelling at that time along a winding track that descended between two thickly wooded ridges, that the group caught sight of the farmstead that had been visited so cruelly by the two men pursued. When Jack first spotted the farmstead, it was about half a mile ahead, lying in an open clearing, which looked as if it had been carved out of the surrounding forest like a sort of bowl. But even from that distance, he realised immediately that something was amiss.

The group came closer, eventually reaching a high point on the track above the dell from which the men were able to get a clearer view. Sanderson held up his arm to bring his little convoy to a halt. The full extent of the site's devastation was now revealed before them and all three fell silent at the sight. The charred remains of what appeared to be two separate buildings still smouldered in the centre of the clearing, sending thin plumes of blue-grey smoke into the air. The smoke from the pyre rose vertically at first but soon spread out to form a layer of wispy haze that extended across the whole basin and into the surrounding trees. It was as if it had been fashioned into a shroud to obscure the disquieting scene, for the air was as still as death itself and filled with funereal foreboding. Sanderson seemed uncertain for a while, but in due course he signalled to proceed, and he led the wagon down into the dell with some evident circumspection. The site looked deserted, except for a dozen chickens scratching about in an empty paddock and also in the lush greenery of a neatly laid out garden set off to one side. The threesome continued closer, soon descending into the smoke layer as if submerging, finding the taste of it at once bitter in their mouths.

Eventually the three men arrived within the curtilage of the farmstead, pulling the wagon off the track to pass along the paddock fence, and finally bringing the lumbering vehicle to a halt in the yard between the two heaps of smouldering debris. They paused to survey the scene of smoking wreckage in some dismay. Only the small outbuildings of the farmstead remained standing. What must have been a cabin and a barn had been reduced to burned-out frames and cinders. Not a sound could be heard save for the incongruously pleasant gurgling of a nearby stream, a sound that jarred with the feeling of sadness that seemed to radiate with the heat of the ashes. It was as if even the birds had been bid to reverent silence by the gloomy pall that hung in the air overhead.

'Indians?' pondered the colonel at last.

Schluntz swung his gaze about the site.

'Only boots and horseshoes,' he said plainly, examining the trodden earth of the yard. 'This is no Indian work.'

A sullen voice, dull and hollow, then came suddenly from behind:

'Two men,' it said.

The three men turned to see the tall figure of a young man standing in the open doorway of the nearby outbuilding. His clothes were charred and shredded; his grimy face, riven with streaks of sweat (or possibly tears); his dark hair, a tangled shock made grey with dust and ash.

Jack leapt from the wagon and rushed over, catching the man just as he lost his steadying grip on the doorpost. Jack had already laid the man down on the ground before the others dismounted.

'Bring some water and dressings from the wagon,' he called quickly.

The sight of Jack's quick intervention had stayed his companions, but now they responded, bringing water and medications from the wagon as requested. It was, even so, some time before the man ventured to speak again, by which time his burns had been bathed and his head and hands soothed with liniment and bandaged in clean cloth.

'They had my wife and boy... tied up inside...the fire was so close...' he uttered, his voice weak and rambling as if he were still only half conscious. 'I...I should not have surrendered...I could have stopped them...' His words were disjointed, yet his tone was earnest. It was as if he were speaking from a different place – from the limbo of lost souls between nightmare and incomprehensible truth. 'I should have rushed them. I could have taken them by surprise. But I dare not... they had guns to their heads...they looked so helpless and frightened...I should have saved them.'

Jack had let him pour it all out, bathing his forehead meanwhile with cool water from the flask. The man continued in this way for some minutes. He seemed desperate to get something off his chest, to be seeking absolution for some sin, as if by giving voice to his guilt it would somehow exorcise the horror and torment that stalked him. His utterances spilled out in such a jumble, that it was difficult to understand.

Jack cut in, meaning to steady the man's thoughts and make them more coherent:

'Your wife and boy?' he pressed. 'What happened to them?' he asked, swinging his gaze about.

The man's face went blank as if some light had suddenly been extinguished. Ceasing his rambling instantly, he fixed Jack's eyes with such a mournful expression that it communicated at once what he evidently could not bring himself to say. His eyes then drifted to the smouldering wreckage that had once been his home, and his gaze lingered there as tears welled up and rolled down his cheeks.

'They were tied up in the far corner of the room,' he said quietly, 'tied to a post.' It seemed now that every word was drawn painfully from his chest, his gaze meanwhile remaining fixed upon the burnt-out pile. The man's thoughts tumbled out in a torrent of disjointed fragments, often repeated, separated by bouts of sobbing and mournful cries. He was clearly re-living the ghastly experience with every utterance.

Jack let the man talk himself out, until eventually his words began to slow and he grew tired. One telling phrase, however, was spoken clearly at the end, a sort of bitter epilogue of self-reproach:

'My darling wife and boy,' he cried, 'I tried to reach them, but the flames beat me back.' He held out his arms to show Jack the blackened scorch marks and weeping blisters that disfigured them. 'My sleeves caught fire,' he went on, 'I should have let myself be taken too…I should be with them now… God bless them both.'

And with that, he fell into exhausted slumber, still cradled in Jack's arms - until he was rolled gently onto a blanket.

It was a grisly business to rake over the ashes and extract the charred remains of the woman and the boy, but it was a necessary act of kindness to spare the husband the grim task. Any man might be driven to madness by such a sight – the sight of a beloved family so horribly disfigured – a sight to fuel his guilt and haunt his nights. And so, while the man slept on oblivious to the three scouts' gruesome labour, his wife and son were buried in a quiet corner of the site, in the centre of a leafy glade that would capture the setting sun. Jack had taken it upon himself to select the site carefully. He thought that the man might like to sit there in peaceful communion at the end of the day, just like he and Rose did back at New Hope in a similar quiet place of remembrance, reflecting on the short life of Rose's sister, Elizabeth, and the death of their son.

It was already late in the afternoon by the time the man awoke, by which time Jack and his companions had erected an awning on the side of the shed, using some timbers and canvas that they had found inside. The temporary edifice would be a useful extension to the man's living space while he got himself reorganised, and would serve as sleeping quarters for his three visitors in the coming night. The preparation of an evening meal was also well underway as the man joined the three scouts at their cooking fire. Arriving without a word, he seated himself on the long, curved log that had been drawn up as a communal perch. At first, he sat silently apart, lost in thought, cupping his chin in his hands as he gazed into the flames. His new companions had turned to welcome him with their eyes, but somehow sensed that it was not yet time to speak. They left him thus to his thoughts, Sanderson soon returning to his earlier, somewhat banal analysis of the coming fight with the French; though while the diverting talk continued, each from time to time threw the grieving man a kindly glance.

Eventually the meal was ready, and Schluntz, an unlikely yet surprisingly competent cook as it turned out, was soon passing around steaming bowls of meaty broth and hominy grits. The aroma of it seemed to bring the man out of his reverie with a start, and he took the offered bowl and consumed its contents with such ravenousness that he surely must not have eaten for some time. The day's labour had left the scouts hungry too and this preoccupation gripped the group as they sated their appetites in silence, a silence broken only by the thrifty scraping of their wooden spoons against their wooden bowls. It was not until the man finished his second helping that he began to sit up and cast his gaze about. His face was still drawn, his expression still as ashen as the surrounding desolation, but quite suddenly he seemed to perk up, his alertness returning in an instant as if he had arrived from some other place. His eyes swept the scene and found the two burial mounds in the grassy glade, where his gaze then lingered. The early evening sun had found the graves too through an opening between the trees; it lit the mounds with oblique rays of golden light that seemed to Jack in some strange way as if the spot were being blessed.

'Thank you,' the man said at last. 'I could not have brought myself to do it. I could not have endured it.'

No one spoke a reply, but Jack offered the man a beaker of liquid poured from his own flask.

'Cider,' he said. 'Fresh in Frederick. Drink it. It will do you good.'

The man accepted the beaker and drank its contents in one long draught, wiping his lips dry with the back of his sleeve. There then followed a short period of awkwardness, with no one seeming to know quite what to say. But Jack leant over to offer more of the golden liquid from his flask, the man offering up his beaker and his name at the same time.

'Blake,' he said gruffly. 'Jeremiah Blake. I'm grateful for your company.' His eyes were alive now, seeming to indicate a readiness for engagement.

Jack introduced himself and the others, pointing with his flask at Sanderson and Schluntz in turn. He filled the man's beaker.

'You mentioned two men,' Jack ventured as he poured, hoping that the alcohol might make his new acquaintance more inclined to open up.

Blake nodded, running his fingers distractedly through his hair. 'Yes, two men,' he said heavily, 'although at first I only saw one.'

He sighed, set his jaw firmly, then began the tragic tale from the beginning as if for the first time: how he had been woken by the commotion in the barn and gone to investigate, how he had found the intruder with the halter in his hands, and how he was then taken by surprise from behind by a second man and knocked out. He shook his head disbelievingly.

'I came to my senses later, finding myself back in the cabin, ' he said. 'My wife and boy had dragged me there. But we weren't about to give up our mares without a fight, so we waited for 'em to come out of the barn...fired a few shots and chased 'em right back in! That's when the fire started...'

He paused for a moment, his eyes once more seeking out the ashen heap and dwelling there wistfully. It seemed as if he were steeling himself, summoning some inner reserve to speak further of the catastrophe that then ensued. Eventually, he continued, relating the story more coherently than before when he had spoken in delirium. He spoke of finding his wife and son tied up when he returned to the cabin again after rescuing the horses, of being struck down by the intruders and left unconscious, regaining it when it was already too late to save his family, only just saving himself by climbing out of a rear window before the cabin was engulfed in flames. It was undoubtedly a painful recollection, for his voice faltered from time to time as the story unfolded. It may have been cathartic too to have a communion of men around him, listening solemnly to his guilty regrets and his tortured analysis of where he felt he had failed. He blamed himself for the disaster and agonised over his fateful part in it: perhaps if he had not done this or that; perhaps if he taken some other action or no action at all; perhaps if he had done differently, he might only have lost his old mares?

'Well, everything gone now!' Blake said, with a tone of finality. He seemed at last to have talked himself out, and he cast a lingering gaze around the devastated site before he spoke again. 'And all for a couple of knackered old mares?' he added incredulously, shaking his head as if he could not believe the hand that fate had dealt him. 'Stubborn old work horses too, and devils as mounts. They'll not get far on them!' He shook his head again.

The three scouts exchanged meaningful glances.

'Would you know them again if you saw them?' Jack asked the man lightly.

It was obvious to Jack's companions exactly who he had in mind.

'You're damn right I would!' spat Blake with sudden vehemence.

Jack pulled out his 'wanted' poster, still smudged with the sooty amendments made in the Frederick saloon, and by now becoming rather crumpled. He straightened it out and held it up.

'That's one of 'em,' said Blake immediately he saw the face of Pettigrew staring out from the paper – with the supercilious twist of his lips that Jack had captured so well. He grabbed the poster from Jack's hands and read it.

'Pah! It'll not just be the reward I'll be looking for if I ever lay my hands upon them!' he said grimly.

Jack nodded his understanding. 'We think that they're headed for the military road,' he said, 'and thence westwards following it to New France where they are probably hoping to find sanctuary of a sort. However,' he added gruffly, 'we intend to catch them up and deal with them before they do, because I have some scores to settle too! You're welcome to join us if you want.'

Blake threw Jack a glance then swung a gloomy gaze across to the burial site of his lost wife and son, and while his eyes dallied there a moment, he sighed heavily. The glade, with its two lonely, earthen mounds, was now in deep shadow; only the tops of the surrounding trees still caught the amber light of a fast retreating sun.

'I can't leave them,' he said sadly, his voice on the brink of breaking, 'not just yet.'

If Pettigrew and Hayward thought that their ruthless plunder of the farm would set them up for their onward journey, they would soon learn otherwise. They neglected the welfare of their stolen horses from the beginning, treating them with the same callousness that they had demonstrated towards the farmer and his wife and son. But unlike the bereaved farmer who they had left for dead, their animals would soon get their own back for the uncaring disregard. The beasts had been reluctant conveyances from the start, but they had become more and more obstinate as the days had passed. Had their riders not been so preoccupied with their own welfare in the trying circumstances of expeditionary existence, they might have made their mounts more willing to cooperate by attending better to their needs. But heedless of the growing equine lethargy, the men had whipped and flogged the flagging beasts onwards even as they faltered - until eventually the animals rebelled. Left to graze on meagre pickings at the roadside while the two men dozed one afternoon, the mares were drawn by the burbling of a brook in a far off grassy glade and were never seen again. And worse yet, the beasts took with them all the spoils of the two men's pillaging that had been securely strapped upon their backs, leaving Pettigrew and Hayward in the virtual wilderness alone and once more empty-handed.

By this time, the two fugitives, still intent on reaching French territory as quickly as possible, had already intercepted the military road and had started along it. But as if transported by some rearward shift of time, they found themselves again destitute of resources, with none of their ill-gotten gains to relieve the hardships ahead. This was a bitter blow, for they were now in territory that was so sparsely populated that there were no nearby opportunities to recoup their losses by any means, fair or foul. Recognising the potential peril of the situation, the two men spent the remaining hours of light that day frantically hacking about the undergrowth in increasing desperation, searching for the wayward mounts and their precious loads. But their efforts came to no avail. If from time to time they caught a glimpse of some distant movement between the trees and set off determinedly in pursuit, their search always came to nought. For when they reached the spot - if they were ever sure of it in the confusion of the forest - an exasperating emptiness always greeted them. The mutely condescending trees seemed to mock their blundering human ways, tripping with their roots and whipping with their sharp branches. And perhaps the illusive animals too had joined in that arboreal conspiracy to punish the two men for their crime, running them in maddening circles unto disorientation and exhaustion?

Many would say that it was a pity that Pettigrew and Hayward did not meet their end in this way - literally run into the ground, or perhaps mauled by the black bears that inhabited the woods hereabouts. But on this occasion, such a just and convenient disposal of these two criminals was not to be. While Pettigrew, in his fury, would have chased every shadow until he dropped, Hayward kept his head. He soon saw the futility of their efforts and called the search off, eventually having to take his companion by the shoulders and shake him to force him to concede. Fortunately for the pair, Hayward, more careful with his orientation, had never lost track of direction, and he was thus was able to lead the pair out of the woody maze. But they emerged back onto the road tattered, torn and beaten as darkness fell.

That night was uncomfortably cold and hungry, and the days on foot that followed in that empty wilderness would become more uncomfortable and hungry yet. It was therefore just as well that Major William Green would come upon the two men some days later, for they were quickly becoming depleted.

Seated on his mount at the head of his battalion of the South Coast Fusiliers, Major Green was astonished to encounter two such apparently ill-prepared and dishevelled travellers on this lonely road. He first noticed them when still at some distance. They walked leadenly, with heads and shoulders bent as if lost in gloomy introspection, and seemed completely unaware of the marching phalanx approaching noisily from their rear. Indeed, it was not until the major's mount gave out a snort that awareness seemed suddenly to spring upon them like some wild thing from the forest. And with a startled glance over their shoulders, the two men leapt aside almost in sheer terror.

'You look like a couple of townsfolk lost on a Sunday stroll!' laughed the major derisively, pulling his horse off the road behind them so as to allow the oncoming battalion to continue past unimpeded.

Neither of the two men replied. They seemed too taken by the spectacle. A hundred and fifty redcoats bore down upon them, stamping up the dust. They marched, or rather strode with broken step on the uneven terrain, in rows of three abreast. On their shoulders were slung their muskets, across their chests, the uniformly crossed bandoliers and webbing straps for their backpacks, all meticulously white against the scarlet of their tunics. And bringing up the rear, a line of wagons and light artillery pieces, drawn by teams of heavy horses, threw out a constant din of clattering harnesses and grinding wheels. The major watched the pair's reaction to this show of military might with mild amusement as the long column of his soldiers tramped past to the driving beat of a marching drum; the pair might have been standing on the high street watching a military parade.

At length, an outrider with silver chevrons on his sleeve passed by, and the major called out to him amidst the clamour of pounding boots:

'Sergeant! Two more strays for you here. Get them into the wagon; they'll need a lift by the look of the state they're in!'

And the mounted soldier reined his horse back sharply and turned it to trot back along the column towards some open wagons in the rearguard.

.'Lost?' called down the major loftily from his saddle.

The two men seemed bemused or bewildered.

'Horses ran off,' answered the taller of the two.

Green raised a disdainful eyebrow.

'Careless if not negligent in this wilderness!' he said flatly. 'On your way to join up, I suppose?'

The major noticed the uncertain glance that passed between the two men before the same man eventually replied:

'Yes, indeed we hoped to, major.'

The major noted that the man had assessed his rank correctly, an unusual insight for these uninformed Americans, he thought. Evidently he must understand the significance of the officers' insignia about him: the silver gorget around his neck, the finer cut and cloth of his scarlet tunic with its dark blue facings, and the braid that edged his tricorn. Green cast an appraising eye over the two sorry specimens who stood before him and shook his head disparagingly. Both men's hair hung about their unshaven and grimy faces in tangled strands; their clothes, completely unsuitable for the rigours of living in the wild, had been torn and badly stained, their boots scuffed and caked in mud. They would need some cleaning up and feeding but they looked in sound enough condition to be conscripted.

'Get them aboard, sergeant;' he ordered as the NCO rode back alongside the open wagon, 'and sign them up once we reach Fort Loudoun. They'll do as orderlies.'

But as he watched the two men clamber into the wagon, something about the one to have spoken attracted his closer attention. The tall man looked vaguely familiar; something about the high forehead and set of the eyes reminded him of someone he had seen before, although he could not recall where or when.

The driver cracked his whip and the two large draught horses started forward in their harnesses with a rattle. The wagon jerked into motion and trundled on, leaving the major behind at the side of the road, still wondering.

Slumping onto the bed of straw that served to cushion the rough ride, Pettigrew and Hayward found themselves amongst the sick, the lame, and others in the wagon who looked as exhausted as they. The vehicle was evidently employed as the battalion's ambulant sickbay, and a foot-weary soldier lying opposite with his boots off offered the new arrivals his flask in a kindly gesture. Pettigrew seized the container and drank from it thirstily before handing it to his companion. Haywood took the flask and began to raise it to his mouth, but then shook it crossly, evidently finding it nearly empty. He flashed Pettigrew an accusing glance but drained the last dregs from it before throwing it aside in disgust.

'Hoped to join up, did we?' he muttered scornfully to his selfish companion under his breath, while wiping his mouth dry with the back of his hand. Another flask was passed back by a medical orderly stretching back from the driver's seat. Hayward took a longer draught.

'No choice in this wilderness,' replied Pettigrew, dropping his voice to a murmur. 'Besides it will get us where we want to go.'

If there had been an inkling of recognition in Major Green's mind, the same had not been true for Pettigrew. Nothing about the major had seemed familiar to him - not that he had taken the opportunity to study the officer's features at any length before. And yet the two men had once stood face to face - on the deck of the *Miranda* in the lower Chesapeake when Pettigrew and his henchmen had made their escape. It is unlikely that Pettigrew had forgotten this brief but highly charged encounter. But he failed to recognise the major nevertheless, most likely because Green had not then been wearing the silver wig and tricorn that now lent him such a haughty air.

In that earlier encounter, it had been an angry and forceful Major Green, with his dark hair tied back and his tunic undone, that had led his men onto the deck to confront Pettigrew and his gang as they stood at the ship's rail preparing to escape. Indeed, the major's bold manoeuvre might have been successful had it not been hindered by the scores of transportees recently transferred from the stranded *Rotterdam*. Moreover, panic had erupted amongst this frightened hoard when one of Pettigrew's knuckle-headed thugs let go a reckless shot, bringing down one of the major's subalterns. In the ensuing mayhem, Pettigrew's escaping cohort had slipped over the side into the waiting boat and made off, protected from the major's musket men by the doomed father-and-son hostages used as human shields.

But not connecting that event with the silver-wigged officer who had rescued him from the wilderness, Pettigrew now lay back in the wagon unconcerned. And while he quietly contemplated how he might exploit this unexpected opportunity to further his own ends, it did not enter his mind that the seeds of his discovery had already been sown.

Chapter Fifteen

'I just cannot bring myself to believe that those two could have committed such an atrocity,' said Sanderson as the threesome left the dell behind, once more travelling northwards towards the military road.

'Pettigrew is capable of anything,' returned Jack plainly. 'Perhaps he didn't start the fire; perhaps it was an accident; who knows? But even if it wasn't deliberate, Pettigrew would have exploited it to the full, believe me. And he wouldn't have given a toss for the consequences – as long as he got what he wanted!'

Jack turned in his seat to look back. The threesome had followed the road up a steep, curving gradient since departing the farmstead, and the ground now dropped off sharply to his right. Through a gap between the trees Jack caught an elevated view of the stricken site, not more than a quarter of a mile away as a crow might fly. He pulled the reins up sharply and brought the wagon to a halt before the view of the farm disappeared. He could see Blake stooped in his kitchen garden, where he must have returned after seeing the three men off some ten minutes before. Jack put his finger and thumb between his lips and gave out a shrill, piercing whistle. It was a skill that he could not remember using since childhood and was surprised that it was still so effective. The distant figure straightened at once and looked about, catching sight of the wagon and its outrider straight away (he could hardly have missed Sanderson's conspicuous white mount). He raised his arm in farewell and Jack returned the gesture, standing in his seat. In the few hours that they had spent together around the cooking fire the previous evening, and again over a shared breakfast before leaving, he had grown to like Jeremiah Blake. He felt a certain kinship with the man. Jack judged that they were probably of similar age, and like Blake, he had had his tragedies too, the most recent, not at all dissimilar. Jack also recognised in Blake the same resilient spirit. No doubt the horror of the night of Pettigrew and Hayward's visitation would leave deep and lasting wounds, but Jack was certain that Blake's spirit would rise again and be stronger for it. He would soon find the strength to make a fresh start, Jack reckoned; he had his kitchen garden and his poultry to sustain him, which thankfully had survived the fire - and the donated tools and supplies from the wagon's inventory would help too. Jack raised an arm in a final salute then cracked the reins to start the wagon off. He thought that he would never see the man again.

Colonel Sanderson had been in a pensive mood ever since arriving at the burnt-out farmstead, and even now, walking his horse alongside the lumbering wagon, he still seemed rather thoughtful.

'Well, whether they started the fire deliberately or not, Jack,' he replied (using Jack's Christian name for the first time), 'I hold them entirely responsible for the tragedy that followed. Anyone with an ounce of humanity would not have left those people in the cabin with a fire raging a stone's throw away. It's almost as if they wanted them all dead - yet I find that hard to believe. What had those people done to harm them after all?'

'Pure spite or vindictiveness!' offered Jack tautly. 'Or maybe just outright indifference. It doesn't surprise me at all. I've begun to believe that the devil inhabits Pettigrew's soul – and Hayward is his new disciple.'

'These men,' added Sergeant Schluntz disgustedly, 'we must make it our business that they pay for this.'

Jack's hatred for Pettigrew was rooted in the former ship owner's control of a corrupt customs cell in Weymouth that had made Jack the scapegoat for the murder of Captain Middleton - the murder for which Jack had been transported and exiled. Although Pettigrew had cleverly avoided direct involvement in this and other crimes that he had masterminded, Jack already blamed him for the death on the transport ship of his first-betrothed, Elizabeth, who had been transported too and had perished on that awful voyage. He also regarded Pettigrew's sinister influence as ultimately responsible for the cruel death of Ben Proctor, Jack's young apprentice, and for his father's later suicide. And now, these latest in the trail of death that Pettigrew had left in his wake since first escaping from the *Rotterdam*, had enraged Jack even more. Until now it had been a personal crusade to bring to justice those perpetrators of evil that seemed to have stalked him since the beginning of his quest for retribution – Smyke, Pettigrew, and Judd in particular (Hayward's had been a lesser crime). With Smyke already hanged and the escaped Judd now reportedly dead, only Pettigrew (and his new prodigy, Hayward) remained to be dealt with. It was a mission which some might see as a revengeful obsession, but for Jack it was a sacred commitment to all those who had suffered under Pettigrew's cold hand. Now, however, he seemed no longer to be alone in his crusade: Schluntz and Sanderson had witnessed the aftermath of Pettigrew's latest crime, and it had apparently deeply angered them. The names of Jeremiah Blake's wife and son could now be added to Jack's crusading banner, and his companions were now rallying to it. It lent their joint mission added fervour.

By the middle of the following day, the three men had reached Brigadier General Forbes' new thoroughfare and had started along it; and a day later they arrived within sight of the first of the military fortifications erected by his vanguard for re-supply and defence. The site had been formed in a shallow, stream-fed depression by clear-felling several dozen acres of virgin forest, and it was thus well sheltered by surrounding trees. The perimeter of the site was still littered with tree stumps and other woody debris, but the large central area was already laid out in some order. Dominating the site, situated on a low hillock that rose on the far side of the stream, a square stockade with ramparts had been built from solid tree trunks, all marshalled shoulder to shoulder in a row and sharpened to a point. A Union flag flew proudly above the stockade's main gate, which was wide open, and through it, several log-built buildings could be seen inside. Beside the most prominent of these, a number of white-distempered flagpoles stood in a cluster, all proudly flying different regimental colours.

'That's the headquarters,' said Sanderson superfluously, for it was quite obvious to any observer that the stockade would be the administrative hub of all the activity now taking place around it. Outside its tall, forbidding timbers, lines of canvas ridge-tents radiated like the spokes of a wheel, each line identified with a different pennant.

'British troops,' said Sanderson again unnecessarily, for it was apparent from the sea of scarlet-clad troops taking their ease amongst the tents and cooking fires that they could be none other than a contingent of Brigadier Forbes' amassing army. Jack pulled the wagon to a halt to marvel at the splendid scene of military might laid out before him, a grand, impressive sight that took him by surprise, even after all the talk of war and his own involvement in the preparations for it. Around the array of tents, a vast caravan of laden wagons had been drawn up into a defensive circle. Amongst these transports, a score of wheeled cannon could be seen, their muzzles, bound in oiled canvas, protruding here and there like heads keeping watch. Amongst the several hundred uniformed men that moved about within Jack's view, there were some dressed in hide clothing, like that adopted by Sir Michael's militia, and other men of a swarthy complexion, with beads around their necks and feathers in their jet-black hair. He flashed an enquiring look at Schluntz.

'Scouts and Indians,' returned the sergeant. 'Hired by the British – Forbes is coming better prepared than Braddock ever was. I'll wager he'll not make the same mistakes – see how they build these defences now along their route - and they take more heed of those who know this land well.'

Jack had never set eyes upon Native Americans before. Although he had once, as a boy, seen caricatures of American Indians in an English periodical displayed in a Portland shop window, he now realised such depictions, etched in black and white, could never do their colourful subjects justice. He could not seem to drag his eyes away from these extraordinary figures; he found himself studying them closely. Some were clad like himself and his companions in the uniform of a scout, but others were scantily dressed and garishly ornamented and tattooed, with chests, arms and legs quite bare, even in the cooling air of autumn. Colourful indeed, he thought.

Schluntz caught his gaze.

'Can't trust them,' the sergeant said flatly. 'They'll switch sides if and when it suits them. The British will have to work hard to keep their loyalty – the Indians have reason to be cautious with their alliances.'

'Hmmm. And so do we,' added the colonel, petulantly. 'Anyway,' he said, gathering up his reins, 'I had better ride down to introduce myself to the British commander and see what I can find out about Sir Michael's progress. We'll camp here tonight, then press on first thing tomorrow. But wait here until I'm back - I'll find out where they want us to put the wagon before you take it in.'

And with that, he rode off, leaving Jack and Sergeant Schluntz still sitting on the wagon's driving seat.

'Maybe not such a bad chap?' offered Jack as a testimonial to the retreating rider on his white charger.

Schluntz smiled ruefully as he flicked his shaven head dismissively.

'Doesn't trust us yet though!' he said, watching the diminishing figure. 'He's taken the saddlebags with him. Look!' he said pointing. 'Never lets them out of his sight!'

Jack felt rather let down by Sanderson's mistrust. With the recent distractions of the burnt-down farmstead, he had quite forgotten the money being conveyed to Sir Michael to fund his continuing mission. But at least he had been relieved of the responsibility for it, he thought, as he returned his gaze to the military panoply lit up before him in the afternoon sunshine.

It was indeed a spectacle, and it seized his interest like a small boy at the circus for the first time. The clearing was roughly circular, and bordered by mixed woodland, the conifers standing tall and dark amongst the reds, yellows, and golds of their broad-leafed neighbours, already turning their autumn hues. The road continued past the camp and disappeared over a low ridge beyond, through a narrow opening cut cleanly through the trees as if with surgical precision. In the gap, distantly above the tree line beyond, several ridges of the Appalachian mountains rose up in succession like ocean waves. Nearer to, the high ridges looked dark and brooding, further away, a hazy blue. The route ahead would be hard going sure enough, Jack thought, as he mused idly that somewhere in that foreboding terrain, Sir Michael's militia and countless other units of Brigadier Forbes' army would already be winding their way towards the Ohio valley.

In that vast and seemingly impenetrable forest, it was difficult to imagine war being waged, let alone won. Yet here he was, supposedly a part of it! Still questioning of its nature and fiercely independent of mind, he somehow knew that he would not resist the call to arms if and when it came. And like all those distant, disparate figures marching on before him in that woody wilderness, he would pick up his musket and shoulder his pack and follow orders, and march inexorably onwards until battle was joined. There was something both glorious and deeply troubling about man's willingness to engage in such endeavours – as miniature, individually dispensable components of a vast fighting machine – a machine steered by erratic political forces, and fuelled, as likely as not, by acquisitive self interest. Jack wondered at the scale of it all.

His eye was drawn eventually to the far end of the encampment, near the road where some ordered movement seemed to be taking place. Uniformed men were forming up in ranks as a bugle called. A few flags were raised amongst the gathering throng, but in the shelter of the trees, they hung limply. Smoke from dying campfires lingered in the still air as packs and muskets were hefted up and shouldered. The leading phalanxes wore the red tunics of a British regiment, but forming up behind were some ranks of green-uniformed men, American platoons, Jack thought, and others in looser ranks: scouts, Indians, and plain-clothed men in varied dress and headgear. Seated in the wagons that trailed the column, a few women, wives and helpers, could also be seen.

The sound of beating drums reached his ears as Jack watched the ranks turn into line and march off, followed by its rearguard of vehicles and artillery pieces. The phalanx receded slowly, striding into the distance to the fading sound of drumbeat, passing through a gap in the trees and over the ridge, until they had disappeared from sight. At that distance, it would have been impossible for Jack to recognise his former travelling companion on the *Miranda*, Major William Green, leading his battalion out on horseback. Nor could he have guessed that amongst the rag-tag tail of civilian orderlies that brought up the rear were the very two men that he sought.

***

Judd brought his strolling mount to a halt as he came upon the burnt-out wreckage of the farmstead on the road northwards out of Frederick. He did not linger there long for he was eager not to lose time in catching up Jack Easton and his companions who he knew from his enquiries could not now be far ahead. He saw the farmer across the clearing in his kitchen garden, working as if oblivious to the large piles of smouldering ash that littered the site. The man seemed quite distracted; he worked with an intensity that seemed almost fervent. Judd shouted to him through the thin smoky haze that seemed trapped by the surrounding trees. Had the man seen a wagon pass by, he asked - driven by two militia scouts? The farmer stopped his frantic hoeing and looked up, apparently startled by the unexpected intrusion to his solitude. But he did not reply. Instead he reached for his musket, propped up on a fence nearby, and brought it across his chest, his right hand reaching for the trigger guard. Judd raised a placating hand and asked again – this time trying to appease the man by lifting his hat and offering a friendly smile. But the man simply stood there staring back, a wary look coming to his face as he cocked his weapon.

Judd decided to move on, leaving the farmstead quickly behind, and pressed northwards, resting himself and his horse for as little as seemed sustainable so as to close upon Easton's convoy before it got too far west. He plodded on at the one speed his mount would go, hour by hour, in daylight and by the moon's light when it lit the way, until eventually he too joined the military road and turned along it.

He paused for rest at noon the following day, filling his canteen from a clear stream by the roadside. In his calculations of the relative distances

151

covered since Frederick, Judd guessed that even at his mount's unhurried pace, he would steadily have closed the gap. As he sipped the fresh water, he knew that he could not now be far behind. And so, when he soon after spotted a stationary wagon on the skyline about a mile ahead, he was quite hopeful that he had finally caught up. He closed the distance quietly at a steady walking pace and brought his mount eventually into the bushes about half a mile short. From there, Judd could make out two figures sitting on the driving seat, looking as if they were watching something as yet out of his sight beyond the ridge. He was still too distant to be sure of the identity of the two men, although he could see that they were both dressed as scouts. This was enough for Judd; he convinced himself immediately that one of the seated figures must be Jack Easton, and moreover, that somewhere in that laden wagon would be the saddlebags that he coveted. Judd could not help smiling smugly to himself. His patience had paid off. The money would soon again be his, put to good use buying him the new life and freedoms which Easton's meddling interventions had so far denied him. And he found himself relishing the prospect too of visiting his vengeance upon the man who had made necessary all the discomfort and sacrifice of the journey. No one could be allowed to cause him so much trouble, Judd resolved grimly, without paying dearly for it.

From his enquiries in Frederick, however, Judd had learned that Jack and his shaven-headed companion had been joined by a third member of the militia who had been seen leading the pair out of town mounted upon a conspicuous white mare. He was puzzled, therefore, not to see the reported outrider accompanying the wagon ahead. But as he continued to watch from his hiding place, he saw a rider on a white mount approaching the wagon from the other side of the ridge. If there had been any residual doubt in Judd's mind of the group's identity, this dispelled it at once, and so he sat back in his saddle and waited for the group to move on, soon disappearing from his view beyond the crest of the rise.

With his quarry so close, Judd could now afford to take his time, and so as not to come too close, he allowed some minutes to pass before following. Judd expected to regain sight of the wagon and its outrider on reaching the higher ground, and had the intention thereafter to trail it at a safe distance until nightfall when his chance to get closer might come. He was therefore somewhat taken aback as he topped the crest to catch sight of the military encampment revealed suddenly to his view. Moreover, the wagon that he had followed was now lost amongst the scores of other vehicles lined up at the camp's perimeter. Furthermore, the white charger that might have been a beacon signalling the group's location was already in the corral, cavorting friskily with a dozen other unfettered mounts. A sudden pang of irritation overtook Judd as he searched the busy scene for sight of those he followed, who he assumed must now be somewhere amongst the lines. But eventually he spied three scouts walking purposefully along a row of tents at the far end of the encampment. There was no doubt in Judd's mind that these three were the militiamen he sought - they had evidently been allocated billets for the night and were now taking up occupation. By this time, daylight was beginning to wane, but in the fading light he watched closely as the men sought out and entered their tents. All three carried travelling bags, but Judd's sharp eyes soon picked out the one amongst them who also had slung over his shoulder a pair of saddlebags.

'Got you, my little beauty!' he muttered under his breath.

'Right, here's where we are - Fort Loudoun…um, here,' said Sanderson prodding his finger at the map, held flat on the earthen floor of his tent by various items from his bag. Jack and Schluntz leaned forward to inspect the identified location; in the gloomy lantern light it was a strain to see what the lieutenant colonel was pointing at. The lantern's flame had drawn in through the open flap a small collection of moths and other more hostile insects that now orbited the hanging light in a sort of frenzy. Outside, but for a half moon that slipped silently in and out of the passing clouds, it was already quite dark. The embers of the cooking fire still glowed dimly; it had served its purpose. The air had grown cold at sunset, and Schluntz had taken charge of domestic duties immediately to cook up something hot to eat. He had proved himself adept in open-air culinary arts (so adept indeed that Jack had learned not to interfere, while Sanderson had not even tried), and the threesome had enjoyed a wild turkey from the sergeant's hunting bag pot-roasted with squash and forest herbs 'borrowed' from the fort's kitchen. It was after the meal that Jack and Sergeant Schluntz had been summoned inside Sanderson's tent for a briefing.

'The commandant has brought me up to date with the army's progress and sketched this map for me. So that's Fort Loudoun, and here's Fort Bedford where we're headed,' he said, running his finger along a wiggly line that wound its way first northwards then westwards across the parchment. 'At our current rate of travel, it'll take us about three or four days to get there. I'm told that your friend, Major Green, set off only this afternoon with his battalion, Jack. And Sir Michael and our militia left soon after and so will not be far behind; we've become the second battalion (volunteers), by the way. Good news, I think!'

'We watched a unit departing this afternoon, sir,' offered Jack, 'while we were waiting for you on the ridge. About a hundred and fifty men, we counted – they mustered in front of these very tents before they marched out - could have been Major Green's battalion, I suppose.'

'Yes, that was almost certainly them,' confirmed Sanderson, 'I thought about joining them, but we'll catch them up soon enough. Besides, the adjutant offered us these tents for the night – and I thought it might save us some effort unpacking all our kit. May as well take advantage of the system since we're officially part of Forbes' army now, not just some back-country volunteers,' he said, puffing himself up grandly. 'Fort Loudoun is serving as a transit camp and supply depot; all the regiments will pass through and replenish here en route to the front.' He dropped his voice, his tone suddenly becoming conspiratorial as if divulging privileged information. 'Forbes seems to be driving a new road westward from Fort Bedford rather than cutting south to Braddock's old Virginian route from Fort Cumberland - if he does, it'll be shorter and more direct. Easier for us! The new road's an old fur-traders' route apparently. It's being widened and beefed, up of course to take upwards of five thousand men, plus all their weapons, supplies, and so on – and that's one hell of a lot to move through all that virgin wilderness!'

'Hmmm! I kind of guessed he might do that,' chipped in Schluntz, a cynical veteran of earlier campaigns. 'And let's hope he does – less distance for us to slog our guts out, as you say. Anyway, I'd say it's also the best line of attack, even though it'll be more effort to make it useable. If he does go that way, it'll please the Pennsylvanians too! The road's bound to become a prime settlement route westwards and extend Pennsylvania rather than Virginia. That's why there's a strong Virginian lobby against it; they'd rather have Forbes use Braddock's old southern route through Virginia instead.'

Jack looked puzzled.

Schluntz rubbed his thumb and forefinger together in the air. 'Whoever gets the road stands to make big profits selling the new land for settlement,' he said cynically. 'In Forbes, it seems at last that we might have a British commander who doesn't pander to the Virginian gentry.'

'Quite,' said Sanderson, frowning. (Jack guessed that the colonel was rather put out to have had his sergeant make such an astute analysis – especially since, as a plantation owner himself, the lieutenant colonel might well have sided with his Virginian neighbours in looking for advantage from the war.) 'Well,' he continued rather shortly, 'I think that'll do for now. We'll make an early start tomorrow morning, so you two had better turn in. I've got to write up some notes before I do,' he said, importantly, ' so if you'll excuse me, gentlemen, I'll wish you good night.'

He picked up the map and began to study it. 'Oh, and Sergeant Schluntz,' he added as the two struggled to their feet, '- get the fire going at first light would you, and put some water on for my morning shave.'

***

From the ridge overlooking the encampment, Judd had watched the three scouts enter their tents in the failing light, and had smiled wryly on noting their disposition. Ever since setting out on his pursuit, he had ruminated cruelly on the pleasing ways he might finish off Jack Easton. Indeed, apart from fantasising about how he might spend the money he expected to find in Easton's saddlebags, he had thought of little else. Now, with the opportunity so readily presented to satisfy both desires, it seemed at last his chance had come. And the plan that formed quickly in his mind was nothing if not brutally uncomplicated: having seen how the three men had divided, he would enter Easton's tent, slit his throat while he slept, and make off with the money he so coveted. It should be said here that while Judd had never slit anyone's throat before, he could at least imagine doing it and the thought of it did not frighten him. In fact, he almost relished the act. In some perverted way, he saw killing Easton as a trial, a necessary ritual by which he must prove himself - although he never asked to whom he needed to make this demonstration in order to gain his spurs, so to speak. He would not recognise that it was merely obsession that now drove him, nor that deluded reason would be his own self-serving judge. But to pass the test with honour, he must do it quickly and without passion. And if he accomplished it in this manner, it would be the badge of honour that marked his transition from apprentice to master. If he had been outside the law until now, he told himself grandly, this act would put him above it; it would free him from the constraints that hemmed most ordinary people in, constraints that made them all slaves. Yes, he reflected, killing Jack Easton would be his liberation. And with this ungodly notion in his mind, he rehearsed the act coolly, over and over in his mind like some surgical procedure, as he made his way around the camp's perimeter, hidden by the surrounding trees.

It was shortly after midnight that Judd was in position at the forest edge, some twenty paces short of his intended victim's tent, and he concealed himself and settled down to wait until the camp fell completely quiet. Only then would he make his move.

A lucky gust of wind in the treetops rattled brittle leaves as Judd's sharp knife pierced the soft canvas of the tent and drew its slow incision downwards until long enough for him to enter. The half-moon's light barely penetrated the tent's interior, but in the centre of the floor he could see the dark shape of a sleeping form, covered in a blanket. He tiptoed closer, hearing the steady rhythm of slumbered breathing, and in the faint light he saw the dark hair of his victim's protruding head, the man's face buried in a pillow of folded clothes. 'Easton sleeps on his front,' Judd supposed, 'good - it will make it easier!'

For a while, Judd gazed down at the form, letting his hatred for Easton brew a little longer while savouring the moment of his coming triumph. Absent-mindedly, he ran his thumb across the blade of his knife, gripped in his right hand ready for the intended action. It would cut cleanly and swiftly, he thought distractedly. But then a somnambulant snort from the sleeping man startled him almost out of his skin. His heart leapt into his throat in sudden fear of imminent discovery and, remembering his mantra, he did not allow himself to hesitate further. He would not fumble either, for he knew he would only get one chance. Bending over, Judd reached out to the recumbent form and grabbed a fistful of hair, his heart thumping in his chest, his breathing stilled in anticipation. And yanking up the sleeping head, he drew his blade across the exposed throat in one quick and deadly motion.

There was no cry, no scream of agony – just the spluttering exhalation of the dead man's last breath. The act had been just as Judd imagined, and a rush of blessed ecstasy filled his veins as the body went into spasm beneath him before falling completely limp. And he stood astride the lifeless form for several long, delicious seconds longer, thrilling to the moment of his victory, his hands bathed in the warm wetness of his victim's blood. It was the baptism of the devil.

The saddlebags were easy to find. And with them now once again draped over his shoulder, Judd left the tent as silently as he had entered, retracing his steps through the woods to his waiting horse. By dawn he was already well on the road back, flushed with a heady sense of self-congratulation. He had passed his test; he had proved himself the master, and he had taken his prize. And confident too that the hunter's body on the other side of the Chesapeake would have been taken for his own, he now felt absolutely free. With this ruse undiscovered, no one would connect him with the bloody corpse at Fort Loudoun. Jack Easton was dead in his tent; the way ahead was clear; no one would hound him now! And the fortune that he carried in his saddlebags, would buy him a passage on any ship from Philadelphia, which was where the military road would eventually lead him. The money would buy him back the good life that he had rightly earned – the life that Easton and Goddard had conspired to deny him.

'Just desserts!' he thought.

***

That same morning, Jack and Schluntz were also up and about in the grey light of the early dawn. Heavy dew had fallen, which quickly soaked their boots and leggings as they moved around the encampment in the wet grass. Their breathing steamed in the cold air as they coaxed the ashes of their cooking fire back to life using tinder from Schluntz's fire box - the woodman's friend as he described it - and twigs and timber brought in under canvas overnight to dry, as had been his habit. A modest fire was soon ablaze and water set to heat, the pair squatting before it to rub and warm their cold hands. On some sudden inspiration, the German scout then rose abruptly and disappeared into their tent, returning shortly with a small fabric bag and two beakers in his hand.

'Fancy a hot drink for a change?' he asked, waving the bag at Jack, '- before our leader emerges from his slumber and demands his breakfast on a tray?'

Taking a large pinch of what appeared to be shrivelled fragments of dark, dried leaves from the bag, he divided it into two roughly equal portions, which he placed in the two containers. 'I traded with some Indians for this – 'black drink' they call it.' He raised an ironic eyebrow. ' – made from roasted holly leaves,' he said, pouring hot water from the steaming pot into the mugs to make an infusion. 'Drink too much of it and it'll make you puke, but a mug in the morning will put more spring into your step than cider. Besides, we're running low on that.'

Elsewhere amongst the tented rows, scores of other men were bent upon their morning rituals too. Uniformed men hung about in clusters in several quarters of the clearing as the white smoke of their fires ascended into the still air, rising in thin columns until subsumed into the thin sheet of haze that hung over the awakening encampment like a shroud.

'D'you think we should wake him?' asked Jack eventually, as he tentatively sipped the bitter brew.

Schluntz cast his eye at the sky. 'Nearly sunrise, so I suppose we'd better,' he said, downing the last draught from his mug with a satisfied grunt. Above their heads, the thin mixture of mist and smoke, tinged by the rising sun, turned pink against the pale blue of the clear sky beyond. 'I'll get him,' he said eventually with a long-suffering look, tossing the bitty remnants from his infusion onto the fire. The embers popped and spat with the arrival of the soggy leaves. 'He likes having an NCO to order about,' he added with a wry grin; and he turned and walked the few paces to Sanderson's tent, lifted the flap and disappeared inside.

Jack meanwhile took the opportunity to get rid of the contents of his mug by tipping it away. The liquid had not been much to his taste, but he had sunk a good measure of it and it had made him feel a little giddy. He was attempting to analyse the brew's effect when Schluntz poked his head out from Sanderson's tent. His expression was grave.

'You'd better come, Jack,' he said evenly, and vanished back inside.

Jack followed his friend in with a rising sense of foreboding. The change from daylight to the gloom inside the colonel's tent was quite marked, and Jack's eyes took a moment to adjust. At first he could not make out quite what he saw, but he knew at once that some terrible calamity had occurred. The inside surface of the canvas walls was splattered all over with dark blotches, as if some coloured liquid had been sprayed around and left to run; he knew immediately that it was blood. His vision cleared a little, and in the centre of the tent, he now saw the colonel's body half-covered in a blanket that lay over him in some disorder, as if the man had thrashed about in his sleep. Jack joined Schluntz at the colonel's side, his hand going down upon the blanket to steady himself as he dropped to his knees. The cloth was cold and wet to his touch. Instinctively, he brought his hand up to his view.

'So much blood…' he said disbelievingly, as he let his appalled gaze wander.

'Throat's been cut,' said Schluntz, levelly. 'Whoever did this took the saddlebags and ransacked the colonel's things. His weapons have been taken too.'

Jack cast his eyes about. Articles from the colonel's bag lay strewn all over the earthen floor, and the saddlebags were nowhere to be seen.

'Who...,' he started to articulate a question, but then saw the long slit in the canvas of the tent wall. It had been so neatly cut that he had not noticed it when he had first entered.

Schluntz followed his friend's gaze. '...cut his way in while the colonel slept – he probably never woke,' Schluntz said, his face, deadpan. 'Ever seen a man with his throat cut before? There's always a lot of blood.'

Jack shook his head as he let his gaze settle upon the colonel's blood-splattered face and neck for the first time, having to overcome an instinctive reverence for the dead man's privacy that had inhibited a close inspection before. Sanderson's eyes stared unseeingly upwards, his throat a glistening and blackened gash that stretched almost from ear to ear. Several small flying insects crawled about the wound. Affronted by the sight, he waved them away, disgusted. Then, suddenly overcome, he felt the contents of his stomach lurch and bile begin to rise, the acid pushing up into his throat. It was as much as he could do to reach the open air before he bent double and threw up. His head was still spinning some minutes later when he felt Schluntz's hand upon his shoulder.

'That black stuff get to yah, eh?' said the sergeant, attempting some consoling humour that was the same colour as the bitter infusion they had recently imbibed. 'I'd better report this to the commandant.'

But Jack pulled himself up to his full height and grabbed his companion's arm just as he turned to go.

'Who could have done this?' he asked angrily. '- to slay a man in his sleep like that?' His face was as incredulous as it was intense. 'Was it the saddlebags that the murderer was after? If so, how could he have known how valuable they were? And why the butchery; he could have just slipped away with the bags while Sanderson still slept?'

Schluntz was silent for some seconds, deep in thought. At last he shook his head. 'Keine Ahnung,' he replied slowly, slipping into his native German tongue, before correcting himself: 'No idea, Jack. It just doesn't make sense. All I can think of is that it might have been a sneak Indian attack – Sanderson's tent was the last occupied in the line and thus the easiest to creep up upon without being seen. On the other hand, there was no scalping, and I'm pretty sure that any Indian raiding party would have taken that as their trophy - whether they were simply having a go at the white man or acting for the French. And they probably wouldn't have stopped there either! *We* would have been next in line!'

Both men pondered for a little longer in silence, both shaking their heads from time to time as if mentally considering then discounting possible scenarios.

'Looks more targeted to me,' said Jack at last. 'It's as if the colonel was a marked man. Perhaps someone spotted him when we arrived and had a score to settle?'

'Hmmm. Sounds more likely,' agreed Schluntz. 'Perhaps this sort of thing has happened before – let's go and report it and see what the commandant has to offer. If we can find the saddlebags or the money in the camp somewhere, the murderer won't be far away!'

But a full scale search of the entire encampment, carried out by the platoon commanders of all the units subsequently assembled for inspection, did *not* reveal the saddlebags, or the money, or any suspicious individuals - military, civilian, or Indian. Moreover, everyone who should have been at the role call conducted at the same time was identified as present.

The following day, a small military honour guard comprising the adjutant, the chaplain, and a few resident personnel administered Sanderson's burial. But, despite the inconsequential search for the perpetrator, no further investigations were proposed. There were insufficient resources, explained the camp adjutant, to devote more time to a single death when other matters pressed so heavily during mobilisation for war. The crime was therefore simply put aside as unsolved, and the business of the camp returned to normal as if nothing untoward had happened. This left Jack and Schluntz that evening feeling somehow cheated as they sat around their fire tending to their thoughts. Neither had any appetite, and both retired early to their tent fully clothed, with weapons at the ready in case of a repeat. And neither could sleep during the long night that followed; each rustle in the surrounding trees or crackle in the undergrowth, imagined as some stealthy approach, raised both men instantly to their feet to rush outside intent upon ambushing the illusory invaders. Jack could not shake the notion that the murderer still lurked nearby and might yet strike again. But in the stillness of the pale-lit night in which they carried out their fruitless searches, a half-moon's face shone down to mock them with its empty and unrevealing stare.

Chapter Sixteen

It was a wet and windy crossing from Princess Anne, and it was just as well that the sheriff had commandeered a vessel suitable for the fluky squalls and biting spindrift of a stormy Chesapeake. Ned's small skiff would have been harbour-bound for days waiting for a calmer sea. The little craft had been lashed down on the after-deck, for otherwise she would have been swept overboard as the forty-foot sloop cavorted her way through the racing combers in a gusty beam wind that threatened at any moment to broach her. Rose and her two companions had wedged themselves into the lee-side bunks of the cabin below, which bucked and rolled vertiginously as the sea and wind outside conspired. The Chesapeake is an inland sea, protected along its length to some small degree from the prevailing wind by the western shores. But the wind was southerly that day; and when a strong wind blows up the Chesapeake from the south, it is squeezed by the encroaching land and accelerated, thus harrying the trapped waters into ranks of breakers that flee northwards before it. The scurrying waves rushed and slammed the sloop's fine hull like wild beasts in a stampede, the wind pressing her tightly reefed mainsail to such an angle that the boom practically skimmed the waves and the gunwales were awash. Below, the planks and timbers of her hull groaned like an old woman with the ague.

With Rose now convinced that Judd was at large and, moreover, set upon revenge against her husband, time was now of the essence. And she had bullied and cajoled the sheriff and the sloop's skipper into setting off from Princess Anne despite the stormy skies and the cautious instincts that had railed against it. But wedged into the cavorting cabin with the roaring sea and howling wind assailing her senses, Rose was now not quite so sure that she had been wise to insist. The last time she had experienced such shuddering seas was aboard the *Rotterdam*, and the present discomfort brought back bitter memories of that awful voyage. Ned sat beside her, his broad face pale, his eyes closed as if he fought some inner battle of self-control. The sheriff, his tall, slim frame bent awkwardly into the bunk's leaning timbers, winced at every jolt. Through the open hatchway astern, Rose could see the skipper at the wheel, dressed in his oilskins. He stood with his legs braced against the binnacle at such an odd angle that he seemed to be defying gravity; and as the dank sky swirled behind him he swayed with every lurch, spinning the wheel first one way then the other as his craft fought the waves. He seemed to be enjoying every minute, for his face was set into a grin, which became yet broader with every wave that broke across the deck, soaking him with salty spray. Rose thought that the sheriff must have paid him handsomely for his endeavour, for why else could he look so cheerful in such frightful conditions.

Thus it had continued for the six hours of the crossing, until the sandy headlands of the Virginian shore at last provided some protection in its lee. And with the change of heading to a more northerly course to run up the Potomac before a quartering wind, the craft returned to a more even keel. With this let-up from their purgatory, the three travellers emerged on deck in time to see the broad mouth of the St Mary's River estuary passing by to starboard. New Hope was within a few miles but, much as Rose yearned for its comforts, no time could be spared for the diversion. In her mind was the terrifying image of her husband pursued by Judd, set upon some evil mission of retribution. She had become possessed with the elemental notion that she must somehow reach Jack and warn him - if, God willing, it was not already too late!

Some seven hours later, just as the clearing sky began to fade to dusk, the sloop arrived at Neal's Landing. As the commercial and custom's port of entry for Charlestown and its hinterland, the landing lay a short distance down river from the town where the water was still deep enough for trans-Atlantic vessels to manoeuvre. A large, square-rigged ship already lay alongside the quay being loaded by its derricks. And it was as a consequence of this that Thomas Harding was already present there, engaged in his duty as shipping agent, checking the ship's manifest. This was a fortunate coincidence, for it spared the arriving threesome the journey to his office in the town a mile or so further on. Rose spotted him immediately amongst a consignment of tobacco hogsheads lined-up within a derrick's reach of the vessel's holds; he stood nearby watching, clip-board in hand, as a pair of the huge containers was hoisted aboard. She waited until the hogsheads had been lowered before hailing him. He came on board the sloop at once.

'Then your intuition was right,' said Harding evenly, having heard the details of the exhumation as conveyed so graphically by Rose and her two companions, 'And if you say that Judd followed you to Charlestown, then I believe you, Rose, since it is just the sort of thing a warped mind like his might be inclined to. I am sorry to have dismissed your concerns so lightly when you were last here.'

With these words, Harding reached across the narrow cabin table and squeezed Rose's hand lightly.

'And if Judd followed you here, then it is certain that he saw Jack and Sergeant Schluntz depart.' Harding paused here, tightened his lips and nodded sagely, as if coming to a distasteful conclusion. 'I think that we must assume, therefore, that he will have followed them as you suggest,' he went on, his expression becoming rather grave. 'Judd has already shown himself to be vindictive, and I am afraid that he is driven by an obsession to get his own back.'

The sheriff had remained mostly silent during the discourse so far, but now he leant forward to speak.

'I shall need to see the Charlestown sheriff as soon as possible, Mr Harding' he said with an air of authority. 'Perhaps you will be good enough to lead me to him. Clearly we have reached Charlestown before the arrival of my report - otherwise I'm sure that he would have made you aware of it by now. I must brief him on the situation quickly. We may need your help. What we do from now on becomes an official matter, of course, but at the very least we shall need to send word of our suspicions to our law enforcement colleagues along Mr Easton's route - so that they keep a look-out for this man Judd.'

Rose flashed a quick glance at Ned then engaged the sheriff with some diffidence. 'I - I had rather hoped that we might follow Jack's route ourselves, sheriff,' she said, somewhat taken aback.

'You must leave this to us now, Mrs Easton,' said the sheriff firmly. 'If our suspicions are correct, we are likely to be dealing with a potentially dangerous criminal who has killed before and seems set to kill again. This is no place for...' (the sheriff hesitated here) '...this is no place for a woman.'

Rose sat back more stunned than cowed by the sheriff's words. His dismissal was patronising to her gender as well as insulting to her personally – especially after all she had been through to prove her intuition correct. But she knew it would be futile to argue her point, and so held her tongue. She would make up her own mind about what best to do, she resolved. Of one thing, however, she was already quite certain: she would not sit idly by and wait for the blundering machinery of the law to grind into action. She had no faith in it at all. Indeed, she felt herself becoming quite angry as she recalled the dismal history of official ineptitude within her own experience as well as that similarly experienced by her husband. Now things seemed to have gone from bad to worse! Smyke, Pettigrew, Hayward, Judd! Only the first had yet been brought properly to justice – and then only by Jack's brave and tenacious efforts. Why were such criminals as these allowed to blight decent lives? Why, after their capture, at the cost almost of Jack's life indeed, had three of them been allowed to escape - on at least two separate occasions? Such incompetence! She fumed inwardly. Decent people should be given better protection than this! Rose attributed the entire catalogue of her husband's calamitous encounters with these evil men to constabulary inadequacy or ineptitude at best – some might call it negligence. And to this indictment, she added the sorry tale of her *own* capture, imprisonment, and transportation too. No, indeed! She was in no mood to sit idly by and let officialdom take over!

It was no coincidence that Captain Goddard arrived in Charlestown during the afternoon of the following day. News of the exhumation in Princess Anne had finally reached him in Annapolis, along with the uncomfortable deduction that Judd was probably still at large after all. The report also alluded to Rose's convictions on the matter of Judd's likely intention to follow her husband with malice in mind. And so, with his ship still under repair in dry dock for its damaged rudder, the captain had wasted no time in arranging transportation to the Tobacco River port. He found Ned outside the shipping office loading up Harding's four-wheeled chaise.

Rose was just coming out of the open double-doors onto the boardwalk cradling half a dozen muskets in her arms when she heard Ned call out a friendly greeting to someone approaching. She stopped and looked up to see a uniformed, merchant-marine officer striding across the quay, carrying a travelling bag. She guessed at once who the new arrival must be, having heard of him often from her husband; but since this was the first time that she had encountered the good captain, she thought an introduction proper (though in her crumpled riding habit, she felt far from presentable). She waited thus on the boardwalk expectantly, watching bemused as the two men greeted each other like old comrades, (as indeed they were from their shared adventure in recapturing the captain's hijacked ship) – a welcome that became somewhat prolonged by the captain's enquiries (and Ned's rambling answers) concerning the recent events. Ned, perhaps not schooled in the niceties of social etiquette, gave no thought to Rose, left standing behind him at the top of the steps, unannounced and still encumbered by the weapons in her arms. But soon growing tired of looking like the props assistant in a travelling theatre group, Rose decided she must assert her presence (and her pique). Descending the steps with an over-heavy tread, she deposited her burdens into the floor of the chaise with a sudden clatter, which, while startling Goddard, prompted Ned to remember his manners.

'At last we meet, Mrs Easton,' said Goddard, after Ned's hurried introduction. The captain's tone was sober, his face managing a quick smile, which just as quickly disappeared. 'Bad news, I hear,' he added. His uniform was not uncommon in the waterside setting of Charlestown quayside, but it was impressive nevertheless; he wore a peaked cap and a long, black barathea jacket emblazoned with gold bands upon his sleeves. 'Jack has talked about you so much that it seems I already know you.'

'Then won't you call me Rose, captain,' she answered brightly, extending her hand to be taken. 'Jack has spoken of you often; it is a pleasure to meet you. A pity that it is in such worrying circumstances.'

'Indeed,' returned Goddard, still grave. 'And if Judd *is* following Jack as was suggested in the sheriff's report, your husband needs to be told of it straight away. He and I share a compelling reason to be wary of this man and to see him apprehended, and I have come here at once to lend as much support as I am able to. What do we know of his movements; do we have any idea how far he is likely to be behind?'

Rose told Goddard what she now believed to be the clear fact of Judd's pursuit, adding some assumptions and calculations of her own as far as relative distances were concerned. She also told him of the disappointing news received from Mr Harding earlier in the day, following his second meeting with the two sheriffs. It seemed that the county administrators had decreed that jurisdiction for Judd's capture must be an individual county matter; in other words, that the Charles County and the Princess Anne lawmen had no authority to act outside their respective county boundaries. And since Judd was already likely to have reached Montgomery County, Frederick County, or even Pennsylvania by now, his apprehension would have to be left to those law enforcement authorities to act. The good officers of these counties would, of course, be put on alert and requested to remain vigilant. But put plainly, the Charlestown and Princess Anne sheriffs, helpful as they had both been so far, were now rendered completely impotent.

'Needless to say, I am furious about this,' said Rose. 'But I half suspected it! And I cannot trust my husband's fate to the competence of some distant and, as likely as not, disinterested sheriff in Frederick or Pennsylvania; nor can I sit here and allow more time to be squandered. Jack needs to be warned without delay; and therefore Ned and I intend to be his messengers (and pray God that it is not already too late)! Hence, as you see, Captain Goddard, we are preparing ourselves to depart on his trail before the day is out.'

'I wonder, Mrs Easton...' the captain began a little tentatively, correcting himself at once to use Rose's Christian name - as he had been invited to do. He started again: 'Rose, I am impressed that someone of the gentler sex has the courage and determination to go to Jack's immediate aid; it is a great credit to you, and no less than I expected from Jack's description of your qualities. But I wonder...I wonder if I could persuade you to leave this matter to Ned and me?'

Ned winced. He knew Goddard meant well, but his tone was patronising. He flashed his naval friend a warning look, for he knew Rose well enough to anticipate her reaction. But if his glance was noticed, the captain ignored it, or perhaps he did not understand the significance of it as he ploughed on undeterred.

'Ned and I have had dealings with Judd before and we both know what we are up against,' he said. 'He is a nasty character and will spare none of his venom just because you are a woman. And, moreover, the journey is likely to be long, uncomfortable and dangerous....'

Rose had managed to bottle her irritation until now, but this stretched her patience too far. She glared crossly and raised a hand in protest (while Ned shrank, knowing what was coming).

'I assure you, captain,' she bridled, 'that the journey can be no more uncomfortable, nor more dangerous than those that I have experienced before! And perhaps I should also remind you, as Jack will also have told you I'm sure, that I have already encountered Judd once before - you might, therefore, very well appreciate that I owe him some revenge of my own!' Rose was incensed that her gender seemed again to be an issue. 'So *no*, captain,' she flared, 'you *cannot* persuade me to leave this to you and Ned! But you may join us if you like, and you can start by helping us load up!' And with that, she turned on her heel and started back up the steps. 'This way please, gentlemen...time is our enemy, we must use every second! And I do hope, captain, that you will not find my determination too unbecoming of a lady!' she added with an ironic smile.

Thus was the relationship between Captain Goddard and the wife of his good friend, Jack Easton, cast. And from this early exchange, the captain learned that Rose Easton was a force to be reckoned with.

The three travellers were ready to set off for Georgetown later that afternoon with the chaise fully provisioned for an extended journey. The helpful offices of Thomas Harding, whose vehicle and pair had been gladly lent, had assisted their preparations. In addition to ample provisions (and a quantity of sailcloth and cord for the construction of a rudimentary shelter), weapons, powder and shot had been added to the inventory. A second pair of horses had been lent too - to accompany the chaise saddled and lightly loaded, to serve either as replacements in harness for the conveyance, or as spare mounts. Mr Harding had been nothing if not thorough in his assistance. Indeed, he might well have insisted on joining the group had he not thought himself a potential liability (his arm wound still caused him some discomfort and, as he admitted himself somewhat apologetically, he was not as young as he used to be).

'You've no need to apologise, Thomas,' Rose insisted as the party finally took their leave. 'You've helped us quite enough.' And with a warm embrace she climbed into the driving seat, forcing her two already seated companions to shunt over to make room.

'Oh, one last thing, Thomas.' She reached into the pocket of her cloak to pull out two envelopes. 'These letters: one to Jack's mother, the other to my dear parents in Portland,' she said, passing them into Harding's up-reaching hand, 'could you find a trustworthy captain to get them back to England for me?'

'Of course,' replied Harding, grateful to be of further service to a woman he had come to admire. 'The news won't be too worrying for them, I hope?'

'I have spared them the details! But they'll be delighted with our main news,' she said, grabbing the reins from Ned's hands and flapping them sharply, thus jolting the mares into forward motion with a clatter of chains and harnesses. 'I'm expecting again!' she called over her shoulder as the wagon took off, giving the agent no time to think of a reply before she was out of earshot. But when she looked back a few moments later, she saw his arm raised in farewell and a bemused expression upon his face. 'Portland,' she mused wistfully, handing the reins back to Ned absent-mindedly, her thoughts suddenly transported; 'it's not such a wild idea. Perhaps when this is all over, Jack and I *will* return!' And the prospect of a homecoming to her sunny island and her dear parents lifted her heart. If she could endure the journey ahead - if she could save Jack from Judd by her intervention - she resolved that she might very well make the homecoming her reward.

Goddard had travelled the journey to Georgetown by road once before when he and Jack, with others of *Miranda's* crew, had raced there on horseback to commandeer the schooner, *Warrior,* in pursuit of Pettigrew and his hijackers. With this geographical familiarity, navigation for the threesome proved not to be the problem it had been for Judd. With Goddard's guidance, the thirty or so miles to Georgetown were thus covered without mishap or error, and they arrived in the port at dusk. They wasted no time upon arrival either - immediate enquiries at the quayside shipping office confirmed quickly that Jack and Sergeant Schluntz had been seen setting off on the road to Frederick soon after disembarkation from the packet boat.

Driven by the urgency of the situation, Rose and her companions decided therefore not to break their journey overnight. They would drive on, taking turns on the reins as long as there remained enough moonlight to light the way, with two resting under furs in the rear of the chaise as well as the bumpy ride allowed. Progress was steady but painstakingly slow; the laden vehicle was ponderous, especially when the tree canopy or passing cloud obscured the moon's light, forcing the driver to slow to a cautious walking pace on the sometimes rutted, sometimes boggy, and often steeply undulating ground. Moreover, day or night, it was necessary from time to time to bring the vehicle to a complete stop to allow some respite from the jarring ride, or to change or rest the horses. But these pauses were minimal; in the minds of all three, it was a desperate race against time, a race to prevent some further atrocity occurring by Judd's malicious hand. Yet the incessant discomfort and snail-like advance denied any sense of a gallant chase that might otherwise have fuelled them. Without this heady stimulant coursing in their veins, frustration piled upon annoyance with each delay, to make the journey a test of patience and self-control.

Where speed failed, however, dogged endurance succeeded. For twenty of the twenty-four tedious hours that passed since the sun had set in Georgetown, the vehicle had been driven three miles per hour on average. And by twilight, therefore, the three travellers were already well north of Frederick, still making steady progress towards their next objective, the junction with the military road. They had not lingered in the town for long. Rose's urgent enquiries at the sheriff's office had confirmed her fears that news of Judd would be slow in spreading by official word of mouth, for the lawman was unaware of any hue and cry. He was sympathetic to her cause, naturally, but could not spare the resources to assist her while other priorities pressed. And neither could the sheriff offer information of her husband's passage through the town, which had not come to his notice. Had she pursued her enquiries elsewhere (for instance at the Town Hotel), she might have established that she was on the right track. But, guided by her intuition and Harding's sketch of Jack and Schluntz's intended route, she would not spare the time.

Hence it was that at dusk on the second day of their journey, cresting the brow of a shallow rise along the winding track, they saw Jeremiah Blake's farmstead in a clearing a mile or so ahead. At first sight, it offered some longed-for possibility of a comfortable night's rest.

The four horses had done sterling work between them, taking their turn in harness, plodding on without complaint, their sixteen hoof falls echoing in syncopation amongst the regiments of trees that were their constant companions. The steady, soporific beat had lulled the three travellers into a sort of mindless reverie that had helped the miles to pass. But now, seeing the farmstead ahead, they craned and peered inquisitively in the failing light, their tired eyes struggling to interpret what they saw. As they drew closer, something about the scene struck them all as distinctly odd. They exchanged glances and looked again. In the centre of the site, two conspicuous mounds appeared to radiate a strange, pale light. Soon, fenced enclosures and patches of cultivated ground could also be seen clearly, set around a large paddock; in the fading loom of the disappearing day the grass was already silvered with dew. But there were no cabins or barns as might have been expected. Of the few outbuildings standing here and there, the largest eventually drew their eyes. It stood at the edge of the clearing against the rim of surrounding trees; the addition of a tarpaulin lean-to erected at one side made it oddly proportioned. Before it, a small fire blazed, in the light of which a lone man could be seen sitting on a log. He sat before the flames strangely unmoving, despite the obvious rattle and clatter of their approach, which must have carried on the still evening air.

Arriving at the site's perimeter, the wagon was pulled off the road onto a rutted track that passed along the paddock fence and close to the two mounds. There was no doubt now what had occurred, and the three travellers gazed grimly at the ash piles as they passed by. Ahead, the man still sat by his fire. Even now he appeared unaware of their approach; and it seemed to Rose that he must be dozing or lost in thought, for out here, alone and vulnerable, any normal settler would have been on his feet and ready with his musket by now. Ned brought the wagon to a halt a mere twenty paces from him, yet he did not respond even when Rose shouted out a greeting. Goddard made a move to climb down, but Rose stilled him with a quick touch upon his sleeve.

'I'll go,' she said quietly, some instinct guiding her.

It was clear to her that something was terribly wrong; the grey shapes seen earlier from a distance were obviously the residues of two buildings that had been burnt to the ground. The pungent smell of charred wood lingered in the air. She alighted from the vehicle and braved an approach, a mood of gloomy apprehension gripping her almost immediately. It was the same dread gloom that she had felt amongst the charred remains of her own farmstead at New Hope.

Someone has died here, she sensed.

She came closer, stopping a few paces short, and waited for a response. The heat of the blaze warmed her face as she stood in silence, watching the man staring absently into the flames. Still, he did not appear to have noticed her. The man reminded her a little of her husband – dark wavy hair, same strong jaw - he might have been a similar age too - although the grime, the stubble, the lines on his forehead made him look older, careworn and tired. Rose waited a while longer, standing quietly, almost reverently opposite him, wondering if she should break the spell. The fire shifted, popped, and spat a stream of sparks into the air, yet still he did not stir. And then some inner sense prompted her.

'I'm sorry for your loss,' she murmured softly.

The man raised his gaze, his eyes focussing at once at Rose's kindly face glowing in the light from the fire. He sighed heavily.

'What's done is done,' he replied in a voice that was as resigned as it was empty.

'Can we help you?' Rose asked simply, her voice still soft and tentative. 'Perhaps you will let us share your fire tonight – and you can share our supper. Whatever has happened here will not be repaired by starvation!'

The man gave out a little grunt, half amused, half reconciled to his lot.

'Aye,' he agreed. 'True enough!'

'What *did* happen here?' Rose persisted, sensing the man's willingness to engage.

She heard his sigh, but he offered no immediate reply. And while she waited in respectful silence she let her eyes wander. The oddly shaped building lay close behind: an old outhouse, Rose thought, extended by a framework of rough timbers, only partially clad in newly riven planks. A tarpaulin had been fastened over it with rope to form a temporary roof. The man had clearly started to rebuild a home for himself after what must have been a catastrophic fire. Several blackened pots and pans had been stacked in a pile outside an opening that was evidently us as a doorway. Behind the edifice, a thinning sliver of grey light had become a backdrop to the tall, dark conifers that spiked the western horizon. Above, the sky had already turned an inky black, peppered with stars in sparkling profusion. In the darkness that had so quickly descended, the fire's light had become a dome of warm amber that seemed all at once to enclose Rose and her new acquaintance in a private world, holding back the cool emptiness beyond. Then, over the man's shoulder, at the furthest edge of the fiery glow, something reflecting the firelight caught her eye. She lifted her gaze to focus upon it, and saw at once two crosses made of new, white wood, sticking up radiantly from earthen graves, one large with a smaller one right beside it.

'Oh, you poor man!' Rose sighed. It was a spontaneous outpouring of sympathy borne of her own bitter experience; and she went to him immediately and placed a comforting hand upon his shoulder.

'Poor indeed; and lonely too,' he replied in a strangely matter-of-fact voice while struggling to his feet. 'The good Lord sends these things to try us,' he said, coming to his full height and raising his eyes to look Rose squarely in the face. 'You are welcome to share my fire - in return for a share of your supper.' He smiled kindly. 'It's days since I last had a cooked meal and I suddenly have an appetite!' He glanced at the chaise, turned orange by the firelight. 'And I suppose,' he said, managing a hint of satire, 'that we had better invite your friends too – although they seem to have fallen fast asleep!'

Rose followed the man's gaze and smiled at the sight that met her eyes. Ned's sleeping form had fallen against the shoulder of his uniformed companion, while the captain himself snored loudly, head back and mouth agape. 'Yes,' she laughed, 'the lazy laggards! I'll put them to work on erecting our shelter for the night while I prepare something for us to eat. And then, sir, we'll have some ale!'

'Jeremiah Blake,' said the man, introducing himself, 'my name!' And he offered out his hand.

Rose's empathy with the stricken settler had warmed his heart, and her sympathy was soon rewarded. Over the meal, the settler told his visitors about the two intruders who had set fire to his farmstead with such tragic and devastating results. And he told them of the three other men, militia scouts, who had arrived a few days later: two driving a loaded wagon, the other riding a white mare. Mention of militia soldiers and a loaded vehicle made Rose sit up with special interest, for she thought immediately of Jack and Sergeant Schluntz. At first, however, Blake's talk of three men, rather than two, puzzled her.

'Did they tell you who they were?' she asked.

'The rider of the mare was a quiet one,' Blake replied, 'I don't recall what he called himself. Then there was the tall one with a German sounding name – spoke with a bit of an accent – Schlitz or Schluntz, I think his name was. The third was a kindly fellow – went by the name of Easton.'

Rose was delighted to hear this news, and showed it.

'My husband!' she announced proudly. 'We are trying to catch up with him – we believe that he may be in great danger. Are you sure that Easton was his name?'

'Definite about it, ma'am!' the settler confirmed. 'Good-looking fellah - brown, wavy hair, dark brown eyes – about the captain's height, I'd say. I remember him better because it was he who helped identify one of the intruders with a wanted poster he had on him. Said I'd get the reward if they ever caught up with him!'

Goddard suddenly sat up, looking most perplexed. 'Wait a minute! What are you saying?' he asked quickly, his tone almost incredulous. 'Was the intruder's name Pettigrew then?'

'That's him; and the other's name was Hayward, they told me - both criminals on the run - and the Pettigrew fellah wanted for murder, apparently,' Blake continued, his voice turning suddenly bitter. 'And if I ever see them again, I'll blow their bloody brains out - both of them!'

All three visitors now looked totally shocked, and no one spoke for a several racing heartbeats. It was not the settler's language that had offended them.

My God!' breathed Goddard and Ned at last, almost in unison.

'Jack's got them to contend with too!' breathed the captain to both his companions. 'What the devil are they doing this far west…' he wondered aloud. But before he could pursue this line of thought, the settler spoke again.

'And your friends were followed,' he said flatly.

This recaptured his visitors' attention straight away; and Blake then told them of the solitary rider, wearing hunting garb and a black, broad-brimmed hat, that had come along the road a few days after Jack and his companions had departed.

'He asked if I had seen the militia scouts pass by.'

'Did you tell him?' asked Goddard.

'I didn't like the look of him,' replied the settler. 'He was a sour-looking cur if I ever saw one…a nasty bit of work, I reckoned. Anyway, he got nothing from me.'

Goddard flashed a knowing glance at his companions.

'Judd!' he spat, without further explanation.

Chapter Seventeen

The death of Sanderson and the loss of Sir Michael's regimental funding had been a double blow for Jack Easton and Sergeant Schluntz, and both were initially at a loss as to what to do on either count. The unfruitful search of the camp the previous day had left them angry and frustrated. It had also left them with lingering doubts that the search had been sufficiently thorough. The perpetrator must surely have been someone within the camp, someone who had seen the three of them arrive on the eve of the killing, they argued - someone who, for reasons as yet not fully understood, had targeted the colonel and/or the money? But since the adjutant had firmly resisted their demands for a further and more painstaking investigation, they seemed to have come to a dead end. Moreover, time was running out fast; units were packing up and leaving for the front hour by hour, and any evidence that might have been revealed by further searching was thus more and more likely to have gone with them.

Sitting around their fire at the end of a day spent in frustrated and inconsequential investigations of their own, Jack and Schluntz returned to their debate. But somehow reason always faltered - nothing seemed to tie up, nothing they could imagine seemed to make any sense.

'Alright,' said Jack eventually. 'Since that line of enquiry doesn't seem to get us any further, let's try a different tack. We've ruled out an Indian attack so we're assuming that the murderer must have been someone who was here in the camp when we arrived – someone who knew Sanderson and who had a grudge...' Jack was recapping.

'Or someone who knew what the saddlebags contained,' interjected Schluntz, helpfully.

Jack nodded. 'Yes; or someone who knew what the saddlebags contained,' he repeated, his voice trailing off thoughtfully as he wrinkled his brow. 'But I have to say that I find it very difficult to believe that anyone here *could* have known that,' he objected. 'But assuming that was the case, and for the moment also accepting that the saddlebags or some other evidence would have been found if the murderer *had* remained within the camp, then...'

'Then, whoever was responsible must have left the camp...' concluded the sergeant.

'But the roll call did not reveal anyone missing,' cut in Jack, taking the next step in the argument. 'And again, let's assume that the roll call was done thoroughly enough to be certain of that.'

Schluntz looked thoughtful for a moment. 'So whoever it was, was not in the camp when we arrived,' he reasoned simply. 'In other words, he watched us arrive, crept in to do his deed, and then left with the saddlebags.'

'How likely is that?' asked Jack provocatively. '...that someone was watching us when we arrived? Someone who either had a grudge against Sanderson, or who knew about the money?'

'Highly unlikely, I'd say, Jack,' returned the sergeant.

'Hmmm, I agree,' replied Jack.

And both men fell into a slump - a pose that they had adopted several times before when they had tried, and failed, to reason out the detail of the crime – a pose that showed that logic had again defeated them.

For a time they seemed no closer to unravelling the mystery.

'Well,' said Jack at last, 'if we've already ruled out a random attack from outside the camp as improbable, that only leaves one possibility...'

'That we were followed,' said Schluntz, finishing Jack's sentence.

Jack nodded. 'That we were followed,' he echoed. 'By someone who had a grudge against Sanderson or who knew about the money and was set upon stealing it.'

'No one else knew about the money - and saddlebags are saddlebags,' said Schluntz plainly. 'It's not as if it was obvious that we were carrying money in them, is it?'

'Then someone must have seen us set out from Charlestown, someone who knew we carried money with us,' said Jack. 'And if it was not the money but Sanderson who was the target, someone must have followed us from Frederick where he joined us.'

'Both unlikely, Jack,' returned the sergeant, derisively. 'In Charlestown, only Mr Harding and his clerk knew about the money, and it's hardly likely it was either of them, is it? And Sanderson didn't spend enough time in Frederick to have made enemies, surely?'

Jack thought awhile then inclined his head. 'I suppose not,' he said sullenly.

'Unless he owed a gambling debt, perhaps?' responded Schluntz, not very convincingly.

And for a while, both fell into another pensive silence, both staring into the fire with blank looks upon their faces.

'Well,' ventured Jack eventually, 'if we take the only *real* evidence we have at face value – that both the search and the roll call proved negative – the logical conclusion is that someone *must* have followed us. And if someone *did* follow us, they would have headed back to where they came from: Charlestown or Frederick…where we might find them…' He was thinking aloud.

'Hmmm,' agreed the sergeant a little doubtfully, 'that would be a possible conclusion *if* we took the evidence, as you say, at face value.'

'Well, we don't seem to have much of a choice do we,' said Jack. 'We could continue on and catch up with the regiment… and incur Sir Michael's wrath when we arrived without his money…which I don't relish one little bit.'

Schluntz picked up Jack's drift immediately. 'Me neither; I don't fancy looking like some *Schulkind in der Ecke* - put in the corner for not doing his homework!'

'And we can't just hang around here waiting for something to turn up, can we?' said Jack.

Both men looked each other in the eye, each guessing what the other must be thinking.

'So that leaves us with just one option,' said Jack, confirming it.

'What about Pettigrew and Hayward?' asked Schluntz.

'They'll have to wait,' said Jack simply.

Another pause ensued while both men pondered.

'Well sergeant,' said Jack at last, caricaturing an officer's commanding tone, 'that's settled then - we have to go back! We have to get ourselves some decent horses and head back down the military road – all the way to Charlestown if we have to! We have to trust our instincts. And if they're right, we'll find Sanderson's killer – and the money!'

'Yes, sir, lieutenant!' agreed Schluntz, in a parody of deference.

The two men had thus come to the correct decision (at least as far of the direction of travel was concerned) - to go back along the military road in the hope of catching up the killer and dealing with him. After two bewildering and frustrating days of getting nowhere, both were glad to have some practical mission on which to focus. It suited both their temperaments: theorising and reasoning could only get a man so far; action was what was needed now! And if both men harboured a residual fear that they might be racing off on the wrong tack, they lost it in the heady anticipation of the chase to come. But it had still not entered either of their minds that Jack had been the target, nor that it was Judd that they would be following.

The quick eyes of a golden eagle, soaring in the updrafts of a standing wave high above the Appalachian ridges, spotted the pair of riders setting out from Fort Loudoun at sunrise the following day. It might have been the dust kicked up by cantering hooves that first drew its sharp glance. These riders rode in haste, and travelled eastwards too - unlike the many others often seen toiling in the opposite direction on this menacing intrusion into its once silent domain. That one of the riders rode a white horse had also caught its eye, but nothing yet detected in its eagle-eyed inspection had represented food. And so its search continued. The raptor's view encompassed a radius of over thirty miles in the transparent, cloudless sky of this new autumn morning. Below, a lush sylvan carpet stretched from horizon to horizon, its undulant contours regimented in roughly parallel ranks like the swell of an ocean swept before the prevailing wind. For the aerial migrant, the ridgelines marked an easy highway from north to south - along corridors of lifting air - to bear its long wings from the icy winds that blew when winter came, towards this temperate and more fruitful land that beckoned and enticed. The morning sun was already warm upon its beak, its low rays bathing the high ridges in pure amber and inching its vivid fingers into the dark valleys between. Viewed from above, the furrowed terrain was brushed by the sunny radiance into bright and dark bands, the pattern running as far as the eagle's searching eyes could see, like ribbons of varied colours ranging from deep purple to burnished gold. And creeping up the hillsides, turbid mists, stirred by warming solar rays, melted stealthily into the trees.

The predator searched for its breakfast, its eyes alert for any movement on the ground that might be prey. It scanned the glistening trails of water, the grassy tracks, the rocky outcrops, but nothing caught its eye. Except that on the yellow road that wound its way towards the rising sun, the two riders still cantered at a brisk pace, the dust still rising behind them like a cloud. If the bird had allowed its scan to trace the road's track eastwards into the far distance, its sharp eyes might have seen two thin plumes of smoke rising into the air.

Beneath the nearest of these dozed Judd, wrapped in his canvas, half in, half out of sleep, now supremely confident that all his trials were behind him and indulging himself in an extra hour of rest. Without rising, he had thrown a few more sticks upon the fire left smouldering overnight; they hissed and smoked but were not yet alight; he would use the fire later to warm his water.

Beneath the second smoking plume, some fifteen miles further east of the first, near the junction of the road north from Frederick and the new military highway, a four-wheeled chaise sat idle, its shaft and swingletree resting on the ground. On the rear seat of the vehicle, Ned Holder still slept, huddled under furs where he had lain since handing the reins to Captain Goddard in the middle of the night. Nearby, Rose and her naval companion squatted on a fallen tree trunk adjacent to the fire. While she idly stirred the contents of a blackened pot, half-buried in the embers, the four horses grazed contentedly at the full extents of their tethers.

'Soon time to go,' said Rose, leaving off her stirring and getting to her feet with a suddenly impatient air. 'We needed the break, captain, but we cannot give up any more time. I'm afraid we'll get no proper rest until we've finished what we started.' She glanced down to receive her companion's unenthusiastic nod. 'So you'd better wake Ned,' she went on, 'he'll want some of this hominy before it goes cold.'

'You're right, Rose, we should be on our way,' agreed the captain with a reluctant sigh. He struggled up from his haunches and stretched himself lazily. 'God, I'm stiff!' he groaned. 'We mustn't squander the time we've gained. Still, we've done well so far; we could be in Fort Loudoun in a few days and I'm sure we'll find Jack there safe and sound,' he added reassuringly. He picked up his cap and put it on. 'Judd won't attempt anything while there are others about,' he said, dusting down his crumpled uniform half-heartedly, as if he had given up on it. He sighed wearily. 'I'll get Ned to help me harness up the horses before you feed him.'

Since leaving the burnt-out farmstead, the threesome had not dared break their journey by more than absolutely necessary. And they had travelled day and night, driven by the urgency of their mission to spoil Judd's pursuit. At last they had reached the military road, and having pressed on so determinedly, they hoped by now to have closed the gap considerably. While this was certainly true, they could only estimate how far Judd or Jack would be ahead by making assumptions of their relative travelling speeds. Harding had provided them with a roughly sketched map, but there were so few navigational features marked upon it that it had been difficult to establish their rate of travel along the marked route.

Moreover, the gradients were now often bringing them to a crawl, the road sometimes climbing and twisting so tortuously in the increasingly mountainous terrain that the actual distance travelled in any day was hard to estimate.

Anticipating a journey into largely uncharted wilderness, Captain Goddard had packed his new octant, thinking that the instrument might prove a useful aid to navigation. And he was soon experimenting with it, using the technique required on land, when a distant terrestrial horizon could not be seen. It was a technique quite different to that employed on the deck of a ship, and one that he was keen to practice. At sea, with decent visibility, the elevations of heavenly bodies could be measured by reference to the real horizon, the circular intersection with the celestial sphere of the plane tangential to the earth at the position of the observer. On land, however, the real horizon was almost always obscured, and since Goddard's octant did not incorporate the innovative *artificial* horizon of newer models (the instrument had been passed on to Goddard by the retiring Captain Auld), some other method of determining the horizontal was required. The special technique entailed measuring the angle between the selected star and its own reflection in still (thus perfectly horizontal) water, and then bisecting the angle so acquired to obtain the star's elevation (from which latitude could then be derived). Goddard had taken to using a shallow cooking pan to contain the reflecting liquid and had taken elevations of Polaris as often as time had allowed, whenever the night sky was clear. The accurate vernier scale of the instrument's index arm allowed measurements of the star's elevation to be taken within one minute of arc, the equivalent of one nautical mile on the north-south scale. And with his two feet planted firmly on stable ground rather than on a tilting, rolling deck, his measurements had been remarkably consistent. He was so delighted with his results indeed that he could hardly contain his excitement; and with almost boyish enthusiasm, he soon cajoled an apprehensive Ned into giving the method a try. The big man had been very tentative, handling the instrument as if he were meddling in some black and dangerous art. And his clumsy fingers had trembled so much that the star's image had shot in and out of his eyepiece like some dancing will-o'-the-wisp.

Goddard had taken his sightings as the group had progressed northwards; and with the latitudes so obtained, he had refined the map's scale, establishing a reasonably accurate measure of distance covered each day. He'd been working on his measurements of the previous night while Ned slept.

With Ned soon awake and breakfasted and the horses back in harness, the journey continued. This time it was Rose's turn to slumber in the rear while Ned and Goddard occupied the driving seat. Ned held the reins.

'I've been working on these calculations, Ned,' said Goddard brightly.

Ned wrinkled his eyebrows apprehensively, but the captain was not to be put off.

'By my reckoning, we've been making a little short of twenty miles per day on average, he said. 'I know the gradients will get steeper and longer from now on as we start to cut through these passes, but I have made some adjustments for that.'

Ned nodded distractedly - his attention was more on the road than the captain's words.

'If my calculations are correct and this map of Harding's is anywhere near accurate,' Goddard continued, 'we'll be in Fort Loudoun inside forty-eight hours – that's assuming moonlight will let us drive through another night.'

Ned seemed suddenly interested - perhaps because the arrival at Fort Loudoun held the promise of a decent bed (a vain hope as it would turn out!).

'Then let's hope Jack and his friends are still there when we arrive,' he said, rather imagining that the fort would be a fortified sanctuary that Judd could not penetrate.

'Well, if my assumptions of their daily distances are correct, they'll have arrived a few days ago - and therefore they should have got there ahead of Judd – that is unless Judd rode through the night too, of course...'

'And if he did...' asked Ned. 'I mean, if Judd rode through the night, what then?'

'Well, I doubt that he could have ridden more than a few extra hours each day – he and his horse would have needed rest. And he's not able to split the driving like we've done, and doesn't have the spare horses to exchange either. Nevertheless, he could easily have caught up by now, so we'd better be prepared when we get there. When we find Jack, Judd will certainly not be far away, probably still waiting for his chance.'

Both men sat in thoughtful silence for a while as the chaise trundled on.

'Well if Judd caught Jack up on the road,' said Ned at last, 'let's hope Jack saw him coming up behind!'

'I'm afraid that his friend's white mare would probably have been a bit of a give-away, Ned – assuming someone told Judd about it somewhere along the route, which is pretty likely. He'd have spotted them ahead and kept out of sight. But even if Judd did catch up, I don't think that he'd risk going in guns blazing – not against three armed men. He'd wait until Jack was by himself before he tried anything, especially if he's got his eye on the money and wants to get away with it without leaving a trail.'

'Then we've got a chance of stopping him,' affirmed Ned.

'Oh yes,' replied Goddard, confidently. 'Of course, Jack won't know yet that Judd is still alive, let alone on his tail; but once we're able to warn him, the tables will be turned - especially with Sergeant Schluntz and this other officer with him. And as soon as Judd loses the advantage of surprise, he'll become the prey rather than the hunter!'

Thus were assumptions built upon assumptions and misleading conclusions drawn. Captain Goddard had allowed his logic and his clever calculations to become tainted by presumption and wishful thinking. Had he considered the possibility that Judd would commit his murderous act on the very night of Jack's arrival at Fort Loudoun, he might also have guessed that Judd would already be on his way back. Moreover, accepting this scenario even as a possibility, an estimation of the time it would take for Judd to retrace his steps might well have shown that an encounter could be imminent. As it was, Goddard had convinced himself (and Ned) that it would be two full days at least before they would need to place themselves on their guard. And so, while Rose still slumbered under furs in the rear of the chaise, neither he nor Ned would be prepared, either mentally or physically, for the confrontation that would face them a little later that morning.

Chapter Eighteen

The distant sound of wheels grating reached Judd's ears, and brought him immediately out of his reverie. He pulled up the reins sharply to bring his mount to a halt and sat listening for a while, eventually becoming sure that a vehicle approached from somewhere ahead, as yet out of sight. Surprisingly, it was the first he had encountered on this well-trodden strategic byway, and it made him immediately wary. The murder of Jack Easton was sure to have caused a major stir at Fort Loudoun, and it was very likely that a furore of enquiries and investigations there was still underway. The last thing he would want at this early stage of his escape was someone arriving at the Fort reporting a suspicious lone rider a day or so back along the road.

Luckily, the telltale sound of the approaching vehicle had carried on the breeze, for he still had time to get out of sight before it came into view. Thinking thus, he coaxed his horse off the road into the undergrowth, soon becoming all but invisible to outside inspection, yet still able to see sections of the road through gaps in his leafy cover. Here he found himself a level footing, but as he cast his gaze about, he saw that the ground fell away quite sharply to his right into what appeared to be a deepening and rocky ravine that swung away into the forest. Tracing its path as far as he was able to, between the obscuring trunks of forest trees, he saw in the middle distance, a stony promontory sticking out like a platform above a vertiginous drop. The platform seemed to mark the head of a narrow, steep-sided gully joining the ravine, and beside it, a torrent issued from a rocky stream that splattered onto boulders far below. He let his eyes follow the cascading water downwards as it fell through dark regiments of trees on either side, right to the bottom of the descent where he saw glints of reflected sunlight sparkling on water – a lake or river, he thought.

The approaching sound of wheels became suddenly sharper - gritty and hard-edged, like iron on stone - and to this had now been added the clip-clop sounds of hooves. From the number of footfalls, he guessed that there must be three or four horses accompanying the vehicle and was glad to have taken cover from such an apparently large group, possibly a small platoon of soldiers with a supply wagon. He craned in his saddle to get a view through a leafy gap and saw now that the vehicle had just rounded the bend – not the wagon and several riders that he had imagined, but a four-wheeled chaise and pair driven by two men, and trailing two extra horses behind. Judd watched as it came closer, needing to shift his eyes from gap to gap in order to keep the chaise in view.

Only gradually as the chaise neared did something about the drivers strike him as out of place. But when he realised what it was, it astonished him. One of the men was dressed in naval uniform, and even from a distance Judd recognised him as none other than Captain Goddard. It was almost beyond belief that Jack Easton's collaborator in his persecution should be delivered to him in this wilderness - with only his thick-set and ponderous-looking co-driver to protect him. Moreover, neither of them seemed armed nor even the slightest bit alert to danger! It took only a moment to convince himself that this was more than lucky happenstance. Retribution was meant to be, he thought. Fate had played its hand to allow Goddard to be dealt with too - just as his revenge on Easton had already been efficiently exacted. And surely it was also meant that a vehicle and spare horses had been offered for the taking too, for he was mightily fed up with the plodding mule he had commandeered from the hunter. Fortune shines upon the clever and quick-witted, he thought smugly, as he primed the touchholes of both his flintlocks and returned the pistols to his belt.

Judd emerged from the undergrowth as the chaise came within about thirty paces. It was not the impressive entrance onto the scene that he had first conjured in his mind - a sudden, dramatic burst from the trees like some highwayman that would have caused the approaching vehicle's horses to whinny and shy. No, Judd's entrance was somewhat more calculated and certainly less spectacular (if only because his mount was not exactly fleet of foot).

But to Ned Holder, once again driving the chaise while Goddard dozed, using Ned's right shoulder as a prop, the effect of Judd's unhurried, almost casual appearance from the gloomy fringes of the forest was ambiguous. The manner with which the rider brought his mount to a halt in the middle of the road ahead both alarmed and confused him at the same time. The rider seemed confident in his comportment, as if he already held some authority over the approaching vehicle, like a lawman might have appeared. Indeed the man remained motionless in his saddle even as the chaise grew nearer, as if to command it to stop. Yet there was something threatening about the figure too. His face was a dark mask in the shadow of his broad-brimmed hat, making him appear mysterious and sinister; and his rain cape was thrown back over his shoulders like folded wings, giving him such a demonic appearance that it might have been the harbinger of all things evil that stood so unyieldingly in the way. Suddenly frightened in his uncertainty, Ned nudged his dozing companion urgently as several conflicting thoughts raced through his mind: should he thrash the reins so as to rush the rider and force him off the road, he wondered, or should he pull up – perhaps to answer some legitimate enquiry – or even prepare himself for a fight? And in his indecision, he allowed the chaise to rumble on. But before he had resolved what best to do one way or the other, he felt Goddard stiffen, then reach behind the driving seat. Ned sensed that his companion must be trying to reach a weapon, or else alert Rose, who still slumbered under furs in the rear.

'Pull up, Ned!' whispered Goddard tersely, even as he still probed behind the seat.

Ned yanked back on the reins and the chaise came to a juddering halt.

The mysterious rider was now some ten paces ahead, still unmoving in his saddle.

'Need some help, mister,' called Ned. He tried to sound confident, but he could feel his heart pounding.

'Damn it! Can't reach a weapon,' growled Goddard under his breath. 'Let's hope it's not trouble!' Then, half turning his head so as to direct his voice behind, he whispered urgently: 'Rose, stay hidden! There's someone on the road ahead - don't know what his intentions are, but better be prepared for anything. If you can reach a pistol, it may come in handy!' He saw the fur stir and heard her acknowledging murmur.

The rider spurred his horse forward a few paces towards the waiting wagon, yet otherwise did not move in his saddle; his face was still shrouded in shadow so as to make it unrecognisable.

'What can we do for you, sir?' demanded Goddard civilly. He felt too vulnerable to be hostile and hoped that his instincts lied. But again there came no reply from the stranger who remained stationary in his saddle, appearing quietly to be studying the pair. It was quite unnerving.

'I don't like this, captain!' muttered Ned at last.

'Nor do I!' said Goddard in a decisive tone as he made to swing his legs over the side to descend.

But as he did so, the rider pulled a pistol quickly from his belt.

'I'll tell you when you can move, Captain Goddard!' he called as he levelled the weapon directly at the mariner. And with this, he took off his hat so that the high sun lit up his mean features – revealing an expression that was as smug as it was malicious.

'You!' Goddard spat. 'I should have known...'

'Yes, Captain,' interjected Judd calmly, 'so you should! But you didn't; and now I've got you – so I can repay you for all the trouble you have caused me.' He drew back the firing arm of his pistol with a click. 'Now, both of you raise your hands where I can see them!' he growled.

The two men did as they were told - but with obvious reluctance.

'Come on Judd,' pleaded Goddard, in a bid for time, 'that's all in the past now. You're making this a personal vendetta. You should have disappeared when you had the chance – and if you kill us you'll just be making more trouble for yourself!'

Judd laughed. 'You think so? I don't! I'm already a dead man - remember? It was *you* who left me dead on the beach! As far as the law is concerned, I probably don't exist!'

Goddard decided for the moment not to reveal that Judd's deception had been discovered. 'Well, even more reason not to lay another trail... there'd be a manhunt!'

Judd smirked. 'Just like there's a posse on my trail after your friend Jack Easton's had his throat slit at Fort Loudoun, you mean?' he replied deridingly.

'You liar!' Goddard spat, as his face flushed. He heard Rose's sharp intake of breath behind him.

But Judd simply patted the saddlebags that straddled his mount's rump and his smirk turned into a triumphant grin as both Ned and Goddard's eyes widened in alarm. Both recognised the bags instantly, and that they were now in Judd's possession lent an awful certainty to his claim.

'Now get down! Both of you!' Judd ordered in an oily tone, pulling his second pistol from his belt. 'And keep your hands where I can see them!'

Goddard and Ned exchanged anxious glances as they shifted to their respective ends of the driving seat. Both faces had turned quite pale now, but Goddard's had taken on the grim look of determination, his eyes already alert for possibilities of escape or counter-attack. He made himself look awkward as he turned to descend from the seat backwards, feeling with his leg for the ground as if it were a long reach. With a steadying arm on the seat covering his face, he took the chance of whispering a message to Rose, still hidden in the furs:

'Wait until his back's turned, Rose,' he said. 'You'll only get one chance, so make it count!' And with this, he feigned an awkward landing so as to finish up several paces from his side of the chaise. This split Judd's aim, his pistols forced to spread widely to cover both men at the same time. Goddard saw Judd's eyes flicking between the two and calculated the chances of reaching him before he could fire. He flashed another glance at his friend on the far side of the chaise. Ned returned it with a barely perceptible shake of his head. It was too risky, his eyes said; they would have to wait.

'Down on your knees!' ordered Judd sharply.

The two men complied, both lowering themselves awkwardly and with some trepidation. One of the harnessed horses shook its mane and snorted. The sudden tension in the air had spooked it. Another at the rear yanked back on its halter, jerking the vehicle rearwards a few inches – the brake had not been applied. The wheels ground the grit on the track.

'Now, flat on your faces!' Judd barked.

The two men did as they were bid, and once their cheeks rested in the dust, Judd took his opportunity to climb down from his saddle. Then, keeping his eyes and pistols on the two prostrate forms, he walked his horse to the side of the road, where he tied its rein it to a branch.

'You can get up now,' he called sharply, and watched with a sot of contemptuous leer upon his face as his two victims struggled to their feet.

'That way!' Judd waved one of his pistols in the direction of the undergrowth from which, a few minutes before, he had emerged onto the road. 'Move!' he growled. 'Or you'll die where you stand.'

With no sensible alternative, both men did as they were bid. In Goddard's mind resided the hope that by cooperating with Judd's instructions, he would more quickly give Rose the opportunity to shoot Judd in the back. The two men moved forward, picking their way through the long grass on the wide verge that ran beside the road. Judd followed at a prudent distance, his aim unwavering. Ahead, a worn, earthen path drew the group towards a narrow opening through a line of tangled vegetation that looked otherwise impenetrable. The path was evidently in regular use by deer or bear or other good-sized animals, for a passable walkway had been trodden right through the barrier into the forest beyond. Goddard held back a little to let Ned lead in. If the chance came to take Judd by surprise, he would not want to be obstructed by his friend being in the way.

'Don't try anything!' called Judd, evidently reading Goddard's thoughts. He had come up close behind and rammed a pistol barrel roughly into Goddard's back. The thrust of it made the seaman stumble forward into his companion, now a pace or two ahead.

Ned grunted, winded by the blow. Half turning he growled: 'Let me get at the bastard!' under his breath.

'Not yet!' replied Goddard quickly, as both were bullied on.

They emerged into a shady arbour deprived of sunlight by the trees' high canopy.

'Keep moving!' rasped Judd as the two men hesitated, their eyes adjusting to the gloom. Another prod from Judd's pistol forced them on.

The pair soon found themselves amongst a phalanx of dark tree trunks, standing as tall as ships' masts upon a dense carpet of dry pine needles and cones. Several distinct paths now led off in different directions, evidence of active woodland life. But if animals resided here, they watched quietly and unseen from their cover, for the wood was as still and as silent as a mausoleum. It was an eerie silence too: a dead, oppressive silence. Neither birdsong nor even the wind's whispering penetrated this vaulted hall, the almost total absence of sound making Goddard's elevated pulse almost deafening in his ears.

Ned's uncertainty over which of the paths to take drew another wave of Judd's pistol. 'Straight ahead!' came his sharp call.

'What're you going to do with us, Judd?' Goddard asked angrily as he picked his way carefully over some woody detritus that obstructed the directed path. 'You shoot us - others will hear and come to investigate.'

'Just keep moving,' barked Judd impatiently from close behind. 'You'll find out soon enough!'

The path led on, both captives forced along it at a stumbling pace, Judd pushing and shoving all the while, barking his directions from the rear. It was only when Goddard caught sight of the rocky precipice ahead that he guessed what Judd had in mind. He intended to dispatch his two victims into the abyss, then take the chaise and disappear. It was clear at once that Judd planned to leave no evidence of his deed behind. Until now, anticipating Rose's intervention at any moment, Goddard had not been afraid. He had played a compliant game to put Judd off his guard, yet had remained ready to react the instant Rose's expected shot rang out. But now he began to wonder what had delayed her – and, worse, to worry that she might come too late. And for the first time Goddard began to fear for his life. Ned's nervous glance over his shoulder showed that he too had seen the precipice and realised what lay in store. Goddard mouthed at him: 'Play for time.' He hoped Ned understood. Rose must come soon, he thought, his anxiety increasing with each step. Her intervention might be their only chance. And if he and Ned were lost, then she might become a victim too, for Judd would almost certainly discover her presence when he returned to the road.

Rose had stifled a gasp when she overheard Judd's assertion that Jack was dead. At first, she could not believe it, her instinct being instead that the claim was just the boastful taunting of a vindictive mind. But there had been a ring of conviction in Judd's tone that struck a dissonant chord in her protesting heart. While the candour of his words had been immediately suspected, an awful dread now hovered like some spectre at the fringes of her mind. It was a spectre into whose cold embrace she would not let herself be drawn. Yet that dread, the putative reality of Jack's demise, had a taken root. It was a looming presence, if still distant and undefined, the seed of fear planted in her consciousness - and now it grew. She shunned it; she held it back; she could not envisage her Jack so easily the victim of this… this *monster*. She heard herself spit out this last word as if it were a bitter pill. The utterance seemed to draw out an almost tangible sense of loathing for the man who had caused the death of her precious unborn child, who had so cruelly destroyed her home, and who now, once again, threatened her life by his very arrival on the scene. That fear soon began to take the form of anger. If Jack *had* been taken from her, then she would count her life as nought and sacrifice it gladly to send Judd into purgatory where he belonged. As she heard Judd barking his orders, listening secretly from her hiding place under the furs, every syllable from his foul mouth fuelled her hatred more. It would not have taken much to provoke her into recklessness – she imagined breaking from her cover, pulling him from his horse, and sinking her nails into his smug face. And if she died in that deliciously gratifying act, then so much the better - for she would greet Jack in heaven with the sweet news of her revenge.

But she resisted that impulse and bided her time.

She heard the men's footsteps move away, first grinding on the stony track, then treading more softly through the grassy verge, eventually crunching through the brittle swathe of leaves and brush, until the undergrowth swallowed any further sound of their movement. And with their going, everything suddenly fell very quiet.

Even then she did not stir. She forced herself to lie absolutely still even though her heart pounded so powerfully in her breast that it threatened to burst out. Then, at last, tentatively at first, she lifted a corner of the fur and peeked out. Of the three men there was no sign, but she could see the opening through the undergrowth where she thought they must have gone. She also saw that her hands were trembling, but it was fury rather than fear that drove her now, and it craved satisfaction. Careful not to make a sound she threw back the furs to reveal the store of weapons under the rear seat: several muskets, a few differently sized metal containers for accessories, and a wooden pistol box. She drew out the box, took out two pistols, and laid them on the seat. The hand weapons had been loaded with shot before setting out on their journey, in case of urgent need. She hoped that the charges had remained dry for there was no time to reload them now. But the powder had run out of the firing pans; they would need re-priming. A quick, nervous glance over her shoulder confirmed that Judd had not returned, but the enduring silence worried her. Hurriedly, she searched for the priming horn. At first, she expected to find it in the pistol box; but it wasn't there! Her heart began to race as she felt panic's grip; every lost second brought death closer. Then she remembered that she had stored the powder separately for safety. But where on earth had she put it? Her fingers scrambled madly to find the right box amongst the others under the seats; with the roughness of the ride, the stores had lost the neat order in which she had carefully arranged them before starting out. But at last she found it, extracted the priming horn and poured some of the fine black powder into each of the touchholes, closing the firing arms to secure it. She primed a musket too, thinking to take it but then rejecting the idea – its long barrel, she thought, would be too unwieldy in the undergrowth.

Finally, she was ready. But in stepping down from the chaise in some haste, she snagged her long skirt on a protruding hinge. She heard a seam tear and swore under her breath in irritation at the encumbrance - these were no clothes for a manhunt, she decided. And without a second's thought, she pulled up a handful of the hem, twisted it to draw up and gather her skirt more tightly about her, and tucked the material firmly into her waistband to free her legs from their constraint. At once, she found herself able to move more freely, her calves now exposed above her boots. Even in such a desperate cause, she felt a momentary coy aversion to revealing her bare flesh to view, a bizarre thought in the circumstances, which she just as quickly dismissed. And with a cross shake of her head, she picked up the pistols and set off.

Entering the forest by way of the same gap used by the men, it felt as though she had entered another world from the one she had just left. On the road, it had been bright and warm; here it was gloomy and cool - and so eerily silent too, that she might suddenly have been struck deaf. Even her footfalls made no sound on the soft carpet of dry pine needles that covered the forest floor; only the pulse beating in her ears told her that she retained her senses. For a few moments, she stood quite still, adjusting to her new environment – listening intently, sweeping her gaze frantically here and there for any clue that would tell her which way her companions had been led. Nothing! Pistols clutched in both hands, she took a few more careful steps, stopped, and listened and looked again. The dark and hefty trunks seemed to stretch in all directions under a high canopy of patchy foliage; her view was limited in this woodland labyrinth to less that twenty paces. It was very claustrophobic. Still no movement seen, nor sound heard. The ground fell away quite sharply to her right into what appeared to be a steep, wooded ravine. She edged closer and looked down. Here and there, great moss-covered boulders littered the descent. And at the bottom, she could make out running water that sparkled in the few shafts of misty sunlight that penetrated those sylvan depths like shining rods. Following the contour around to her left, she moved cautiously, stopping every few paces to listen and look again, her weapons held out like some divining tool to lead her. Gradually she became aware of the faint noise of falling water and moved closer, until she saw a cloud of mist hanging in a deep cleft that appeared to form the head of the ravine. Above the mist, a rocky ledge stuck out like a platform over a sheer drop.

It was on this rocky ledge that she first caught sight of them – yet at that moment only two of the expected three figures could be seen, both rendered unrecognisable at this range in the dim forest light. They seemed to be standing face to face, separated by a few yards as if in conversation. She moved closer, picking her steps with utmost care, passing from the cover of one tree trunk to the next, until she came within some twenty paces of the two men. Now she could see that they were Captain Goddard and Judd, still apparently engaged in conversation on the rocky platform: the former dangerously close to the precipitous edge, the latter with a commanding pistol in one hand. Now she saw that Ned lay face down on the ground some yards away. She was close enough to see the blood on his head and neck; it appeared that he had been hit from behind. Poor Ned, Rose thought, and hoped to God he had not been too badly hurt. Since no shots had been heard, she consoled herself, there was every chance that he was only stunned.

The noise of water splattering onto rocks below, albeit faint, drowned out whatever words were passing between the two men, but Rose could see the sneer on Judd's face. Goddard, meanwhile, appearing to be reasoning with his tormentor, was getting no response. By the agitated movement of the captain's arms, however, it seemed quite likely that his reasoning might soon turn to desperate action instead. But then Judd was seen to raise his weapon and press forward, forcing Goddard to step back, a step closer to the edge. Judd pressed forward again, and again the captain stepped back. Rose saw her friend glance over his shoulder nervously; another step would be a step into the void.

It was obvious to Rose what Judd intended to do, and she must stop him. But there was no time to get closer; she must act now or her erstwhile companion would certainly be forced to fall to his death. Quickly stuffing one of her pistols into her waistband, she brought the other's sights to bear. But even steadying her arm on the bark of her shielding trunk, she found it impossible to keep her aim steady, her heart now beating so fast that her hand trembled. She held her breath, steadied her aim as best she could, and pulled the trigger. But nothing happened; there was no resistance to her pull, and she realised at once that she had not cocked the firing arm. Her hands were visibly shaking now; she had only fired a weapon under her husband's patient instruction, and the lethal devices still frightened her. Time was running out. Quickly, she pulled back the firing arm, took aim and squeezed the trigger again. This time, the arm sprang over, the flint sparked, and the primer ignited with a flash. The intensity of the combustion took her by surprise. Perhaps she had been too liberal with the powder, for in the dim light of the forest, the flash blinded her as the weapon recoiled sharply in her hand. She must instinctively have closed her eyes.

It could only have been some seconds later, after her vision returned and the smoke from her shot had cleared, that Rose regained her view of the promontory, but neither Judd nor Captain Goddard were anywhere to be seen. For a moment she feared that her shot might somehow have done for them both, and she came out from behind her cover to look more closely. Ned's prostrate form still lay inertly where she had seen him before, but there was no sign of the other two men at all. Then, out of the corner of her eye, she saw a streak of movement - and caught the briefest glimpse of a shadowy figure dashing between one tree trunk and the next, moving away from the rocky outcrop and obliquely across her line of sight. She was certain that it was Judd. Her shot had evidently missed its mark, and he may now be positioning for a counterattack. What of Goddard though, she wondered, suddenly terrified that she might have hit him instead. But this was no time to think of him; with her intervention, she had given herself away and had made herself the target. She drew back behind the protective cover of her tree, threw her spent weapon to the ground and cocked the other - then steeled herself for another chance to shoot, her heart pounding in her chest, her ears straining for the telltale sounds of Judd's approach. It was a long time before she heard anything at all, bar the constant splattering of water on the rocks deep down in the ravine. Every few seconds she snatched a furtive glance around her tree, neither seeing nor hearing any further sign of Judd.

After a while, she began to think that he had fled, and she began to relax. But a sudden splintering of dry wood seemingly very close by made her heart leap into her mouth. She dare not take another glance now; if he were near he was bound to see her movement. She held her breath, listening intently for what seemed an eternity; but the constant splattering was like an aural curtain, it masked all but the most deliberate of sounds. When, after a long time, nothing further untoward had been heard, she decided to risk another glance. Perhaps he had not seen her, she reasoned hopefully. Perhaps the crack of brittle wood had been the sound of Judd moving in another direction?

Her pistol led her eyes as she inched around the trunk hoping to catch him out in the open. And this she certainly did. But instead of catching him some distance off as she had hoped, he had already closed to within a few feet; moreover, he had his pistol aimed as if he knew exactly where she was. When their eyes met, both seemed as startled as the other. In a fright, she swung her weapon and pulled the trigger; and in that instant, she saw him do the same. A double explosion resounded, his muzzle so close that she felt the residue of its blast upon her face. But she was not hit; his bullet must have lodged in the bark of her protecting tree. Seizing her chance, she flung her weapon down and ran as fast as her legs would carry her, hoping desperately that her shot had done enough to prevent or slow his pursuit.

She retraced the path she had taken around the edge of the ravine then turned towards the opening to the road. She could not yet see the gap through which she had entered but knew in which direction it lay. If she could reach the chaise, she thought, she could re-arm herself with the musket that she had left there already primed. Her heart thumped, her scorched lungs screamed for air. Even if her pistol ball had not hit him, she reasoned, she must surely be outrunning him. She dare not look behind, yet the sound of her gasping would have masked any pursuit.

It was then that the tuck in her skirt began to loosen at her waistband, and she felt its folds fall heavily about her legs so that suddenly it was as if she were running on soft sand. The entanglement slowed and drained her quickly, but she pressed on using every last ounce of her strength, dodging this way and that to avoid obstructions in her path - until the flying fabric snagged on a low branch and brought her down flat on her face.

She raised herself quickly to her knees, turning at once to pull herself free; but as she did so, she saw immediately that it was too late.

Chapter Nineteen

Jack and Schluntz on the road approaching heard the two shots ring out. The reports had come so close together that the second might have been an echo of the first, but Jack was not deceived. They curbed their mounts and waited in the silence that followed.

'Pistol fire,' said Schluntz at last, 'not muskets.'

'Trouble then!' replied Jack laconically.

The two men exchanged glances that were at once suspicious and optimistic. They had travelled so fast and so relentlessly in pursuit of Sanderson's murderer that they might well already have caught up. A musket shot could have been a hunter's, but pistol fire generally meant strife – and their quarry may well be the object or the cause of it. If he had robbed and killed before, he might rob and kill again. Each checked his weapons – two pistols in each belt, charged and primed. Schluntz drew his hunting knife, checked its oiled and sharpened blade, and returned it to its sheath.

The shots had come from fairly close at hand - Jack estimated within half a mile at most - but a bend in the road immediately ahead limited their view. They spurred forward at a canter to reach the bend quickly, and what they saw on rounding it seemed to confirm that something was indeed amiss. It was a curious sight; a sight that brought puzzled frowns to both men's faces. Just a few hundred yards ahead sat an abandoned chaise and pair, a second pair standing at its rear. A fifth animal, a single, saddled mount, grazed on the verge nearby. The two men reined back, moved forward cautiously awhile, then dismounted, leaving their mounts to graze while they approached the vehicle and horses on foot. Schluntz brought a finger to his lips as they came closer, then signalled Jack to stop when still some twenty paces off. The chaise sat at an angle across the road, its mares evidently attracted to the lush grass of the verge on which they now fed. The sounds of horses contentedly grazing, accompanied by the clinking of their bridle buckles, were strangely out of place at such a tense moment, for the atmosphere seemed suddenly charged. The men stood silently for a while, swinging their gazes, searching for anything that would give a clue as to the circumstances of the abandonment; yet no clue came. Jack pulled one of his pistols from his belt and Schluntz did the same as both tentatively approached the saddled singleton, which continued tearing at the grass, quite indifferent to their close inspection.

'We've got our man,' whispered Jack, pointing at the saddlebags on which the shot-damaged buckle was plain to see. He removed the bags and tossed them under a bush nearby, kicking some brush on top as cover. 'Safer there,' said Jack plainly. Schluntz nodded his approval and led on, until the two men came alongside the chaise. Its left-hand-side door hung open; a fragment of green fabric dangled loosely from a protruding hinge as if it had been snagged; Jack fingered it distractedly. Evidence of a hasty exit, he thought, and drew it to the attention of his companion with an exchange of glances. Both also noticed the musket lying on the back seat, and the boxes and other weapon paraphernalia scattered in disarray. While there were still no clues as to the identity of the missing occupants or their current whereabouts, it was clear that some mischief was afoot. Jack was about to turn away, still baffled, when he noticed something stencilled in black ink upon the lid of one of the boxes. He bent closer to read the faded lettering then straightened, suddenly alarmed; he'd read the name, *T. Harding Esq.* He had to read it again before it dawned upon him that he knew the sturdy vehicle - its four wheels made it unusual and quite distinctive. He should have recognised it before. Indeed, both he and Schluntz had been delivered to Charlestown quay in this very chaise at the beginning of their journey!

'This is Harding's chaise!' he whispered incredulously. And both cast their gazes about, almost in disbelief. Suddenly, the stakes had been raised. The air hung oppressively about them and for late September it was unusually warm. But it was not until now that Jack became conscious of the heat. His brow began to prickle with sweat. What should they do, he wondered? They could not simply wait and lay an ambush for the killer to return - they must pursue! But which way to go? Endless, dense forest extended on both sides of the road. Blundering off in the wrong direction would waste time that could cost someone's life.

'Look for tracks!' whispered Schluntz urgently. And the pair separated to both sides of the road to search along the verges. A fast-moving shadow caught their eyes briefly, and both men glanced up to see an eagle pass across the sun. A chorus of warning calls rose up from the surrounding treetops, but otherwise silence taunted.

'Over here!' called Schluntz, stooping to examine some trodden grasses. Jack joined him quickly and knelt beside him. Tracks, sure enough! And immediately before them lay a path into the undergrowth through a narrow gap in the foliage. Schluntz made to lead the way in.

'Wait! I'll get the musket,' said Jack. And without waiting for a reply, he ran back to the chaise and returned moments later with the weapon in his hand. 'We might need it!' he said breathlessly.

It seemed that no sooner had they entered the leafy tunnel that a female scream rang out. But it was difficult to be certain from which direction the cry came for the sound echoed amongst the standing ranks of dark tree trunks with which they were now faced. Instinct led them straight ahead, and before they had loped forward ten paces, a movement caught Jack's eye. And in a gap between the intervening trunks, he saw a figure standing in a shaft of sunlight with a pistol in his hand. Jack pointed the figure out to his companion, and they moved closer – more cautiously now, for they did not want to alert him to their presence. Schluntz led the way, making for the decaying stump of a fallen tree to use as cover. He crouched behind it.

'He's got a woman on the ground!' exclaimed Schluntz in a low voice as Jack arrived beside him.

Jack shifted his position to get a better view, and saw a female on her back amongst the fallen leaves. It looked as if she had just been thrown there. Although her words were muffled, it was quite evident from her protestations that she was in great distress. Jack could see that she was desperately working herself backwards on her elbows, trying to get away, her upturned face covered in a tangle of long dark hair, shaken loose in the struggle. But the man then lunged forward, grabbed a leg, and yanked her roughly back to where she had first lain. And with that, her skirts were dragged up around her thighs to reveal her bare legs. She kicked out wildly, but fell still when he hit her across the face. The attacker then stood astride the woman's unmoving form like some conquering beast displaying his kill; and, while sweeping his gaze about as if to check he would not be disturbed, he began to loosen his belt. If it had not been obvious what the man intended until then, his lascivious mutterings now made it abundantly clear. Only fragments of the man's oily monologue reached Jack's ears, but it sickened him. Without hesitating, he raised his musket and took aim. But just as he squeezed the trigger he recognised the face brought under his sights. 'It's Judd!' he gasped in utter disbelief; and his astonishment threw off his aim even as his bullet accelerated down the barrel.

The shot went wide, splintering bark rather than Judd's head, and by the time the smoke had cleared, his intended target had disappeared. Jack knew that Judd must have taken cover behind a trunk, but in the leafy shadows of the high canopy, he could not be sure which it was. The woman stirred, raised her head and shook her hair free. She swung her head to look in Jack's direction, no doubt relieved at this stranger's intervention. Both realised at once, and with some evident astonishment, whose features they now gazed upon; but in his moment of recognition, a movement beside a nearby tree drew Jack's eye. Just in time, he saw Judd taking aim, and just in time he ducked. He felt the sonic pressure wave part his hair as the speeding ball zipped by an inch above his head and thudded into the tree behind. Schluntz had gone down with him, seeking the cover of the stump, and both now pulled out their pistols and came up to their knees to return fire. But Judd had used his shot to cover his escape and was already dodging between the tree trunks as Jack and Sergeant Schluntz brought their weapons to bear. Both let off a shot, but both missed; and without a moment's hesitation, both leapt up to give chase.

As the two men started after Judd, Jack flashed a worried glance towards his wife who was by then struggling to her feet.

'Stay where you are, Rose!' he shouted, but he saw her hitching up her skirt and knew that she would not obey.

'He's fired both pistol's, Jack!' Rose shouted back through cupped hands. 'I don't think he's got another.' And then she shouted something else that was drowned out by the pounding of his feet.

The two men ducked and weaved between trunks and fallen wood, dodging this way and that, never losing sight of Judd for more than a few seconds at a time. Sometimes Jack led, sometimes Schluntz, but both ran with grim intent, crashing through the undergrowth, their pistols clutched in their hands. As he ran, Jack flashed a glance into a steep ravine encroaching from his right, and he saw that Judd's course had altered to follow its curving rim. Soon a rocky promontory came into view ahead, and beyond its precipitous edge, the deep void of a chasm opened up. Jack must have taken his eyes off Judd only for the briefest of moments to register its potential danger, but when he looked back, Judd was no longer to be seen. While moments before the fleeing villain had been clearly in Jack's sight not more than twenty paces in front, Judd had now suddenly and inexplicably vanished. It was as if the forest had swallowed him whole.

'Lost him!' shouted Schluntz, who, still racing headlong had at that moment edged ahead and thus partially blocked Jack's view.

'Keep going!' Jack shouted back from close behind.

And both men kept up their pace until they came to where Judd had last been seen, before skidding to a halt. They found themselves now in a gloomy, circular opening about thirty paces across, which formed a sort of woodland antechamber to the promontory and the void beyond. The ravine echoed with the sound of distant water splattering on rocks far below. The two men, dishevelled and flustered from their exertions, stood panting in frustration as they cast about their gazes, searching for some indication of which way the fugitive had gone.

'Where the hell...' Jack started to say; but he was interrupted by a voice coming seemingly out of nowhere.

'Drop your weapons or your friend dies!'

Judd's voice was dark and threatening. And it came from so near at hand that it startled both pursuers. Only now did they see him, down on one knee in the dappled shadows, half-hidden by a boulder not ten paces from where they stood. Rose had been right: Judd had fired both his pistols and had had no time to reload. But he still had his knife. And as soon as Jack saw the glint of its steel blade, he knew that Judd had regained the upper hand, for propped up before him as a human shield was Ned's unconscious form.

Judd had wedged the big man's broad shoulders against his thigh. With his left hand, he held Ned's head up by his hair, and with his right he held his knife at Ned's throat. Both Jack and Sergeant Schluntz had swung their pistols instinctively when they heard Judd's voice, but now they let their aims drop. With Ned's large frame partially in the way, neither would dare to shoot.

By his sneer, it was clear that Judd thought that he had turned the tables in his favour.

'Now disarm your weapons,' he called, 'and lay them down. Careful now!' he snarled, this last order spoken sharply as Jack took a step towards him.

Judd's threat was made manifest by pressing the point of his knife deeper into Ned's exposed neck. Jack noticed a trickle of blood ooze out under the blade. Reluctantly, both men closed the firing arms of their pistols and laid them on the ground.

'Now kick them towards me,' said Judd tensely.

Again, Jack and Schluntz did as they were told. Perhaps they should not have been so cooperative, but with Ned in obvious peril, neither wanted to test Judd's resolve. Jack had not been slow to piece together the evidence; he realised now that it was Judd who had slit Sanderson's throat. Moreover, cornered as he was, the murderer might be driven to do the same to Ned - even though he would be playing his only ace.

Judd manoeuvred to pick up the nearest of the weapons keeping his knife never more than a few inches from Ned's throat. And once he had the pistol in his hand, he cocked it quickly and trained it on Jack. Now he raised himself to his full height and came out into the open, leaving Ned's limp form to slump back onto the boulder.

'So we meet again, Mr Easton,' Judd sneered. Without taking his eyes or his aim from Jack for a second, he slipped his knife into his belt and picked up the second pistol from the ground. 'And here was I thinking that I'd already slit your throat back at Fort Loudoun,' he mocked. 'Well, I've got your money, and now I really *have* got you! And you and this big oaf (he cocked his thumb at Ned) will soon join your friend Goddard who, poor man, seems to have gone over the edge!' He threw back his head and gave out a loud, triumphant guffaw, revealing a mouthful of yellow teeth. 'For which I have your mad wife's fine shooting to thank!' he added cynically.

Captain Goddard had indeed gone over the edge, having done just that when Rose's shot had distracted Judd at a crucial moment. As the smoke of Judd's returning pistol fire still hung in the air, Goddard had seized his chance to jump down onto a narrow ledge, a feature spotted in his nervous rearward glance as Judd had backed him to the precipice. It was a risky move, for the ledge was barely three feet wide and the abyss of the ravine beyond threatened, but it saved him from any more of Judd's hostility. Moreover, his disappearance seems to have convinced Judd that the mariner had fallen to his death, for the potential threat posed by him thereafter appears to have been discounted.

Once on the ledge, however, Goddard had found there to be no easy route off it. Below, the chasm beckoned with certain death if he missed his footing. Above, the rock face was so sheer that he could see no easy purchase. And until he heard the exchange of pistol fire some minutes later, he had searched tentatively along the ledge with his back pressed firmly against the wall. Not until hearing those distant discharges did it dawn upon Goddard that his escape had made Rose the sole target of

Judd's pursuit. He had already seen Ned clubbed unconscious with a pistol butt from behind, and now he feared that Rose, alone and unprotected, would become easy prey to Judd's spite. The period of silence that followed that second exchange of fire left him thus imagining the worst, which dreadful thought galvanised him immediately to bolder and more determined action. Frantically, he now probed and toed every likely fissure, several times managing to climb so high that he nearly gained a handhold on the lip of the precipice above. But on each occasion, he lost his footing and slipped back. He tried time and time again and was still no closer to extricating himself when, after what seemed a long time, he heard another, more distant exchange of fire. With those reports came the apprehension that Rose was still engaged with Judd, still fighting to defend herself, and that thought at once spurred him into yet more urgent exploration.

'God, get me off this damned ledge,' he swore, furiously sweeping his eyes about the rock wall for a different route of escape.

The answer lay at his feet, and when he saw it, he chastised himself for not thinking of it before. He would build his own foothold! Falling to his knees, he set about at once prising loose rock from the ledge, tearing at it with his fingers. The crumbling strata, penetrated through millennia by rain and frost, came away more easily than expected, and it was possible to pull up some quite substantial slabs. Before long, he had accumulated enough to start building his steps.

It was while he was arranging his stone into a rough but stable platform that he heard voices coming from close above. He could scarcely believe his ears when amongst them he recognised the voice of his friend, Jack.

Rose meanwhile had started after her husband and Sergeant Schluntz as they had raced off in pursuit of Judd, but she had trodden more carefully and less noisily through the trees than they. Thus, as she approached the clearing near the precipice, some minutes later, she became aware of Judd's ambush without giving her presence away. It did not take her long to gauge the scene, appreciating at once the perilous trap that her husband and companion had blundered into. Judd seemed to have regained the initiative remarkably quickly; somehow he had managed already to capture the two men's weapons, which he now brandished at his two new captives threateningly. She could see by his swaggering manner that he revelled in his apparent victory. He must be stopped, she knew; but how, she wondered? Ned could be no help. From where she hid, her old friend still looked unconscious. Curiously, he now appeared to be leaning on a large boulder, not flat on the ground as she had last seen him, but she did not have time to wonder why; she was more worried that Judd's blow might have injured him seriously. And Captain Goddard was still nowhere to be seen. Perhaps he hid somewhere nearby and would come to her aid, she thought hopefully, for she could not believe that she had hit him with her shot. Yet the worry of that dreadful possibility still nagged her.

Either way, Rose knew that for now she would have to act alone and act quickly; Jack and Sergeant Schluntz faced certain execution unless she could intervene. Without a weapon, however, what could she do? A wrong move on her part could seal their fates and leave her again at Judd's lascivious mercy. She wished she had returned to the chaise to rearm, but things had moved so fast, and there was certainly no time now. But she had to do something, anything to interfere with Judd's obvious intentions. She decided that she would have to brazen it out – and simply hope for the best.

Judd enjoyed taunting his two new captives, and as he did so he shifted sideways, away from the unconscious Ned so that he could keep all three within a tight arc of his view. But with his back to the ravine, he did not see Goddard pulling himself up silently over the rocky edge some ten paces to his rear. And with his gloating eyes fixed upon Jack, neither did Judd see Rose rise from the undergrowth on his flank and start slowly towards him. Jack and Sergeant Schluntz would later say that they had seen both, and had thus been ready to rush their captor when the opportunity came; but at that moment neither gave it away. Judd was taken by surprise when Rose spoke:

'You can't kill us all, Judd,' she said coldly as she approached him, upright and unafraid, her wild hair and her intense, hating stare making her presence all the more threatening. She saw the sudden indecision in Judd's eyes as he swung a glance and a pistol towards her, thus splitting his aim.

'Too many of us for you now, Judd?' she jibed.

Jack and Schluntz began to inch apart as if readying to spring should a chance to do so arise from the distraction.

Unfortunately, Judd saw their movement.

'That's far enough,' he sneered, bringing both pistols quickly back to bear.

While the men stopped, Rose kept coming. 'You might shoot two of us with those pistols, Judd,' she said, 'but you can't shoot all three. One of us will get you, and if it's me, I'll claw out your eyes!' She sounded as if she meant it.

'Stay back or you'll be the first to die!' Judd snarled, flashing her an angry glare. But he seemed to have been rendered uncertain, even frightened by her audacity; and as she continued towards him, he started to back away.

When she had run from him before, Rose had run in fear - a woman alone in the wilderness, pursued. Judd had caught her and dominated her with his strength and would have forced himself upon her had not Jack's shot interfered. But now, she was not afraid; somehow she felt empowered by the evident effect on Judd of her boldness. Perhaps she also recognised this reckless approach as a last resort - that there was nothing else left in her armoury. If it failed, then better to get death over with quickly by pistol shot rather than suffer something far worse. Some instinct told her too that he would not shoot while she held her nerve. Her womanly self-assurance had become her shield. She had been aware of this effect on men before, even as a younger woman, that self-assurance seemed both to intimidate and inhibit at the same time. She would use it as a weapon against Judd. She pressed closer as she taunted him, and he continued to back away, his glances now flicking anxiously between her and the two men, who now postured with menace, bridling for a chance to act. Yet as she came nearer, Rose began to see the first flickers of panic in Judd's eyes and knew then that she could not force him too far – a rat cornered might spring into the attack in an act of desperation. And recognising this, her confidence began to wane, fear taking its place as she became unsure where her bold experiment would lead.

Jack had seen this too.

'No further, Rose!' he called quickly. 'He's a mad man; you'll push him too far!'

Rose stopped uncertainly, but Jack saw that her brave approach had backed Judd so far across the clearing that he was now much closer to the rocky precipice. And just a few short steps behind him, Goddard now lay quietly, having gained some partial cover behind some low rocks. It looked as if he was waiting for a chance to move again. Jack had been aware of his movements out of the corner of his eye, but would not betray his friend's presence with a direct glance.

'All right, Judd, let's make a deal,' Jack suggested quickly, hoping to keep Judd engaged and thus distract him.

Judd shook his head derisively. He had begun to regain his composure and the spiteful cast had returned to his eyes. 'No deal for you Easton,' he spat. 'You and Goddard have already cost me too much.'

A fortuitous gust of wind then rattled the high branches and rustled the leaves. A movement in Jack's peripheral vision told him that Goddard's movements had resumed. When he risked a brief glance in that direction, he saw that his friend had raised himself into a half-kneeling position. Goddard was now poised to spring but was still too far away to reach Judd before the latter's weapons could be levelled and fired. The forces against Judd were gathering but they were not yet ready to strike.

Then Ned stirred, which Jack sensed rather than saw, for again, he would not risk a direct glance. He continued to play for time.

'Let us go free, Judd, and we'll split the money,' Jack persisted. And as he spoke he took a small oblique step sideways to draw Judd's gaze further away from his waking friend.

Temptation seemed to flit across Judd's face, as if he were considering the proposal. But just as quickly his expression hardened.

'And leave you to come after me again?' he sneered. And with this taunt he waved his pistols sharply. 'Now, all of you – down on your knees! You too!' This last order was directed at Rose who still stood several paces off to Judd's side.

Although he did not know it, Judd was now all but surrounded. With two cocked pistols in his hands, however, he could not be rushed, even by Goddard from behind, without a real risk that someone might be fatally wounded in the attempt. The odds were simply stacked too high. Something was needed to change those odds and tip the balance in favour of Jack and his companions.

Sergeant Schluntz provided it. Feigning to stoop as if responding to Judd's instructions, his right hand slipped his hunting knife from its hidden sheath and threw it in one swift and practiced motion at Judd's throat. But Judd was clearly on his guard. He must have seen the weapon leave the sergeant's hand for, despite the speed of its trajectory, he dodged it nimbly, his pistols hardly wavering. The moment was not lost, however, for while Judd's attention was distracted, Goddard sprang up and pounced on him. With his left arm wrapped roughly around Judd's neck, he yanked backwards, arching Judd's spine. At the same time, he grabbed Judd's flailing right wrist in an attempt to shake the lethal instrument from his grip. The pistol fired into the air while he struggled, while the other waved about wildly, its random aim swinging dangerously. Picking the timing of their approach to avoid the cavorting line of fire, Jack, Schluntz, and then Ned, once more on his feet and very angry, closed in. Before they could reach the struggling pair, however, the second weapon fired, sending its projectile zipping within a hair's breadth of Jack's ear. The explosion stopped the two scouts momentarily in their tracks as they ducked instinctively, while Judd broke free, sending Goddard sprawling to the ground. Ned however was not to be so easily deflected, the momentum of his heavy frame making his charge unstoppable. But as he lunged after the fleeing Judd, his foot caught one of Goddard's outstretched limbs and he stumbled. His now staggering form at once became a projectile, propelled forward by sheer inertia and fuelled by Ned's ungainly efforts to right himself. This all happened within a few racing heartbeats as the others watched, left behind and helpless in those fleeting moments to intervene. It would have looked comical but for the adjacent danger of the precipice. Judd meanwhile had begun to sprint ahead, but his lead amounted only to a few paces. So that when Ned's sprawling form finally lost the battle with gravity and went flying headlong, his outstretched hand caught the heel of Judd's rearmost boot. The force of Ned's brief touch was slight, but it was just enough to deflect Judd's leg so that when it came forward for the next stride, it caught upon the ankle of his leading foot. Now it was Judd who tripped and stumbled. But for him the consequences would be far more serious, for he also lost control of his direction. And he was still clawing desperately at the air for balance as he went over the edge. His scream echoed briefly in the ravine.

When Jack and Sergeant Schluntz reached the precipice and looked down, Judd's tumbling body was in the final seconds of its descent, having been set spinning by its impact with a rocky outcrop half way down. Both saw the splash when Judd hit the water far below, although another sudden rustle of leaves in the canopy overhead masked the sound of it. Jack glanced up to see the treetops swaying wildly in a gust of wind. The breeze seemed to have come from nowhere, and it roared and hissed loudly before dying just as quickly. It was undoubtedly happenstance that the sudden flurry had coincided with Judd's fall, but Jack fancied that it might have been the angry passing of Judd's unloved soul.

The others soon gathered around the two scouts at the edge and craned down into the abyss, waiting for the body to surface. Perhaps all craved one last sight of the man who had caused so much pain and strife. But they waited in vain for that final satisfaction, for he never re-appeared.

And in that sense, Judd had cheated them again.

Chapter Twenty

Throughout most of 1758, Brigadier General Forbes was gravely ill and thus forced to direct the advance of his brigade from his sick bed at the rear. He would be brought forward eventually to a newly constructed fortification at Loyal Hannon creek, only fifty miles from Fort Duquesne, from where he would plan and direct the intended assault. Meanwhile, under the supervision of his second-in-command, the Swiss-born Lieutenant Colonel Henry Bouquet, his new road and fortifications were being literally hacked out of virgin forests across the four ridges of the Alleghenies, which lay like obstacles between his supply base in eastern Pennsylvania and the Ohio River valley in the west. All this was accomplished while the French and their Indian allies continued to harass the frontier, even advancing deep into Pennsylvania and Virginia with their continuing, often brutal, raids upon British settlements. It was a Herculean undertaking to move six thousand British and American troops through such an outlying and hostile wilderness, with a supply chain that stretched hundreds of miles along rudimentary roads and in tortuous terrain.

The going had been difficult enough during the benign summer months, but the coming winter would represent a different prospect altogether. Time would thus be of the essence. But while his new route was shorter and had fewer troublesome rivers to negotiate than the old southern route, the cutting of it had not been universally welcomed. The old route, used by General Braddock in his disastrous attempt to take Fort Duquesne from the French two years before, lay only thirty miles to the south in adjacent Virginian territory. With an eye on land acquisition and profits from its sale, the Virginians still pressed for this route to be used again. Indeed, a road cut between Fort Bedford and Fort Cumberland connected the two routes, and Forbes had had work parties out clearing and grading both, just in case the Virginians won the debate. But he was also being canny. With two possible routes available, he might elect to use either, or indeed both. And by keeping his options open as long as possible, he would also keep the French guessing and stretch their defences to cover the two lines of approach. The troops' assembly at Fort Bedford, however, signalled that it would soon be time for a decision to be made one way or the other.

Fort Bedford was also the point at which Pettigrew and Hayward made their decision to desert. Both had realised soon after their recruitment into Major Green's company on the road to Fort Loudoun that they could not safely remain within the Regiment for long. But they also recognised that once they escaped, they could not use the same line of approach into French territory as that used by the British. If they did, they would risk being overrun by British troops or else sandwiched between the two approaching sides and become potential targets for both. And since at first they were unaware of an alternative to the new road west (that is, striking south along the link road to join Braddock's old route), they were placed in something of a dilemma. Without knowing of this alternative, it appeared that their only recourse would be to navigate their own way through the wilderness, a thought that was so dauntingly unfeasible as to be ruled out of the question. For a time, therefore, it seemed that they were stuck.

It was only after arriving at Fort Bedford that the pair learnt of the connecting road to the old southern route, and moreover, that both routes had been maintained as tactical alternatives. They were also to learn soon after, that Brigadier Forbes had finally won his argument to use the new northern route as the line of approach. With this intelligence, the route and strategy of Pettigrew and Hayward's escape became clear – they would make their way down the now redundant link road and pick up Braddock's old route west. It was longer, certainly, but with any luck, they would be able to travel along it unmolested - and while the British and American troops slogged it out along the northern route to the battlefront, they would slip across the border further south to make overtures to the French. This time they would be better prepared for their expedition than they had been before, for they had taken the trouble to cultivate friends within the Company who would help them. And they would also go armed with new information on the British troop configuration that might buy them the French favour that they sought.

***

Following Judd's summary disposal to the bottom of the ravine, Jack Easton and Sergeant Schluntz returned to Fort Loudoun to make their report, expecting that the good news of the death of Sanderson's killer might be received with interest and their efforts congratulated. It was somewhat deflating, therefore, when the commandant referred the pair offhandedly to a tight-lipped adjutant rather than receive the report himself. From behind a desk piled high with requisitions, the adjutant explained curtly that investigations into Sanderson's murder had anyway been suspended due to other operational pressures on the camp. Nevertheless, the officer said with a smile belying his disinterested tone, he was pleased to note that justice had been done. And with that cursory conclusion, he scribbled in the file and tossed it aside, at once returning his attention to his pile of paperwork.

Despite Jack's earlier uncharitable feelings about his dead superior, he left the office quietly incensed. That the perpetrator had met a just end might seem enough to the adjutant, but Jack had wanted something more. Somehow, he expected the officer's manner to be more reverential on the passing of a willing servant than the casual dumping of his file in his out-tray. On later reflection, he came to resign himself to the truth of war that individual lives were as grains of sand on the beachhead of such grand ventures as these. And he found himself musing for the first time on the possibility of his own untimely passing, recognising without emotion that it would be just as indifferently marked by those in power, at least those who rated conquest greater than its human cost. He paused a moment to recall again his wife's objections to the current battles with the French, and realised that he would not argue with her insights now. A pity, he lamented, that such fine sentiments as hers were so easily swept aside by arrogance and avarice, both cloaked in a worthy rhetoric that took most people in.

Early the following day, somewhat despondently, the two scouts hitched up the wagon and climbed into the driving seat. Schluntz's borrowed mount had been returned to the livery, but Sanderson's valuable white mare would accompany the pair, perhaps one day to be returned to Sanderson's plantation when Jack eventually returned to Maryland. The handsome beast, secured by its halter to a hitching rail behind, tossed its head, whinnied, and shook its mane as if protesting its subordination, but the two plain workhorses harnessed to the swingletree took not the slightest notice of the ostentatious display. Schluntz, having volunteered to be the first to drive, let go the brake, picked up the reins and cracked them sharply. If until that moment, the mares had stood quietly ruminating, they were now awoken rudely, both fairly leaping into action with a whip across their rumps. And with a clattering of chains and the creak and rattle of fully loaded coachwork, the next stage of Jack and Schluntz's journey had begun.

Three dawns had now come and gone since Jack had taken his leave from Rose, putting her on the road back to Charlestown in the good company of Captain Goddard and Ned Holder. And still somewhat morose after the previous day's gloomy introspections, Jack soon found himself reflecting on that parting. After the euphoria of Judd's dispatch, it seemed an unsatisfactory conclusion that they should again be forced to go their separate ways. Moreover, the farewell had been a trite and rushed affair in his anxiety to get back on the road to make up for lost time. As he thought about it further, he realised that it had been insensitive to be so hasty, and he wished that he could recapture that moment and put matters right. It was his very haste that seemed to trigger her displeasure, creating that same coolness in her manner that he had felt at New Hope on the day of his departure, a coolness that seemed to have melted when they later met at Charlestown but seemed, unaccountably at the time, to have returned. Now he began to understand it. He recalled her parting words – words that had been gently spoken yet in retrospect seemed very plain - words that he should have responded to at the time but did not think enough about to appreciate what lay behind their articulation. As he considered their implication more carefully, Jack came to comprehend that his wife had been trying to make her position clear regarding their future lives – together or apart. Her meaning only now sinking in, he came to appreciate that he had ridden roughshod over her sensibilities and desires, and that he had miscalculated what he saw to be her wifely duty - a duty that he had evidently taken too much for granted. For the present, he would have to focus on matters in hand for he had duties of his own to attend to, but her unspoken ultimatum would have to be addressed. And with their new child growing in her belly, Rose would be impatient for his answer - and his promise. Jack now began to understand that he might lose Rose if he could not return to New Hope soon and tell her what she wanted to hear.

The two scouts spared no time in getting to Fort Bedford, travelling the forty or so miles on the rough new road in two days flat with hardly pause for rest. They arrived at the Fort to find Sir Michael's militia already encamped in neat order near other units outside the palisade. Leaving the wagon and horses in the care of the livery sergeant, they set out at once to seek Major Lawrence, the scouts' platoon commander, and were directed to a large circular marquee in the middle of the encampment. Two red-coated soldiers standing guard at the tent entrance barred their way as the pair approached, apparently unimpressed with the scouts' improvised and travel-ragged uniforms. If Jack's hackles rose, he managed to contain his irritation. But Schluntz was more forthright.

'We're here to report to Major Lawrence,' the sergeant said brusquely, pushing his way past. Jack followed close on his friend's heels, both barging into the tent with no concessions to military ceremony. The two guards, taken by surprise, protested and pressed in behind, grabbing the two intruders roughly by the shoulders and making to eject them. By this time, all four were inside the entrance where an unseemly struggle ensued. Jack had already caught a glimpse of Lawrence in conversation with the British Major, William Green, and Colonel Michael (as he now insisted on being called in the latter's presence). Now, with his and Schluntz's rowdy invasion of their peace, however, this conversation came to an abrupt halt. The three officers at once swung their gazes towards the entrance, their expressions ranging between affront and astonishment as the two intruders resisted restraint with yet more vigour than before.

'Corporal!' shouted the Colonel crossly to one of the struggling redcoats, 'Get those damned ruffians out of here!' But almost as soon as he had said it, he realised who they were.

'Wait! Leave them be, corporal.' His tone became resigned. 'Ragged as they are, I am afraid to admit that they are my men.' He said this with an ironic glint in his eyes. 'You may return to your posts outside.'

'Ah, Jack!' smiled the colonel as the guards departed, and made his way across the tent with the others in his train.

The last time the two had spoken, Jack had still been recuperating in his sick-bed from his gunshot wound, and Sir Michael was therefore quite clearly delighted to see his new lieutenant in such good shape.

'And Sergeant Schluntz too! Well done to have made it here!' he added, apparently congratulating the NCO for his successful escort duty. 'Jack, I think you already know Major Green from the South Coast Fusiliers?'

'Indeed I do, sir,' said Jack, straightening his jacket after his tussle with the guards. 'We shared a cabin on the *Miranda*, sir. Good to see you again, William - I'd heard that we were to join you.'

Jack reached out to shake the major's proffered hand. Schluntz did the same.

Sir Michael gave out a little murmur of satisfaction. 'We were beginning to wonder if you'd gone off on another of your escapades, Jack!' he said with a hint of irony. 'Anyway, I'm glad that you've finally joined us! And just in time...' He paused abruptly in mid-sentence, flashing a puzzled glance towards the entrance. 'Where's Sanderson by the way? Polishing his boots?' he laughed.

Jack's demeanour did not mirror his superior's.

'I'm afraid he won't be joining us, sir!' he said soberly, handing over the saddlebags. 'And you very nearly didn't get these!' He exchanged a glance with Schluntz, and then related the account of Sanderson's murder and the theft and recapture of the money sent from Charlestown. Judd's demise was covered merely as a postscript without triumph or celebration. Some brief clarification of the facts then ensued between the three, but when all questions had been answered all fell into a sombre and reflective mood.

'Well I'm sorry to hear about Sanderson,' said the Colonel at last. 'And I will, of course, try to get notification back to his family in St Mary's as soon as possible.' He stopped, frowned, and paused for a moment's thought. 'But perhaps not,' he went on more considerately, 'perhaps I'll deliver the sad news myself when all this is over – his family deserves better than to be told by a mere messenger.'

Others in the group nodded their approval but the atmosphere remained grave.

'Anyway,' the colonel continued, injecting a more businesslike tone into the proceedings, 'right at the moment, Jack, we've got other demands to sort out; and your arrival may well be part of the solution.' With this he flashed an enquiring eye at Green. 'Major?'

Major Green stepped forward. Decked in his silver wig, he wore the scarlet tunic, black breeches and long gaiters of a British infantry officer; and hanging on a chain about his neck was the silver gorget that marked his royal commission. By comparison, the uniforms of his militia companions were as dowdy moths to a flamboyant butterfly - and might attract less attention from a sniper's aim, thought Jack wryly, glad to be wearing the hide jacket of the Southern Maryland Scouts.

'We lost six of our men yesterday, Jack,' Green said plainly. 'Deserted. We've lost regulars at other times, but on this occasion all of the absconders were relatively new recruits - provincials picked up along the route from Philadelphia - men who'd volunteered but who'd clearly had second thoughts and decided to go home. I cannot condone it but, in a way, I can understand it – they're untrained, the going's been tough, and with our stretched logistic support, food and medical supplies have become short. They're not the first to go either – nor will they be the last to try, I'll warrant!' Green gave out a heavy sigh, flashing Jack an almost embarrassed glance. 'Anyway, suffice it to say,' he continued, 'that it has become a serious enough problem across the brigade to cause headquarters to fret about it. They think that it's got to be tackled fast or else the current trickle might become a flood that will damage our capability. To get to the heart of it, Jack, they've decided that an example has to be made of these men to deter others. They want them tracked down, brought back and dealt with summarily.' His steadfast gaze shifted uneasily with this last remark, but he answered the unspoken question forming on Jack's lips. 'And that means a court marshal and probably a firing squad - at least for the ring-leaders.'

Sir Michael had seated himself on a canvas field chair during the major's explanation and had sat with his legs crossed while he listened attentively, his elbows propped upon its arms, his hands clasped contemplatively to his chin. But now he uncrossed his legs, gripped the chair arms, and brought himself more upright in his seat.

'The long and the short of it, Jack,' he explained, 'is that we've been asked to lend some of our scouts to help round these men up. I gather that a party of redcoats is already on the trail, but the major wants some scouts out there as well – in case the deserters are not keeping to the main routes.'

'My redcoats won't be especially comfortable stalking in the forest; they're just not used to it,' Major Green added, as if by way of explanation.

'We were discussing it as you and the sergeant arrived,' Sir Michael continued. 'I have been arguing against it,' he sighed resignedly, 'I *had* claimed that we could not spare more scouts from Major Lawrence's unit with you two away. But I suppose that now that you are back it might change things…' He turned to the scout commander and raised an enquiring eyebrow. ' Major Lawrence?'

Major Lawrence was Sergeant Schluntz's immediate superior as scout platoon commander, and would become Jack's now that Jack had rejoined Sir Michael's militia. Distinguished by his neat, trimmed beard, Lawrence was perhaps an inch shorter than Jack and stockier in his build;

he wore the same worn, faded hunting jacket that he was wearing when Jack had first met him in the briefing tent at New Hope. Jack knew him by repute to be an experienced backwoods fighting man, a former British soldier with plans to settle in Maryland in due course. He was a straight-talking man who commanded the respect and liking of his scouts.

'You already know my opinion, sir,' the scout major began robustly; it was at once clear by his tone that he had resisted the proposal, 'Between here and the new post at Loyal Hannon, we'll be moving through increasingly dangerous territory. We've all heard the reports of French and Indian advances - even so far eastwards as Cumberland and Augusta - so we have to be prepared for ambush at any time from here on. If we lose scouts to this mission, it will leave holes in our forward and flank lookout just when we are most likely to come under attack. We'd be sending good fighting men off on a...on a housekeeping errand, sir, all just to find a few strays!' The major flashed an irritated glare at Green, then added darkly: 'Especially since we'd probably be bringing them back to be shot!' He swept a glance around the others in the tent, clearly hoping to rally some support.

But Major Green spoke up before anyone could come to Lawrence's aid. 'I understand the major's reluctance, sir.' He spoke calmly, directing himself to Sir Michael now. 'And I share his and, no doubt, your own unease and misgivings about the nature of the mission. But I have to remind you,' he said more stiffly, 'that you, like my colonel, now fall under headquarters' command, and they evidently think the issue important enough to warrant this commitment. It is their direct order that I merely convey.'

Sir Michael shook his head gravely and shrugged his shoulders. 'Well I hope that your lords and masters know what they are doing!' he sighed resignedly.

Major Green took off his wig and scratched his head. 'If it's any consolation, sir,' he said, visibly relaxing, 'we are not scheduled to move out for at least ten days. I'm sure that your scouts could be back by then, couldn't they?' Green threw the colonel a meaningful glance. 'And if not, at least they'll know where to find us.'

Sir Michael nodded a tight smile; he seemed to see some sense in that. 'Hmmm! A reasonable compromise, sir, I think. Major Lawrence, could you work with that?' Sir Michael was addressing his subordinate.

The scout commander nodded a resigned agreement. 'Then may I suggest that Lieutenant Easton and Sergeant Schluntz here be the only ones detailed to go,' he said. 'They seem to work well enough together acting on their own initiative. With the lieutenant colonel dead, sir, I am assuming that I shall take his place as far as discipline and training are concerned.' The colonel nodded grimly. 'And in light of that, sir,' Lawrence continued, 'I shall need a good strong core of subalterns and NCO's around me to keep up morale and motivation. Losing Lieutenant Easton and Sergeant Schluntz would be bad enough, but to let more officers and men go might court a desertion problem of our own!'

Sir Michael gave out a short but humourless laugh. 'Nicely argued.' he said, throwing an enquiring glance at Major Green. 'Would that satisfy their lordships, major?' he asked.

The redcoat seemed amused. 'I think that I need only to report to my commanders that a search party has been sent out supported by provincial scouts,' he said, 'I shall spare them the details!'

Jack and Schluntz exchanged frowns.

'Ten days before you depart, you say?' Jack questioned. 'And they are already ahead of us by a full day? Then we'll have our work cut out to catch them, major! How are they travelling?'

'They stole horses, Jack,' said Major Green, tightly. 'I'll give you a full briefing if you'll come over to the regimental headquarters tent as soon as you are ready.'

Jack waited for a consenting nod from Sir Michael then made to leave; Schluntz went with him. But as the pair reached the tent-flap, Jack turned back.

'Oh, one thing I didn't mention…' he began. Sir Michael and the others had fallen back into conversation behind them, but now they looked up.

'Before we got diverted into going after Judd,' Jack went on, 'we were on the trail of two others involved in *Miranda's* hijack. Sir Michael - you'll remember them: Pettigrew and Hayward. I gather you heard about the escape from Mr Harding before you left Charlestown?'

The colonel frowned. 'Yes, but what the blazes would they be doing out here?'

'We're not sure, sir, but we think that they're probably making for French territory - using the military road most likely.'

Jack had noticed the look of puzzlement that furrowed Green's forehead at the mention of Pettigrew's name, and so decided to press the matter further.

'Major Green, you'll remember Pettigrew, I think? He was the one who led the escape from the *Miranda* - taking that father and son hostage.'

The redcoat nodded. 'Indeed,' he replied in a strangely distracted tone. It was clear from his expression that something troubled him, but Jack continued regardless:

'We got a pretty firm identification from a settler on the road north of Frederick about a week ago – he recognised Pettigrew's face from my poster – so if he and Hayward are using the military road, any number of soldiers might have come across them by now. It may be worth putting the word out just in case – I've got a copy of the poster if you want it.'

Green's eyes narrowed suddenly. Something seemed to have thrown him into introspection. 'We *have* picked up a few strays along the way,' he said, nodding thoughtfully. 'It is quite possible that these two might be amongst them, and there's a couple in particular that come to mind,' he said mysteriously. 'Bring the poster with you when you come over, Jack; ' he said. 'I'll get my recruiting sergeant to look at it too – he's had more to do with them than I.'

About an hour later, Jack and Schluntz arrived at Major Green's tent for their briefing, and they found the major waiting, accompanied by a redcoat sergeant major. Jack had brought his 'wanted' poster as had been requested, carrying it rolled up in his hand. The major spotted it immediately.

'Let me have a look at that, Jack,' he said, holding out his hand impatiently. He took the paper, unfurled it, and held it up for his sergeant major to inspect. 'I remember you doing this sketch on deck while we were waiting for our orders in Annapolis, Jack,' he said as an aside as he examined it. 'You've added to it since, I think?'

'Oh, the hat and the goatee?' asked Jack, reminded of his rough amendments. 'Yes, but I can rub those out - I added them in Frederick. That was how he was last reported - he could look different now, of course.'

'What do you think, sar'nt major?' asked Green.

'That's him, sir,' the sergeant major replied after hardly a moment's inspection. 'No doubt about it, sir; we found him and the other feller on the road in a bit of a poor state - a couple of days before we reached Fort Loudoun.'

'God damn it!' retorted Green, crossly. 'When we picked them up, I thought I'd seen one of them before!' He punched one hand with the other, chastising himself. 'We came across the two of them on the road on foot - in the middle of nowhere! They said they'd lost their horses – cooked up some story about wanting to volunteer. It crossed my mind then that one of them looked familiar, but both were unshaven and dishevelled. And I'm afraid to say that, with one thing and another, I quite forgot about them after that.' He shook his head in self-reproach. 'What did they say their names were, sar'nt major?'

'Smith and Jones, sir!' replied the redcoat sergeant major with a derisory smirk. 'I should have twigged the bastards, begging your pardon, sir. Trouble from the start they were! Within a few days of joining they was building a little cadre of rebellion in the ranks. The poor food hadn't helped morale, of course, sir – it had given the men something to gripe about anyway, and I think these two men of yours used the general discontent to stir things up.'

'And we're pretty sure that it was these two who led the desertion, Jack,' admitted the major. 'All of the deserters were employed as orderlies and quartermaster's assistants and so were well placed to lay their hands on equipment and supplies. Seems obvious when you think about it - if I were going to desert, these are just the sort I would recruit. They'd know what was going on too.'

'Didn't last long together though, sir,' put in the sergeant major. 'I got a report back this morning from the tracking party, sir; they've found trails going off in all sorts of directions. They've split up apparently. The lieutenant in charge is asking for more help, sir.'

'Hmmm, clever!' groaned the major.

'Pettigrew's just being true to form,' answered Jack, simply. 'He's used the others to cover his own escape! He and Hayward probably needed their help to prepare and equip, but once they'd made their break, the others would have become a liability. They'd be more useful to Pettigrew laying trails of their own to confuse the trackers! My guess would be that he planned it this way from the start for that very reason!'

'Quite possible,' agreed Major Green, nodding sagely. He pondered for a moment as if considering options. He then seemed to make up his mind, for his manner became suddenly quite decisive.

'Jack, you have my permission to make Pettigrew and this other fellow your priority,' he said. 'If we're going to put anyone in front of a firing squad, then it should be Pettigrew. I share a particular interest in seeing him brought to justice too; his gang shot one of my men aboard the *Miranda* when we tried to stop them escaping - remember?' (Jack nodded.) 'The soldier survived, by the way,' the major went on, 'but lost his arm, poor chap - we had to leave him in Annapolis. That fifty pound reward on Pettigrew's head would keep him from an English poorhouse when he's eventually shipped home; he won't have an easy time of it without a pension.'

Jack grimaced. 'Pettigrew owes a good many others too, William,' he said wryly. 'Those hostages he took were found washed up on a beach with their hands tied. Then in Charlestown, his thugs slit the throats of Captain Goddard's deck-watch when they hijacked his ship. And even on the trail here, Sergeant Schluntz and I came across a farmstead on the road out of Frederick that'd had a visitation from the pair of them. They stole horses and ransacked the place, then just left it to burn – leaving a woman and her son tied up inside to burn with it!'

Jack shook his head, still incredulous at the thought that such a pitiless murderer may yet go unpunished for his crimes. But this was Pettigrew, he reflected bitterly. It was his callous indifference that had led directly or indirectly to the deaths of Elizabeth, Captain Middleton, young Ben Proctor, *and* his own father. All would still be alive but for the activities of this manipulative bastard!

'He owes a debt for his crimes on *both* sides of the Atlantic, William!' he added. 'I do not want him shot – death should not come too tidily for the likes of him. I want his end to be drawn out and painful; I want him to suffer before he takes his last breath!'

Major Green lifted an eyebrow at Jack's vehemence, but nodded soberly. 'Then you'd better get yourselves equipped and get going as quickly as you can, Jack,' he said. 'Go with the sar'nt major here when we're finished – he'll sort you out with whatever you want and brief you on whatever you need to know.' He paused in thought for a moment. 'I would suggest that you try to catch up with the tracking party first - Lieutenant Hawkins is the officer in charge – then decide between you how to split up your resources. It's possible that his men might have already recaptured some of the deserters and extracted information about the others' intentions...they must have discussed between themselves where each would be heading?'

'We think we already know where Pettigrew and Hayward are making for, William,' said Jack firmly. '- into French territory where they probably think they'll be safe.'

'Hmmm. Bring that map case over to the table, sar'nt major,' ordered Green, flicking a directing glance to a leather tube propped upon a large travelling trunk at the end of his long tent. And he waited while the sergeant major retrieved the case and brought it back. The map was withdrawn and spread out on a trestle table that occupied the centre of the earthen floor. Propping his arms on the table for support, Green leant forward to study the map closely. After a moment or two, he straightened and shook his head.

'Well they won't be following the new road, Jack,' said the major adamantly, 'not with all our sister units already en route to the new post at Loyal Hannon. It would be too risky for them with so many already on the lookout for deserters; and anyway, beyond the Loyal Hannon the road's not finished - they'd probably have found that out. I'll pass your poster up the line just in case, but if Pettigrew wants to make contact with the French, he's more likely to have headed down the link road to Cumberland to join General Braddock's old route west. Here, look,' he said, running his finger down the map. The others clustered around the table to examine it. 'Here,' he repeated, pointing again, to be sure that his companions could see where he meant. 'We had reports that the French used the southern route to make one of their raids from Fort Duquesne earlier this year, so we know they won't be far away.'

Sergeant Schluntz broke in, his brow puckered in a frown.

'It looks like it'll be about thirty miles longer for them that way than on the northern road, sir, but still not much more than a hundred miles in all,' he said. 'That's only five or six days on horseback if the going's fair. And they'll be able to carry enough supplies to get them all the way there, so won't need to lose time foraging for food.' He turned to Jack. 'If we're already a whole day behind, Jack, there's not much chance that we'll be able to catch them before they make contact with the French, especially if they've got forward pickets out watching the road.'

'And what we don't want,' said the major most emphatically, 'is for the French to learn too much about us. They'll probably know that we're coming by now, but they won't know when, or which direction we're approaching from, or how large the force is. That's all potentially decisive intelligence! If Pettigrew trades that information for his safety, it could tip the tactical balance and give the French an advantage!'

The major fell into a thoughtful silence, his eyes seeming to grow wider as he pondered his own words. It was as if the full import of his analysis was only now dawning – the thought that his unit might be the source of French intelligence, intelligence that might cause the failure of General Forbes' carefully planned expedition. History would render a harsh indictment, and he would not want his career blighted by association.

'Jack,' he said at last, his voice becoming suddenly quite urgent, 'this changes everything! Pettigrew and Hayward must be prevented from making contact with the enemy at all costs!'

Green was clearly agitated now, for he began to pace as he spoke, thumping the fist of one hand into the palm of the other repeatedly.

'Forget Lieutenant Hawkins and his search party - making contact with him now would be a waste of your time. I prefer to back your hunch about Pettigrew's intentions. You must follow them with all haste – you must go south to Cumberland then onto the old southern route to Fort Duquesne and catch them up!'

Jack and Sergeant Schluntz exchanged questioning glances. Perhaps both had had the same thought; but it was Jack who spoke.

'Look, William,' said Jack waving his hand at the map, 'these routes eventually converge in the Ohio valley. It would make more sense for us to try to cut the corner somewhere here (he traced a possible interception route with his finger), rather than simply follow the same road. The northern route's clearly more direct isn't it? So we could get ahead of them if we stayed on it and cut across later – here perhaps?'

Schluntz nodded. 'And the southern route winds a lot more, sir,' he said, pointing, '- so it's a lot longer; and these river crossings might slow them down too. Now here,' he said emphatically, moving his finger further along the line on the map, 'the southern route swings sharply north again for the best part of thirty miles. So if we took the more direct northern road like the lieutenant says, there comes a point - here (he indicated) – where the two routes come within about ten to fifteen miles of each other.' (He waited for the major to lean over to inspect the map more closely.) 'You see, sir?' continued the sergeant. 'They will have to travel nearly three times our distance to reach almost the same point. So if we were able to find a decent trail going south – say, around there somewhere (he indicated an arc to the south and west of Loyal Hannon) - we should come out ahead of them.'

'Hmmm, yes,' said the major, approvingly, 'that might well work. I'd say it's certainly worth a try. I'll write out some official orders to authorise your passage along the route, otherwise you'd be challenged and stopped. The papers should also get you some assistance if you need it – you'll want to stock up on provisions at Loyal Hannon, at the very least.' His expression now turned more serious. 'You'll just have to be careful not to run into the enemy down there, Jack,' he said soberly, tracing his finger along the proposed route. 'Like us, they're going to have scouting parties sniffing about; so tread quietly or they'll hear you coming.'

Chapter Twenty-One

Jack and Sergeant Schluntz had been on the road only two days when they heard of the attack on the post at Loyal Hannon. If until then, Jack had imagined war with the French as a series of classic set-piece battles on open ground, this news disabused him of that notion immediately, for it was anything but that. And by the number of British prisoners and casualties reported, it was also clear that relative superiority in terms of size was no guarantee of victory.

Reports of the attack had travelled back along the new road, passed by messenger from one unit to the next as each progressed in column from Bedford towards the new post. Jack and Schluntz were told the story by a mounted sergeant who rode flank to the rearmost of these units, with which the pair had just that morning caught up.

'Seems that we might have brought it on ourselves,' said the sergeant, having dropped back to ride alongside.

He had to raise his voice over the constant grating and grinding of marching feet and carriage wheels. His unit, an artillery regiment trailing several large cannon and howitzer carriages, stretched ahead into the distance, a thick line of scarlet snaking through unending verdant forest. The din of hooves, chains, and carriage wheels was almost deafening.

'And we don't appear to have been at our best in repulsing it either.' He said wryly. 'Anyway, it's apparently all over now. The French have gone back to Fort Duquesne, so it shouldn't affect your plans.'

To boil the details of his tale down to its essence, it seems that about a month previously, around mid-September reportedly, the new post's commander, the Swiss-born Colonel Bouquet (previously mentioned), had sent a force of over seven hundred men to the forks of the Ohio to reconnoitre the general lay of the land. Irritated by the sniping raids that had been hindering his new fort's completion, the colonel may also have hoped that a show of British strength in the area might deter the French from making further mischief. The commander of that force, however, seemed to have strayed somewhat from his brief! Instead of the authorised reconnaissance, the officer evidently took it into his head to mount a direct attack on Fort Duquesne in an attempt to capture it, possibly motivated by the prospect (and the glory) of a quick victory before Forbes arrived in theatre. But he seems to have been outsmarted by the French commander, a Colonel de Lignery, who received intelligence of the British force's approach and laid a trap. Despite a numerical advantage, the ill-planned assault resulted in the capture of its reckless leader and the death of nearly half his men.

This latest attack on the post at Loyal Hannon, just a month following that debacle, was the predictable reprisal. Yet the officer left in charge of the post, deputising for Colonel Bouquet who was away at the time, seems to have been caught completely by surprise. It took his men at arms a whole day and night to repulse the attack despite a numerical advantage of more than three to one.

It was suggested that the de Lignery's objective might have been to capture British supplies. His own, it seems, were running low following the recent fall to the British of Fort Frontenac, the French logistic distribution hub at the bottom of the Saint Lawrence. And, undoubtedly emboldened by his easy victory a month before, he seems not to have been deterred by the odds stacked heavily against him. A British-American force of around two thousand men was garrisoned at Loyal Hannon at the time against only four hundred and forty French troops and one hundred and fifty Delaware warriors. To give the British commander his due, he had stationed soldiers to guard the supplies within the larger retrenchment outside the palisade. But he did not fully appreciate the danger he had put them in, for the defensive enclosure that might otherwise have protected them had not yet been completed. Pickets had also been detailed to guard the expedition's livestock grazing some mile-and-a-half distant but these were even more exposed.

It was these dispersed and unprotected sentinels that were the first targets of the French and Indian attacks. Bouquet's deputy had completely underestimated the boldness and tenacity of the French force, and the stealth and guile of their approach. When firing was first heard to break out, two hundred American troops of the Maryland Battalion were quickly dispatched towards the action but were forced back. A second battalion (of Pennsylvanians) was then sent out to reinforce the first, but these men too were forced to retreat to the stockade. Finally, it took a bombardment from British artillery to turn back the French and Indian advance.

It soon became apparent, however, that the enemy withdrawal had been tactical. Under darkness, they returned and renewed their assault, this time on one of the redoubts. Again the attack was repulsed by artillery, but the enemy remained near the fort throughout the night, sniping at sentries and continuously testing the defences. When the French commander finally withdrew his largely unmolested force, he had in his possession the coveted British supplies, about two hundred horses, several dozen prisoners, and a number of British and American scalps. He left behind twelve British soldiers dead and eighteen wounded. In all, thirty-one men were reported missing at the end of the engagement.

Jack and Schluntz had listened to the unfolding account with mounting despair.

'Oh dear God,' exclaimed Jack when the sergeant had finished.

Schluntz just shook his head.

It was not an auspicious opening to Forbes' campaign.

There followed days of almost continuous drizzle as Jack and Sergeant Schluntz, choosing now to travel in the company of the military phalanx, continued westwards along the military road. The drizzle was composed of such fine water particles that it looked more like drifting mist than actual precipitation; and visibility within it was so poor that it was rarely possible to see more than twenty yards ahead. A rider might be aware of the road's meanderings, its obstacles, its ascents and descents, but the view from the saddle seemed to change little, hour after hour: the same rough-cut road fading into grey invisibility, marshalled by the same, seemingly unending avenue of tall and thinning trees. The woodland backdrop was streaked with wisps of vapour caught like wool on a hedge. The up-reaching branches became a conduit for moisture, which coalesced to fall as droplets upon the brittle leaves below, striking with the percussive pitter-patter of marching drums. They beat out a rhythm with which the leaden feet of marching men could not hope to keep time. The cold, thin air of the high passes seemed so laden, that just to breathe it made a man choke. The scarlet cloth of uniforms was soon sodden, the flesh beneath soon chapped and cold. Men muttered, sniffed, and spat out phlegm, the column pressing on relentlessly, across dry streambeds turned to gushing torrents, on soaked earth trodden into bog.

The military column soon slowed to a snail's pace as feet got stuck in cloying mud and wheels sunk up to their axles. What had been an orderly flow along the road became a series of miserable waits and faltering starts as queues built up – to be relieved eventually by platoons of roving engineers, moving from one hold-up to the next, finding ever more ingenious ways to bridge or circumnavigate the obstacles. This was a routine that was repeated time after time as the army crawled its way westward. And with all this delay and frustration, Jack and Sergeant Schluntz soon began to feel that their short cut might not have been such a good idea after all. They feared that the advantage they had hoped to gain over Pettigrew and Hayward was fast being whittled away.

'At this rate, Jack, we'll be lucky to intercept them,' said Schluntz gloomily from the saddle of his stationary horse.

The pair waited impatiently behind a queue of drenched soldiers, so glum in their discomfort that they had fallen into a surly mood. The road ahead had been washed away, and a sort of corduroy road was being constructed from the trunks of trees, felled at the roadside then dragged into place by several pairs of oxen. It was the second such delay of the morning.

'Well, let's hope that this weather is causing Pettigrew and Hayward as much difficulty as it is us – though they won't have this chaos in front of them to slow them down!' said Jack, despondently. He cast a weary glance over the logjam of vehicles, men and horses that jostled for position as the work approached completion.

'But nor will they have these engineers to help them,' replied Schluntz more optimistically.

There was a sudden lurch amongst the throng and a weary cheer rose up as the roadway was reopened. The jostling column then surged forward as if a dam had been broken. There was some shouting and cursing from a few who had been taken by surprise. Those that had not been quick enough to pick up their packs, would have no chance of fighting the scarlet tide that now swept everyone along in its path.

'One thing in our favour, at least as far as Pettigrew is concerned,' added Jack, a little more upbeat as he spurred his mount forward, 'is that the French will have interrogated the prisoners taken in that last raid by now...and the more they already know about British troop movements, the less Pettigrew will have to bargain with.'

'Depends,' said Schluntz doubtfully as he brought his mount into step alongside Jack's. 'The average soldier's head is filled with rumour and gossip – scuttlebutt, I think you say,' he said, trying out some of his recently acquired English vernacular. '...and most of it's likely to be conflicting too; so the French won't get much that they can rely on. Anyway, they must already feel very confident. They have easily beaten British and American units two times now in just a few weeks:' (he shook his head despairingly and glared at Jack as if he were personally

225

responsible for all the failures) '– first, by repulsing that reckless raid on Fort Duquesne, and then by mounting their successful counter attack on Loyal Hannon, when the response must have looked weak and uncoordinated! Why, it's only a couple of years ago that Braddock's army was defeated trying to take the same fort!' Schluntz shrugged his shoulders and threw a hopeless glance into the heavens. *'Der Colonel De Lignery brauchte um sein Leben nicht Fürchten!'* he muttered disparagingly. (Schluntz was not easily riled, but these examples of British and American ineptitude had clearly vexed him, for he had lapsed into his native tongue.)

Jack inclined his head. 'True – none of them impressive military performances, were they?' he admitted, smiling at his friend's fluster. 'It doesn't bode well, does it? But then again, de Lignery probably won't know that he was only fighting a fraction of the total British and American force, will he – and led by a subordinate too. I suppose Pettigrew's usefulness depends on how much he knows about all the other units coming up behind, and whether Forbes is directing them all along the same route. Let's hope he doesn't know too much!'

'Pettigrew was a clerk in the headquarters, Jack!' argued Schluntz, as if that proved his point. 'From where he worked, he could have overheard anything and everything! He could be very valuable to the French.'

Jack clamped his jaw and nodded glumly.

With so much congestion on the road, especially with so many bottlenecks caused by stricken vehicles stuck on boggy ground, it had been impossible to overtake the straggling convoy and press ahead as they had first hoped. Thus, eventually abandoning aspirations of making better progress, the pair (using Major Green's orders as authority) arranged to be adopted by the regiment they had by chance been following at the time. It was at least a small compensation to be billeted in relative comfort under regimental canvas and fed on the hearty if narrow menu of the regimental mess.

The pair arrived at the post at Loyal Hannon in the late afternoon of the fifth day, having put Fort Bedford now some forty miles behind - five days for a journey that, unimpeded by traffic and weather, should have taken two! By this time, however, the overcast was already lifting, with brighter skies at last becoming visible in the west. And with this Jack's mood lifted too - as if a burden had been lifted from his shoulders. Suddenly everything seemed possible after all.

Jack and Schluntz's adopted regiment was allotted an area within the retrenchment near the artillery revetment, a crescent-shaped earthen embankment that projected from the west wall of the fort. As the soldiers set about erecting their tents in the prescribed area, a low sun made a late appearance under the dark mantle of lifting clouds. But it was a cool sun and its weak rays bathed the encampment in a watery yellow light that held no comfort. Looking across the esplanade, a roughly level area within the outer retrenchments defended by several artillery batteries, Jack counted at least twenty lines of tents already erected. Here and there, regimental colours, made vivid in the sunshine, flapped lazily in the breeze; Jack counted five already flying, and the colours of his adopted regiment would soon join them.

The walls of the fort towered close by, a sturdy, solid pine construction of perhaps two hundred feet square, with defensive bastions projecting from each corner. A score of red-coated guards with muskets on their shoulders patrolled the ramparts, their watchful gazes scanning the horizon. Echoing and reverberating within the walls, the staccato sounds of carpentry told Jack that work was still underway. A union flag hung lazily from a tall flagstaff that crowned the centre of the palisade.

The undulating ground around the fort became more and more crowded as other units arrived within the retrenchment. It seemed that the recent attack had injected a sense of urgency, for no sooner had one regiment entered the encampment and unloaded their wagons than another appeared at the gates. And by the sweat on the horses' flanks and the flushed faces of the marching men arriving at the gates, they had not spared any of the shortening daylight hours to rest. Jack guessed that orders must have been passed back along the road for all remaining regiments to make haste into the protection of the post; a military unit stretched out within the narrow confines of a rough forest road would be vulnerable to ambush, and the sooner they were off it the better. He wondered if Major Green's regiment and Sir Michael's militia would be hurried forward too.

He wondered too if the recent French raid had focussed minds; this fortification certainly seemed better located and defended than Fort Bedford, though admittedly the latter at the present time was more of a supply hub than a bastion and did not need quite so much protection. For a start, the river and cliffs running along the post's southern perimeter would be relatively easy to defend, and from Jack's elevated position near the palisade's high walls, other approaches looked well covered too. The reported weaknesses in the outer defences, a ring of pointed stakes and earthen embankments that encircled the tented esplanade, must also have been attended to since the French raid, for Jack could see no gaps along its entire length. Indeed, with its profusion of batteries and lookout posts, each with an attendant cluster of red and fawn tunics, the fortification seemed to be at a high state of readiness.

And by every appearance, the fortification would be a relatively comfortable place to spend the winter too, with its officers' mess, storerooms, and barracks, all substantially built or in the process of construction for an extended stay. There was even a smokehouse for meat preservation, a sawmill, a smithy, and a hospital with resident surgeon. And the fact that Brigadier General Forbes had ordered a hut built for his own occupation gave every impression that his army would spend the winter here before marching on Fort Duquesne next spring. It was, after all, an established axiom that fighting was not a practicable winter activity: an army got bogged down or frozen in; powder got wet and would not fire; and cold, wet soldiers could be surly and uncooperative, especially if the cooking fires would not light. It was thus confidently assumed that the brigadier would be too careful a soldier, and his health too poor, for him to risk leading his tired troops into battle against Fort Duquesne so late in the year. And with that expectation, there might have been a general air of ease within the headquarters building when Jack and Sergeant Schluntz visited it later that evening looking for advice on possible routes south. The atmosphere was anything but.

The sentry at the gate let the two pass by with a suspicious glance, and stepping through the tall entrance gates that hung open on massive iron hinges, they saw the administrative office immediately to their left. Identified by a painted sign 'Adjutant' pinned to the wall alongside its open door, the office lay at the near end of a long building that evidently accommodated a number of different service functions. A boardwalk running the length of the building connected several doorways, and in front of some of these, red-coated soldiers stood on guard. Directly opposite this building, a second of similar proportions appeared to be a barracks, with several platoons of soldiers forming up in ranks in front of its open doors. The space between the two buildings, a grassy square with the tall flagstaff at its centre, was clearly an assembly area of some sort. A number of artillery pieces were positioned here and there with groups of soldiers receiving instruction clustered around them. There was an air of intensity about their drill.

Jack and Schluntz entered the office to find themselves at the rear of a briefing of some sort. It was a relatively confined space - bare wood walls, low ceiling, one small window - and the half-dozen men now standing in the room seemed to fill it. Facing the assembly, two officers, one sitting behind a desk, the other perching half on it, listened intently as an imposing bare-chested, black-haired Indian scout spoke out. Jack and Schluntz moved sideways so as to hear and see better past the shoulders of the men in front. The Indian spoke in a strangely deep and guttural tongue, using his hands in a sort of semaphore as if to emphasise what he was saying. He had an air of assurance about him, as though he felt anything but inferior in the company of uniformed men. The officers studied him as he spoke, but from their puzzled expressions, it appeared that, like the two newcomers, they did not understand a word of what was being said. After a while, during which time everyone else in the room seemed frozen in attentive poses as if in awe of the native presence, one of the other men cleared his throat and began to translate. It became clear at once that the Indian was making a report on intelligence gathered during his recent reconnaissance. The seated officer, by his grey hair and gravitas evidently the more senior of the two, listened soberly with his arms folded across his chest; the other - younger, his scarlet tunic casually unbuttoned revealing the white cotton of his shirt beneath - seemed to be taking notes. The report continued thus for several minutes more, the Indian talking in his strange language, interrupted from time to time by translation, until piece by piece, the full report was eventually completed.

It appeared that after the recent French raid on the post, the scout had followed the raiding party back to Fort Duquesne, some fifty miles away, where he reported activity soon returning to its normal routines. He had counted fifteen uniformed British-American prisoners taken inside the Fort's gates but had seen nothing more of them in the two days that he remained watching from his hidden viewpoint. Two small scouting parties, each of several Delaware warriors and one or two white scouts (probably French non-commissioned officers, the Indian suggested), were observed to leave the Fort in that time, one heading north up the river valley, retracing the raiding party's returning path in the direction of Loyal Hannon, the second heading south. Significantly, he had noticed a sudden upturn in the amount of troop activity within the enclosure during the morning of his departure – in particular an assembly of soldiers and

Indian warriors - which suggested that a further expedition of some sort was imminent.

There followed a few questions from the officers, which were answered and translated in the same manner, before the briefing was terminated and the men dismissed. This left Jack and Schluntz standing by the doorway as the four men exited past them, and they hovered there uncertainly as the two officers reflected on the Indian's report. It seemed that neither had noticed the two strangers still in the room.

The senior officer shook his head resignedly.

'I fear that we must expect another attack,' he said. 'They won't just sit there and wait for us to come. They'll do everything they can to interfere with our build-up.'

The younger officer nodded thoughtfully. 'Then I hope, sir,' he said in measured tones, 'that we shall send out a suitable contingent to intercept it...'

It was at this point that the senior officer's surprised glance caught the two visitors standing near the doorway, and with a lift of a finger, he silenced his subordinate.

Without waiting for an invitation, Jack stepped forward and saluted, hoping to take the initiative before the officers could react adversely to their presence, introducing himself and his companion smartly. And by presenting Major Green's orders into the senior officer's hand, he neatly forestalled the officer's incipient objection.

The senior officer seemed a little taken aback by Jack's forthrightness, but he unfolded and read the orders, eventually handing the paper to his subordinate with a nod of his head.

'Sort them out will you, captain,' he said gruffly, without so much as a glance in Jack's direction. 'I've got other matters to attend to.' And with that, he rose from his chair and left in somewhat of a hurry, leaving the captain still perched on the desk reading the note.

'Looks like you've drawn the short straw with this one – damned traitors these deserters!' he said at last, getting to his feet.

He was a tall man, perhaps as tall as six feet in his boots, and his head came close to the ceiling beam as he reached his full height. His short, dark hair was slicked back and flattened as if he had just taken off his wig.

'Are you sure you know what you're doing?' He raised a doubtful eyebrow. 'As you'll probably just have overheard, there's likely to be a fair bit going on out there at present. Not easy to see who's who in those woods, you know; and everyone's so touchy these days that either side could open fire without asking questions first.'

'We intend go on foot from here, sir,' said Schluntz, 'so as to travel quiet - so as to make sure we see or hear them first!' He flashed a glance at Jack who, though taken by surprise by the suggestion, nodded in approval. Horses can't be hidden and they make a lot of noise, he realised. Anyone on the lookout, friend or foe, would hear them coming miles away.

'Hmmm,' uttered the captain, stroking his chin thoughtfully. 'All right, I'll help you as much as I can with supplies, but you'll be on your own; I can't spare any of my men to guide you! Come over here; I'll show you on the map.'

He led the pair across the room to a map pinned to the wall facing the only window, which despite the approach of dusk let in enough light to see the detail clearly.

'There's an old trail that leads southwest to connect up with General Braddock's old road,' he said, running his finger down the map to indicate the route. 'It crosses this ridge here, and runs down the other side...along the valley here, until it meets the Braddock road, here, where it fords the Youghiogheny River.' He stumbled over the pronunciation and gave out a little laugh as he corrected himself. 'It's one of the tributaries to the Monongahela River' (he got that one right) 'which it joins just before its confluence with the Allegheny River coming south to form the Ohio...here. And where the two meet,' he said with a sharp prod of his finger on the map, 'are the famous forks that Fort Duquesne commands! So if you get as far as that, it'll probably be as captives – assuming you haven't already been scalped! The French pay the Indians a bounty for British scalps, you know, so they're quite keen to collect them.' The captain flashed Jack a wry glance at his audience, waiting for a reaction; but Jack simply bent closer to the map and studied it more closely.

'This ford,' he said thoughtfully, 'it looks about twenty miles from Loyal Hannon?' Jack wanted the captain's confirmation to be sure he understood what lay ahead.

The captain checked the scale bar. 'About right, yes,' he said, 'perhaps a little less; and still fifty from Fort Duquesne so relatively safe, I'd say; although don't bank on it. A good place to await this Pettigrew fellow. If he's on the road, he has to cross the river there – otherwise it's pure untrodden wilderness. It's not a bad path down there, but it'll take you a good two days. How much of a lead has he got?' he asked.

Jack outlined the relative timing of Pettigrew and Hayward's desertion from Fort Bedford, and his and his companion's departure a day later and their progress since.

The captain checked the map's scale bar again and measured out the distances with his hand, marching his outstretched thumb and index finger along both routes in turn like a set of navigational dividers.

'It will be quite a lot further for them on the southern route so there's a good chance you'll get there first, even if they started a day or so ahead – especially if they've been slowed up like you have by the atrocious weather. And there are two major river crossings on the southern route before they reach this one, so if *you've* had trouble getting here from Fort Bedford, they'll probably have had it even worse!'

'I hope so!' said Jack. 'But as we can't depend on that, we'll set off at first light tomorrow.'

'Well, if that's the case, gentlemen, may I wish you goodnight and the best of luck!' the officer said, offering his hand, 'I'll put the word out amongst our scouts that you're out there, but I can't guarantee that it will protect you. You'll have to keep your wits about you!' The officer returned to his desk as the pair made for the door. 'See the quartermaster if you need anything,' he called, as they reached it. 'Tell him I've approved it.'

Chapter Twenty-Two

The desertion from Fort Bedford had gone according to Pettigrew's plan. He, in league with Hayward and four other malcontents who had been easy to disaffect once the going had got rough, had been planning it for days. All local volunteers who had been allocated support duties within Major Green's company, they had been well selected by Pettigrew as likely candidates - orderlies, cooks, and livery hands – the sort who could ferret out useful information, the sort who could keep their mouths shut, and the sort who could lay their hands on the wherewithal required without drawing too much attention to themselves. But however well organised and equipped they might become they could not just flee into the wilderness. They needed an escape route that would take them speedily away from the main stream of the army's advance, yet also one that would not be too difficult to navigate. It had been the lack of intelligence in this respect that had stayed Pettigrew's hand. Indeed, he and Hayward had begun to wonder if the military machine they had artfully sought to use for their own benefit had in fact become a trap, for as the days passed, it looked more and more likely that there would be no escape. When they arrived at Fort Bedford, however, two decisive pieces of information reached Pettigrew's ears. The first of these was of Brigadier Forbes' decision to take the new, more direct northern route to the Ohio forks; the second was that not only did a passable escape route exist, but also that it led directly to Braddock's old southern road. With this knowledge, everything in Pettigrew's plan fell into place. The coincidence could not have been more opportune. On horseback, the thirty or so miles to intercept the southern road, passing down the valleys of the Appalachian ridges rather than across them, could be achieved in a day, or two at most. And once there, his co-deserters could be sent their separate ways to confuse pursuit. He and Hayward would then have a clear run westward into French territory.

And so it was - at least for this first part of Pettigrew's escape strategy, which played out just exactly as he had planned. Spread out in ones and twos in a long and uncommunicative line, the group followed the link path southwest at a steady and uninterrupted pace. Having slipped out of their tents in the dead of night, moreover, their desertion remained unnoticed for some hours, and they reached Braddock's old road before nightfall of the same day. Once there, Pettigrew and Hayward lost no time in ridding themselves of their compatriots who now turned east and south, making for destinations that Pettigrew could not care less about – except that in doing so their fellow deserters would continue to serve their purpose by leaving a number of trails for any tracking party to follow.

Pettigrew need not have worried; his ploy would work just as intended. Lieutenant James Hawkins and the men of his small platoon, arriving at the same spot some five hours later, were presented with a dilemma. The Lieutenant's Indian scout had tracked the hoof prints of Pettigrew's six horses in the soft ground of the link road quite easily, and now saw their dispersal in several directions. But, as he would later report, there were too many to follow them all, especially since the recent onset of precipitation would make the tracks short-lived. Though two sets of tracks were observed to go west and another south, three of the horses appeared to have turned eastward. And so, not wanting to split his small party, the lieutenant elected sensibly to follow the larger group, reckoning it would leave an easier trail. But he and his men would return to Fort Bedford empty-handed some three days later, demoralised and soaked to the skin. His report to Major Green, however, would at least lend credence to Jack Easton's assertion that Pettigrew and Hayward had gone west, for who else in that party of scoundrels would have wanted to head towards the enemy. Furthermore, this intelligence would prove yet more helpful in due course, for soon afterwards, a certain Jeremiah Blake would arrive at Fort Bedford fresh from the gravesides of his wife and son. And he was a very angry and determined man.

The old fur-traders' path leading southwest from the post at Loyal Hannon initially followed a tumbling stream, meandering through low, rolling hills that had taken the place of the mountainous ridges at last left behind. By degree, the stream withered to a narrow brook and then a trickle, until finally it disappeared into a rocky gully, leaving the path to strike out on its own. Schluntz, a veteran of skirmishes in similar territory further north, had used old paths like this before and had little difficulty in following it. He said he liked them because they always seemed to seek out the least arduous routes, following the shallowest gradients, valleys, and gorges wherever possible. Marked and eroded over decades of use, the paths were once part of an extensive network that connected Indian fur suppliers with European traders, and neither would have considered it a virtue to make life difficult. In such hilly terrain, therefore, the paths were rarely direct, but because they were also rarely strenuous, they were fast.

Although they did not know it, Jack and Schluntz were treading a path with a long history. Even before the days of significant settlement in these relatively new colonial territories, the export of animal fur to Europe was a major and burgeoning trade, a trade spearheaded by the French but quickly emulated by the British and the Dutch. In fact, it might be said that it was the market for fur that drove early exploration deep into the continent to satisfy demand (largely from the European hat trade of all things!). And it was those fur traders who forged the first alliances with Native American nations, bartering for beaver with European goods. Indeed, it was those alliances, either with the expanding British or the resisting French (the Dutch had since quit New Amsterdam, now renamed New York), which characterised the present conflict over territory. Some of these old paths had returned to nature, but others, like the one that Jack and Schluntz now used to lead them to the Youghiogheny River were still well trodden. They had endured because they still linked the settlements that had grown up around a trade that even now flourished. Yet it was a trade retreating westwards from ever encroaching settlement and the accompanying destruction of habitat.

The pair reached the river at dusk, arriving at the ford where the old Braddock road crossed it. No one was in sight. Opposite, the empty road appeared as if out of a solid wall of trees and descended obliquely to the river; it was a part earthen, part stony track, wide enough for a wagon and well worn. On the near side of the ford, the track emerged from the crossing at the same oblique angle, and climbed a steep wooded ascent before disappearing quite quickly out of sight over a ridge. Schluntz stooped and spent some minutes examining a stretch of the road nearest to the river, looking for any telltale signs of use. The ground was mainly gravel here, but there were patches of bare earth made soft by the recent rains. He moved carefully, treading with an agile step from one stony patch to another, so as to avoid leaving any imprints of his own.

'No recent tracks,' he said laconically, when he returned.

'Not too late then,' Jack replied hopefully.

Jack had been surveying the immediate area for a suitable place from which to observe the crossing point and mount an ambush.

'Unless they're long gone - and their tracks with them with the rain!' said Schluntz.

'Well, let's hope not,' Jack replied. He pointed towards a small, rocky outcrop a few paces up river. 'A likely lookout post for us, I'd say.'

Schluntz cast a critical eye at it, swinging his gaze about to check its lines of sight. He inclined his head favourably. 'Should do,' he agreed.

The outcrop stood a few feet above the river, enshrouded in leafy vegetation that merged without a break into the dark overhang that lined the riverbank. Indeed, so complete was the concealment, that at first it appeared impenetrable, even through the thinning leaves of autumn. But Schluntz persisted and, climbing up from the water's edge using tree roots as rungs, he found a way in. Eventually, he called for Jack to follow.

Inside the thicket there was a clear, level area, open to the sky, with enough room for a rudimentary camp – it would be a tight fit, but both thought it tolerable for the short stay envisaged. They shed their backpacks and checked and re-primed their weapons. It was prudent to leave nothing to chance; a misfire could ruin the only opportunity they would get of a clear shot. Next they set about removing some of the branches and foliage here and there, trying their muskets for size in the newly cut openings, testing the lines of sight over the ford and its approaches. Eventually they had done enough, and in the dwindling daylight, they inspected their new domain proprietarily, for it seemed that they had made themselves a temporary home. All soon fell quiet; only the odd, shrill croak from small fowl seen strutting amongst the weed on the far side of the river fractured the descending peace; and save for the slow movement of the water below, little else stirred as the rosy hues of twilight turned the river red.

Settling down to watch the fading scene, the two looked out upon their new domain. Around the crossing point the river widened to about fifty or sixty paces, where the banks had been eroded to form shallow beaches of gravel. Elsewhere, the river seemed a little narrower, perhaps because of the overhanging vegetation encroaching on both sides, which bounded the river darkly like a long avenue, until eventually it wound out of sight. A line of drying flotsam was visible on each of the ford's approaches a good foot or so above the present water level, evidence of the recent rain. But the river appeared now to be flowing relatively slowly, rippling soundlessly from some unseen unevenness of its bed. Jack wondered how easy the crossing would be to ford, guessing from the shallow gradient of the beaches and the rash of stones protruding about half way across, that it could not be more than axle depth in its deepest parts. Up and down stream, however, the water looked darker, quieter, and much deeper.

Throughout that long day, they had moved quickly and silently along the fur traders' path, through densely wooded terrain - hardly daring to speak and picking their steps carefully, so as not to announce their passage. And now they settled down for the night with the same circumspection, eating cold from their backpacks, not daring to light a fire. Night fell. Neither thought it likely that Pettigrew and Hayward would travel at night, even by the moonlight that soon bathed the scene, turning the river into a glistening silver carpet. But others might be less inhibited by the darkness. And consequently the pair slept lightly and fitfully, each starting from time to time at some slight sound, only to dismiss the noises as from the passing of creatures of the night.

Jack awoke with the greying light of early dawn and raised himself from the hide ground sheet he had carried rolled up across his backpack. His first instinct was quickly to survey the scene outside, expecting to find things just as he had left it the night before. And through the first few of his leafy peepholes, those that gave lines of sight across the river to the opposite bank and its approaches, it was indeed as he expected. He almost didn't bother to look at the near bank at all, taking his time to stretch and rub his face awake before he brought his eyes level with that final opening. At first, the scene seemed as still as those viewed moments before, but just as he was turning his eyes away, something about the scene registered in his mind as out of place. He looked back, and what he then saw not ten paces away made his heart skip a beat. There, crouching on one knee, motionless as a statue at the water's edge, was a single Indian; his skin colour and clothing blending so well with the gravel background that, unmoving, he had been all but invisible to Jack's first sweeping glance. The native was bare-armed despite the cold of the morning air. He wore a sort of hide jerkin above a breechcloth and long leggings. On his feet, he wore moccasins, and from his belt hung a tomahawk and a knife in its sheath. His head was shaven bald except for a sort of topknot and pigtail of jet-black hair from which dangled several long feathers. He seemed to be examining the near side road's approach to the water's edge.

Jack could not tear his eyes away from the crouching form, and found himself watching intently as the Indian turned his head slowly and deliberately, sweeping his fierce gaze first one way then the other. It was the manner in which he did this that made the native appear so menacing; he was otherwise so still, so calm, yet his glances were suspicious and intense. It was as if his every sense was alive to his environment, as if the slightest sound, the smallest thing out of place would immediately be detected. Jack hardly dared to breathe. Without moving his head, he extended his arm to feel for his still-sleeping companion and shook him awake. In an instant, Schluntz was at his side, peering through the same gap in the foliage. By this time the Indian had swung his gaze towards the very outcrop from which the hidden pair returned the examination. He seemed to be studying it closely. To Jack, it felt at once as though the Indian must have seen or sensed his presence, for his scrutiny seemed to dwell upon the outcrop for an unduly long time. Jack had an almost irresistible urge to duck away from the peephole, but held himself steady despite the racing heartbeat that thumped against the inside of his ribcage like a hammer. He felt his muscles tense as if preparing for flight but knew that the slightest movement might give them both away. Suddenly he felt vulnerable; the thicket that had been selected as such an ideal observatory could now so easily become a death trap. Schluntz must have felt the same, for he too froze, holding himself as motionless and as rigid as the ring of slender trunks forming their stockade. It was a stockade that might become a prison.

The Indian's piercing scrutiny of the outcrop lingered only for a few seconds longer, yet it seemed like an eternity to the two men holed up inside. And there was a long, mutual exhalation of relief when the native scout eventually stood up and turned away. Jack realised that he had been holding his breath for a long time and had a struggle bringing his breathing silently back under control. If the roar of each regulated breath was as loud outside Jack's head as it was in his ears, he must be broadcasting his presence like a beacon.

But the Indian appeared not to have detected the watching presence nearby, for after a moment he stood and raised his hand, appearing to be making some sort of 'all clear' signal, for it was neither urgent nor alarming by its nature. And very soon this was confirmed, as three more men appeared separately from the undergrowth along the far side of the track. The three moved no further for a while, but stood perfectly still, partially concealed by the vegetation, looking warily about them as if expecting trouble. One was fair-haired and quite obviously European from his features and complexion; the other two were Indians dressed like the first, and wearing similar head adornments. Another signal seemed to reassure them and bring them out into the open, coming together at the edge of the track as the first returned to join them. After a brief exchange of words amongst the group, the European was seen speaking out tersely and assertively, making rough hand gestures as he did so. Jack imagined that he was issuing instructions because soon after, the four men dispersed, melting back into the trees from whence they had come. And then they were gone, almost as quickly as they had appeared, leaving the scene apparently as empty as before. If Jack had not spotted them in those brief moments, he would never have known that they were there.

'Three Ohio and a Frenchman - an officer or NCO,' whispered Schluntz. 'Looks like a picket to me – keeping a lookout for any redcoats on the southern route, probably. Just our luck!'

As the four men had stood out in the open, Jack had sized them up, gauging how much of a threat they posed.

'Mean looking too,' he returned, succinctly coming to a conclusion.

The European had been wearing the tunic, breeches and boots of a French soldier, but the fabric of his clothes and leather of his boots had looked badly soiled and scuffed, probably from weeks of living rough. He was tall and willowy, yet seemed to have a commanding presence, for the Indians deferred to him despite their surly demeanour. Their tattooed faces and forearms had made them frightening to behold.

'At least we arrived before them,' said Jack wryly. 'If it had been the other way round, they'd have had our scalps by now.'

Schluntz snorted. 'If they get wind of us, they may yet get their chance, Jack! And likely as not, they're here for a bit, so we're going to have to keep our heads down.'

'Perhaps they'll do our work for us if Pettigrew and Hayward come along?' quipped Jack with a smirk. 'Save us the trouble.'

With the enemy presence nearby, Jack and Schluntz spent the rest of that day on tenterhooks. Neither was the patient sort. Simply sitting and waiting for something to happen would have been difficult enough, but knowing that their room for manoeuvre had now become severely limited, the confinement would be even harder to bear. If they had ever contemplated crossing the river and proceeding along the road to intercept Pettigrew and Hayward before they arrived at the ford, this was now ruled out, for leaving the sanctuary of their hiding place brought obvious dangers.

'We might get across in darkness,' thought Schluntz aloud, 'but if they're alert, we'd make easy targets; they'd probably hear us on that gravel. And if there's moonlight again tonight, we'd be sitting ducks.'

'We could drop into the water here behind the bluff and swim for it?' suggested Jack without much conviction. And both men exchanged doubtful glances, suggesting that neither was very keen on that wet and frigid option.

And so they sat tight and waited. And they waited throughout that long day, taking turns at their peepholes, while hoping for something, anything to happen that might break the impasse and present an opportunity. But nothing did happen; neither Pettigrew nor Hayward, nor any of the picket party, nor indeed anybody else made an appearance at the crossing. And when the moon rose from the horizon to bathe the empty scene again in its ghostly light, the two men went on taking turns as look out, both growing more and more frustrated at their impotence. The worst of it was that they had been caught in a trap of their own making.

Chapter Twenty-Three

Back at the post at Loyal Hannon, events were moving apace, and although Jack would know nothing of the course of the campaign over the coming days (at least not until he was told by Sir Michael much later), he would come to feel its effect.

Brigadier General Forbes and his entourage arrived at the post shortly after Jack and Sergeant Schluntz departed to set up their ambush at the ford. The brigadier was, by all accounts, still a sick man, and the long, uncomfortable journey through the Pennsylvanian frontier lands had not helped to improve his condition. He was accommodated in the quarters constructed for his use near the main gate of the outer retrenchment, from where, reportedly languishing on his sick bed, he would continue to direct operations.

Sir Michael's account of the events that followed may not be completely accurate since he was to receive his information by word of mouth from several sources, including some who were not directly involved. But it appears that soon after his arrival, the brigadier called his senior officers together in a council of war to take stock of the situation and consider options. The war council had first to consider the question of whether to press on to Fort Duquesne immediately or to rest and prepare for an attack in the spring. The army was now only forty or fifty miles from its objective, and an assault upon it was still a practical proposition before the worst of the winter weather set in, providing, of course, that the attack was swiftly and efficiently executed. However, having struggled for months across the tortuous terrain of the Appalachian Mountains, the troops were in poor shape. The going had been rough and the men were exhausted. Food and medical supplies had also been in short supply due to the stretched-out logistic chain; and sickness and malaise had taken hold (the latter evidenced by the high level of desertions). Moreover, the strength of the enemy contingent at Fort Duquesne was probably overestimated by many of the officers at the table. Indeed, in light of the recent audacious and stinging French successes, the prudent military judgement would be not to rush in; to recoup and consolidate before moving forward; and to treat the French and Indian force with considerable respect. With all this in mind, the decision, it seems, was an easy and quick one to make: it was resolved to remain at the post at Loyal Hannon and make the assault on the Ohio forks early in the spring. All but the most headstrong of Forbes' regimental colonels must have pressed for this outcome in the debate; and Forbes himself must also have recognised that his troops would need to be in full fighting condition before pitching them into battle, his caution undoubtedly heightened by the recent military embarrassments. Moreover, appointed directly by Secretary of State, William Pitt, for this key mission within the wider campaign to rid North Eastern America of the French, he would certainly not have wanted a repeat of General Braddock's ignominious defeat two years before.

Forbes' decision to remain at Loyal Hannon over the winter, however, did not mean that the pressure was off. The Brigadier General and his British and American colonels now faced an extended stay in hostile territory and needed to remain vigilant. The French had attacked the post before and they might very well try to attack again. Indeed, reports that a medium-sized enemy force was manoeuvring between the two outposts had already been received from scouts. This intelligence prompted a quick and commensurate response: two large defensive patrols were dispatched at once to deal with the feared marauders before they came too close. These two units, each comprising about five hundred American foot soldiers, headed out from the post on different routes reportedly with the intention of trapping the enemy force in a pincer movement and attacking it on both flanks. The reports that eventually filtered back to Sir Michael's ears from his various sources vary in detail, but there seemed to have been a consensus on what followed.

It appears that one of the patrols soon encountered the enemy, putting it to flight and capturing a number of prisoners. The intelligence obtained from interrogations of these unfortunates was to prove crucial in due course for, contrary to earlier belief, it revealed that Fort Duquesne was not as strongly defended as was supposed. Colonel de Lignery's Indian allies it appears, apparently under the belief that there would be no more fighting until the spring, had begun to drift back to their tribal homelands to prepare for the coming winter.

With the benefit of later information, it seems that a more likely explanation for the Indians' homeward drift was the new treaty negotiated between the British and the Iroquois Confederacy (described more fully later), which had removed the principal cause for them to fight. Under this treaty, the British agreed to restrain settlement west of the

Appalachians and guarantee the Ohio Indians possession of their homelands. And, as a quid pro quo, the leaders of the Iroquois nations (but not others) agreed to abandon their support for the French.

These discussions had taken place only a few weeks earlier (in Easton, Pennsylvania) and spreading news of it may have been distrusted at first, or perhaps even resisted by some of the smaller tribes in the Confederacy who trusted the French more. Moreover, word of the terms of the treaty would also have travelled slowly in the densely forested terrain that surrounded and separated the French and British posts, both so distant from where the negotiations took place. In any event, it seems clear from events described earlier, that the agreement did not precipitate a uniform and sudden Indian withdrawal of support from their former allies. However, accepting that the intelligence of the reduced strength at Fort Duquesne was at least partly true, it seemed safe for Forbes to assume that the balance of power had shifted in his favour - Fort Duquesne might well be ripe for the taking after all, despite the earlier reservations of most of his officers. With this analysis, the brigadier would waste no time in revoking his earlier orders, deciding instead to launch an immediate attack.

Before Forbes' orders would be issued, however, fate was to play a spiteful hand during the return of the two patrols. Conveying what would prove to be such valuable intelligence back to the post at Loyal Hannon, it was unfortunate to say the least that in coming upon the other suddenly in the darkness, one of the patrols should be mistaken for the enemy. One bright flash of nervous musket fire sparked a swift retaliation in kind, and before anyone had time to correct the misapprehension, the furious exchange of red-hot musket balls between the two American units had left forty men dead or dying amongst the trees.

As has been said, Jack would remain unaware of any of this for some time yet. And neither did it seem that the French and Indian picket party hidden in the undergrowth nearby had taken any notice of the new treaty (if they were aware of it at all). And so for a while, at least in this small part of the contested lands of western Pennsylvania, where the old Braddock road crossed the Youghiogheny River, nothing much changed.

Pettigrew and Hayward meanwhile had had a difficult time of it, encountering the same sort of weather-induced obstacles along the southern route as Jack and Sergeant Schluntz had experienced on the northern. But now, they were approaching the ford; and with only two or three days' ride ahead of them to reach their supposed sanctuary at the forks of the Ohio, they must have thought that they had got clear away.

It was mid morning of the third day of Jack and Sergeant Schluntz's vigil when two mounted riders appeared on the other side of the river. They had come out into the open from the trees and vegetation that had shielded both sight and sound of their approach, so that it seemed that the pair had been dropped suddenly and silently into the still scene. They paused on the bank, looked briefly around, and then descended to the water where they paused again. Both Jack and Schluntz happened to be looking out from their leafy hiding place at the time, and they exchanged hopeful glances, but at their distance from the ford, neither could be sure of the riders' identity. The figures were partially concealed under long greatcoats, darkened at the shoulders from a recent shower, and the drooping rims of their hats obscured their faces so that neither could be clearly seen. Both riders rode mares laden with bags and bundles secured behind their saddles. If these were Pettigrew and Hayward, Jack thought, they seemed well prepared for their journey - perhaps too well prepared for the likes of the two men he had begun to know well. And for a moment he began to doubt that they were the individuals that he and his companion had been waiting for.

'Can you make them out?' he whispered. 'D'you think it's them?'

'Not sure,' replied Schluntz slowly as he reached for his long musket and brought it to his side. 'But better be ready just in case. We can't let them get across, or they'll be away up the road, and we won't catch them on foot.'

Jack picked up his pistols, checked the firing pans, and stuffed the weapons inside his belt. He too then brought his musket to his side, settling himself back onto one knee to resume his observation.

'Unless that picket intercepts them!' he said, hopefully. 'If they're still there, they'll be watching the horsemen as carefully as we are – probably trying to assess whose side they're on.'

A few moments passed in silence as Jack and Schluntz watched and waited, both fearing that the picket might be biding their time too. But when after several minutes there was still no sign of movement from where the picket had last been seen taking cover, Jack grew impatient.

'Perhaps now's the time to slip out the back door?' he proposed. He flicked a glance to the rear of the leafy den where a long, narrow tunnel through the undergrowth had been cut away, a quiet labour that had occupied the pair during the two long days of their incarceration. It was their escape exit, a way out hidden from the view of anyone at or around the ford.

Schluntz nodded. 'Then circle round?' he suggested, indicating what he meant with a sweep of his arm. But neither moved for a while longer, both seeming to be pondering the situation while still monitoring the newly arrived pair on the other side of the ford.

'Perhaps they're fur traders,' Jack wondered aloud. 'They look too relaxed.'

Schluntz watched the two riders closely for some moments in silence. 'Hmmm, quite possible,' he returned slowly. 'Better wait a bit longer. We don't want to risk leaving our cover if they are.'

The two new arrivals did indeed seem not to be in any hurry, nor did they look especially concerned to be exposed in this open arena to the full light of day. They appeared now casually to be surveying the river – looking first one way, then the other. One then stood up in his stirrups, appearing to be searching out the route of the crossing. He resumed his seat, then with a pointing finger indicated the gravel island that divided the river into two wide streams. During all this, the riders allowed their steeds to come to the water's edge to drink. The pair looked rather too confident to be fugitives on the run.

The heavy overcast, which all morning had threatened rain, chose this moment to break up, allowing a few glimpses here and there of blue sky through the fracturing cloud. With this, the dull light that had flattened the scene viewed through Jack's lookout porthole into a dull monochrome, suddenly brightened, throwing colour and contrast into the picture as patches of sunshine shone through. The two riders, caught in a ray of the warming light, straightened as if revelling in the comfort that it must have brought. One of the men took off his hat, and threw a glance at his companion as if to say 'thank God for small mercies'. The other seemed to respond in kind, removing his hat too; and for a few moments, both men lifted their faces towards the sun.

Observing this distant gesture, two thoughts passed through Jack's mind almost simultaneously. The first thought contradicted his earlier assessment that the two men had been relaxed and casual in their demeanour. It now seemed more likely that they had been travel weary and worn down, for the sunlight appeared suddenly to have enlivened them. The second thought came fast upon the heels of the first; indeed it was not so much a thought but more of a revelation. By warming their faces in the morning sun, the two riders had given Jack a straight-on view, and recognition at once began to dawn. Bearded and dishevelled the pair might be, but he was sure that he now held Hayward and Pettigrew in his view. Having earlier begun to convince himself that the pair had been fur traders, he had to study them hard before he could allow himself to believe what he saw. But he quickly became quite certain, and uttered more in a gasp than a whisper: 'It's them.' And he turned towards his companion and nodded fiercely, as if his assertion might be doubted.

Schluntz, who's attention at the time had been on re-priming his pistols and not on looking out, brought his gaze back to his gap between the leaves in a trice. Jack did the same. The two riders had by this time already started to wade their mounts into the water, which appeared deeper than it had first looked, for the water rose quickly up the animals' legs, almost to their breasts.

'Now, we go!' Schluntz said urgently, at the same time turning towards the escape tunnel at the rear, making to leave the den according to their earlier plan.

Jack was quick to follow. But just as the two men had fallen to their knees in readiness to crawl their way out, a single loud report split the air.

'A musket shot,' thought Jack, alarmed; and for an instant he feared that their movement might have been detected, drawing fire from the picket. He leapt to his feet, returning to his look out in an instant, his hand instinctively reaching for one of the two pistols in his belt. He half expected to see weapons already raised towards their concealment. But what he saw was more puzzling than threatening. The two horsemen had now reached the middle of the first stream, well separated, heading for the gravel island. It was the second rider that drew Jack's attention immediately, for he had slumped forward in his saddle, his body bent over the saddle post so low that his head was hidden from Jack's view behind his mare's withers. The man's hold appeared so tenuous that Jack thought that he was bound to fall off soon. He switched his gaze to the leading rider whose hat, now back upon his head, made it impossible to identify which of the two it was. Whether Pettigrew or Hayward, he seemed more interested in his own survival than his injured comrade. Indeed, after a panicky glance over his shoulder, he spurred his mount so brutally that his mare whinnied, reared, and made a lunge for the island, its hooves skidding and clattering on the shingle. But the rider did not rein back there; instead he spurred the bolting beast onwards into the second stream without ever looking back. Meanwhile, the wounded rider's mount seemed to have come to a complete stop mid-stream.

Jack's first thought was that one of the hidden picket must have opened fire, and he swung his gaze immediately to the near bank. But there was no sign of anyone there, and no revealing cloud of powder smoke that would certainly have lingered had the shot come from that quarter.

Then Schluntz called out: 'Someone's on the far bank, Jack!'

And Jack jerked his head to an adjacent gap in the foliage and saw a lone figure standing on the far beach in full view. The man seemed enveloped in a blue haze, shot smoke still hanging about him in the still air; he was rodding his musket furiously. It was clear immediately that he was intent upon shooting the escaping rider too, for moments later he brought his reloaded weapon to his shoulder and took aim. But before he could fire, another shot rang out, this time so near and loud that Jack started. Dodging adeptly from one leafy porthole to another, he switched his view in a flash to the near bank. On the beach, not fifty paces from Jack's hiding place, stood the French officer, his musket raised and powder smoke about him. The officer lowered his weapon so calmly that Jack guessed that he had hit his mark; and a quick glance across to the far bank revealed indeed that the stranger had fallen to the ground.

When Jack returned his gaze to the near bank, he now saw the three Indian scouts sprinting along the beach, clearly intent on intercepting the escaping rider, who, seemingly well aware of the encroaching threat and trying desperately to outrun it, whipped his mare furiously up the gravel towards the road. But he had no chance; his mare's galloping hooves skidded and slipped on the loose stones, gaining so little purchase that the animal seemed unable to accelerate away. The scouts went for the beast's reins, pulling the mare to such a rapid halt that the rider was thrown off, losing his hat in the ensuing tumble on the ground. And with that, Jack saw instantly, even before the man had picked himself up, that it was Pettigrew. With another quick glance back across the river, Jack saw the second mare now walking sedately up the bank away from the water's edge; rider-less and apparently indifferent to the unfolding drama, she headed towards a grassy bank that seemed to have attracted her attention.

The injured man, who Jack knew now to be Hayward, must have fallen from his saddle for he was nowhere to be seen. Jack scanned the river quickly, sweeping the glassy surface with his eyes as the murky water moved languidly downstream. After a few moments he saw what he was sure must be Hayward's body, face down and quite still, drifting slowly away, the shoulders of his coat puffed up by trapped air, his hat floating buoyantly nearby. He watched the body for some moments longer, unable to wrench his gaze away from the second of his persecutors to meet their end in a watery grave. But it was not satisfaction that he felt at that moment. As it had been with Judd's demise, it was more a sense of disappointment that gripped him - disappointment that there would be no corpse to gloat over to vent the destructive hatred that only now he realised had begun to consume him.

It was Pettigrew, however, who was of the greater interest to Jack at this moment. It had been *his* callous deeds that had cost Jack most dearly, and it was thus *his* end that Jack most relished. As Jack repositioned himself to regain a view of the near beach, he exchanged glances with Schluntz who seemed to be doing likewise on his side of the den. No words passed between them, but the expressions on their faces revealed keen anticipation. They seemed to have become mere spectators in the finale in which they had expected to play leading roles, the work they had set out to do being done on their behalf by strangers. Pettigrew might already be dead if the Frenchman had not intervened, but his capture created a new uncertainty in the outcome of events, an intriguing twist in the final scene leaving Jack and Schluntz on tenterhooks. Would he be slaughtered as an intruding Englishman, Jack wondered, or would the prisoner persuade his captors that he was worth a reprieve? Jack and Schluntz both recognised that they may yet be called upon to play the parts they had prepared for.

They resumed their observations to find Pettigrew now faced with three hostile Indian scouts who poked and pushed him roughly backwards, shouting in a strange and threatening tongue. The French officer stood back, holding the captured horse's reins, observing the melee with evident humour. The Indians played with their new captive like cats with a mouse, their provocative movements so vicious and belligerent that it would not have surprised Jack to see Pettigrew bludgeoned to a bloody death there and then; the Indians all brandished tomahawks, repeatedly swinging them in a sort of wild frenzy to within an inch of Pettigrew's cowering form, sneering contemptuously as he whined and whimpered. Several times Pettigrew stumbled and fell as he was backed relentlessly along the beach. Each time he staggered back to his feet so quickly that he seemed in terror of what further brutality might ensue should he leave himself defenceless at their feet. Again and again, Pettigrew called out a desperate appeal to the Frenchman who watched dispassionately from a distance as the orgy of violence continued. Jack's ears caught Pettigrew's frightened voice above the angry shouting of his provocateurs; though he spoke in the French language, the Frenchman still did not intervene. Until finally, exhausted and beaten, Pettigrew fell to the ground almost in a faint, where he lay in a foetal curl with his arms and hands wrapped tightly around his head. The three Indians then gathered around him in menacing silence, raising their sharp-bladed weapons as if jointly to administer the coup de grace.

And unrestrained, they certainly would have done so, so seemingly unstoppable was the fever of their passion; and soon thereafter they would have taken out their knives and removed Pettigrew's scalp as a trophy and a prize. But it was just at this point that the French officer chose to make his intervention, shouting out an order in harsh native vernacular. Jack did not understand what the Frenchman had shouted, but the meaning of it was unmistakable. With remarkable swiftness, the warriors lowered their weapons and pulled back, glowering at their former plaything, as if at the slightest provocation they might finish what they had started. Another guttural order was shouted from the same mouth, and the three Indians responded instantly, grabbing Pettigrew by the arms and pulling him to his feet, whence, still quivering in evident fear, he was brought face to face with the Frenchman.

The conversation that was then seen to take place between the two Europeans could not be heard distinctly by either of the two distant observers, but from Pettigrew's agitated gesticulations and expressions, it was clear that he was pleading for his life. He spoke in a torrent, all the while flashing anxious glances at the three Indians who hovered threateningly at his shoulders. The officer interjected from time to time, his manner sceptical and short; he seemed to be asking questions to which Pettigrew appeared only too eager to respond. His normal calm composure had been entirely lost. Jack was now seeing this hated figure for what he was, naked of his armour, at last stripped of his props, those self-interested companions of his, the lackeys and henchmen through whom he had once wielded power, now gone once and for all. Oh, how it pleased Jack to witness Pettigrew's grovelling, to see him humbled in his desperate entreaties. Oh, how sweet it was to see the man begging for mercy, mercy that he had so often denied others who had had the misfortune to cross his path.

But then the nature of the conversation seemed to change. The Frenchman was seen suddenly to frown, at once turning serious and attentive, leaning forward as if to take in fully whatever it was that Pettigrew was saying. Now Jack remembered the useful intelligence that Pettigrew might convey to the enemy camp, intelligence, he had been told, that could change the course of the war unfavourably. Suddenly, it seemed vital that the exchange be stopped. He brought his musket to his side and reached across to tap Schluntz sharply on the arm.

'I'll take Pettigrew,' he said urgently; 'you take the Frenchman!'

And without waiting for an acknowledgement, Jack cocked his flintlock and raised his musket to his porthole. But bringing his eye along the sights, he found the broad backs of the Indian scouts obscuring his line of fire. He uttered an obscenity under his breath; he would have to wait for a clear shot. He must be sure of his aim, for he knew that there would only be one chance. If he or Schluntz missed their allocated target, the cat might still be out of the bag, for the information was potentially conveyable by either (it did not occur to him that the Indians might also have been capable of understanding whatever it was that Pettigrew had revealed and thus be equally capable of transmitting it). Moreover, as soon as the weapons had been fired, the pair would give themselves away immediately to the three natives who, as he had already seen, could turn into swift-footed and spiteful foes. And these were adversaries too who could melt into the undergrowth and encircle them before a second shot could be brought to bear, leaving him and his companion trapped in their sylvan cage like rats. He thought long and hard before he curled his finger around the trigger for there was a lot at stake, but he did it all the same and steeled himself to fire. Jack had never been one to shy away from what he thought to be his duty; indeed, that he might be martyred in an honourable cause seemed to make it both more worthy and more difficult to retreat. Such is the stuff called heroism, while a cooler head might call it recklessness. Once set upon this self-appointed and deluded mission - to kill Pettigrew and the Frenchman and thus in his mind potentially save British and American armies from defeat — the die was cast. To Jack, it would have been ignoble, cowardice even, to shrink at such a potentially decisive moment. In that fleeting instant, the course of history might be resting in his hands; he felt its gravity pulling him inexorably onwards as if he were its instrument; the chance lost now might never come again, and he would be judged forever on how he had failed to measure up. He was thus cornered by his own foolish pride, for a challenge once thrown down could never be refused.

And so it was just as well that Sergeant Schluntz appreciated the futility of Jack's intentions, brave and well meaning as they were. It was he who reached across and tapped Jack on his arm just as the Portlander stilled his breathing in readiness to fire.

Jack's quick glance was hostile, his face angry. His friend's intervention may have cost him the one firing opportunity he was ever going to get. But Schluntz shook his head slowly, fixing his eyes on Jack's so that he could not look away.

'There'll be a better time, Jack,' he said calmly and insistently.

And Jack knew at once that his friend was right. Schluntz the veteran, whose judgement he had learned to trust; thank God for him, Jack thought with relief as he lowered his weapon, his pulse at once beginning to subside. And he counted himself lucky to have had his friend's counsel at that moment, for it had saved him from the sort of impetuosity that had got him into trouble before.

Chapter Twenty-Four

When Jack and Sergeant Schluntz resumed their lookout, they saw the picket already moving away from the riverbank towards the road, the Frenchman leading, sitting astride Pettigrew's horse. His captive walked some ten yards behind. Or, perhaps more accurately described, Pettigrew with hands tied at his front, was drawn like a slave by a long rope, tied at one end around his neck and at the other to the Frenchman's saddle post. One of the Indians trailed some distance behind the captive as rearguard, sweeping his gaze in all directions as the party moved off the beach. The other two straddled the prisoner, one at each shoulder, jostling him roughly at the slightest hint of tardiness or recalcitrance. Indeed, they seemed to be taking cruel delight in goading him, laughing and sneering at his frightened glances, and held back from worse by the sharp words shouted back by the Frenchman twisting in his saddle. Without him there to restrain them, it looked as if the Indians would have shown no mercy at all.

'Maybe we should leave it there, Jack?' said Schluntz. 'Let them have him. I wouldn't risk a day's pay on his chances of surviving anyway.'

'You don't know Pettigrew like I do,' replied Jack evenly. 'He's a slippery customer. However slim his chances might look at present, I'll give you ten to one he'll live to gloat one day in some French tavern about how he turned the tables. I won't be satisfied until I see him dead.'

However, in delivering this bold indictment, Jack paused to wonder how on earth he could now be a witness to Pettigrew's end, especially the fitting end that would give Jack the satisfaction he sought. By this time, the Frenchman's little procession was already well up the road, which wound first one way and then the other as it negotiated the steep rise out of the river valley. They moved slowly, hindered by Pettigrew's stumbling slowness, but it was not long before the five men were out of sight, swallowed by the forest on the ridge over which the road eventually disappeared. For a while thereafter, Jack could not take his eyes off the spot where he had last seen Pettigrew's distant form, yanked roughly in that final moment by his out-of-sight captor into the cover of the trees, still hounded by his truculent Indian escort. It was too much of an anticlimax for Jack to see him go so meekly; this was not the end he had imagined in his most vindictive of dreams. Pettigrew should not simply have vanished from sight. Jack stared at the empty ridge as his disappointment turned first to bitterness and then anger, craving the sweet fulfilment of seeing Pettigrew pay most painfully for all the harm that he had caused. But how could this now be achieved, he wondered? For all his earlier rhetoric, the odds did indeed seem too highly stacked against him - the cost of justice likely to be too high a price to pay if he should perish in the attempt, a price that would ultimately fall on others too dear to him to disregard. Perhaps Schluntz *was* right, he pondered. Perhaps this *was* as far as they could go without pushing their luck too far? And for a time he flirted with the idea of giving up the quest that had driven him for so long. Then, all at once, he knew how he would do it; he knew what had to be done to ensure that Pettigrew was appropriately dealt with.

Jack and Schluntz waited patiently until the distant grating of hooves on the rocky path died away before moving from the safety of the den. And when the pair eventually emerged from their leafy tunnel, it was with some caution and nervousness. What they had observed of the Indians had unnerved them both – these Native Americans seemed masters of their wilderness - able to lie unseen in wait for days, then spring a deathly trap - able to move swiftly and silently, then act with cunning and sullen maleficence. The sudden freedom after so long in confinement gave Jack an intense feeling of vulnerability in this vast and empty backcountry, a foreign country in which deadly hatred lurked, watching and waiting for its chance to strike. Some small part of his consciousness harboured the niggling fear that the natives might have circled back, might even now be observing the pair's tentative exploration. Until his nerves were finally stilled, every whisper of wind, every sudden rustle in the branches made his heart jolt, causing him to swing this way and that, pistols in hand, ready to shoot the imagined foe leaping from the undergrowth.

But no attack came.

'We'd better see who that is,' said Jack at last, flicking a grim glance across the river to the inert form of the stranger, still lying on the beach where he had been felled by the Frenchman's musket shot. And with a nod of agreement from Schluntz, he led the way across the river, holding his weapons high above the water's reach, making directly for the recumbent body. But as they approached it, the noisy grinding of their footsteps on the gravel seemed to spark a most dramatic effect. The pair had come no nearer than ten paces, when the body seemed suddenly to spring to life. Moreover, it sprang into a defensive, half-kneeling position, at the same time raising a pistol in one hand and a long knife in the other, which it brandished at the approaching pair thus stopping them dead in their tracks. Jack was dumbfounded. Clearly the man was not dead at all; indeed he seemed quite unscathed. And in that instant, Jack realised that he must have feigned death for protection or else to lay a trap. And if these had been his motives, he had been entirely successful with both, for Jack and Schluntz were now at his mercy, having been taken completely by surprise.

The next moment, however, that surprise seemed to become mutual, the menace on the stranger's face turning, with a blink of his astonished eyes, into a beam of great delight.

'Why it's Jack Easton and Sergeant Schluntz!' he yelled, stuffing his weapons into his belt. And he came towards them grinning, holding out his hand in greeting.

It took a while for Jack to realise who it was he had encountered in this unlikely place; the man's face was strangely familiar but so out of any earlier context that Jack could not place him at first. Then it dawned.

'Jeremiah Blake! What in God's name are you doing here?' he said as their hands clasped. Schluntz had recognised him too, and he in turn shook Blake's hand warmly.

'Same as you, by the sound of it,' Blake said, still grinning like a wild cat. 'Got one of 'em, didn't I? Hah! And fooled them others too! The bastard 'ud need a rifled barrel like this one to be sure of a hit at that distance! Much more accurate! Heard a shot whistle over my head; saw at once that there were too many of 'em for me; so decided to play dead.'

'Just as well you did,' slipped in Schluntz. 'That was a French and Indian picket!'

Jack nodded. 'Well, it seemed to satisfy them, at least. It was Hayward you got, by the way. I saw his body floating away with the current...dead in the water,' he said. 'But how the devil did you find us out here?'

Blake related how Rose, Ned, and Captain Goddard had returned to the burnt-out farmstead on their way back to Charlestown to spent a second night there; and how, over an evening meal, they had told him of Judd's ambush, and of Jack and Schluntz's timely intervention.

'They also reminded me, Jack, about your plan to catch up with Pettigrew and Hayward,' he said, looking a little discomfited. 'You already told me the last time I saw you, didn't you? I guess I should have come with you then, but…but somehow I wasn't ready to leave. Anyhow, when your wife reminded me of what you were up to, I felt a bit lame jus' wallowing in my own misery, leaving all the dirty work to you and the sergeant here. Perhaps I wasn't ready before, but suddenly it seemed jus' the right thing for me to do.' With this admission, his face crinkled into a sly smile. 'You know,' he winked, 'I had this terrible urge to inflict some dire retribution of my own!' (Jack and Schluntz laughed at this.) 'Well anyway,' Blake continued, 'once I'd told your Rose and her friends what I'd decided, they set me up with some supplies and gave me one of their spare mares…' (He flicked a glance to where the road curved out of sight behind him where he had left his horse tied up.) '…and this pistol too!' he said patting the weapon in his belt. 'And as they set off south for Frederick the following morning, I set off northwards for the military road, jus' like you'd told me.'

Blake continued the story of how he had then travelled along the military road to reach Fort Bedford, where he had been told by Major Green of Jack and Sergeant Schluntz's plans to get ahead of the fugitives and intercept them at the river crossing.

'So I decided to take the link route south to Cumberland and follow the old Braddock road to come up on them from behind – that way I figured we'd have them caught between us. And good thing I did, by the look of it!' he said. 'You two were a bit late getting here, weren't you?'

Jack's lips wrinkled. 'We've been here for two days,' he admitted; 'but got pinned down in that outcrop over there by the picket. Saw everything that happened after you arrived on the scene, but couldn't do a thing.' With this remark Jack flashed Schluntz a meaningful glance by way of acknowledging his friend's helpful intervention. 'If we *had* tried a shot, I've a feeling that we wouldn't be here now,' he owned.

In the reflective pause that ensued, Jack found his eyes drawn to the musket lying on the ground behind Blake's back. His brow furrowed.

'Anyway, that musket of yours?' Jack asked, suddenly intrigued. 'You say it's rifled and more accurate?'

'Better range too,' exclaimed Blake proudly. 'Got it from your Major Green; his scouts use them for sniping, apparently. The barrel's got a sort of spiral groove in it that spins the ball and keeps it flyin' straight. Trouble is, the shot has to fit so tight that it's a devil of a job to ram it home – takes, I don't know, three or four times as long to reload as a smooth bore musket!' He raised his eyebrows in disgust. 'Alright for deer stalking if you've got the time, I guess, but definitely no good for soldiers on the front line! Should have realised that from my practise firings, I suppose – a bit of a liability if you've got more than one target!'

Schluntz smiled indulgently. 'Standard issue for us,' he said, patting his own musket proudly. He threw Jack a glance. 'That's how Major Lawrence brought Judd down on the beach, by the way; it would have been a real fluke to have hit him at that range with a standard musket. I'll admit it's a bit slower to load; but even at two hundred paces, it'll bring down nine out of ten targets...in the right hands, that is!' he jibed, throwing a sideways smirk in Blake's direction. 'The smooth-bore would hardly *reach* that far, let alone strike home – good for smoke and noise, but if you hit anything, it just happened to be in the way!'

'Hah! Nine out of ten?' retorted the farmer; 'Perhaps if they stood still long enough!'.

Schluntz was about to respond when Jack intervened. 'Well, each to his own, I suppose.' He flicked a glance across the river to where the old Braddock road wound its way up into the trees. 'But, gentlemen,' he said in mild rebuke, 'we've got more important matters to attend to right now.'

'Yeah! Let's be after 'em!' said Blake, turning and making as if to collect his weapon.

'Hold on, hold on!' said Jack quickly, stopping Blake in his tracks. 'Not you, Jeremiah!' he said more calmly.

Blake turned back, his brow puckered.

Jack had to think quickly; the last thing he wanted was a third man with him now. Especially one with unknown field credentials like Blake, someone whose lust for vengeance might be difficult to restrain once Pettigrew was once again in sight. While Blake's tenacity and motives could not be questioned, it was stealth and patience that Jack would need to accomplish what he had in mind. Another pair of feet on the ground was bound to increase the risk of detection. Besides, with Pettigrew's capture, it had dawned on Jack that he owed one *very* important duty to his comrades in arms waiting at the post – and one that should be discharged without delay. With Blake available as a runner, it now could be.

'You've done your bit in dealing with Hayward,' continued Jack smoothly; 'without your timely action, Jeremiah, I've a feeling that we'd still be stuck in that leafy hideout of ours, wondering what to do!' (Schluntz gave out a little grunt of agreement here; '*Ja, stimmt,*' he muttered.) 'I want you to leave Pettigrew to us now;' Jack went on, 'we'll have a better chance alone. I need you instead to take a message back to

Major Green at the post at Loyal Hannon. He'll have arrived there by now, and it's vital that he learns that Pettigrew has made contact with the French. Tell him that it must be assumed that the enemy will get to know everything about Forbes' army – size, disposition, strengths, weaknesses – everything that Pettigrew will have made it his business to find out before he deserted. Can you do that for us? We'll put you on the path that'll take you practically all the way.'

Blake's eyes widened. 'Of course,' he said, puffing himself up, clearly appreciating the importance of the assignment.

'Then, collect your horse – and that one too while you're about it,' said Jack, nodding a glance at the grassy bank on which Hayward's animal had been grazing contentedly meanwhile, 'and follow us across the river.'

Blake had already turned on his way when Jack added:

'And I'll borrow that musket of yours - and the ammunition,' he called. 'I think I may have a use for it.'

It would have been about an hour later that Jack and Sergeant Schluntz left the ford to set out in pursuit. And treading carefully to avoid detection by the picket's rearguard, it took the pair most of the remaining daylight to come within earshot of the group. A sudden outburst of raised voices somewhere not far ahead first signalled that they had caught up. This stopped them dead in their tracks to listen as the exchange continued just out of sight around a bend: apparently an argument of some kind between the Frenchman and Pettigrew, whose irritable remonstrations were unmistakable.

'A handy twist of fortunes,' reflected Jack, with an ironic grin, 'that it should be Pettigrew himself who warns us with his protests, and stops us from blundering too close!' But as a precaution, the pair slipped quietly off the road and under the overhanging boughs of a large and droopy evergreen for cover.

Dusk was falling early. A leaden overcast, harried by bitter winds into spiteful outbursts of precipitation, had dogged the day. And having pushed on without a break in such wearisome conditions, treading silently and always on their guard against ambush, the two scouts were cold, wet, and close to exhaustion. The heavy cloud would mean no moon tonight, and neither pursuers nor pursued would travel much further in the total darkness that was soon to fall. But if for the picket, the blackout would frustrate progress, for Jack and his companion, it would present a blessed opportunity to rest.

'It'll be the same for them; they'll need to stop too,' said Schluntz, unrolling his groundsheet in one practised flourish onto the thick, dry bed of coniferous detritus.

'Then we won't be far behind them in the morning,' replied Jack wearily, swinging his gaze around the evergreen vault in which they had by chance taken refuge.

In the centre of their arboreal cavern, a huge, gnarled trunk ascended into a gloom of its own making. As it rose, the column sprouted tier upon tier of drooping, feathery branches, which cascaded to the ground like overlapping fronds to form a sort of living roof. Only a few chinks of dusk's dwindling light penetrated the embracing shroud to make the two men's drawn faces greyer yet as they rummaged in their bags.

'Made for us,' mumbled Jack dully, unloading the contents of his backpack onto his groundsheet. 'Pity we can't have a fire,' he added in a similar, tired monotone. 'It would have been a home from home!'

An hour later, the pair were in a somewhat better state having consumed some of their rations – a chunk each of dried meat, a piece of corn bread (a bit stale by now) with some squash and apple pickle, and a spoonful of the precious fruit compote that Jack had stolen from the quartermaster's stores at Loyal Hannon – all beginning to run a little short after the unexpected delay at the ford. At least there had been a plentiful supply of good, clean water from the many gushing streams passed during the day. After such a volume of rain over recent weeks, their flasks were not likely to run dry. And with the luxury of a change of shirt and breeches, their damp garments were soon hanging from the array of branches overhead so that the heat from their bodies might dry them overnight.

By the completion of all these domestic duties, the darkness had become as impenetrable as tar, and both men had to feel their way onto their groundsheets to settle down for the night. Curiosity about the picket would nag for a while, but there would be no exploring along the road on this black night to where they imagined the group might be encamped. Indeed, to venture out at all with the enemy undoubtedly so close at hand would court almost certain discovery. And thus the two men wrapped themselves tightly in their groundsheets to suffer the long, cold night, impatient for the confrontation that the morrow was sure to bring.

Schluntz fell almost at once into a deep and apparently untroubled sleep. Perhaps the veteran found this safe and cosy arbour and its soft, dry floor a luxury after the watchful crouching and hard ground of the lookout den. But for Jack it was a long and restless night, achieving slumber in such short snatches that it seemed that he hardly slept at all. On tenterhooks with the French picket probably very near, every rustle in the undergrowth, every creak of ancient boughs, brought him back to wakefulness. On each occasion, he would raise his head and listen, eyes wide and pulse racing, imagining the random sounds coherent and connecting, while he waited with bated breath for the next. But, soon tiring of his vigil, he would drift once more into a fitful sleep. And throughout Jack's long and worrisome night, Schluntz's breathing continued evenly and undisturbed, as if the massed armies of the entire French nation marching past their tree would not have woken him.

A sudden, splintering crash brought both men awake and to their feet in an instant. They saw at once that dawn had broken. Little chinks of light now peppered their enclosure so that the alarm on each other's face was plain to see. For a while, neither man dared to move; each seeming rooted to the spot, ears pricked, they listened out intently for further clues as to what might have had been the cause of their rude awakening. Gingerly, they trod towards one of the tiny openings through their cover and peered out. One glimpse told them all. The road immediately in front of their sheltering yew was now a mess of leafless brush and broken boughs; a large maple opposite had evidently shed a rotten limb. Weakened, no doubt by the wind that still played in the upper branches, it had chosen this moment to fall. The men exchanged glances; the event had been a natural, rather than a man-made phenomenon. But no sooner had the pair breathed out a collective sigh of relief, when a movement further up the road caught Jack's eye.

'Back!' he whispered urgently, bringing his finger to his lips to silence his companion's response, even as Schluntz made to utter it.

Beckoning his friend to follow, Jack retreated to the darker core of the arbour, where the spots of daylight hardly reached.

'One of the Indians,' said Jack in a low voice. 'Come to take a look at what caused the noise, no doubt.'

Schluntz nodded, then stooped to retrieve his knife from his belongings, left in a neat pile by the backpack he had used as a pillow. He unsheathed his weapon and held it up. 'Just in case,' he said, smiling grimly.

Jack leant forward, intending to arm himself too - one of his pistols lay within an arms length - but Schluntz restrained him as he reached out.

Schluntz shook his head and frowned. 'A shot would bring the others running,' he whispered.

In the very next moment, the brittle cracking of trodden brushwood signalled that the Indian was near. Instinctively, Jack and Schluntz pulled back further into the darker core, pressing against the trunk to make themselves invisible from outside. Another splintering crack rang out - very close this time. Jack found himself holding his breath, anxious not to make the slightest sound. In his mind, these natives of the wilderness were gifted with superhuman powers of detection. He released his lungful slowly, lips parted, struggling not to let go all at once. His heart thumped in his chest; he needed to gulp in new air desperately but he held the urge in check, sucking in the air silently with utmost restraint. He could hear the native's careful footfalls now, picking a way through the fallen debris outside, the tread coming ever closer, tentative and cautious, as if he already suspected a hostile presence nearby.

A few lonely clouds, scurrying before the breeze aloft, dashed across a clear, cold sky that had replaced the previous day's overcast. The rising sun had found an early entry into the awakening forest, shining its rays directly along the clear-felled canyon of the approaching road. The fiery orb lingered in the opening before moving on, its piercing glare setting the avenue momentarily aflame.

The Indian came closer still, his long shadow now stretching out before him like a dark, exploring hand that slid beneath the low boughs and reached into the arbour. The fierce light found every chink in Jack and Schluntz's leafy shield, the dark recesses of their cavern pierced at once by a thousand bright needles. And one by one, these dazzling pinpricks were extinguished as the creeping form drew closer yet, blanking out the light. The Indian must then have reached the tree's perimeter for the shadowy movement then seemed to stop; he was now just a step or two away from the two souls that held themselves so deathly still against its trunk. Jack could hear the Indian's breathing. Through a gap, he could see the Indian's eyes shifting first one way then the other. Jack's heart began to race; it felt as if the whites of his eyes must be shining like a beacon, yet he could not tear his gaze away.

Then suddenly, the outer branches moved as if brushed with an impatient hand; it seemed at first as if they may be parted. Jack was aware of Schluntz bringing up his knife, and he too readied himself for the fight he felt certain was now imminent. He cast a gaze around the dingy arbour – the two men's belongings were strewn about untidily, their drying garments still slung over the branches. If the Indian once caught a glimpse inside, the pair would be undone. They waited in this frozen pose for several seconds, poised and ready to spring, to catch the Indian by surprise at the very moment of his discovery.

But the next event was not the explosive entry that they had feared, or even a shout of alarm to call the others to the Indian's aid. Amazingly, the next sound to enter Jack's ears was that of gushing water - accompanied by the rip of breaking wind. It took a moment for Jack to realise that the Indian was urinating against the very branches that separated them; the snaking, gently steaming rivulet of piss even penetrated their sanctuary! He flashed his companion a glance that was at once incredulous and relieved, and found his own feelings reflected in Schluntz's face. Miraculously, their presence had not been detected.

Chapter Twenty-Five

It was a good hour later, well after the inquisitive Indian had withdrawn in the direction from which he had come, that Jack and Schluntz were ready to venture out into the open. They rounded the first bend warily, staying under the cover of the woody overhang as much as possible lest the picket had posted a lookout. But they need not have been so careful, for coming soon upon a small clearing at the side of the road, the kicked-out residue of a campfire was clear evidence that the picket had long gone. Schluntz passed his hand across the dying embers.

'They're getting careless,' he said. 'They must think they're home already.'

'Tomorrow, they probably will be!' replied Jack. 'We have to catch them tonight or lose our chance.'

The pair set off in pursuit along a road that negotiated its way through a rocky and thickly forested land, sweeping this way and that to mitigate the steepness of the contours. It forded streams and followed valleys; it climbed upwards, crested, and descended again. And all the while, Jack and Schluntz were guided ever onwards by its navigation. Picking up the traces of the picket here and there, they were always wary, always on their guard lest a rearguard might be lurking; but step by careful step, they closed the gap. The day remained bright and dry; the cool autumnal wind played boisterously in the upper branches, stripping off the last of the leaves; the ground, soft in parts from previous rain, was largely firm and easy going. The pair's progress was steady and unimpeded.

It was early afternoon when once again the sound of hoof falls could be heard echoing on the road ahead. Careful not to come too close, the two men dropped back, taking up a pace that kept the tell-tale sound just on the edge of hearing, yet rounding every bend with utmost caution. The afternoon wore on in this manner, until at last voices could be heard floating faintly on the air. The voices came and went from moment to moment, growing louder and more persistent as time went on. The picket seemed to have become careless of their noise, for the voices soon became more strident, with Pettigrew's tones rising above the rest. It sounded as though he might be protesting again, or else pleading, perhaps for rest? Jack's enemy was providing another helpful distraction with his remonstrations; and under its cover, the pair were able to close the gap.

Then, rounding a sharp bend, they caught sight of the group, and found themselves suddenly and uncomfortably exposed. Had any one of the picket turned a rearward glance at that moment, Jack and Schluntz's secret pursuit would have quickly turned to flight. For an instant, both men froze, fearful that the slightest further movement might draw an enemy eye. The pair could only have been fifty paces behind - so close indeed that every detail of the group was clear. But the picket ambled on, its attention evidently taken entirely with Pettigrew's churlish recalcitrance and unaware of the presence close behind. Hardly believing that they had not been seen, the two scouts began to inch towards the cover of the trees, each half-expecting to hear the sudden shout of alarm that would signal their discovery.

But no cry came, and after a while, the two men poked their heads tentatively from their cover and looked ahead. The picket and their prisoner had continued on without pause but remained in clear sight. The Frenchman still sat astride the mare with Pettigrew still walking, or rather stumbling behind, his Indian escort clustered around him menacingly with muskets in their hands.

The two men waited until the picket had disappeared beyond the next bend, then moved swiftly, running along the road with a crouching, silent gait. When they reached the bend, they hid again. The picket was only fifty or so paces ahead, but the background scene in which the retreating group was set was now quite different to the oppressive, mixed woodland through which they had trudged all day. Quite unexpectedly, they had emerged into an extensive glade of long grass and patchy scrub that stretched at least a mile into the distance.

Roughly oval in shape, the ground first descended towards a stream-fed pond two hundred or so yards from the near boundary, before climbing again towards the trees on the horizon at the far edge of the clearing. Jack wondered at the sudden lack of trees, thinking them to have been clear-felled at some time in the past, perhaps by a native population – yet there was no visible evidence or residue of habitation. Broad swathes of long, dry grasses swayed in the wind with rhythmic pulses like waves on open water, in which the scattered spindly tees and clumps of scrub stood firm as islands. In the distance, a herd of startled deer made a bolt for the cover of the surrounding trees; and from the pond's muddy banks, a flock of black-headed geese took off and clattered into the air, honking in protest at the intruders who had entered their domain.

The road meandered through the middle of the clearing, passing close by the pond before climbing the shallow gradient beyond, eventually disappearing into the tree line. Jack and Schluntz lay still and watched the picket descending along it towards the water. With the paucity of decent cover, the pair could not prudently follow until the picket had moved further away, when careful pursuit might again be possible. Until then, they must lie in wait. But as he watched the picket winding down the slope, Jack realised that the open ground presented him with just the opportunity he had hoped for. It would allow the clear shot he needed at long enough range to give him and his companion time to make a safe retreat. He must wait awhile yet, however – the picket was still too close – but the time would soon come. He removed his pack, took out his powder horn and shot flask, and unwrapped his musket from its oilskin cover.

'Load and prime!' he whispered to his companion, who was already mirroring Jack's own preparations.

Both men worked quickly, but when it came to ramming his shot down the barrel of his borrowed weapon, Jack got a tangible reminder of what Blake had told him. At first he wondered if there was something wrong - he had never loaded a rifled weapon before. He frowned, flashing his companion a worried glance.

'Keep ramming,' said Schluntz, seeing his friend's difficulty. 'It'll get there!' he grinned. 'See that mark on the ramming rod?' (Jack squinted at the tool, then nodded.) 'You've got to get it to there before you stop,' continued Schluntz. 'Otherwise the shot will be too far from the powder, and it will fall short.'

'Won't need any wadding!' Jack grunted as, finally, he rammed his shot home and laid his weapon down for priming.

When the two men had completed the preparation of their armoury, they swept their gazes across the clearing, seeking out the picket on the road. By now, the five men had reached the pond from which the horse was being allowed to drink. The Frenchman meanwhile had remained in his saddle, while the three Indian scouts simply stood restively around their exhausted captive, his head thrown back in an agonised gasp at the heavens. Then suddenly Pettigrew fell to his knees, from which position he appeared emphatically to be refusing to get up - despite much prodding and taunting from his escort. It did not take long for the three native scouts visibly to become quite agitated by Pettigrew's refusals; yet at the distance, none of the altercation carried to Jack's ears. He could only imagine what was being said with such evident hostility. For a time, the Frenchman merely looked on without interfering, but after a while he seemed to grow impatient with his cohort and dismounted. The Indians pulled back as he walked back to the prisoner, whom he attempted to coax to his feet in a more moderate manner – but still without success. Pettigrew was quite clearly done for the day!

The light by this time was beginning to fade fast, with nightfall probably not an hour away, and this must have been in the Frenchman's mind when, with a resigned shrug, he signalled his intention to camp. A heated exchange then appeared to break out between him and the Indian trio who shook their heads and gesticulated wildly, pointing up the road away from the pond. Perhaps the three scouts disliked the suggested campsite and wanted to move on; perhaps Pettigrew's frailty was frustrating some cherished objective for the night that they would now fail to reach? Whatever the reason, they turned upon Pettigrew and tried to lift him up, all the while shouting in his face. But each time they got him to his feet, his legs buckled and he fell back to his knees. The Indians eventually gave up when the Frenchman shouted angrily, leaving them standing sullenly as he turned his back and led his horse away. It was what the three did as the officer retreated that made Jack smile grimly, for they took out their knives and gestured luridly at the kneeling prisoner behind the Frenchman's back.

Jack now revealed to his friend what he had in mind to bring Pettigrew to a fitting end, and as dusk fell the pair set out to come closer to the pond. The scattered clouds meanwhile had dispersed, leaving a clear sky that turned red in the west before fading to a sort of colourless translucence as stars began to shine. The air quickly became still and cold.

Having stashed their packs and loaded pistols in a nearby thicket that would serve later as a hiding place, they crept through the long grasses, half crouching, half crawling with their muskets strapped across their backs. Eventually they found a dip in the ground some hundred yards or so from the Frenchman's camp and slid quietly into it, resting there for a moment while Jack took stock of their position. The indentation offered cover and an encircling mound on which to bear and aim their weapons. Jack took up a prone position, resting his elbows on the mound, and used the long barrel of his musket to clear a sighting line through the grasses. He checked his aim along the muzzle pointing directly at the camp.

By now, the three Indians had lit their fire and were sitting around it. Over the blaze, they had erected some sort of tripod of sticks, from which a small pot was suspended. Jack wondered what they ate, for in all these days of contact, albeit intermittent, he had not seen them hunt or snare, and their backpacks were so small that they could not have been carrying much by way of sustenance. He wondered if their rations too were running short - for this might be the reason the Indians had been so impatient to move on. The Frenchman had placed himself and Pettigrew apart, half a dozen strides away, around a fire and tripod of their own; the Frenchman stooped on one knee over his pot while Pettigrew sat cross-legged with his hands tied in his lap, looking on morosely. There was a strange unease about the camp that puzzled Jack; it was as if a rift had developed between the two groups and each had retired to its own corner to brood upon it.

Jack threw a glance over his shoulder. Behind him, the eastern sky was already black except for a pale loom of faint grey light just visible above the dark rank of evergreens that marked their refuge. Moonrise would not be long in coming, he thought. The Frenchman's camp would get its rays first, leaving him and his companion in shadow for a time - time enough, he calculated, to make good a retreat. On the opposite horizon, the last vestiges of the past day were retreating fast, the pond mirroring the sky's dull shades. Against those fading hues, the five faces clustered around their fires' warm light, shone amber like beacons in the dark.

'Perfect set up,' said Jack, half to himself, as Schluntz came up alongside and poked his musket through the grass to take a look for himself.

Jack waited for him to settle, snatching another glance over his shoulder at the eastern sky.

'Not long now,' he said.

Schluntz took a sighting down his muzzle. 'You won't need to allow for much gravity drop, Jack, so don't aim too high,' he whispered. 'At this range, a head's height should be enough.' He wet his finger in his mouth and held it up. 'No wind to take account of either.'

Jack grunted as he shifted his weight, experimenting with lining up his sights. 'Our shots have got to count,' he muttered, distractedly. 'You know the target. You fire the moment I fire - and as soon as you have, run for the thicket, staying low!'

The two men waited thus for what seemed an eternity as the moon's loom grew stronger, making stark silhouettes of the treetops, which stood like tall observers watching from behind. Darkness had descended over the camp while the fires blazed, and the air had grown colder yet, so that Jack's breath steamed as he kept his sighting eye on activities there. His stomach churned to watch the contents of the cooking pots consumed. Soon afterwards Pettigrew was seen to be led off into the darkness by the Frenchman; but they were soon back. And in their turn, the Indians went off too, all leaving then soon returning into the hemisphere of fire-glow that had become their haven for the night.

At last the lunar light touched the far side of the clearing, lighting up the distant trees. A lone wolf's eerie calling could be heard in the far distance.

'Ready?' Jack asked calmly. He could feel the presence of his friend lying alongside but could hardly see him.

Schluntz seemed to take his time lining up his sights.

'Yep,' came Schluntz's eventual reply.

The moon's light descended towards the camp like a slow-moving tide. The pair would wait until the picket fell within its sweep before taking their shots. In just a few minutes, Jack thought, the bright lunar orb would rise above the trees to dazzle enemy eyes, and blind them to the musket fire that was about to be unleashed. Jack's finger rested on the trigger with his target steady in his sights. If he achieved what he intended, his shot would mark the end of a long journey - a journey started as a young and carefree mason in the quarries of Portland and finished here in this dark wilderness as a hardened and embittered man. Yes, he had come to recognise that this was what his long quest for revenge had made him, and while he hated himself for it, he knew that he must see his plan through. Perhaps when it was done, he could return to being more the man he was before? There, in his sights, was the cause of all the tragedies and hardships that had befallen him since that fateful night at Church Ope Cove. There, in his sights, was the man behind the assassination plot into which Jack had inadvertently strayed and made its scapegoat. Pettigrew! Without him, the train of events that had led Jack here would never have begun – Jack's imprisonment, torture, and transportation - the deaths of his betrothed, his father and his son. None of this would have come to pass without Pettigrew, the shadowy manipulator, the puller of strings. Smyke had been his murderous instrument, and Judd and Hayward, his greedy acolytes. But it had been Pettigrew's callous hand that had drawn back the bow and let the dart fly to blight Jack's life as if dispatched by the devil himself. Now only Pettigrew remained to be dealt with: Pettigrew the betrayer – seeking to save himself - prepared to sell his own countrymen to the enemy!

There in Jack's sights was the man he held responsible.

The tide of moonlight crept closer. Half a minute more and the Frenchman's camp would be lit up in its full glare. Jack's finger curled around his trigger.

Pettigrew had dodged the law twice before. Now, unknowingly, he may be moments away from the just and fitting end that Jack had carefully schemed for him these past two days. Not a sudden passage into oblivion, but a journey that would allow him time to reflect on his past and come to know as punishment.

'Nearly there,' Jack whispered into the darkness.

He heard his companion adjusting his position.

'Uh huh,' came Schluntz's breathy acknowledgement.

Jack's trigger finger tightened as the lunar penumbra merged with the radiance of the campfires below. And soon the camp was bathed in bright moonlight, making the fires' light puny by comparison. In that moment, as if caught by the sudden exposure, Pettigrew turned his gaze upon the moon's all-seeing face, thereby giving Jack a frontal view. He found himself studying the man's hated features as if for the first time, seeing fear in the man's expression. It was as if Pettigrew sensed the danger skulking in the shadows not far away.

At last the time had come, Jack thought; at last he could take his shot and finish what he had set out to do. But a strange mood came over him that stayed his hand. It was as if he needed to reflect upon this moment just a little longer, as if there were something yet to be resolved within his mind. His shot would bring death, a slow death that would give Pettigrew time to ponder his cruel past, and perhaps come eventually to understand that he was reaping what he had sown. This moment of retribution had been long in coming and should not be rushed; it demanded a certain reverence. When Jack had shot at men before, his blood had been up; it was kill or be killed. But this was different. His eyes blurred, and as he blinked them clear, the image of his father came into his thoughts. And with this revelation he realised at once that it was for his father that he had come so far; it was for his father that he had striven for revenge – for the man who had nurtured and guided him, had given him his start - the man who had been broken by the events and consequences of that fateful night - the man whose tortured soul had driven him to take his own life. And for this, Pettigrew was responsible just as he bore the ultimate responsibility for Elizabeth's death on the transport ship, and for countless other deaths too. And for all this, Pettigrew must suffer.

Jack squeezed the trigger and held his aim steady on its mark as the firing arm sprang over. Flint sparked against steel. Powder flashed in the pan. But Jack did not flinch as the burning residue spluttered about his face, the particles of red-hot sulphur stinging his cheek like a hundred tiny needles. Half a second later, the musket kicked back into Jack's shoulder like an angry mule as the ball sped forward on its course, spinning straight and true. Almost simultaneously, he heard Schluntz's weapon fire too, the smoke from both muzzles mingling briefly to obscure the view. The flash had blinded Jack, but as his sight returned and the smoke dispersed, he saw that both shots had done the work intended.

The Frenchman was flat on his back, his face dark with blood. He had been blown backwards by Schluntz's shot with such force that he lay a yard from where he had sat. Death would have been instantaneous. But it had been Pettigrew that had been Jack's target. A flesh wound was all that had been intended, a wound that would incapacitate but not kill, and Jack was gratified to see his victim lying on his side, clutching a bleeding thigh, his face set in a grimace. The Indians were nowhere in sight. They must have run for it, probably thinking that they might next become targets themselves. Jack guessed that they lay hidden somewhere near, and he imagined them squinting into the moon's full light whence the shots had come, blind and fearful of another strike. He scanned the low bushes around the pond, but if the natives had gone to ground there, he could not see them. Then suddenly, Schluntz grabbed him by the arm and shook him roughly.

'Come on, Jack!' the scout rasped urgently, already on his feet. 'Time to get out of here while the moon's in their eyes.'

Jack had allowed precious seconds to pass unheeded. A few more and the pair would both have been caught in the moon's full glare. His companion's rough call had brought him back to his wits just in time. Jack leapt to his feet and followed his partner straight for the tree line, guided by the loom. They reached its cover quickly, then took up a curving path, running silently on the thick litter of pine needles carpeting the forest floor. It did not take them long to locate the thicket of dense undergrowth already fashioned as their lookout and their hiding place, and they hid themselves within it and settled down to wait.

Jack expected to see the Indians appear at any moment, tracking the path that he and Schluntz had blazed through the grass in their flight to the trees; those traces must inevitably become visible as the moonlight encroached. He had begun to endow the Indians with animal-like senses – senses that could sniff out the presence of two alien Anglo-Saxons. The rustle of tiny creatures foraging in the dry grass, a night-owl's call from the trees, the snuffling of a hedgehog as it waddled by unseen – any of these sounds might have been the stealthy approach of a native closing in for the kill. But no one came. And after a time, the two scouts began to relax their guard.

Meanwhile at the campsite, nothing seemed to change. In the moon's pale light, the scene looked like a still cameo painted in shades of grey: the mare, tethered to a bush where it had been left, stood motionless, apparently asleep; the Frenchman lay quite still, certainly dead and seemingly forgotten by Pettigrew who rocked gently where he sat, both hands clutching his outstretched leg as if pressing on his wound. His plaintive moaning could be heard faintly on the still night air. It sounded like the distant sobbing of a lost child - a pitiful, mournful sound that echoed in the vast emptiness. Occasionally, he would call out more loudly in French, perhaps hoping that the Indians would come to his aid? But no one answered his call. And as more time passed and the moon continued its steady trajectory across the starlit sky, his cries became weaker and more desolate.

Schluntz soon fell asleep while Jack remained wide-awake and watchful, his eyes scanning the entire clearing for any sign of movement. But he found his glances drawn constantly back to the lonely, sagging figure of Pettigrew sitting by his dying fire. Somehow, this was not the end he had expected for his foe. His scheme had been to leave a cripple to the mercy of the Indians or the wolves – to suffer a death of horror and drawn-out torture befitting his crimes, not a gentle fall into unconsciousness while bleeding to death.

But as Jack listened to the pathetic groans floating on the night air, a surge of sensibility came over him that took him quite by surprise. Some almost forgotten chord chimed deep within his being that made his heart go cold. Instead of feeling the righteous glee of satisfaction he had expected at Pettigrew's approaching demise, a terrible feeling of guilt suddenly seized him. And in that instant, he realised that he had become just as depraved and callous as his victim. Where was the honour in this, he chided himself? Where was the principled conscience that had always guided him to do the right and proper thing? His quest should have been for justice not revenge. How could his life's course have been so perverted; how could he have sunk so low? He began then to see himself as others might see him, as a mean and vindictive man - a man who coolly employed torture to gratify a base and savage lust. Rose would never love such a man as this; and neither could he. This was a man infected by the same devil that had possessed the four men that he had so tenaciously sought, and this dark stranger lurking within his soul had to be cast out.

Chapter Twenty-Six

Anyone who has experienced the sort of shame that Jack felt so acutely in his moment of self-revulsion will not find it difficult to understand the abrupt reversal of his outlook and purpose. Where earlier he had craved the satisfaction of seeing Pettigrew writhing in his death throes, screaming for a mercy that would be denied, now suddenly, his conscience demanded that he rescue him from the fate that he himself had engineered. And it was clear at once that in order to set things right, Pettigrew must face justice under the King's law and not his own. Moreover, he realised that he must act immediately or else miss his one chance of redemption, thus condemning his soul forever. Jack would never have described himself as a religious man. He had never feared the wrath of God because of the strict rule he applied to himself always to do what he thought was right (apart perhaps from a little smuggling in his Portland days, which he ignored in this analysis). But in recognising that his designs for Pettigrew's execution had taken him seriously away from that righteous path, he now felt God's eyes keenly and expectantly upon him.

This heady notion propelled him into a state of such single-minded urgency to find absolution that his heart began to race. He grabbed Schluntz's shoulder and shook him roughly awake.

'I'm taking Pettigrew back! We'll let the army deal with him!' he whispered fiercely in his friend's ear. 'Cover me!'

And stuffing a pistol in his belt he left the den, leaving Schluntz drowsily awakening, wondering if he had dreamt it. Jack was now operating at his impetuous best! And in his mind was a simple plan, a plan that minimised such possible impediments as might be put in his way by the three Indians - who he hoped incautiously had conveniently withdrawn or, at least, had gone to sleep. In his mind's eye, he saw himself reaching the campsite unseen and administering a tourniquet of some sort to Pettigrew's leg. Then he saw himself bundling the wounded man onto the mare and leading him away, eventually back to the post at Loyal Hannon where he would face a court marshal.

The moon had by this time risen to its apogee in the night sky so that it clearly illuminated his entire route to the pond. Not, however, totally insensible to the odds-on chance that the Indians might still be watching, he kept himself concealed in the long grass by crawling on all fours or on his belly. Homing onto Pettigrew's moans like some slithering predator of the night, he picked his way towards the pond with such care that his passing was no more than the gentle hissing of night zephyrs through the sward. The moon had already begun its descent when he reached the periphery of the trodden area around the pond, and as he parted the grass, he got his first clear view of Pettigrew, now just ten paces away. Jack lifted his head tentatively at first, then seeing and hearing no reaction to his movement, he rose to a crouching position, his senses now acutely tuned. He held himself stock-still like that while he swung his gaze about, then, satisfied that no immediate danger threatened, he trod carefully and silently into the open. Pettigrew sat propped up on a bedroll (from the saddle of his stolen horse) with his wounded leg outstretched as if immovable, the material of his breeches, ragged and bloody. With his eyes squeezed shut, he seemed completely unaware of Jack's nearing presence, and rocked himself gently as before, making curious little grunting noises in the back of his throat. Jack reached him and crouched down before him on his haunches. The moon threw its pallid light across the wounded man's face, making him deathly pale and gaunt. His lips quivered; his body was beset with shivers. He seemed in a stupor, yet he was not unconscious for he muttered something inaudible in a sort of moaning chant. His hair hung about his ears, unkempt and matted; his unshaven chin was bruised and bloody, his brow furrowed as if concentrating very hard. Jack could hear the rasp of his breathing as he stared into his face; his high forehead and hooked nose were so familiar, yet somehow in their present state, the sum of his lineaments was hardly recognisable at all. Jack dropped his gaze and examined Pettigrew's exposed wound; the blood seemed to have congealed around it in a dark circle of torn, suppurating flesh, the lack of present bleeding suggesting that Jack's shot had not severed an artery. He decided that the application of a tourniquet could wait.

Jack raised himself once more to his feet and looked about, his senses probing the still night air, the hairs on the back of his neck bristling to the imagined threat behind his back. Reassured, he flashed a glance towards the leafy refuge that he had left behind. An almost straight line of deep shadow cutting through the tall, moonlit grasses marked the path that he had made with his approach; and with the whole clearing laid bare in full moonlight, he realised that it would be impossible to find an easy sanctuary now. He knew Schluntz would be out there somewhere hidden in that moonlit scene, vigilantly marking his every move with his rifled musket at the ready. Jack was glad that he could not see his friend, but he hoped that he was near.

The mare stood dozing on her feet close by; Jack retrieved her and led her back to Pettigrew's side. Positioning himself at Pettigrew's front, he pulled the man upright with a hold on his arms, pinning his feet with his own to make a fulcrum; the limp body was lighter and more compliant than Jack expected, perhaps depleted by his ordeal. Then, stooping, Jack let the wounded man's head and upper torso fall over his bent back, and straightened to his full height with Pettigrew dangling across his shoulder like a carcass. The prisoner made neither protest nor sound, save from the wheezing of air from his lungs or an occasional groan; it crossed Jack's mind that to all intents and purposes, his captive was indeed dead meat, for his execution would not be stayed for long. Jack next tried in vain to swing the limp form across the mare's rump, but it was more difficult than he had imagined. He tried several times more, but on each occasion, the beast moved a step or two away, and whichever way he manhandled his unwieldy burden, he could not seem to achieve the geometry required to effect a transfer. With all this futile effort, Jack soon became exhausted, and anxious too about being out in the open for so long. Exasperated, he finally came to accept the error of his plan; he could not do what he had set out to do alone. Moreover, Pettigrew's weight had become too heavy and uncomfortable on his shoulder to consider carrying him further, and he unloaded him with relief to the ground. Then, taking the mare's reins to stop it wandering away, he swung his gaze about the clearing, hoping to attract his friend's attention and beckon him to his aid. But what he then saw frightened him almost out of his wits.

Not ten paces away, creeping towards him with their muskets in their hands, were the three Indians spread out in a wide arc. Jack was so astonished that they had managed to come so close without him having been aware of it that, in that instant, he could only stare aghast. The Indians meanwhile, caught by Jack's startled glare, had straightened, and now glared back with fierce intent upon their faces. But they did not their weapons, and some instinct told Jack not to reach for his own.

Instead, playing for time to give Schluntz an opportunity to intervene, he squared up to the three and spoke as confidently as he could manage.

'This man is a traitor and a murderer,' he said, pointing at the body at his feet, trying to keep the tremor from his voice. 'I have followed him here, and now I intend to take him back to face the King's justice.'

At this moment, alerted by Jack's voice, Schluntz rose silently from the grass some ten or so paces away on the Indians' left flank. At first they did not see him, but when they did, Schluntz's musket was already aimed upon them. Before they could react, however, the tall German called out in a native dialect that Jack could not understand. He spoke in an abrupt and forceful tone yet it was clear by the length of his monologue that he was articulating more than the simple warning that Jack had expected. And while the Indians listened, Jack pulled his pistol from his belt and cocked it quietly by his side. It was two weapons against three now; the odds had improved but with the Indians spread defensively, they still had command of the situation. Jack saw their recognition of this by the quick glances that passed between them, but they did not appear to want to press home their advantage. Their attention seemed to have been arrested by whatever it was that Schluntz had said. One of the three replied in his own tongue.

It was now Schluntz's turn to listen.

'I told them what you said,' he called to Jack eventually from the side. 'He's asking which king.'

'Tell him, King George the second,' said Jack, 'the King of British America, Great Britain and Ireland. Tell him that the king expects this man to be brought back for punishment under his law.' Jack was trying to impress his audience; he wondered if it would work.

Schluntz translated and, after a pause during which the three conferred, the first spoke again. Schluntz then replied at some length, which seemed to spark off yet further discussion.

'He asked if we followed them here,' relayed Schluntz finally. 'I told him that we were at the ford over the Youghiogheny River when they arrived there, and that we have been following them since. They seemed impressed with that, and also with the fact that we appear to have achieved our objective with some precision. There is apparently a new treaty between the British and the Native American peoples living west of the mountains, those that have until now been allied to the French. Word of it has been passing amongst the tribes, he says, but until tonight he did not trust it. That we did not kill them when we had the chance, he says, has persuaded him of it now.'

Jack nodded. He knew nothing yet of the treaty that had been mentioned, but he was glad to hear of it - and flattered too that his intentions had been recognised as honourable, which in respect of Pettigrew they certainly had not been until his change of heart. In some strange way it seemed to Jack that the evil that had had him in its grip was already letting go, that he was being pardoned for his earlier errant intentions.

'Tell him that we have no quarrel with them. Tell him that they should return to their homes and care for their families in the coming winter,' he called, and he waited while his friend translated his words.

He saw the Indians register his sentiments then watched them keenly as they conferred, sensing from their manner that this would be the end of the exchange. This was as close as he had ever been to their kind. They were impressive indeed to behold close to - tall, proud, muscular figures, their heads shaven, leaving just a topknot and pigtail of jet-black hair. All three were similarly dressed in shirts of coarse fabric under sleeveless hide jerkins decorated with rows of beads or horn. Below their waists, they wore breechcloths, leggings, and soft hide boots. Jack realised then that they were studying him with just the same interest, but their gazes were wary. At first he was uneasy at their interest, but then remembered that his pistol was still clutched in his hand. With an acknowledging nod, he raised its barrel upright, uncocked its mechanism, and pushed it into his belt. He expected that to be the end of the matter - that the Indians would be satisfied, turn away, and melt into the night. What they did next, therefore, took him by surprise. All three lowered their muskets to the ground and came towards him, coming to a stop just a pace or two away, the leader coming even a step closer. Jack caught the smell of musk and earth about them. The expressions on their faces were austere, so aloof and so expressionless that Jack could not read them. He felt awed, almost intimidated by their powerful presence, but he held their appraising gazes confidently. He stood face to face with the leader of the group wondering what would come next, but feeling at ease nevertheless. Eventually, it seemed that some gesture was required, and so, instinctively, he held out his hand. The Indian simply glanced at it, then lifted his eyes to search Jack's face. Jack felt under intense scrutiny, as if the native were peering into his very soul, and for a moment, he thought that he might have done the wrong thing. But just as he began to let his arm fall, the native grasped it with both of his big hands, reaching right up to Jack's elbow. All this time no words had been uttered between them, but now the Indian spoke.

Schluntz translated from behind Jack's shoulder:

'He says this new treaty protects their homeland from further British settlement. He expects this King George of yours to honour it so that there can be a new and lasting peace.'

Jack nodded gravely; it was indeed a worthy aim. He wanted to offer some fine words that would express his solidarity with that notion, but the three Indians turned and walked away before he could speak. He watched thoughtfully as they retrieved their weapons and set off up the road, expecting them to cast a rearward glance, thinking that if they did, he would lift his arm in farewell. But they never looked back. And as they disappeared into the night, retreating into the moonlit wilderness that eventually swallowed them up, he found himself feeling pessimistic about the future for these proud peoples. Although he wanted fervently to believe that their homelands could somehow be protected as had been promised, he doubted that the flood of European settlement could be so easily contained by an edict from a little island across the sea. As ever, supply would try to meet demand where there was a profit to be made, and a line of principle drawn in the sand could be too easily kicked over by those who stood to gain.

It was a minor miracle that Pettigrew survived the journey back to the Post at Loyal Hannon, for he went three days with hardly anything but water to sustain him. Indeed, had he been more than only intermittently conscious, he might have begged to be put out of his misery, rather than suffer the relentless discomfort of being strapped to the back of horse for so long and rough a trek.

The medics kept him in a hospital bed under an armed guard of two redcoats, but he was in no state to escape; Jack's musket ball might have done no more than torn Pettigrew's flesh, but it was still the best part of a week before he had the strength to stand, even supported by crutches. As soon as he was mobile, he was led before a court marshal and charged with desertion and theft, to which he could hardly plead anything but guilty since he had been caught red-handed, so to speak. Two others of his deserting cohort, having got lost in the wilderness, had handed themselves in to face similar charges. By turning King's evidence and making ardent reaffirmations of loyalty, they had escaped a capital disposal, but Pettigrew would not get off so lightly. He had been the ringleader and mastermind of the group, and he also faced the more serious charge of consorting with the enemy.

Until the moment he was led into the office-cum-courtroom set aside for the purpose of hearing this additional and contested prosecution, Pettigrew had no more than a hazy recollection of his capture or of his captors. Jack therefore expected to get some satisfaction, facing the defendant in the courtroom, of seeing the astonishment and chagrin in the man's reaction. But he was disappointed. There may just have been a flicker of recognition when Jack stood before him and presented his evidence, but Pettigrew's face seemed to have lost all life. He seemed a broken man, brought low by his ordeal; and when defending himself, his answers were half-hearted and even off-hand, often trailing into incomprehensible murmurings. The military chairman (a provost lieutenant colonel who was not known for equivocation) quickly lost patience with all of this, and cutting Pettigrew's ramblings short, found him guilty of the charge. Had the sentence been less than the summary execution pronounced by the learned officer, Jack would immediately have demanded Pettigrew's remand on murder charges to be brought before a civil court; but there was no need. That afternoon, Pettigrew was taken out and shot by firing squad.

Jack was more or less compelled to witness the event, having been the prosecutor, and he found himself a reluctant member of the party required by protocol to be present in the square. With most of the units already mobilised and marching on their surprise attack to Fort Duquesne, the barracks and esplanade had an abandoned air about them, with none of the usual military hustle and bustle within the stockade that might otherwise have been the case. A few camp-following wives paused on the boardwalks as Pettigrew and his guard came out into the square; they had seen such spectacles before and knew what gruesomeness came next, yet they seemed unable to avert their gazes. Four red-coated musketeers with shouldered muskets marched behind the party in a column, flanked by a sergeant. As the group approached the rear wall of the stockade, he barked his orders, bringing his little squad into a firing line, while Pettigrew was secured to a post some ten paces in front. Jack had watched the procession cursorily, since in some way it seemed intrusive to study a man too closely in the last moments of his life. But when Pettigrew was left standing at the post alone, now blindfolded at his own request, Jack found himself transfixed. Pettigrew shivered uncontrollably. He could be heard sobbing quietly; his lips moving as if muttering some last words to himself. Jack thought he might be offering a prayer, and wondered that a man so pernicious could ever expect to make his peace. This man who stood before the firing line so miserably had reached the just end that Jack finally had come to see as right; Pettigrew was paying with his life for the error of his ways after due process. A man who had abused his position and used others in a murderous inventory of wrongs deserved to feel the full weight of proper law. The man who had once cynically administered justice as a magistrate was at last on the receiving end.

The sergeant brought his men to the firing position with a sharp order, then gave the order to fire. The detonations of four muskets shook the air, and from behind the ensuing cloud of smoke, a piercing cry rang out. The smoke drifted clear. Pettigrew still stood upright at the post, his linen shirt turned scarlet. His left arm and abdomen had been hit but he was not dead. He rolled his blindfolded head in agony, uttering an awful, haunting moan that echoed around the stockade's high walls. Some of the women gasped, bringing their handkerchiefs to their mouths in horror. The sergeant unhurriedly gave the order to reload, and heedless of the bloody man convulsing just before them, the soldiers did as they were told. A second firing order followed a minute later. This time the muskets were better aimed and the lethal balls did the work intended. Pettigrew's head fell to his chest like a string had been cut, then his legs gave way and his body crumpled like an discarded doll.

A few days after Pettigrew's execution, a large body of Forbes' troops returned to the post in unexpectedly good shape and humour. Colonel Michael de Burgh's Southern Maryland militia was amongst this company, which, as it turned out, had not been needed after all. The story of the assault on the French fort was thus soon circulating around the post like a whirlwind. Jack and Schluntz heard it from Sir Michael himself, to whom the two scouts had reported as their returning comrades dropped their backpacks in the esplanade. The story is worth retelling:

It appears that the Brigadier's columns were only a day's march from Fort Duquesne when the French commander abandoned it, razing it to the ground. The conclusion drawn was that Colonel de Lignery knew of the imminent British attack, and realising that his dwindling garrison was hopelessly outnumbered, decided to destroy his fort rather than surrender it. The resulting explosions in the fort's armoury and powder stores had been heard by Forbes' vanguard ten miles away. And when Forbes reached the fort the following day, the enemy had already fled back to Illinois and Louisiana, leaving behind a deserted pile of smouldering wreckage. The Brigadier, still very ill, was carried to the site on a litter to see it for himself, but he was not too ill to celebrate the victory. He declared immediately that the fort would be rebuilt stronger and several times larger than before, renaming it Fort Pitt and the nearby settlement, Pittsburgh, after William Pitt, his patron.

Sir Michael related all this somewhat piqued that he would now not see any action at all, despite all his efforts and considerable personal expense. Nor would he gain any recompense from the customary spoils of war. With the recapture of Fort Duquesne, the southernmost prong of the British 1758 campaign was now successfully accomplished. The two other principal thrusts against the French were taking place further north: General Amherst and his army of fourteen thousand had already taken Louisburg on Cape Breton Island, leaving the way open for an assault on Quebec down the St Lawrence; and eight thousand British and twenty thousand provincial troops were on their way northwards from New York, with Montreal as their ultimate target. All this meant that Sir Michael's volunteer unit was now superfluous to requirements and could return home, the borders of Maryland and Pennsylvania regarded no longer as vulnerable to French attack.

'So it seems, Jack,' ended Sir Michael with a sigh, 'that our little adventure has come to an end – and yours too from what I have just been told. I will have to lead the men back to New Hope after we are rested, but I know that you'll be anxious to return more quickly, so I release you.'

As Sir Michael's account of his march had unfolded, Jack's thoughts had turned to this very possibility. 'I'm grateful, sir,' he said soberly, hiding his excitement at the prospect. 'I have a home to rebuild - and a wife to pacify,' he added with a crooked smile.

'Then go as soon as you are ready, Jack, and tell my good lady that I shall not be long behind you. But you'll be on your own, I'm afraid; Sergeant Schluntz here won't be joining you. He'll be heading northwards with Major Lawrence and the other scouts of his platoon.' Sir Michael turned to Schluntz. 'You're to be seconded to Major Green and his boys, sergeant - to help them find their way through the Adirondacks to Lake Champlain!'

Schluntz raised his eyebrows. 'Well, I've managed to navigate one Englishman through the Appalachians, so I guess I've served my apprenticeship!' he laughed. 'But d'you think Jack will ever make it home without me?'

'I think I'll manage,' said Jack wryly.

Historical Notes

Jack Easton and all the characters and events in *An American Exile, Fortune's Hostage,* and *The Road to Fort Duquesne* are entirely fictional, but the setting in which they are placed is historically accurate (as far as can be deduced from a wide range of sources). In particular the background references to Brigadier General Forbes' campaign to retake Fort Duquesne on the forks of the Ohio River represent the author's understanding of actual events. The following is offered as a somewhat simplified overview of the 1750s in that part of British Colonial America where the plot of the three novels unfolds.

Relative Populations

In 1750, (when Jack Easton first arrives in Maryland as a convict transportee) the population of all the Native American ('Indian') nations in northeastern North America was about 175,000. This compares to about 60,000 French settlers between Canada and the Mississippi and about 1,000,000 settlers in the British colonies from Virginia to New Hampshire. By 1770 the population of all the British colonies had grown to over 2,000,000.

The 'Indian' Nations around the Ohio River Valley

The Ohio River valley, Pettigrew's assumed sanctuary, was inhabited mainly by the Seneca, the Lenape (or Delaware), and the Shawnee peoples (nations) with a population of about 3,000 to 4,000. (Maryland's European population at the same time was about 140,000 and Pennsylvania's, 120,000.)

Further north, based in and around what is now central and western New York state, the powerful League of the Iroquois (comprising the Mohawk, Oneida, Onondaga, Cayuga, and Seneca nations) controlled and coordinated Indian activities, policy and trade for the whole of the region. Other Iroquoians (not members of the League) were the Hurons on the upper St Lawrence and east of Lake Huron, and the Cherokees of the southern Appalachian region and adjoining areas. The Tuscaroras of North Carolina (further south) joined the League to make the 'Six Nations' of the 'Iroquois Confederacy' referred to in Chapter 23.

The Indian economy was based on hunting, fishing and agriculture. Fur, skins, and food were traded principally with French and British traders in exchange for metal products, cloth, firearms and other items.

New France

New France had three colonies: Canada (along the St. Lawrence River), the Illinois Country (the mid-Mississippi Valley), and Louisiana (New Orleans and west of the Mississippi). There were about 70,000 colonists throughout the French settlements.

The French depended on the Indian trade as the basis of their economy, and so resented it when the British colonies of Pennsylvania and Virginia started trading with the Ohio River valley Indians. This area was on the eastern edge of their main trading routes and they did not want to lose control of any of the trade. They also used the Ohio River Valley and its river systems as routes of transportation between Canada and their other colonies, allowing their traders, priests, and soldiers to travel freely through the region. While the French did not appear to want to settle the area, they were fiercely determined to maintain authority over it.

The Dispute

By the 1750s, colonial settlement of western Pennsylvania, Maryland, and Virginia had reached the Appalachian (and Allegheny) mountains. Beyond the mountains, the immense and fertile valley of the Ohio River stretched to the Mississippi and offered tantalising scope for further expansion. British colonial traders involved in the Indian fur trade were already making fortunes there, and wealthy Virginian landowners now saw an opportunity to acquire and sell land for settlement at a profit. Although there were still no settlers (either French or British) in the Ohio River Valley in 1750, the British colonies claimed the land. Virginia, in fact, laid claim to all the territory as far west as the "islands of California."

In 1752, the Marquis Duquesne was made Governor of Canada and his instructions from France were "to make every possible effort to drive the English from our lands . . . and to prevent their coming there to trade." In 1753, he therefore began building a series of forts along the waterways in the Ohio River Valley as a line of demarcation.

The Lieutenant Governor of Virginia, Robert Dinwiddie, however, was already granting land in that same area to citizens of his colony. In 1753, he received instructions from the King to commence "erecting forts within the king's own territory" to protect it from the French. Dinwiddie was so concerned about all the French activity that he sent a young volunteer (and fellow land speculator) George Washington, to demand that the French leave the region, but not surprisingly, the French refused.

In the spring of 1754, the French erected Fort Machault, (about 100 miles south of Lake Erie, at present-day Franklin, Pa). At the same time, the British started to build a fort at the forks of the Ohio (about 100 miles further south, at present-day Pittsburgh Pa). But the gates of the British fort had only just been hung when the French artillery arrived! The British commander, realising that he was badly outnumbered, abandoned the fort without a fight. The French took possession at once and began building a much stronger fortification, renaming it Fort Duquesne (after the Marquis). Dinwiddie, however, keen to reassert Virginia's jurisdiction (and promote his own interests), would not accept this defeat and hastily dispatched a small regiment of colonial troops to retake the fort. Unfortunately, the unit (under the command of Washington) was hopelessly out-manoeuvred by the French, and forced into an embarrassing surrender (but were soon released – somewhat ignominiously).

Although then officially not at war, both France and Britain then decided to send troops and supplies to the area to support their conflicting territorial claims. Thus early in 1755, Major General Edward Braddock was sent to take command of all the British forces in North America. Later that year, he led an expedition of 2,200 regular and provincial troops to recapture the Forks of the Ohio (with George Washington as his aide), cutting a new road from Fort Cumberland through the forested mountains towards Fort Duquesne. In *The Road to Fort Duquesne*, this road is variously called the 'southern route' or the 'old Braddock road', and it is this road that Pettigrew and Hayward use to make contact with the French.

The French at Fort Duquesne, however, were well informed by their Indian scouts of Braddock's progress. And on July 9th, 254 French and 637 Indians left the fort to intercept the approaching British force. It was only eight miles east that the French and British armies spotted each other. The American Indians under French command quickly took the high ground and were able to dominate the battle, killing or wounding two-thirds of the British troops and most of the officers. Braddock suffered a serious wound from which he died four days later. George Washington inherited the command and resourcefully led a retreat that saved the remnant of the army.

Although his army was numerically superior, Braddock had blundered into an ambush because he lacked the Indian (guerrilla fighting) expertise, and he did not employ the scouts and partisans vital for forest warfare. Only 8 Native Americans accompanied Braddock's army, and he ignored their advice. Brigadier General Forbes would learn from General Braddock's mistakes in his 1758 campaign to retake the fort (see below).

As a result of Braddock's defeat many previously ambivalent Ohio River Valley Indians were emboldened to side actively with the French, and for the next few years Fort Duquesne became the launching base for hundreds of French and Indian raids on the Pennsylvania and Virginia frontier. By the spring of 1756, Indian raiders had already killed or captured at least 700 settlers from colonial settlements in Maryland, Virginia, and Pennsylvania, the survivors abandoning their farms and fleeing eastwards to within 100 miles of Philadelphia.

It was not until May 1756, that Britain officially declared war on France and the two countries began fighting in Europe. French and British colonies in the West Indies, India, and Africa were also drawn into the conflict. In Europe, the war became known as the Seven Years War.

The new commander of the French American colonies, Major General Louis-Joseph de Montcalm arrived in Canada in May 1756 to continue a successful campaign against the British in North America (capturing British forts on Lake Ontario in 1756 and on Lake George in 1757).

In 1758, William Pitt, Secretary of State in Britain, (effective head of government) appointed more competent and adaptable generals to command the growing forces deployed against New France. He also repealed some unpopular existing policies and enacted new ones that were advantageous to the colonies, and in return, at last received colonial support for the war by way of manpower and funding. Of the 45,000 troops employed in the 1758 campaign, about half were British regulars and half colonial volunteers (pitched against about 7000 French regulars and about 3000 provincials, supplemented by Indian warriors and drafted Canadian militiamen.

Pitt's 1758 objectives were as follows:

1. General Jeffery Amherst would attack the fortress at Louisbourg, which guarded the mouth of the St. Lawrence River.
2. General James Abercromby was assigned to take Fort Ticonderoga (on Lake Champlain).

3.   Brigadier General John Forbes was given the task of recapturing Fort Duquesne.

In July 1758, General Amherst's army captured Louisbourg, which opened the St. Lawrence River and a water route into Canada. Although not ordered in the plan Lieutenant Colonel Bradstreet also successfully captured Fort Frontenac, the strategic French supply base for the entire western French army and an important trading post for trade with the Indian population.   General Abercromby was not able to take Fort Ticonderoga (which was later taken during General Amherst's march northwards up Lake Champlain to capture Montreal).

For his campaign to retake Fort Duquesne, Forbes believed in a strategy known as a 'protected advance'. As the army moved forward, it would build forts or supply-bases at regular intervals. He ordered the construction of a new road across Pennsylvania, (referred to in *The Road to Fort Duquesne* as the 'northern route' to distinguish it from General Braddock's road of 1755) guarded by a chain of fortifications. The last fort built in September was to be the Post at Loyalhanna (Loyal Hannon in the novel), which lay about 50 miles from Fort Duquesne. The fort was built as a supply depot and a staging area for a British-American army of about 6,000 troops.   The principal British contingent was the 77th Highland Regiment of Foot, to which were added several companies of the 60th, the Royal Americans, whose ranks consisted mainly of Germans with officers comprising some British but mainly Swiss German and Swiss French. The Colonel Bouquet mentioned in Chapter 21 was one of the latter. Although several smaller units from Maryland and the Carolinas participated, the principal provincial contribution came in the form of three battalions of the Pennsylvania Regiment (mostly Scots-Irish) and two Virginia Regiments (one of which was commanded by George Washington). Sir Michael de Burgh and his 'Southern Maryland Volunteer Militia', and Major William Green and his 'South Coast Fusiliers' are all entirely made up.

While Forbes was moving forward, an important conference was taking place in Easton, Pennsylvania. Representatives from the Iroquois Confederacy (see above) and from the Shawnee and the Lenape nations (of the Ohio River Valley) met to make peace with the British. In return for not fighting for the French, they sought promises that would prevent settlement on all of the lands west of the Allegheny Mountains after the war. The British agreed, and also acceded to the Indians' request to remove forts from Indian lands. The Treaty of Easton was signed in October 1758 (that Jack Easton shares this name is purely coincidental). It is worth noting here that other more northerly Indian nations, in particular those around the Great Lakes and along the St Lawrence River, remained staunchly loyal to the French, and would continue to support the French strongly (notably during General Wolfe's long battle for Quebec during 1759).

It was by now so late in the year that Forbes was considering ending the campaign for the winter to resume his approach to Fort Duquesne in the spring. On November 12th, however, Washington captured a French soldier near Loyalhanna and learned that the French at Fort Duquesne were very weak; it appeared that they could no longer count on help from the American Indians, and with the fall of Fort Frontenac they had very few supplies. This intelligence was the useful outcome of the otherwise catastrophic 'friendly fire' incident described in Chapter 23, and led to Brigadier Forbes mounting an immediate attack.

As the reader will know from the account in Chapter 26, by the time Brigadier Forbes' army arrived at the French fort, it had been abandoned and destroyed. He occupied the ruin nevertheless on November 25th and renamed it Fort Pitt, which was to later to be built up to become one of the largest English strongholds in North America. Brigadier Forbes, still very ill, left the fort in December and was conveyed back to Philadelphia, where he died on 11th March 1759 at the age of only 49.

In 1759, the British continued their successes in North America. The Iroquois Confederacy, politically neutral until this point after the Treaty of Easton, decided to side actively with the British, and during the summer of that year, Fort Niagara, Fort Ticonderoga, and Crown Point were taken from the French. The opening of the St. Lawrence River (after the capture of Louisburg), moreover, allowed the British to sail largely unmolested to Quebec, where General Wolfe's troops put the French fortification under siege and eventually took control. Both the French commander, General Montcalm, and General Wolfe died from wounds received during the decisive battle for Quebec on the 'Plains of Abraham', just outside the city.

The French colonial government then moved to Montreal, but were effectively marooned after the destruction of the French Fleet in November 1759. Without essential supplies, the French army could not retake Quebec.

In 1760, the British captured Montreal, and the war between France and England in North America ended.

Also by Ron Burrows

An American Exile – ISBN: 978 1 84549 217 5
Fortune's Hostage – ISBN: 978 1 84549 381 3

Both published by arima Publishing and
available through Amazon and good bookshops

Lightning Source UK Ltd.
Milton Keynes UK
UKOW030323281212

204148UK00001B/9/P